# A TWIST OF TIME

A TWIST OF TIME
Copyright © 2020 Michael Banas

This is a work of fiction. Names, characters, businesses, places, events and incidents are either the products of the author's imagination or used in a fictitious manner. Any resemblance to actual persons, living or dead, or actual events is purely coincidental.

ISBN: 978-0-9890713-7-6

## ALSO BY MICHAEL BANAS

*The Key to the Future*
*In Plain Sight*
*Last Words Spoken*
*Twelve Men in the Huddle*
*The Chief Resident*
*The Center of Excellence*
*Pennsylvania's Finest*

# A TWIST OF TIME

### A NOVEL

BY
MICHAEL BANAS

## CHAPTER ONE
### THE GURU
### 2020

"He disappeared from this very spot," declared Dr. John Sullivan as he ran his hand up and down a wrought iron fence, as if feeling for a slot. "I was looking in the opposite direction."

"That's his epitaph?" asked his brother. He leaned forward to read the bronze plaque anchored to a brick pillar just outside the Christ Church graveyard, near the corner of 5$^{th}$ and Arch Street. "He wrote it himself?"

"Yes."

"Who writes his own epitaph?"

"Benjamin Franklin writes his own epitaph. He called it his 'grand clue' stating 'it couldn't be more obvious.'" Sullivan peered through the fence at Franklin's grave. "In retrospect, he was absolutely right. Why didn't anyone ever figure it out? I mean, millions of people have visited this tomb since 1790. They've all read his epitaph. It jumps out like a public notice."

"*For it will as he believ'd... appear once more,*" read George Sullivan from the placard. "*In a new and more elegant edition, corrected and improved by the author.*" He paused. "You're right, John. It couldn't be more obvious. Ben let it be known that he was a traveler of time. Of course, deciphering the clue brings into play the knowledge of a time tunnel. *That, my friend, is the critical piece of the puzzle."*

A group of schoolchildren turned the corner in excitement, swarming around the two brothers. A few eagerly tossed some pennies toward Franklin's grave.

"Are you going to tell them?" whispered George to his brother.

"Tell them what?"

"That Ben's grave is empty," snickered George. "They should get their money back."

"It's another portal site," ruminated John. "Another wormhole to the year 2065, but my key doesn't trigger it." He visually scanned the area. "Nor is there a key slot anywhere. I've searched the entire site over and over."

"So, there are two portals in Philadelphia? Is that what you're saying?"

"Yes. One recently destroyed in West Philly and the other one here, perhaps in the crypt of Benjamin Franklin."

"So why didn't your buddy Zachary Schmidt just transport back with Ben?"

"It must have been impossible. Zachary knew that R.S. was Benjamin Franklin. He would have certainly used the portal if possible."

"A penny saved is a penny earned!" bellowed the voice of a man from behind.

The Sullivan brothers turned around to stare directly at Ben Franklin, wearing his trademark coat, britches and high socks. Before they could speak the schoolchildren and some tourists swarmed around the Philadelphia icon.

"Ben Franklin! Ben Franklin!" shouted the third graders.

"Welcome to my city!" shouted Franklin. He glanced at Sullivan as he held out his arms. "Welcome everyone!" A cane steadied his frame as he leaned forward. "What a glorious day!" He pushed his bifocals upward on his nose. "Now children, can anyone tell me what the word 'Philadelphia' means?"

"Brotherly love," blurted out an adult tourist.

"Yes, very good," lamented Franklin. "Now… ahem, can any of the *children* tell me who sailed up the mighty Delaware River to discover the city of Philadelphia?"

"George Washington!" shouted an eager boy to Franklin's right.

"Well, not exactly," replied Franklin in a polite tone. "You have the correct river but the incorrect man. General Washington sailed across the Delaware to surprise the British during the Revolutionary War, but that was a tad north of here." He patted the child on the head. "A good try, though."

"William Penn," came the response from a young girl.

"Correct," said Franklin. "William Penn from the town of London, England. There's a magnificent statue of Mr. Penn atop City Hall, which you can see just over your shoulder." He pointed to the sky with his cane. "Oh my, what has become of my city? Who put all those tall buildings there? I used to be able to see clear across the Schuylkill River."

Some of the children began to giggle.

"Well, trust me," continued Franklin. "If you stroll a few blocks west, you will encounter the 37-foot high statue of Philadelphia's founding father, William Penn. Hence the name of the great state of Pennsylvania… which means Penn's woods."

As he spoke, the crowd surrounding the founding father increased in size.

"Now, who wants to head over to Independence Hall?" asked Franklin. "I'd like to show you where we signed the Declaration of Independence."

A few of the tourists began to clap and cheer as Ben moved forward.

"Can anyone guess the name of the oldest man to have signed the Declaration of Independence?"

"Ben Franklin!" shouted the boy to Franklin's right.

"Now you are correct," said Franklin. "I was 70 years young when I signed that document… oh how quickly time passes by. Always remember, lost time is never found again."

As the elderly man shuffled forward, so did the crowd.

"He's back!" shouted Dr. Sullivan joyfully with his hands clenched together. "I knew he would return sooner or later. We can't let him out of our sight, George! Not this time."

"That's the real Ben Franklin?" asked George. "He looks a bit frail."

"He's in his nineties, George! If you ask me, he looks fantastic." Sullivan looked up and down Arch Street in anticipation. "Professor Bookman should be here any minute. So, I'm going to have to count on you to keep track of Ben. Can you do that, George?"

"I'll give it my best," quipped George. "It's going to be tough... he's got a head start on me."

"Get going," smiled the doctor. "I'll be waiting right here. He has to return to this spot, in order to transport back. Don't lose track of him, George."

"I'll give it my best."

Over the next ten minutes, John Sullivan reexamined the surroundings of Ben Franklin's grave. Three months had passed since Franklin's abrupt disappearance over the Labor Day weekend, and since then there were no sightings of the man in the city. Even the sentry outside the Independence Hall Visitor's Center thought his prolonged absence peculiar.

"Dr. Sullivan?" asked a tall, slender man wearing a tweed jacket. He held a pipe in his left hand.

"Yes. I'm Dr. Sullivan. Professor Bookman I presume?"

"I am Professor Alabaster Bookman, from the University's Department of History." The man bowed in regal fashion. "A pleasure to meet you." He didn't offer a hand to shake.

"Thank you for meeting with me, Dr. Bookman." Sullivan had to look upward at the professor while speaking, directly into a long, skinny nose that had a slight bump midway down. Nostril hairs protruded from his nares in haphazard fashion and bushy eyebrows sat above drab brown eyes. His rosy cheeks suggested rosacea.

"The pleasure is all mine, Dr. Sullivan. I live nearby so this is a perfect meeting spot." The professor slowly scanned the area. "How can I be of assistance?" He put the pipe into his mouth and took a puff. "You're doing some historical work on Mr. Benjamin Franklin?"

"Well yes, professor. I'm a member of the West Philadelphia Historical Society and we're conducting some research on Benjamin Franklin's gravesite. Perhaps you've heard of our group?"

"No. I have not."

"We meet once a month up on Baltimore Avenue, near the University. Attorney Frederick Mills is our current president. The society has been in existence for over fifty years."

Bookman didn't respond.

"Well anyway, our organization tried to halt the destruction of the Philadelphia General's Franklin Wing, but we failed. You may have read about our exploits in the *Philadelphia Chronicle*. The society garnered some significant notoriety in the process."

"No. I did not. I was away on sabbatical for six months in France. Paris to be exact. I just returned to town." The professor took another regal puff from his pipe.

"Well, again… thank you for answering my call."

"I always answer the call when it comes to Mr. Franklin. I've dedicated my life to researching the man. So when anyone wants to talk 'Ben Franklin'… count me in." The personal declaration was followed by a jut of the jaw.

"Yes. Well then… I guess my question is what can you tell me about his gravesite? I mean for such an accomplished man, it's a bit underwhelming. Why did he choose this site and more importantly, why isn't there a much larger memorial dedicated to his life's work?"

"That's a broad set of questions, but I'll answer to the best of my ability." He sneered at a couple of tourists trying to take a selfie at his side. They laughed and brushed up against his shoulder. "Do you mind if we walk as we talk?" It was an unusually warm December day in the city.

"Not at all, professor."

Over the next twenty minutes, Dr. Alabaster Bookman unleashed an avalanche of information concerning the death and burial of his idol, Benjamin Franklin. Together they walked several blocks around the perimeter of the historic district. During the tutorial, it became apparent to Sullivan that Bookman was indeed the leading authority on the life and times of Ben Franklin.

"He died from complications of pleurisy on April 17, 1790," said Bookman. "His final words were 'a dying man can do nothing easy.'"

"Was anyone else in the room with him?"

"His two grandchildren were nearby," continued Bookman. "William and Bennie. He passed at the age of 84."

"How did they announce his death? I mean, it must have been a big event back then."

"A man named Dr. Edward Casey informed the public of his demise. He was Ben's longtime personal physician. The following day a full-page article came out in the *Pennsylvania Gazette* announcing his death, which of course was composed some time earlier by Benjamin himself."

"So, it sounds like the announcement of his death was well thought out?"

"Absolutely… by Franklin and his personal physician. Ben Franklin managed his public persona quite well. Like many other things, the man was ahead of the curve when it came to his social media profile. It should come as no surprise that he tightly controlled the sequence of events surrounding his death. At the time of his passing, Benjamin Franklin may have been the most famous person in the world." Bookman took out a white handkerchief and loudly blew his nose. "Sorry, allergies." He carefully folded the hanky and placed it into his jacket. "He and Dr. Casey were considered inseparable, the best of friends."

"Kind of like his wingman?"

"Excuse me?"

"Dr. Casey… his wingman. You know, Ben's sidekick. Every pilot needs a trusted co-pilot, or wingman."

"That's not nomenclature I commonly use," countered Bookman. "But I understand your point."

"What about his funeral?" asked Sullivan. "I understand 20,000 people showed up."

"An epic event. The citizens of Philadelphia carried his coffin through the streets. Benjamin wanted it that way. Immediately behind the casket were the printers of the city and their apprentices. Franklin always considered himself a common man, a leather apron worker. He frequently stated, 'Keep thy trade, and thy trade shall keep thee'. Hence, a common man's grave."

"Interesting."

"He was buried next to his wife, Deborah. She preceded him in death by about 25 years. Their relationship stood cordial at best. Simply put, Ben Franklin outgrew his spouse and the city of Philadelphia. The man was idolized in France and England where he spent an inordinate amount of time. Believe it or not, Deborah never saw Franklin during the last seven years of her life." Bookman stopped as if distraught. "Sad, if you ask me." He paused and continued walking. "He joined his son Francis in the graveyard, who died at age four."

"Were people embalmed back then?"

Bookman stopped walking and stared at Sullivan. "That's a peculiar question."

"Just a thought."

"No. He was not embalmed. The preservation of corpses only came into vogue in the United States around the time of the Civil War, when formaldehyde was first identified."

"I see." Their stroll together returned to Franklin's grave. "So why did he pick this exact spot?" He pointed directly at Franklin's flat tombstone. "Did it have any significance?"

"To my knowledge… no. Christ Church was Episcopal at the time and Ben's religious allegiance to this date remains a point of considerable debate. His father Josiah raised him as a Puritan."

"So why Christ Church graveyard?"

"He did tremendous charity work for the church," replied Bookman. "And of course his son and Deborah were waiting there too."

"Dr. Bookman, would you ever be interested in coming out to one of our Historical Society meetings as a guest lecturer?" asked Sullivan. "I would love to have you meet the other members of the group."

"Well, uh… certainly. That is, if my schedule allows." He cleared his throat. "I'm teaching two graduate classes this semester and for some reason I have no teacher's assistant. But, thank you for the invitation. I'll have to check with my coordinator. Let's keep in touch."

"Surely," countered Sullivan. "And thank you so much for coming down to Ben's gravesite to talk with me. I greatly appreciate it."

"You are welcome, Dr. Sullivan. The pleasure was all mine. Good day." The professor turned and began to step away.

"Professor Bookman, one last question," shouted Sullivan.

"Yes?" Bookman turned back and looked at his watch.

"Can you tell me what Ben's favorite saying was? Did he have a favorite? I mean there were so many."

"Certainly," replied Bookman as he raised his pipe to relight it. "Ben Franklin's favorite saying was 'Early to bed and early to rise, makes a man healthy, wealthy and wise.'" As he puffed the pipe's mouthpiece, a few flames flickered from its bowl.

Sullivan didn't respond.

"What? You look surprised? That was his favorite saying… without a doubt."

"No, it's just that… "

"I'll bet my professional reputation on it. I'm frequently asked that very question."

"Well you see… ah, it's nothing."

"Go on, Dr. Sullivan. What's your opinion on the matter? Tell me, what do you think Ben's favorite saying was?"

Sullivan paused but then responded. "Ah… the used key is always bright?"

"Was that a question or an answer?"

Sullivan had a brief flashback to his grade school days. "An answer," came the still tentative reply.

"Don't tell me you've been listening to that impersonator over at the Visitor's Center!" howled Bookman as his cheeks flashed a brighter shade of red. "That guy is a thespian, an entertainer. His amusing little act of anecdotes is a disservice to the historical preservation of Benjamin Franklin. He portrays Mr. Franklin as some sort of affable buffoon as opposed to the brilliant politician, inventor and Philadelphian that he was!"

"Well, actually…"

"The used key is always bright. Bah!"

"It kind of makes a lot of sense."

"Promise me one thing, Dr. Sullivan!" huffed Bookman.

"Yes?"

"When you have questions about Ben Franklin…. talk to me. Don't listen to that actor." He waved his pipe in the air. "I understand his purpose and the importance of tourism in the area but when it comes to the essence of Ben Franklin and the facts of his vast accomplishments… talk to Professor Alabaster Bookman. I *am* the Ben Franklin guru. Understand?"

"Yes sir. Thank you."

"You're welcome. Good day."

The professor pivoted, turned and walked away. As he departed a stream of angry smoke billowed from his large head.

Thirty minutes later, Sullivan's cell phone rang.

"John, he's done," declared his brother.

"Already? Is he on the way back?"

"Nope. He bolted in the opposite direction, for some manly sustenance after a long, hard day at the office."

"Ah, he must be at *Firenze's*. He loves the cheesesteaks there." Sullivan took a step westward. "I'll be there in a minute."

"Nah. It's a few blocks up from *Firenze's*… closer to 9th Street. I'll meet you on the corner of 9$^{th}$ and Arch."

"Be right there."

Sullivan hustled away from Franklin's grave. As he passed *Firenze's*, the touristy atmosphere of the historic district began to fade. He spotted his brother standing on the corner of 9$^{th}$ street. Behind him lay a homeless man atop a rectangular subway vent in the pavement, his body wrapped tight in a tattered blanket.

"The British are coming! The British are coming!" declared the homeless man as Sullivan approached.

"He made it all the way up here?" asked John to his brother. "It's a bit outside of the tourist district." He sidestepped the vagrant.

"Yes… with quite the spry step I may add."

"No taxation without representation!" howled the street person.

"Where's he at?" asked Sullivan while pulling his brother a few feet away.

"Right across the street," answered George with a grin. He pointed at a series of shops, most of them closed up with security gates rolled across their entrances.

"Where? I don't see any restaurant."

"Right there. To the right of the laundromat."

Sullivan peered across the street. Just to the right of the laundromat stood a narrow building with painted black bricks. A dimly lit sign sat above a wooden door that centered the edifice.

"What does that sign say?" asked Sullivan. "*Liberty Belle*?"

"Keep reading."

"*Liberty Belle… Gentlemen's Club*! What?" John looked at his brother in disbelief. "Are you sure? Ben Franklin went into a strip joint?"

"One hundred percent certain. He strolled in there like he owned the place."

Dr. Sullivan paused to gather his thoughts. He looked up and down the street.

"You better check it out, John. I'll sit this one out."

"I don't believe it," countered John as he bolted across the street. "There must be some explanation as to why he would walk into a Gentlemen's Club. It doesn't make any sense."

Sullivan didn't hesitate as he walked through the doorway into a long dark hallway. At the end of the walkway sat the sketchy silhouette of an elderly man on a bar stool. The twang of provocative music filled the air as did the stench of stale beer. Sullivan stopped in front of the man.

"Are you a member?" asked the man, his face pitted with acne scars.

"No. No I'm not."

"Would you like to become a member?"

"No," answered Sullivan. He glanced over the man's right shoulder to spot a circular bar. In the middle of the bar stood an elevated stage with a shiny gold pole running up to the ceiling."

"Hey buddy, no peeking," warned the doorman. "Five bucks to get in with a two drink minimum… and no taking photos of the staff."

"Sure," stammered Sullivan as he pulled out the cover fee from his wallet. He handed the money to the man.

"Do you want a receipt?"

"A receipt? No. Why would I want a receipt?"

"You look like a businessman. Just asking."

"Thank you," said Sullivan as he brushed past the watchman. He glared through a film of cigar and cigarette smoke to spot a smattering of patrons at the bar, gawking upward at a topless dancer. They all held a mug of beer in their hands as loud disco music played overhead.

"What'll it be?" shouted the barmaid over the noise.

"Diet soda," answered Sullivan. He took a seat next to a heavily bearded, mountain of a man.

"Go Bennie!" shouted the mountain man as he stared across the stage. "My brother from another mother!"

The comment prompted Sullivan to look across the dance platform. There, he eyed the backside of a dancer leaning forward to accept a well-placed tip from a patron. Between a set of spiked high-heels he spotted the face of Benjamin Franklin, looking upward in delight.

"What the..." muttered Sullivan.

"Bennie! Bennie!" went the barroom chant.

Sullivan rapidly walked around the stage and approached the man as the dancer continued to gyrate in a provocative manner.

"Ben... Ben Franklin!" shouted Sullivan over the din.

Franklin tilted his head to the right and looked over his reading glasses. His eyes were bloodshot and his breath stank of brandy. He held a wad of five dollar bills in hand.

"Bennie! Bennie!"

"Mr. Franklin, it's me... John Sullivan."

"Who?"

"Dr. John Sullivan! We met a few weeks ago... at the Visitor's Center."

"Beat it, buddy. I'm off duty." Franklin raised a greenback high into the air and waved it back and forth. "Can't you see I'm busy?"

"But Mr. Franklin..."

"I said beat it!" Franklin pushed his seat back and stood up in anger. "Leave me alone!" He began to walk to the men's room.

"But, I need to talk to you about the skeleton key. Why doesn't my key work at your portal?"

Franklin stopped and turned toward Sullivan. "What key?"

"The key to the future. Your key, the one that was struck by lightning during your kite experiment."

"You found my key?"

"Yes." Sullivan leaned closer to Franklin. "Are you O.K., Ben. You look a bit more frail than what I remember."

Franklin paused as if trying to render a witty reply. He then burst into a hysterical fit of laughter interrupted by an occasional blast of phlegm from his nostrils. He pointed at Sullivan. "Hey everybody! This guy thinks I'm the real Ben Franklin! What a nut job!" He cackled louder. "Somebody call security."

Scattered laughter rose from the crowd.

"What? You're not Benjamin Franklin?"

"Do I look like Ben Franklin?" asked the man. He peeled off a wig to expose a crop of black hair. "Mr. Franklin died about 200 years ago. Perhaps you didn't hear the news?" He grinned. "I'm Gus Thomas, from Camden, New Jersey. Please to make your acquaintance." He bowed in regal fashion.

Sullivan went silent.

"Now if you'll excuse me, I'll be in the washroom. You're certainly welcome to come along. Tonight's topic will be the Constitution... my evening constitutional that is."

"I'm sorry, sir. I just thought..."

"Don't be sorry," replied Gus as he put his wig back on. "Get back to the bar. There's a two drink minimum here. Remember... beer is proof that God loves us and wants us to be happy."

"Did Ben say that?"

"You better believe he did! It was his favorite saying, too." The man burped.

"Really?"

"Absolutely."

"Are you sure?"

"Of course I'm sure. I *am* the Ben Franklin guru."

## CHAPTER TWO
### THE SUPER-USHER
### 2065

Forty-five years later, in the basement of the Pagano Orthopedic Institute, Vincent Pagano sat in bed with his leg elevated on two pillows. A bag of ice covered his lower extremity and Dr. Schmidt paced the room from side to side. Five days had gone by since the surgeon reappeared in 2065 with a badly injured ankle that required a cast application.

"Quite the conundrum," stated Schmidt as he continued to pace. "It's déjà vu all over again." He nervously rubbed his hands together. "With one exception, however."

"What's that?" asked Vince.

"The key. It's not lost. We know who has it… Dr. Sullivan."

"He must have made it out alive since his name isn't on the memorial plaque in the lobby."

"One would hope," followed up Schmidt. "But our problem is the granite wall and time tunnel. I'm assuming they've both been blown to smithereens."

"I have no doubt that the wall is gone. Once those sirens start blaring, there's no stopping the detonation." Pagano rubbed his bloodshot eyes. "Oh, my poor Mom and Dad. They must be absolutely distraught."

"Well, we have no key... that much I know," declared Schmidt. "So you can't transport back." He stopped pacing and looked at Pagano. "We have to just hunker down and wait for Dr. Sullivan to somehow get back to us. There must be a way. If anyone can figure it out, John can."

"Maybe there's another tunnel?" suggested Pagano as he repositioned the ice.

"Actually there is," came the terse disclosure from Schmidt. "Across the river in the historic district. We call it Tunnel #2."

"What!" shouted Pagano as he bolted upright in bed. "Let's use it! What are we waiting for?"

"It's not that easy," cautioned Schmidt with a pointed finger. "Actually... it's impossible. A veteran voyager utilizes that wormhole, but a person can only transport back in the tunnel that they arrived in. Yet another cardinal rule of time travel."

"Are you kidding me?"

"No. I'm not. I tried to transport back in Tunnel #2 multiple times, but it just doesn't work. I'm sorry, but it has something to do with the distortion of your bodily molecules, at least that's what we've hypothesized."

"Wow, another tunnel. How many time travelers are walking around in Philadelphia?"

"Just two," answered Schmidt. "I think."

"Great. I'm stuck in the future and my parents and fiancée think I'm dead. Any other good news?"

"You're alive."

Pagano didn't reply, thankful for that. He winced as he repositioned his cast on the pillow, the tips of his toes a bit purple and edematous. The surgeon reached for a rectangular piece of glass to his right. He leaned forward to speak into the portable computer. "Find me Jordan Ally McCarthy... Philadelphia... Bryn Mawr College Class of 2009."

"Vince, don't do it," ordered Schmidt as he stepped toward the bed. "You'll make yourself crazy!"

"Too late." He immediately began to read about his fiancée. "Hmmm, she still lives on the Main Line. Let's see… in the old family homestead. Interesting."

"Give me that!" snapped Schmidt as he pulled the computer out of Pagano's hand.

"Wait! She's 77 years old!"

"I will not allow you to destroy yourself with information that may be too painful." Schmidt powered down the device. "You're new to this, but I'm not. The future can be bitterly cruel. Do not let it alter your own destiny. Understand?"

"No. I don't. Give me back the computer!"

"You decide your future, Vince. Don't condemn yourself to knowing what will happen. You'll regret it forever. No one knows that better than me."

Pagano quickly got up out of bed and hobbled his way across the room. "Excuse me," said the physician as his crutches grazed Schmidt.

"Where are you going? That leg needs to remain elevated. I'm your treating doctor."

"I need to freshen up and I can take care of my own ankle," grumbled Pagano as he awkwardly made his way into a small lavatory. "I'm a board certified orthopedic surgeon."

"The doctor who treats himself has a fool for a patient," retorted Schmidt. "And besides, your certification expired over forty years ago. Now, get back in bed!"

Pagano began to wash his face and brush his teeth, during which time Dr. Schmidt delivered a stern lecture, imploring Pagano to remain calm, warning him not to do anything rash in an attempt to return back to 2020. The theme of the sermon centered upon the concept of time and the need for patience.

"Someone has to be here when John arrives," stated Schmidt emphatically. "It's absolutely paramount. He's going to reappear in this very room. We don't know what's happening on the other side of the tunnel, so your window of opportunity may be brief."

Pagano made his way out of the bathroom. "Don't miss your

opportunity, Vince. Do you understand what I'm saying? You may only get one chance to return home."

"Sure I understand, but I'm a surgeon, so I've got to do something." He made his way to the door. "When I'm stuck in the middle of an operation I just don't stand there dumbfounded. I have to act… it's in my DNA."

"Where are you going?"

"Outside to get some air."

"Vince, you need to be careful. Do not draw attention to yourself."

"Nothing is going to happen. I've walked around West Philly before."

"Do not cause a commotion. It's 2065 and cameras are everywhere. Facial recognition has been taken to a whole new level."

Pagano opened the door. "Big deal. I've got nothing to lose."

Schmidt grabbed his upper arm. "It *is* a big deal, Vince. Because we're not sure if you exist in the year 2065." He tilted his head. "Do you understand?"

The possibility generated only a brief pause in Pagano's thought process. "Thanks. I'll be careful." He made his way out into a hallway.

"Wait," said Schmidt. "Take this." He put a visitor's pass lanyard around his neck. "Any troubles, use my name immediately. I'll be here, waiting for John."

"Thank you."

Pagano hobbled into the lobby of the Pagano Orthopedic Institute, his injured frame blending in well with the crowd. He made his way to the plaque that bore his name, a reminder of his fate that was ignored by the drove of people passing by. To the right of the memorial stood a young security guard at attention. His name tag read, 'Reginald Washington'. Pagano stared at the sentry.

"May I help you?" asked the guard politely.

"Yes," answered Pagano. "Your name is familiar to me. May I ask if your father worked in the old Philadelphia General? I used to know a man they called Reggie Washington."

"That was probably my grandpa, or great-grandfather," chuckled Washington. "I'm like the fourth generation working here." He looked at the plaque on the wall. "My dad actually told me that his grandfather used to work with Dr. Vincent Pagano, back in the old Franklin Wing." He paused out of respect. "Around the time he died in the explosion."

"I see."

"He knew him very well."

"Interesting, do you know anything else about this Vincent Romeo Pagano?" While speaking, Pagano pointed at the memorial with his crutch.

"No sir. I don't. Except for the fact that he died on July 4$^{th}$, 2020."

"He's not on staff here at the Institute?"

"Excuse me?"

"Dr. Vincent Pagano. Do you know if he works here at the hospital?"

"No," replied the guard slowly. He pointed at the plaque. "Dr. Pagano passed away around forty years ago. It's says right there… in the year 2020."

Pagano went to speak but held his tongue, recalling Schmidt's words of advice. "Right. Thank you Mr. Washington." He went to turn away but stopped. "Your great-grandfather would be proud of you." Pagano grinned and gimped away.

"Thank you," said the somewhat bemused guard. While watching Pagano navigate across the lobby he reached over to a microphone attached to his lapel. "Reggie here… at the front door. Keep an eye on the dude on crutches moving away from me. He's wearing a visitor's tag and doesn't appear to be oriented to time."

"Roger," replied the voice in Reggie's earbud. "We're tracking him."

Pagano worked his way up to a large computer screen on a wall. He reached forward and tapped on the heading 'Orthopedic

Department". His action generated a list of 20 surgeons listed in alphabetic order, along with their face and brief biography. He quickly scanned down the list in search for the Pagano name, but there was none. A pang of sorrow rattled his soul.

"Son of a..."

"May I help you?" asked an energetic male receptionist at Pagano's side. "Are you looking for a specific doctor or department?"

Pagano peered at the hospital employee, immediately spotting two security guards over his shoulder, staring him down.

"You're a visitor here?" asked the receptionist.

"Yes. Yes I am," stammered Pagano.

"Where are you from?"

"Actually, I'm from Italy." He held forward the I.D. tag. "I'm here on conference... as a guest lecturer."

"I see."

"I'm looking for a place to eat in town. Do you have any recommendations?" Pagano began to hobble away. "On second thought, can someone call me a cab?"

"A cab?" laughed the worker.

"An Uber perhaps?"

"Just head outside," pointed the receptionist. "The valet will secure transportation for you."

"Thank you." Pagano nodded to Washington as he exited the building. A parking attendant immediately summoned a nearby transport. Once the vehicle pulled to the curb, he lowered his injured frame inside. There was no one in the front seat.

"Where to?" asked the car.

"Excuse me?" stammered Pagano. "Ah, where's the driver?"

"You are currently in a ninth generation Super-Usher transport. Driverless cars have been proven much safer that human controlled vehicles. Your risk of fatality in this transport is sixty-times less as compared to a manned car. Do you accept that risk?"

"Yes. I guess so."

"Excellent. To whom can I charge the ride?"

"Um, Vincent Pagano."

A brief pause occurred before the car spoke. "We have no Vincent Pagano on our preferred transport list. Do you have another account?"

"Ah, how about Dr. Zachary Schmidt? Does that work?"

A small screen on the front dashboard immediately pulled up a photo of Dr. Schmidt. His face then appeared live.

"This passenger is charging your account for a Super-Usher ride. Do you permit such a charge?"

"Vincent," said Schmidt in a fatherly tone over the car's speaker. "Where are you headed?"

"To the old neighborhood, to look around."

Schmidt paused with a look of concern. "Technology is light years ahead, Vince. You're being tracked by the Internet of Things. Trust me. Every step you take will be on record."

"I'll take the risk."

"As you wish," said Schmidt. "Good luck. I approve of the charge."

"Thank you for your patronage, Dr. Schmidt," stated the computer. Schmidt's face vanished. "Where would you like to go, Vince?"

"Bryn Mawr," came the reply without hesitation.

"Do you have a specific destination in Bryn Mawr?"

"The McCarthy Estate."

The vehicle pulled away from the curb, its electric motor extremely quiet.

"Bryn Mawr means 'big hill' in Welsh," stated the Super-Usher. "It was named after an estate in Wales owned by Rowland Ellis."

"Hmm," said Vince. "I didn't know that."

"Here's another fun fact," continued the car. "Up until 1869, Bryn Mawr was formerly known as Crankyville. Imagine that!"

"Ha!" laughed Vince. "I'm sure not many people know that."

"First time to Philadelphia?" asked the vehicle.

"No."

"Can I interest you in a snack or liquid nourishment… including the option of an adult beverage?"

"No thank you."

"Would you be interested in our frequent rider club? All passengers today are being offered 500 free miles to be used in any city across the United States with no blackout dates. This limited-time offer automatically enrolls you in our loyalty program and includes a 30% discount from our already low prices. As a frequent rider you will be the first to benefit from future…"

"No thanks."

Pagano stared out the window as the vehicle continued on an orderly approach toward the Schuylkill Expressway.

"Where are the traffic lights?"

"Traffic lights were removed from the city of Philadelphia in 2050," came the reply. "The Super-Usher that you are riding in adheres to the Internet of Things' Recommended Rules, Regulations and Routes for driverless transport. A two car length distance will be maintained by complying vehicles at all times."

"Interesting," mumbled Pagano and he watched the Philadelphia skyline pass by to his right. "So, no more road rage?"

"Twenty percent of vehicles in the metropolitan area still operate via human driver. They account for 97% of accidents and 100% of road rage… sad."

Boat house row remained unchanged as did the topography of Fairmount Park. The vehicle took the City Line Avenue exit. It was here that Pagano felt transported to another world.

"What the heck?" said Pagano. "Where are all the stores? The strip malls?" He looked out at green space that was intermittently scattered with aesthetically pleasing apartment complexes. "There used to be retail stores here."

"Suburban box stores and shopping malls capitulated to online commerce between 2035 and 2045. Would you like me to connect you to one of our sponsors for an enjoyable shopping experience? Your purchase may be available by the time we reach your destination."

"Are you kidding me?" laughed Pagano. "No more box stores or retail outlets? What about the King of Prussia Mall?"

"A historical footnote that was leveled in 2050. The site was used to host the 2060 Olympic Games."

"Wow. My fiancée loved that mall. It must have broken her heart."

"Congratulations on your engagement. Who's the lucky girl?"

Pagano laughed at the computer. "You're pretty funny."

"Why does a man twist the wedding ring on his finger?"

Pagano looked at the empty front seat. "Are you telling me a joke?"

"Yes. Why does a man twist the wedding ring on his finger?"

Pagano let out a chuckle. "I don't know. Why?"

"Because he's trying to figure out the combination!" Canned laughter played over the car's speaker system.

"Good one."

"How many divorced men does it take to change a light bulb?" asked the Super-Usher.

"I don't know," said Vince. "How many?"

"It doesn't matter, they never get the house anyway!" Some more corny laughter followed.

And so it went for the remainder of the ride, the driverless car amusing its passenger with a series of jokes, fun facts and anecdotes. Vince even agreed to a baguette sandwich while approaching the town of Ardmore.

"Wow, Bryn Mawr hasn't changed a bit," said the surgeon as he peered out the rear window. "These homes have been here for hundreds of years." He wiped his mouth with a napkin. "Good old Crankyville." He crumpled up the sandwich wrapper. "Thanks for the snack."

"You are quite welcome, Vincent Pagano. Is Bryn Mawr your hometown?"

"No. I was born in South Philly."

"Do you work in the area?"

"I used to, a long time ago."

"What's your occupation?"

"Hey, you missed the turnoff," exclaimed Vince while looking back over his right shoulder. "You should have made a right turn."

"Thank you for that information."

The vehicle continued forward for two blocks. Vince thought he heard the doors lock.

"What's going on here? Where are you going?" He rapidly turned his head from side to side. "You're off course. Turn around!"

"Recalculating." The vehicle came to a stop at a traffic light. It put on its right side blinker. "Recalculating."

"Let me out," ordered Vince. "Now." He tried to open the door but it wouldn't unlatch. He pushed it a few times to no avail.

"For your safety, all doors are kept locked until we arrive at your destination."

The light turned green and the vehicle turned directly into the Bryn Mawr Police Department parking lot. Standing outside were two uniformed officers. One of the policemen pointed for the car to stop directly in front of him. The car came to a halt and the doors unlatched.

"Thank you for choosing Super-Usher. I hope your trip was enjoyable."

"Why did you bring me here?"

"Rules and Regulations of the Internet of Things," came the automated reply. "Please exit the vehicle to your right. Look both ways for oncoming traffic."

The policeman opened the door.

"Step out of the car, sir," said the officer.

Vince just looked upward.

"I said… step out of the car."

He hobbled out with crutches in hand. "What seems to be the problem, officer?"

"Have a good day and live your best life!" proclaimed the Super-Usher as its door shut automatically. The vehicle slowly pulled away from the curb.

"We need to see some identification," said the officer.

"What?"

"Do you have some I.D.? A driver's license perhaps?"

Pagano had no identification on hand since his wallet was lost in the last transport. "Ah, no. I do not. I only have this visitor's pass from the hospital." He surrendered the lanyard to the lawmen. "I left my wallet at home." He looked to his left at the older policeman. "What's the problem? Why did that vehicle drop me off here?"

"Sir, you've been tagged by the vehicle's facial recognition program as a 319."

"Which is?"

"An undocumented," said the officer. "An illegal. Are you an American citizen?"

"Yes."

"Where's your hometown?"

"Philadelphia."

"But you have no identification to prove that?"

"No. I do not."

"Can you please come inside with us, Mister … "

"Pagano. Vincent Pagano. That's my name."

"Thank you, Mr. Pagano." The two officers escorted Vince to a stark office in the building's basement. "Please, take a seat," said the officer. "Would you like a cup of coffee or a doughnut?"

"No thank you."

Over the next thirty minutes, Vince Pagano failed to convince the officers that he was a United States citizen. He intermittently mentioned the name of Dr. Zachary Schmidt but dare not play the time travel card. The officers had no other option but to arrest Vince and prepare him for transport.

"You're sending me where?" asked Vince as he was fingerprinted.

"Downtown…North 8th Street," replied the officer as he scanned the fingerprints beneath a scanner.

"North 8th Street?"

"Yep. Philadelphia's Immigration and Customs Enforcement office."

"This is unbelievable," muttered Vince.

"I'll say so," agreed the officer as he squinted at the computer screen. "Wow. That's strange. Your fingerprints do match perfectly to a 'Vincent Pagano.'"

"Now we're getting somewhere."

"But there's only one problem," continued the officer as he looked over his glasses at Vince.

"What's that?"

"According to the computer… you're officially dead."

"What!"

"I'm sorry to inform you Mr. Pagano, but you died on July 4$^{th}$, 2000." He took off his glasses and slowly placed them on the desk. "Is there any way you can explain that?"

# CHAPTER THREE
## ELFRETH'S ALLEY
## 2020

"Elfreth's Alley is our nation's oldest residential street, dating back to 1702," boasted Benjamin Franklin as he stood in the middle of a cobblestone lane framed by Federal style rowhomes. "The passageway is named after Jeremiah Elfreth, a skilled blacksmith and good friend of mine. In fact, Mr. Elfreth's hand was instrumental in the development of the Franklin stove, which during its heyday warmed many a hearth up and down the eastern seaboard."

As he spoke a crowd of tourists looked up and down the alley, nestled between the Delaware River and Second Street. Colorful flags jutted out in haphazard fashion including the occasional Betsy Ross. A fat cat stood on a concrete step enjoying the winter sun. Franklin led the crowd forward with a cane in hand.

"Good morning, Mr. Franklin," shouted a denizen of the lane as he exited his front door.

Franklin doffed his cap. "Hello, friend."

A slow-moving, horse-drawn carriage forced the tour group to step aside.

"A beautiful steed indeed," commented Franklin as the transport passed by. He turned about and pointed his cane at a picturesque home with brightly painted red shutters and front door.

"One of my old homesteads," quipped Franklin in a nostalgic tone. "It hasn't changed a bit."

"You lived in that house?" asked a middle-aged woman in the group. She quickly scanned a collection of tour pamphlets in her left hand. "It's not on my map?"

"Absolutely… in the late 1700s." He continued to gaze upward while speaking. "My bedroom on the third floor faced the alley." He chuckled. "I got so tired of running up and down three flights of stairs to answer the door, that I invented the busybody mirror. See?" He pointed to a three-mirror contraption anchored to the upper windowsill, the device ubiquitous to the historic lane. "It allowed me to peer out the window and see the street below in a rather inconspicuous manner."

"Kind of like today's doorbell camera," opined a lanky male in the tour group. "You should have patented the idea."

"Perhaps," said Franklin. "But I never patented any of my inventions."

"Really?"

"Absolutely. I wanted all of society to benefit from my discoveries, hence my personal mantra."

"Which is?"

"Doing well by doing good," came the measured response. "That's right." He pointed to a second story window. "The meeting parlor was on the second floor. Once a month the Junto met there."

"The Junto?"

"Yes. The Junto, otherwise known as the Leather Apron Club. I established it in 1727. An assembly whose members were drawn from a wide range of occupations and backgrounds, the main goal being the mutual improvement of everyone involved."

"A secret society?" asked the lanky man.

"No. It wasn't a secret at all. We gathered to improve ourselves, our community and those in need. In the club were printers such as myself, surveyors, merchants, cobblers and bibliophiles." He grinned. "We even had an astrologer who studied the movements and relative position of celestial objects. Oh, it was a grand alliance." He pointed an index finger to his head. "The seeds for so many of my future endeavors were planted in the midst of the Junto fellowship."

"Who lives there now?" asked the woman.

"Well, I don't know," answered Franklin. "I sold it some time ago to a merchant from Barbados, an honorable man with a large sugar plantation in the Caribbean. I believe it's changed hands a few times since then."

"Did any other famous people live on the street?" asked a teenage boy as he took a panorama with his cell phone.

"During my time... let's see." Franklin held a hand to his chin. "Well, Betsy Ross had a home across the way and to the right lived the Hamilton clan from New York, and oh yes, my next door neighbor." He pointed to the home directly to his right with black shutters. "How could I forget? The man was a bit of a rapscallion. In fact, he may have been the reason for me selling the place." Franklin laughed. "Perhaps the walls were a bit too thin."

Just then the neighbor's door to his right opened and out backed a tall man with a long overcoat and a deerstalker hat in herringbone pattern. He put a pipe in his mouth as he fumbled with the deadbolt. After latching the door, he turned toward the crowd with a look of disdain.

"Hello neighbor!" bellowed Franklin with a mighty wave. "Are you one of the Arnolds?"

"Excuse me?" mumbled Professor Bookman.

"The Arnolds, originally from the colony of Connecticut... are you a descendent of their namesake?"

"No," snarled Bookman. He took a puff of pipe and began to make his way through the crowd as it clogged the lane. "Excuse me."

"Do you know who the original owner of your flat was?" asked Franklin with a canny grin. "He was a rather infamous man to say the least."

"You know right well who lived there," snapped back Bookman.

"Yes. I know who lived there. But do you?"

"Of course I do."

"So you are aware of the Arnold name?"

"No. I'm not aware of the Arnold name. I've researched the history of my home extensively, and no one with the last name 'Arnold' ever lived there. I can assure you of that."

Franklin's grin turned a bit mischievous as he continued to interact with Bookman. "Well then, if I may ask… who originally owned your home?"

Bookman paused with a sigh. He looked at Franklin and then the crowd. "All right, I'll play along. Once upon a time, the great Benjamin Franklin lived in my home," proclaimed the professor sarcastically with a raise of his hands. "The founding father of this great nation of ours. The man who snatched lightning from the sky." He looked back at Franklin. "There, are you happy? Good day." He spun and walked away.

"Well, I respectfully disagree," countered Franklin. "I lived in the house next door, with the red shutters… not the black."

The declaration froze Professor Bookman in his tracks. He waited three seconds to gather his composure before turning back toward the tour group. He took the pipe out of his mouth as he slowly approached Franklin.

"Listen here, man," grumbled Bookman. "Benjamin Franklin lived in my home. That's an absolutism. What makes you think anything different?"

"I'm Benjamin Franklin."

A few chuckles emanated from the crowd.

"Do you know who you're talking to?" asked Bookman.

"Well, if you're not a direct descendant of the Arnolds, then no. I do not." He reached out a hand. "A pleasure to make your acquaintance… I'm Benjamin Franklin."

Bookman didn't shake Franklin's hand. "I am Professor Alabaster Bookman, the Chairman of the Department of History at the University. I know everything about Benjamin Franklin including where he lived in Philadelphia." He took one step closer to Franklin and looked down upon him. "Trust me when I say that… I *am* the Ben Franklin guru."

"Oh," said Franklin a bit surprised. "I never knew I had a guru."

Some more laughter occurred.

Bookman ignored the comment and turned to the tour group. "Benjamin Franklin lived in the home to your right, with the black shutters… *my* home, roughly between the years 1750 and 1788. He then sold it to a plantation owner from Barbados, for a handsome profit, I may add." He turned and sneered at Franklin. "He needed the money, to help raise his illegitimate son."

"Barbados, handsome profit and a son out of wedlock… yes," countered Franklin. "But you, currently residing in my old home… no."

"Well then, sir," huffed Bookman. "Can you please enlighten us as to who you believe originally lived in my home? I know it's been a few hundred years… but think hard." Bookman smirked as he looked at the crowd. "Perhaps George Washington?"

"No. Not George and Martha! They lived over on Market Street," countered Franklin. "Your current dwelling was originally owned by the Arnold family… that much I am sure of. During my stay here on Elfreth's Alley, their son Benedict and his second wife, Peggy resided in your home. As a professor of history, I'm sure you'll recall Peggy's father, Judge Edward Shippen, a loyalist with deep ties to the British Crown."

Bookman stared down Franklin with an incredulous glare. "Are you trying to tell me that the former inhabitant of my home was the biggest traitor in the history of America? That being…"

"Benedict Arnold," said Franklin. "Yes. That is exactly what I'm trying to tell you, professor. I'm sorry to inform you of that. Benedict Arnold and his wife Peggy lived in your home along with their servant."

Bookman tried to take a puff of his pipe but the tobacco had burned dry. A concerning frown overcame his face as he looked up at each home, trying to digest the possibility. Benedict Arnold did indeed marry the 19 year-old daughter of a Philadelphian named Judge Shippen, her role in the plot to overthrow the United States government significant. He was unaware of their address in the city but the initials 'B.A.' were carved into the doorjamb of an upstairs closet. He slowly relit his pipe before returning his attention to Franklin.

"What was the name of your first school, Mr. Franklin?"

"Boston Latin," came the enthusiastic reply. "Our motto was Sumus Primi... we are first!"

"And your father was?"

"Josiah... from the village of Ecton, England! He emigrated to the United States in 1682."

"Who was Richard Saunders?"

"My second favorite pseudonym," chuckled Franklin. "Benevolus was my first."

"What was the name of the print type used in your newspaper?"

"Oh, that would be *Franklin Gothic*," answered Franklin boastfully. "I developed it for the *Pennsylvania Gazette* after buying the newspaper in 1729. The paper was faltering and I quickly learned that loud headlines sell... thus the development of my characteristic print." He looked at the crowd stating, "You'll still find *Franklin Gothic* on your computers under the 'Font' section. It continues to be used to this very day. I'm rather proud of that."

The series of correct answers given in a folksy tone irked Bookman. He stared down the tour leader while searching his memory banks.

"Would you like to know anything else about my life?" asked Franklin. "I appreciate your enthusiasm. It's quite commendable."

"Yes I would," countered Bookman with a queer grin. "Why don't you tell everyone the name of your mistress in France?"

"Whoa Nelly!" hollered Franklin, his voice echoing in the alley. "That's TMI Professor Bookman... too much information." He chuckled. "I'm taking the Fifth on that one." He looked at the crowd with a pointed index finger in the air. "You have a Virginian named James Madison to thank for that amendment… an insightful safeguard protecting the accused."

Boisterous laughter erupted from the group, the tourists enjoying the historical banter as if it were staged.

"Oh, isn't that convenient," shot back Bookman. "You recite only what you conveniently know about Mr. Franklin. How lame is that? Personally sir, I find your schtick unbefitting to the legacy of Philadelphia's premier citizen." He pointed a finger at Franklin. "If Mr. Franklin were alive today, I'm sure he would disapprove!"

Several seconds of silence passed between the two men.

"I'm very sorry to disappoint you," said Franklin in an apologetic tone. "I was merely trying to answer your questions to the best of my ability. Please… take no offense. However, the suggesting of me having a paramour in France was somewhat…"

"Don't waste my time with your poppycock," snarled Bookman. "How dare you suggest Benedict Arnold lived in my home!" He stepped away. "And quit congesting the street with your tour groups or I'll report you to the police."

An angry pall of pipe tobacco doused the tour group as Bookman stormed down the lane and out of sight. Franklin took a white handkerchief out of his front coat pocket and slowly dabbed his nose.

"What a pompous idiot," commented the lanky man.

"No. No," said Franklin. "Don't feel sorry for me. Critics are our friends for they show us our faults." He put away his hanky. "Perhaps I need to work a little bit harder on my so-called 'schtick.'"

"This is the best tour I've ever had," declared the woman with the map. "Don't listen to him. He's just mad that a turncoat lived in his home."

"Perhaps," countered Franklin. "The truth can hurt."

"I'm giving you a five-star review right now!" blurted out another tourist with cell phone in hand. "That guy was a jerk."

"Thank you for the kind words," replied Ben. He cleared his throat and took a deep breath. "Well, let's move on."

"Mr. Franklin?" asked the teenager.

"Yes, young man?"

"What's the biggest difference between living in Philadelphia now as compared to the 1700s?"

"An insightful question," said Ben as he began to walk down the lane. "There are certainly pros and cons to living in each century."

"It must have been tough without the internet," commented the teenager. "I can't imagine life without it."

"Believe it or not, we survived without the internet," chuckled Franklin. "It was tough, but we persevered." He continued to pace forward in thought. "I'd have to say the most notable difference in Philadelphia is, believe it or not, the noise. Back in the day, there were no buses, car horns, police sirens or overhead jets muddying your thought process. It was deliciously quiet. The populace was free of the internet and its relentless interference. So, I'd give the 1700s an A+ for a stillness and tranquility that is impossible to obtain nowadays."

"Interesting," said the lanky man. "What would you give the 1700s a failing grade for?"

"Running water and the lack of a public sewer system," came the quick reply. "Quite frankly, many sections of Philadelphia smelled rather wretched back in the day. I'm talking cesspools, flies, maggots and every conceivable disease spawned by such filth! Our drinking water was putrid."

"Yuck!" came the unified response.

"Yuck is right. I survived many a cholera and dysentery epidemic," declared Franklin with a painful grimace. He rubbed his protruding stomach. "So never take clean, running water for granted."

"How about life in Philadelphia today?" asked the map woman. "What gets an 'A' and what gets an 'F'?"

"A passing grade to technology," came the reply. "Your ability to store, retrieve and disseminate information is absolutely astonishing. The founding fathers would be envious. Think about it, you can see and talk to anyone else in the world by tapping a button on your phone. During the Revolutionary War we communicated via messengers and letters that took days or weeks to transmit. For heaven's sake, it took me two months to traverse the Atlantic in order to speak to the King of France!" Franklin shook his head in amazement. "So many breakthroughs... including the fields of medicine, energy and commerce."

"So you like the internet?" asked the teenager.

"It's a love-hate relationship. But I'll admit... more love than hate. I'm a social media addict."

"So what fails?" asked the woman. "What stinks about living in today's world?"

"Oh boy, that's a tough one," sighed Franklin. "So much has changed." They came to a halt at the end of Elfreth's Alley before Franklin spoke again. "I'd have to say the lack of basic respect for your fellow man," declared Ben while making slow and somber eye contact with the tour group. "That's what's failing today in grand fashion and I say that with a heavy heart. It's sad."

"What do you mean?"

"In the 1700s there was a lot of strife and confusion... no doubt. We were young, cocky and full of bluster, trying to dissociate ourselves from the Crown. There were a lot of strong headed and fiery opinions as to the best course of action, yet we talked it out... we worked it out and in doing so, forged a great nation." He smiled. "We respected each other's opinion."

Several of the tourists nodded in agreement.

"Nowadays it's a bit more toxic," continued Franklin. "Everyone is irate and upset, for what reason I'm not exactly sure. My beloved Socratic method of discourse has been replaced by a screaming match, a punch in the face or worse yet... gunfire." He frowned. "Violence is the default button and people are killing each other in the City of Brotherly Love at an alarming rate! We've somehow lost respect for our fellow Philadelphian. Why just this past year... 2019, we set another record for homicides in the city... over 350, mostly by gunfire. That's absolutely horrid."

"So what would you have done different?" asked another tourist.

"Excuse me?"

"If you could go back in time? Knowing what you know now... what would you, Benjamin Franklin, have done differently?"

"Hmm, an excellent question," answered Franklin as if caught off guard. "I guess I've never thought about it. That's strange, because I've thought of just about everything else."

"Why haven't you ever thought about it?"

"Because backward time travel is impossible," declared Franklin emphatically. "Time cannot twist in reverse fashion. So it would be a waste of effort, an exercise in futility. Man can only travel forward per the laws of physics."

"Really? How do you know so much?"

"How do I know so much?" grinned Franklin. "Well, to start with... I *am* Benjamin Franklin."

## CHAPTER FOUR
### WELCOME HOME
### 2020

"Why wouldn't he come to the meeting?" asked Wally. "Is he too good for us?"

"No, I didn't say that," replied Sullivan as he stood in front of his West Philadelphia Historical Society brethren. "He mentioned something about not having a teacher's assistant this semester along with a heavy course load."

"Can someone please crack a window in here," moaned Burt from the rear. "I'm ready to pass out." It was an unusually warm January evening in the city. "It's like we're in one of Dante's circles of hell!"

Fred Mills stood up from the front row and walked over to an aged window. "It's these old cast iron radiators in this house, Burt. They're hard to regulate." He hoisted up the window to allow some fresh air to gush inside. "There's a warm air front moving in tonight. We're in for some thunder busters."

"Professor Bookman was able to provide me with a plethora of information as to Mr. Franklin's gravesite," continued Sullivan. "The man is quite knowledgeable. It's unfortunate that he can't join us."

"Can someone refresh my memory as to why we're researching Ben Franklin so much," asked the Walrus Man. "I mean, Ben's been researched to death. He wrote his own autobiography. What more do you want?"

"Yea," added Burt. "Enough with Franklin already. Let's move on."

"Gentlemen," said Sullivan. "We're still trying to work out the history of the granite wall and the saying "the used key is always light". I believe it should have read "the used key is always bright", which is one of Mr. Franklin's favorite sayings."

"Light, bright... who cares," howled Burt. "Let's talk about something else. That wall was blown to kingdom come."

"Like what, Burt?" asked Mills. "What would you like to discuss?"

"I'd like to discuss where else we could hold these meetings!" He took a white hanky out of his rear pocket to dab his brow. "I'm sweating like a hound dog."

"That's because you're wearing long johns!" shouted Wally.

Just then the sound of hoofbeats could be heard outside the window, the characteristic cadence louder with each approaching step. The rhythmic beat brought a sense of calm to the room.

"Whoa!" came the cry of the coachman followed by the sound of a horse nickering. "Whoa!"

"What the heck," said Fred as he walked over to the window. The club members followed and gathered around his side.

"A horse-drawn carriage," exclaimed Wally. "Cool."

"What's it doing here?" asked President Mills. "And who is that guy in the back?"

They watched the coachman hop down from his seat and open the carriage door. The lone passenger stepped out and looked up and down Baltimore Avenue. He walked toward the front door as it began to lightly rain.

"Hey, wait a minute. That looks like Ben Franklin!" declared Mills with a glance at Sullivan.

Sullivan didn't respond as he hustled downstairs to open the front door.

"Good evening, Doctor Sullivan," bellowed Franklin as he slightly bowed. "Excuse me for the unannounced visit, but I was up in the neighborhood visiting the Children's Hospital and thought it convenient to stop by." He took off his hat. "I hope you don't mind." He slowly slid down his collar to show Sullivan his key.

"Ahem, excuse me," garbled Mills as he brushed by Sullivan. "Attorney Frederick Mills here, President of the West Philadelphia Historical Society. Can I help you… ah, sir?"

"Attorney Mills… a pleasure indeed," said Franklin with an extended hand. "B. Franklin here, printer."

"Yes, how can I help you?"

"I was hoping to spend a few minutes with your society, Attorney Mills. In today's day and age I find it grand that you meet with your fellow Philadelphians to discuss matters of importance. It would be an honor to join in the discussion."

"Yes, well." Mills looked up the crowded stairwell at his fellow members.

"John, is this a joke?" asked Wally.

"You've lost your marbles," added Burt. "Enough with Franklin already." He thrust his arms forward in disgust.

"Oh, I apologize," said Ben. "Perhaps another night?" He went to put his hat back on. "I'm sure there's strict decorum for a guest to attend your meetings."

"No, wait!" said Sullivan. "Stay!" He looked at Mills. "Fred, let him come in."

"Well," replied Mills with a concerned frown. He cleared his throat. "I'd have to query the other members… "

"Fred," interrupted Sullivan sternly. "Give him a few minutes with us. I guarantee you'll all be amazed by his wealth of historical knowledge. Trust me on this one."

"Let him in," said another member of the group. "He's the guy from the Independence Visitor Center. He's good."

"Yea, let him in," chimed in the majority of the membership.

"Well, alright then," followed up Mills with a rosy cheeked grin. "Let me be the first to welcome Mr. Benjamin Franklin to our monthly meeting." He swung forward his left arm. "Do come in, sir."

The group escorted Franklin upstairs to the meeting room as an approaching rumble of thunder could be heard.

"Yes, this reminds me of the old Junto days," beamed Franklin as he inspected the antique map of Philadelphia on the wall. "What a delight!" He respectfully walked to the front of the room and scanned the assemblage. "May I ask if we first go around the group with each member telling me their name and trade?"

"I'll go first," volunteered Burt. "Burt Bilkins here, from up on 49$^{th}$ Street. I was raised in Philadelphia and became a professional boxer at the age of seventeen, my career cut short by World War II. I served in the Army and landed on Omaha Beach on June the sixth, 1944... at exactly 1053 hours."

"Thank you for your service, Mr. Bilkins," said Franklin.

"You're welcome," came the gruff reply. "After the war, I worked for the Postal Service as a carrier for forty-five years before retirement."

"Wonderful!" exclaimed Franklin. "A most illustrious career. What was your record as a pugilist?"

"Eleven wins and only three losses," came the proud reply. "Five of the wins were by knockout."

"Watch out for the right cross," quipped Franklin with a shoulder dip and short jab. He looked at the Walrus Man sitting next to Sullivan. "And you sir, can you tell me about yourself? I must say, I do envy your mustache."

"My name is Wally Roberts and I'm a retired chemist. I was born and raised in the Olney section of Philadelphia and worked for DuPont Industries in their polymer division. My expertise centered upon acrylics as an alternative to glass products. I officially retired seven years ago but still serve as a consultant for the company."

"Marvelous," added Ben. "My understanding is that the word 'chemistry' derives from the word 'alchemy', which has an Arabic origin. True?"

"That's right," said Wally. "It's from an ancient term describing the Nile Valley region of Egypt, that being 'Khemia', which means 'land of black earth'."

"Interesting," said Ben. He looked at Mills. "Attorney Mills, what can you tell me about yourself?"

Mills stood up. "Yes, of course. I was born and raised in this very home, my father an attorney and my mother a nurse at the Philadelphia General Hospital. I earned my Juris Doctorate from Temple and have devoted my life's work to family law and real estate. I'm semi-retired but still lecture at the local University where I maintain an assistant professor position. I've been president of the West Philadelphia Historical Society for the past ten years or so."

"Bravo and caveat emptor," stated Franklin. "Let the buyer beware."

"Absolutely," followed up Mills. "That's a maxim that I adhere to on a daily basis in the world of real estate." He took a deep breath of accomplishment. "Caveat emptor."

And so it went, with each member giving a brief synopsis of their upbringing, occupation and current interests. With each summary, Franklin added a brief commentary with an occasional anecdote in regard to their field of expertise.

"You have quite an interesting and accomplished membership," proclaimed Franklin as the session came to an end. He looked at Attorney Mills. "Congratulations to you all." A louder clap of thunder was heard outside.

"Yes, thank you," replied Mills as he stood up to close the window. "Now, Mr. Franklin… how about you tell us something about yourself?"

Franklin grinned at the invitation. "I most certainly can." He turned toward the crowd. "I am B. Franklin, originally from the colony of Massachusetts, but I certainly call Philadelphia my home. I ran a print shop here in the city until age 42 when I sold it to my partner. I then embarked on a journey of scientific exploration that led to several breakthroughs in a variety of fields to include

A TWIST OF TIME

electrical engineering, medicine and oceanography. I devoted my latter years to public service and the birth of our democracy. I'm proud to say that I'm the only person to have signed all four key documents establishing the United States as a sovereign nation, that being the Declaration of Independence, the Treaty of Alliance with France, the Treaty of Paris that brought peace with Great Britain and the United States Constitution." He nodded his head in a satisfactory way.

The audience sat in awe of the speaker.

"Let's see, have I forgotten anything?" asked Franklin to himself. "Oh yes, one of my prouder local accomplishment's was aiding in the establishment of our nation's first hospital, which is here in center city, that being Pennsylvania Hospital."

Several jaws went agape.

"Oh, and the University of Pennsylvania... I founded that too." He grinned with an upward pointed index finger. "That one turned out quite well." He scanned the crowd. "Would you like to know anything else about my career? I mean, that was only a brief summary of the highlights."

"Wow," stated Mills. "That's quite the resume, Mr. Franklin."

"Holy smokes. How did you do it all?" asked Wally. "I mean, where did you find the time?"

"Yea," snickered Burt. "What did you do for fun?"

"For fun? I swam as a hobby," replied Franklin. "Thank you for reminding me of that, Mr. Bilkins. I enjoyed many a refreshing dip in the Delaware River and in doing so invented swim fins. In fact, I was inducted into the International Swimming Hall of Fame in the year 1968."

Just then a tremendous flash of lightning occurred followed by a clap of thunder that shook the overhead chandelier. The bolt caused the horse outside to neigh in a frightened fashion.

"Whoa, Freedom!" screamed the horseman. "Whoa, old girl!"

"Wow," exclaimed Franklin. "That was close... bad night to fly a kite."

Laughter cut through the room as did another flash of electricity. A car alarm could be heard on the block.

"Sounds like something got hit," stated Wally with wide eyes. "There's a weather alert out for lightning strikes."

"President Mills, do you have lightning rods protecting this domicile?" asked Franklin.

"Well, ah… in the past we did, but then a storm back in the late 1980s damaged a section of the slate roof, which if I can recall…"

"No. He doesn't," interrupted Burt.

Another round of lightning and rolling thunder segued the discussion to another topic.

"So what's on your agenda, gentlemen?" asked Franklin in an inquisitive tone. "What's the purpose of your meeting?"

The question seemed to catch the congregation off guard.

"Well," stammered Mills. "We were deeply involved in trying to prevent the destruction of the Franklin Wing, which as you may know, ended rather abruptly. Since then we've been a bit adrift. I'll admit that."

"I'm still researching the granite wall," stated Sullivan.

"We're looking for a project," interjected Burt with a growl. "Do you have anything in mind?"

"How about the Best Cheesesteaks in Philadelphia?" suggested Ben with a quirky grin. "That's been a hot topic for centuries."

An eruption of eatery names rained down upon Franklin, the enthusiastic shouts drowning out his vote for *Firenze's*.

"Yes, perhaps a conundrum left well enough alone," cautioned Ben. "Let me see." He paced back and forth in front of the group. "What needs to be addressed in our fair city… from a historical standpoint that is?" He stopped pacing but continued to ponder with a downward gaze. "I've got it!" He turned toward the membership.

"What? What is it?"

"It has come to my attention that a controversy is brewing on Elfreth's Alley as to which home was previously owned by Benjamin Franklin."

"I didn't know you had a home there," stated Sullivan.

"I had several residences in the city," declared Franklin. "Everyone is aware of my Franklin Court residence and the West Philadelphia estate that ultimately became the grounds for our Philadelphia General Hospital. However, one of my lesser known dwellings was indeed on Elfreth's Alley… a cozy little retreat where I liked to entertain and actually, where the Junto would meet."

"So what's the controversy?" asked Burt.

"A local history buff whose name escapes me has pegged the wrong house as my previous address," stated Franklin. "The man currently resides on the street. I engaged in a spirited discourse with the gentlemen but it ended with a rather reprehensible exchange of words. Sad, because as you know… whatever is begun in anger ends in shame."

"So, our goal would be to identify the correct residence that Ben lived in?" asked Wally.

"Yes. That would be the objective. I'm quite confident that I lived in the home attached directly to the left of the history maven's dwelling. We would just have to prove that and the rest they say… is history."

"Sounds interesting," added President Mills. "I can certainly see the long-term relevance to such an endeavor."

"Will you help us?" asked Sullivan with a coy smile.

"Yes, help us!" came the cry from the membership. "Please!"

Ben scanned the crowd in a slow and methodical fashion. "Well… alright, I'll help," came his earnest reply. "It would be my pleasure to work hand-in-hand with the West Philadelphia Historical Society on such a noble venture."

"Hear! Hear!" went the chorus.

"Fantastic!" shouted Mills as he stood up to regain control of the meeting. "Now we're getting somewhere. I would like to personally thank Mr. Franklin for spending some time with us this evening. It certainly has been an honor having him here."

"You're quite welcome," said Franklin over a round of applause.

"Perhaps we can all retreat down to the rathskeller and seal the deal with a draft beer?" suggested Mills with a nervous bob up and down on his toes. He looked at Franklin. "Do you imbibe, sir?"

"Is the Pope Catholic?" chuckled Franklin. "Of course I imbibe young man! I've never met a quaff I didn't like."

"Hurrah!" shouted the gang as they bull rushed their way downstairs for a round of libation.

If was after the second round of brew that Sullivan was able to pull Franklin aside.

"I've been looking all over for you," whispered Sullivan over the clamor. "Where have you been?"

"I got hung up in 2065," answered Franklin. "Had a bit of a medical hiccup, but everything is alright now." He took a sip of beer.

"Are you sure?"

"Absolutely. The old ticker ran a bit awry. But I'm fine, thanks to modern medicine."

Sullivan patted Franklin on the shoulder. "It's so good to see you, Ben."

"It's good to see you, too," replied Franklin as he finished off the beer. "Oh yes, before I forget. I reconnected with Dr. Schmidt in the future and he wanted me to deliver a message to you."

"Dr. Schmidt? What did he say?" Sullivan leaned closer.

"His exact words were..." Franklin paused as if searching his memory banks. "Let's see, oh right." He looked at Sullivan. "Tell Dr. Sullivan that Vince has been arrested and he's in police custody."

"WHAT!" shouted Sullivan, his outburst drawing immediate attention from the group. "Did he say anything else?"

"No. That's all he wanted me to convey. Vince has been arrested and he's in police custody."

"Who's been arrested?" asked Mills as he stepped into the conversation.

"Nothing... I mean nobody," stammered Sullivan with a look of grave concern.

"Gentlemen!" shouted Franklin. "It's time for old Ben to pull the pin!" He put the mug down and waved a hand high in the air. "If I'm not home by eleven o'clock, my Deborah calls the police."

Laughter erupted with a few hoisted mugs of beer. "To Ben Franklin!"

"To Ben Franklin!" shouted the fellowship.

A series of heartfelt handshakes delivered Franklin to the front door.

"I'll escort you home," said Sullivan as he put on his jacket.

"If you insist," said Franklin. "That is if you don't mind the smell of horse manure."

"I don't mind and thankfully it stopped raining."

The two men climbed up into the carriage, their ride downtown relaxing and entertaining. It seemed that Franklin's persona garnered attention at every intersection stop. He waved at passing vehicles, took a few selfies with some pedestrians and even got out of the transport at 30th Street Station to wish two newlyweds the best as they prepared to jettison off on their honeymoon.

"My BFF!" shouted the woman as she waved good-bye, still in her wedding dress. "Goodbye, Mr. Franklin!"

"Send me a postcard from Jamaica!" shouted Ben. "Godspeed new friends!" He waved and pulled a blanket over his lap. "What an enchanting couple, she a physical therapist and he a plumber. They just got married by a justice of the peace against their parents' advice. How wonderfully rebellious!"

"You like a good rebellion, don't you?"

"Absolutely," came the quick reply as the carriage traversed the Schuylkill River. "Always remember to challenge authority, John… contest the establishment and dare the elite."

"I'll remember that."

As the carriage approached the historic district, the crowd began to noticeably thin out. The coachman stopped at the corner of 5th and Arch Street and helped his passengers out. It was nearly midnight.

"Thank you, Jerome," said Franklin. "All the best to Sally."

"Goodnight, Mr. Franklin… goodnight sir." The driver tipped his hat.

"Well John, it's been a pleasure. I'm heading forward to 2065."

"Now?"

"Yes. I have an appointment with my cardiologist tomorrow. If I no-show it's a twenty dollar charge." He sighed. "God heals yet the doctor takes the fees."

"I'm coming with you," declared Sullivan. "I've got to help Vince. Is that possible?"

"I suppose," said Franklin as they approached the iron gate in front of his gravesite. "As long as you're at my side when…"

"Yikes!" interrupted Sullivan as he gazed into the darkness of the graveyard. There, on top of Ben's tombstone lay the remains of a massive oak tree that had fallen to the ground. "Lightning must have struck that tree."

"Oh no," cried Franklin. "I planted that tree in honor of my little Franky. It was a favorite."

They stared through the gate at the collapsed carnage with branches and twigs strewn across the drop zone. The grave beneath the tree's canopy could barely be seen. Several seconds of silence ensued.

"Well, what's done is done," whispered Ben. He scanned the area for any other people in sight and then reached down to pick up an acorn from the tree that had rolled forward. "It can be replaced."

"So I can come with you?" asked Sullivan.

"I don't see why not." Franklin held the acorn tight in one hand.

"I have my key, too."

"Interesting," countered Ben as he began to walk directly perpendicular to the midsection of his grave marker. "I've never travelled before with both keys."

"Where? Where's the key slot?" asked Sullivan as he looked around in anticipation. "I couldn't find it."

"Surprise… there is no slot," chuckled Ben. "The wormhole is exactly thirteen feet on a right angle from the midsection of my grave. He took hold of Sullivan's arm. "Are you ready, John? Let's step forward in time together."

"I'm ready."

Both men reached up and took firm hold of their respective keys.

"Let's do it," said Ben.

They stepped forward and vanished.

It was exceptionally dark and cold when each man opened their eyes. Sullivan was the first to notice the unfamiliarity of the surrounding area.

"Ah, Ben," uttered Sullivan as he gazed upwards. "Where are all the tall buildings?"

Franklin rapidly blinked his eyes as he scanned the neighborhood. "Heavens, I'm a bit unfamiliar with this terrain." He squinted forward. "Wait a minute. No… it can't be!" He let go of his key.

"What? What's wrong?"

"But it's impossible," mumbled Ben. "Per the laws of physics."

Just then the approaching voice of two men could be heard in the stillness of the night. They were singing.

*"We drink until the drink is gone, no matter if it's dusk or dawn…"*

"That voice," stated Sullivan. "It sounds familiar."

Over a grassy knoll appeared two men, their gait staggered.

*"Me lady will be waiting home but I'll be sleepin' with dog and bone…"*

"Ahoy!" shouted one of the two drunkards as they stopped in front of the time travelers. Their bodies reeked of liquor. "Benny Franklin? Is that you?" asked the taller of the two. He leaned forward to better view Franklin's face and smiled a toothy grin. "It *is* you!" He put both arms around Franklin. "Welcome home mate. Are you back from London?"

"Yes," sputtered Franklin, his face aghast. "Yes I am. God save the King."

"Let's go celebrate with a brew," suggested the stranger. "First pint is on me!"

"Ah, no. No thank you… ah."

"What? You forgot our names, have you?" asked the shorter of the two.

"Well, I've been away for quite some time," explained Ben as he continued to stare around. "So much has changed."

"It's me, Mario," said the taller man as he took off his hat. "And my brother, Antonio… the Pagano brothers!"

Perhaps for the first time in his life, Ben Franklin stood speechless. He shook his head as if trying to wake up from a bad dream. Several men on horseback trotted behind the brothers.

"Something odd is going on here," stated Ben.

"Has the drink gotten the better of you, Ben?"

"Mario, what year is it?" asked Franklin hesitantly.

"What year is it?" laughed Mario. "Benjamin Franklin is asking me what year it is?"

"Yes. Yes, I am."

"Why Ben… it's 1779. Welcome home to Philadelphia!"

# CHAPTER FIVE
## MINGO
## 1779

"I've been Benjamin's personal physician for some time now," declared Dr. Edward Casey as he strolled down Pine Street. To his right walked John Sullivan in amazement, watching Philadelphians going about their daily business. The dirt covered thoroughfare smelled like rotten eggs with a pungent dash of ammonia. Mangy appearing dogs were ubiquitous and an occasional horse trotted by. "Mr. Franklin has been reasonably healthy to date, except of course for gout and pain from bladder stones. I'm afraid he'll be battling those two maladies until his final days, especially with his penchant for Madeira wine."

"Wine?" asked Sullivan. "I thought he liked beer?"

"Beer, wine… whatever. You have to realize in today's day and age, that being 1779, water isn't all that safe to drink."

"Interesting."

"So the populace in general finds it safer to drink wine and beer." The two men dodged a man pushing a wooden cart full of circular cheeses. "Hence the propensity for gout and alcoholism in the colonies."

"In wine there is wisdom, in beer there is freedom, in water there is bacteria," laughed Sullivan.

"Hmm. I haven't heard that one yet. Did you just make it up?"

"No," came Sullivan's reply. "That's a Ben Franklin saying. You've never heard it?"

"No, and trust me, I've heard them all. So, you better let Ben know about that one, so he can claim it. For some reason he loves to stockpile witty quips. He insists they're going to be his lasting legacy."

Sullivan eyed up the physician, a tall and robust man with a distinguished thick mustache sporting a touch of grey. He wore a black derby hat. After spending the previous night at Franklin's Elfreth's Alley home, he was introduced to Dr. Casey and offered a tour of the city's first hospital. They were in route to the facility near the corner of $8^{th}$ and Pine Street. To their right rose a stately eight foot high brick wall that ran the length of the block. An occasional ivy vine crawled up the wall.

"When was the last time you time traveled?" asked Sullivan.

"My one and only trip was about ten years ago," came the response. "Unfortunately I suffered an apoplexy in transit so Ben arranged for some physician in 2065 to operate on me." He brushed back his front left hairline to expose a curvilinear scar. "The man clipped a ruptured vessel in my brain. Can you believe that? I'm lucky to be alive! Unfortunately, I haven't much of a recall of the entire incident."

"An apoplexy? I'm unfamiliar with that term."

"Oh right. Ben calls it something else. It's when a blood vessel in your head bursts and bleeds." He began to rapidly snap his fingers. "What's the name of that … "

"A stroke?"

"Yes, that's it!" Casey pointed emphatically at Sullivan. "A bit of an emergency from what I understand."

"Indeed. You are lucky to be alive, even by futuristic standards. So you've never traveled to the future again?"

"Never. Too risky. I'm darn glad to have made it back. I've got a wife and seven children here in Philadelphia."

The two men turned to their right and walked through an arched iron gate. Before them ran a stone walkway that led to the hospital's main entrance, a double wooden doorway flanked by three tall gothic columns on each side. The gothic columns occupied the top two floors of the three story construct. A series of circular sidewalks symmetrically dissected the front lawn.

"Welcome to Pennsylvania Hospital," said Casey. "The first hospital in the nation. You're looking at the Pine Building, completed between 1755 and 1756." While speaking he led Sullivan into the hospital grounds.

Sullivan gazed up at the structure before him, well aware of its classic Colonial and Federal architecture. "Wow, it looks exactly the same," said Sullivan. "I mean in a forward sense… 2020 that is. I've always loved the cupola on top."

"Do you know the reason for the cupola?"

"Yes, for light to come into the facility. I believe a surgical amphitheater is beneath the dome."

"Correct," said Casey. "But for what else?"

"Hmm. I'm not exactly sure."

"A fire escape," stated Casey. "To let the patients out in case of a fire."

"Interesting."

"The hospital was founded in 1751 by Dr. Thomas Bond and Mr. Franklin," continued Casey. "Their goal being the creation of a medical oasis for the poor, destitute and sick, especially the insane. In fact, the current number of insane patients outnumbers that of the medically ill." He pointed toward the hospital. "The mentally corrupt are kept on the ground floor, the men's ward occupies the second and the third floor is for women only. The cornerstone was set in 1755."

"What are the most common conditions that prompt an admission?" asked Sullivan as Casey veered their route toward the building's southeast corner.

"Well, insanity is number one. Of course that includes the more specific diagnoses of hysteria, lunacy, madness and delirium."

Sullivan didn't respond.

"From a nonpsychiatric standpoint, the most common reason for admission would have to be grippe with consumption being a strong second." Before Sullivan could reply the physician pointed to the base of the Pine Building's foundation. "Here's the corner stone. Benjamin wrote the wording that's etched in the granite."

"He sure likes engraving statements in stone," laughed Sullivan as he approached the keystone. Leaning forward he read the inscription aloud:

> In the year of Christ
> MDCCLV.
> George the second happily reigning
> (for he sought the happiness of his people)
> Philadelphia flourishing
> (for its inhabitants were publick spirited)
> this building
> by the bounty of the government,
> and of many private persons,
> was piously founded
> for the relief of the sick and miserable;
> may the God of mercies
> bless this undertaking.

"It's ironic that he mentions King George," said Casey. "But that was over thirty years ago. Ben was quite loyal to the Crown before the Stamp Act."

Sullivan took pause in an attempt to register the historic timetable of events. The Revolutionary War was never his forte.

"The British only withdrew their forces from the city last year." Casey's tone became more serious. "Dr. Sullivan, the Revolutionary War is still going on today… as we speak here in Philadelphia. General Washington just appointed someone named Benedict Arnold as Commander of Philadelphia. To my understanding he's a rather controversial chap."

The Arnold name struck a chord with Sullivan. He saw a rather distinguished man with a limp exiting the home adjacent to

Franklin's earlier in the day. The man was in uniform and sneered at Sullivan while stepping into a carriage.

"We also just received word of a heroic captain named John Paul Jones defeating the British at sea off the coast of England. How grand is that!"

"I have not yet begun to fight," declared Sullivan proudly.

"Excuse me?"

"John Paul Jones... I have not yet begun to fight. The British ordered him to surrender but he sent back that immortal message." Sullivan paused. "You're unaware of that famous line?"

"I'm unaware of such a proclamation. Captain Jones uttered those exact words?"

"Well, maybe," countered Sullivan, not wanting to get ahead of the historical curve. "Perhaps I'm getting my sea battles mixed up. Believe it or not a few more naval engagements occurred after the American Revolution."

"I don't want to hear about it," ordered Casey while placing his hands over his ears. "I've made that clear to Ben. Don't spoil the future on me. I prefer not to know my fate."

Sullivan nodded his head. "I understand. Forgive me, doctor. It won't happen again."

Casey dropped his hands and continued on, unphased. "There's talk of a Constitutional Convention in the works once this war is over, here in the city. I'm sure that's why Ben came back. He would never miss that." Casey led Sullivan back toward the main courtyard. "He loves to hobnob."

The two men meandered back toward the front lawn where the spring sprouts of a well-manicured garden poked through the ground.

"Here is our medicinal garden," proclaimed Casey proudly. "All the plants grown here are used to treat the sick." He began to walk around the rectangular plot as he spoke. "Of course we have the basics... garlic, ginger and St. John's Wort." He pointed across the garlic row. "And there we have some foxglove shoots."

"This is magnificent," quipped Sullivan as he scanned the garden, some butterflies and bees drifting through the beds. "How convenient to have your own pharmacy just outside."

"Excuse me?"

"Your own pharmacy." Sullivan paused as he sensed some bemusement. "Oh, pardon me. Your very own, home grown... what's the word I'm searching for? Apothecary?"

"Yes! Indeed. I agree." Casey continued to navigate around the green space. "And of course, no apothecary would be complete without one of my favorites, chamomile. It's very soothing when combined with a proper cup of tea." He squatted down to reach across a low fence, stroking a chamomile leaf. "Next to it grows the cure for the common cold."

"Which is?"

"Echinacea, of course. That's well proven." The physician stood up. "Now, Dr. Sullivan. Would you like to take a look inside?"

"I would love to."

The two physicians strolled up a set of granite steps and through the front entrance of the hospital. Beyond the doors opened a capacious foyer with two stairwells curving along each flanking wall. Broad windows along the front facade allowed sunlight to flood inward. A large candle chandelier centered above a black and white marble floor drew the visitor's eye forward in a pleasing fashion.

"How beautiful," remarked Sullivan. "Everything is so perfectly balanced."

The visual tranquility of the scene was promptly disrupted by the crazed shouts of patients inhabiting the ground floor, their screams of horror echoing through the chamber.

"Yes," said Casey with an extended hand. "Let's move forward through the mental unit." He led Sullivan across the foyer and into the ward.

They quickly encountered a disorganized scene as male attendants dressed in white tended to male patients dressed in drab grey outfits that resembled pajamas. Many of the patients sat in chairs, their gaunt bodies rocking feverishly back and forth in rhythmic fashion. A few sat around tables playing checkers. Others simply stared forward and rapidly moved their hands while talking gibberish to no one in particular. Sullivan estimated about twenty patients to occupy the common room. An attendant had to occasionally redirect a patient's roaming attempt to exit the room. No one seemed to be in charge.

"This is our day room," said Casey. "We believe that free time to interact is crucial to the management of their respective diseases." He continued walking. "That is for those deemed safe enough to enjoy it."

"I see. The beginnings of group therapy."

They continued through another set of double doors that led them into a narrow hallway flanked by individual rooms. Each room had a closed and bolted, thick wooden door with a single rectangular slot along its upper third. Across the open slot ran a narrow bar of steel. The smell of urine and fecal material infiltrated the area. It was along this hallway where the screams emanated.

"I am King George!" shouted one patient. "Off with their heads!"

"They're controlling me!" screeched another. "In the walls… from the basement. They're turning the wheels. Make it stop!"

Dr. Casey ignored the shouts as they passed by a burly attendant with a thick beard and protruding stomach. A ring of skeleton keys hung from his belt. The sentry nodded to Casey.

"Good morning, Walter," said Casey to the strongman.

"Must have been a full moon last night," stated Walt. "They're all wound up." He held a night stick in his hand and flashed a horrid grin of rotting dentition.

"Walt, this is Dr. Sullivan. He's going to be spending some time with us."

The two men exchanged greetings with a handshake, the attendant's hairy hand engulfing that of Sullivan.

"Welcome," said Walt in a gruff tone. "Watch your back." An unsightly scar ran in an oblique fashion across his right cheek.

"I will," muttered Sullivan as he gawked upward at the behemoth. "Thank you for the advice."

"Walter has been here forever," continued Casey as he stepped away. "He's our head orderly." He slapped Walt's broad shoulder. "He's good at maintaining discipline, too… right Walt?"

"The beatings will continue until morale improves," snickered Walt.

"Alright," whispered Sullivan.

The two men walked up to the viewing slot of one room and peered inside. There, in the starkness of the room, stood a naked and scrawny man with his back to the doctors. A low guttural hum generated from his upper torso and a patch of black hair graced his sacrum. With his right arm he rapidly ran a thickened and curled one-inch long fingernail across the stone wall, his actions slowly etching a line in a surface already littered with bizarre doodle similar to cave paintings. A wretched stench drifted out of the confine.

"Classic madness," stated Casey in a professorial tone.

"His forearms? Are those burns?" asked Sullivan.

"Electrical burns indeed," came the reply. "You're quite perceptive, Dr. Sullivan. Believe it or not we've been applying Mr. Franklin's knowledge of electricity to treat patients here at the hospital. Benjamin recommended it himself."

"Fascinating," said Sullivan as he squinted at the wall markings.

"We've been using electrical energy to treat madness, hysteria and certain neurological conditions such as lameness," bragged Casey. "In fact, we're seeing some promising results in the treatment of a young soldier struck by a musket ball in the lower back, the wound resulting in an inability to walk."

As he talked Sullivan continued to stare at the far right wall, trying to make sense of the mishmash of markings. In the midst of the madness appeared two rectangular bars of equal length in upright fashion. Surrounding the columns were crude stick figures of humans a tilt on each side. Some stick figures lay flat on each column side.

"Do you have any questions before we head upstairs?" asked Casey as he pulled out a handkerchief to cover his nose.

"No," mumbled Sullivan as he continued to study the scribble. Above the scene were a few straight lines crossed by shorter lines at ninety degree angles. "Are those airplanes?" mumbled Sullivan as he stepped away.

"Excuse me?" asked Casey. "What did you say?"

"Nothing," stammered Sullivan as he turned away and shook his head. "My eyes are playing tricks on me."

The tour ascended a stairwell to the men's ward on the second floor. A classic open ward greeted Sullivan with ten beds lining each side of the room. A series of clunky white pillars ran in unison along the foot of every other bed. In direct contrast to the floor below, a sense of calmness and order permeated the floor.

"Looks like a Veteran's Administration Hospital," commented Sullivan.

"Pardon me?"

"A VA hospital. Where we treat military veterans."

"We do have a few wounded patriots in house," countered Casey. He stepped up to a bed where two male attendants were working on a patient's left arm. "You're in luck. A bloodletting in progress."

Sullivan stepped forward to witness a young man in his early twenties with a bloodied wrap around his chest. His left arm was held out over the side of the bed. One attendant gripped his upper arm while another held firm to a tubing that penetrated the skin of the patient's extended elbow. The tube ran downward several inches to gravity, allowing blood to slowly drip into a metallic half basin on the floor. Sullivan estimated at least two units of semi-clotted blood to be in the reservoir.

"We're using the antecubital vein," stated Casey. "Not an artery in this case. We've been bloodletting him now for three straight days with positive results."

"What's the diagnosis?" asked Sullivan.

"A bayonet wound to the chest and gunshot to the leg." He pulled a white sheet off of the patient's lower torso, exposing a gangrenous leg from the knee downward. An open, ghastly wound dominated the mid shin area.

"Are those…"

"Maggots? Yes indeed," said Casey. "We're trying to clean the wound as best we can. Our protocol involves draining an amount of blood equal to what would be in this patient's injured leg… in order to balance the humors." He flipped the sheet back over the lower extremity.

Sullivan's gaze slowly moved upward to make eye contact with the wounded warrior. The man's face was ashen white and the membranes below his eyes pale. The soldier reached out his right hand to Sullivan as if trying to save himself.

"Help me," whispered the boy. His lips were parched and his voice weak. "Please… help me."

Sullivan reached down to grasp the soldier's cool hand. He slowly leaned forward and ran his opposite hand gently across the man's forehead. "Thank you," he whispered. "Thank you for your service."

The patient nodded and held his grip for several seconds. He then let go.

"Come along, doctor," ordered Casey. "Ben is expecting us back for lunch."

The two doctors exited the ward and hospital.

"Pretty exciting stuff," stated Casey as they strolled toward the front gate. "The avant-garde of medicine in the colonies." He cleared his throat. "Are you aware that Mr. Franklin developed the first urinary catheter?"

Before Sullivan could respond a horse-drawn carriage galloped up to the entryway. After coming to an abrupt halt, two attendants dressed in black garb jumped off the front seat. They hustled to the rear of the carriage where a person thrashed about wildly. The attendants dragged the man to the ground via a series of ropes and chains attached to his extremities. As they yanked on the cords the madman howled in a ludicrous manner.

"Collusion!" he shouted while standing up. "Global warming... the ice caps are melting! We're all going to be boiled alive!"

"I don't believe my eyes," declared Walt as he walked past the two physicians. "Is that Mingo?" He slapped the night stick into his palm. "Where in the hell have you been?"

"What's going on?" asked Sullivan.

"An ambulance drop off," answered Casey. "That looks like one of our old patients that escaped months ago."

"Don't believe the media!" screamed the man in a psychotic rage. "They're all liars! It's all fake news!"

Extra medical personnel arrived as the man's arms were rope-tied to his torso and his legs shackled. The medical team pulled him to his feet and walked him over to Walt. His clothes were ragged yet he wore a tailored, grey short sleeve shirt. Filth covered his frame.

"My, oh my," declared Walt as he stared down at the patient. "It is Mingo. We've been looking all over town for you. Where have you been hiding?"

"I've been to the future!" shouted Mingo. "The future!" His tongue rapidly darted in and out of his mouth. "The planes... they came out of the sky! The towers... they're gone!" He spit at Walt.

The head orderly administered a tremendous blow to the victim's jaw, knocking him to the ground. He then delivered two kicks to his midsection. Mingo curled up and squealed like a wounded animal.

"No spitting on hospital grounds," snarled Walt. "Obey the rules." He put his foot on Mingo's forearm and pressed downward, the action opening up the patient's clenched hand. "So... you did steal it," declared Walt as he reached down to grab a ring on Mingo's thumb. "I thought so." He forcefully pulled the ring off, the action prompting Mingo to unleash a string of profanities. Walt delivered two more cracks of the club to Mingo's legs. "No cursing on hospital grounds!"

The attendants waited for Mingo to gather himself before bringing him upright. They marched him toward the hospital entrance.

"They're crossing the border!" screamed Mingo as he walked past Sullivan with crazy in his eyes. "The illegals... they're underground... in the tunnels! We have to stop them!"

Sullivan squinted to read some stitching that adorned the madman's left front shirt pocket. It read "Schmidt's of Philadelphia".

"I've been to the future!" squawked Mingo. "The future!"

# CHAPTER SIX
## THE GRANDFATHER PARADOX
## 1779

"We have to be extremely careful," stated Franklin as he sipped some tea. "We're in uncharted waters. A rather odd twist of time." Next to him sat Sullivan slowly rubbing the back of his neck. The two men were seated in the second floor parlor of Franklin's home. It was ten o'clock in the morning and a drizzle of rain fell softly outside.

"In the past I've always been transported back to time as it progressed, as you have too," continued Franklin. "But somehow we've been jettisoned well behind that point. I've always suspected the time tunnel would close once 2065 arrived. Perhaps it was the lightning strike or the presence of both keys?"

Sullivan didn't respond as he nibbled a stale piece of moldy bread.

"Have you ever heard of the grandfather paradox?" asked Ben.

"Maybe," mumbled Sullivan. "Is it cold in here?" His body shuttered. "I'm freezing."

"It's a theory that refutes backward time travel by examining the ability of a person to travel back in time to kill his grandfather, before the conception of their very own mother or father." Ben took a bite of biscuit before continuing. "So in essence the action prevents the very existence of the time traveler."

"That's the paradox?"

"Yes, but the crux of the paradox refers to any action from the traveler that alters the past." Franklin turned toward Sullivan. "John, we're both well aware of what's about to happen here in Philadelphia. We defeat Great Britain and in 1787 a grand convention will be held in this city to create the seminal document of our nation, that being the Constitution of the United States. However, we must be extremely careful not to alter any current events, no matter how tragic the outcome." Franklin took off his bifocals and turned his gaze outside. "If we intercede in the slightest way, no matter how innocent... the result can be both irreversible and exponential in scope. Even the slightest suggestion..."

"Did you hear all that screaming last night?" asked Sullivan.

"Excuse me?"

"The shouts of terror from next door? It went on for about an hour."

"No. I sleep rather soundly." Franklin took another sip of tea. "Well, perhaps a tad. I thought it may have been a dream."

"I know you heard it. Everybody on the street heard it." Sullivan pulled the blanket over his back up to his neck. "It was a woman's cry. It sounded like she was being murdered... or worse." A moment of silence passed. "Why didn't the police arrive?"

Franklin allowed some time to pass before responding. He took a deep breath and pushed his frame out of the chair. "John, allow me to remind you... it's 1779."

"I don't care what year it is," snapped back Sullivan. "Somebody was being abused last night and it came from the Arnold house. I'm sure of that."

"I've no doubt where it came from," continued Franklin. "But..."

"But nobody did anything! That's the problem. Everyone is walking around this morning like nothing happened. Look outside." He tossed the bread down. "I'm ashamed of myself. I should have intervened."

"John, reset your thought process," ordered Franklin in a firm tone. "A women's life in colonial America is drastically different from what you're accustomed to. The infancy of the suffrage movement only takes root in the middle of the next century. We're a long way off from gender equality."

Sullivan continued to brood as the lecture continued.

"John, I'm going to be blunt. Colonial women are subordinate to the dominant male in their lives. It's that simple… first to their father and then as a wife, to their husband. By age 20 a woman is expected to be married with at least one child. They usually remain pregnant throughout their reproductive years, that is if they survive multiple childbirths. Believe it or not, women in New England average around seven childbirths during their lives."

Sullivan stood and walked over to the window. He peered down gravely at the street.

"But please, don't misunderstand me," continued Franklin with a raised index finger. "Women are a most valued asset. For you see, women in the colonies are in short supply as compared to Europe and as you know, they are a rather integral part of the equation when it comes to the propagation of the species. They form the nucleus of any good functioning family." He paused to reload his thought process. "They've even been permitted to work alongside their husband in his trade. That's a significant step in the right direction." He hoisted his finger even higher into the air. "Now take Deborah and me, we have a wonderful working relationship. In my prime I tended to the print shop and she maintained order back home. Our marriage is based on a pragmatic approach…"

"What about spousal abuse? Is that considered acceptable?"

"John, in no way do I condone the physical abuse of a woman. Let me make that perfectly clear. However, now… in the year 1779, a married woman has few legal rights. They are expected to obey the man in their life… without exception. Their legal identity is represented by their husband."

Sullivan sighed.

"John, bad husbands mistreat their wives. From my experience in colonial times, it's the exception, not the rule." He paused to respect the subject at hand. "Yet, as sad as it sounds, there are no repercussions for such heinous behavior in today's society. If an abused wife runs away, she is either shunned or forcibly brought back to her husband."

"There's the culprit now," muttered Sullivan as he looked down upon Elfreth's Alley.

Franklin walked over to the window. He asked Sullivan to step back and out of sight.

"Use the busybody mirror, John. Let's not call attention to ourselves."

"Is that him?" asked Sullivan.

"Who?"

"Benedict Arnold?"

"Yes, it is. He's officially the military governor of Philadelphia, per the orders of General Washington himself. That's a rather coveted position given to Benedict in recognition for his service to our country so far. Benedict is a battle proven leader, that's indisputable. He distinguished himself grandly in the Siege of Boston and Fort Ticonderoga alongside Ethan Allen. Many people consider him a war hero."

"He's got a nasty limp."

"His left leg was severely wounded in the Saratoga Campaign. A gunshot to the femur. Hence the altered gait."

"Who's he talking to?"

"His coachman," replied Franklin. "He must be preparing for a journey." Both men watched Arnold speak to his driver while pointing to the front end of a horse-drawn carriage. Beside the transport stood a uniformed soldier at strict attention with musket rifle in arm. "Perhaps a problem with the front hub or the brake block."

"Everyone on the street is gawking at him," observed Sullivan. "Like he's a rock star."

"John, listen to me," pleaded Franklin as he put his hand on Sullivan's forearm. "We all know what's about to transpire with Mr. Arnold over the next calendar year… at least I do." Franklin checked the busybody mirror again. "He's going to take immediate advantage of his position and in the process make some powerful enemies in Philadelphia. Both he and his wife will live lavishly and consequently find themselves in horrible debt. He'll then start secret negotiations with the British to surrender American forces in return for money and a command in their army."

"He's starting to walk over to your front door," interjected Sullivan as he leaned farther backward.

"In about a year, his plans to hand over West Point to the British will be foiled and he'll flee the country, disgraced and branded the greatest turncoat of all time. He'll take that moniker to his grave and his name will forever be synonymous with the word 'traitor.'"

A rap from the doorknocker sounded from downstairs.

"Let it play out, John." Franklin held his grip. "No matter what the circumstances… don't tilt our hand."

Sullivan didn't reply.

"Do you understand? Please, place your emotions in check. You're only passing through a brief snapshot in history."

Sullivan paused before answering. "I understand." He turned defiantly toward the stairwell. "Let's go meet Benedict Arnold."

Ben put on a hat and the two men headed downstairs.

Franklin opened the door and before him stood Major General Benedict Arnold in full military garb. At a height of five foot and nine inches he stood taller than the average British-American man of the day. An aristocratic nose with a slight bump dominated a pair of thin lips, and a whitish wig made from the hair of a yak covered his skull, complete with ponytail. Slate grey eyes with some surrounding wrinkles belied an age of 38 years. He wore a scarlet coat with plain silver buttons atop a ruffled shirt, breeches and black leg stockings. A pair of high top boots completed his commanding presentation.

"Ah, Benjamin," stated Arnold in a deep and firm tone. "It is true. Someone told me you've recently returned from overseas." He put a hand on Franklin's shoulder. "How grand. Welcome home my friend."

"Yes. It's always good to be back in Philadelphia," answered Benjamin. "Would you like to come in for a spot of tea?"

"No, thank you," answered Arnold with a glance at Sullivan.

"Oh forgive me," declared Franklin. "I'd like you to meet Dr. John Sullivan. He's from the north of Penn's Woods and will be spending some time here at our hospital, caring for the wounded."

"Very good," said Arnold with an extended hand. "Our troops deserve the best."

Sullivan reached out and shook the commander's hand, noticing his grip to be firm and resolute.

"Congratulations on your Philadelphia command," said Franklin. "A well-deserved honor for your service."

"It took a bit of maneuvering but General Washington finally came through. His ungrateful staff initially passed me over for some junior officers, but thankfully George intervened… and here I am. Ben, we've got the bloody British on their heels."

"How grand," blurted out Franklin. "Liberty or death!"

"Victory will be ours soon!" countered Arnold with a clenched fist.

Sullivan stood to the rear left of Franklin, refusing to partake in the bravado. He noticed some scratch marks on top of Arnold's right hand.

"How's the leg?" asked Franklin.

"From what they tell me as good as can be expected," answered Arnold. "Of course it's one of the main reasons I've been put in command here. My battlefield days I'm afraid are over."

"Would you like Dr. Casey's opinion? He's my personal physician."

"No, thank you, Ben. There's daily pain but nothing a good blast of rum can't handle."

"And congratulations on the recent nuptials," continued Franklin with a gleam. "I know the judge well, but not his daughter. She comes from a fine family. You're a lucky man."

"A most gorgeous bride indeed, my dear Peggy. She adores this little street. She can't wait to meet you."

"Is she home now?" asked Franklin.

"Unfortunately, no," came the response that caught both Ben and Sullivan off guard. "She been down in Virginia with her father for the past week settling some accounts."

The horse attached to the waiting carriage suddenly let out a series of neighs, prompting all three men to look backward in a reflexive fashion. It was then that Dr. Sullivan first set eyes upon her.

She stood five and a half feet tall and her frame was lean but well-rounded. Her skin was black with a lighter tone that suggested an African lineage with a mixed Caribbean trait. A white three-quarter sleeve blouse and blue skirt covered her torso to ankle level and her feet were bare. She wore the patched outfit with pride, yet it was her face that immediately struck the beholder, a youthful and perfectly symmetric display of beauty set above a set of full lips and framed by a blue kerchief head wrap. She fumbled with a rectangular suitcase in hand and quickly turned her gaze away from the men.

"My new house servant," mumbled Arnold. "Put it in the carriage and be careful!" he hollered before turning back to Franklin. "She's basically useless… no wonder Jefferson gave her to me for cheap." He laughed. "Caveat emptor."

"Where are you headed?" asked Franklin.

As the military governor disclosed his travel plans, Sullivan watched the servant struggle in an attempt to hoist the baggage into an overhead slot. She repeatedly tried but failed, the travel trunk too cumbersome to manage. The driver ignored her plight as did the soldier on guard.

"Wait, let me help!" shouted Sullivan. He bolted toward the girl.

"John!" shouted Franklin.

Sullivan approached the servant and reached up to help her push the baggage into place. Their bodies bumped together in the process.

"Look here," shouted the driver. "Don't help her."

"There you go," said Sullivan after completing the task. He let go of the bag and brought his gaze upon the girl, perhaps in her late teens, immediately noticing a bruised and slightly swollen left cheek bone. Blotches of black and blue covered her wrists and an angry scratch ran across her neckline.

"Are you OK?" asked Sullivan.

The servant spun away and walked back into the house.

"Did the luggage hit her?" asked Sullivan as he looked up at the driver.

The coachman smirked. "I suppose," came his sarcastic reply. He spit on the sidewalk. "Yeah, that's what happened."

Sullivan looked at the sentry. "Is that what happened?"

The guard didn't reply as he kept his attention forward.

Sullivan turned and walked back toward Arnold. "Was that young woman in an accident? I mean… she's bruised all over."

"What's it your business?" snarled Arnold.

"I'm a physician," retorted Sullivan as he stopped in front of the military leader. "She appears to be a bit banged up. Did anything happen? She may need medical attention."

"So what if she's hurt," scoffed Arnold. "Never you mind. She's fine."

"It looks like she was assaulted," declared Sullivan. "Is that possible?"

"It's none of your business what happened to my servant," barked Arnold. "None whatsoever."

"Take it easy, John," interjected Franklin.

"I respectfully disagree," continued Sullivan. "It is my business. I've taken an oath to care for and protect… "

"Do you know who you're talking to!" blurted the military officer with a menacing step forward. His frame loomed over that of Sullivan's. "I'm Major General Benedict Arnold of the Continental

Army and current military governor of this city. What are you suggesting man… an impropriety on my behalf?"

Franklin intervened as the exchange escalated. He tried to position his body between the two men.

"John, let's say we head back inside for a spell," suggested Ben in a calm manner. He looked at Arnold. "Benedict, forgive my friend for his words, he's been up all night in turmoil, perhaps from exhaustion."

Benedict Arnold kept his gaze on Sullivan, awaiting a response.

"Let's go, doctor," implored Franklin as he took hold of Sullivan's arm. "The governor must be on his way."

An anger roiled in the soul of John Sullivan as he locked eyes with the military leader. He started to speak until Arnold slowly raised his right hand as if ordering someone to halt. Sullivan then felt a pointed object touch the base of his lower spine. He turned around to espy the sentry with his rifle drawn and bayonet pointed at his abdomen. No one moved for several seconds.

"You were saying, doctor?" asked Arnold. "Let's hear it. Voice your concern."

Sullivan looked up at the soldier, his face weathered and scarred. Several insignia stripes ran across his left shoulder and a peculiar bloodlust emanated from his sordid grin as he waited for a command. He peered down at the bayonet which was long, rusted and a tad crooked near the tip.

"He was saying that he's sorry," implored Franklin. "Forgive him, Benedict… for he is a country doctor from the woodlands, unfamiliar with the ways of our city. He is here to help… I can assure you of that. Why just yesterday he toiled long hours at the hospital, helping the cause. I can vouch for the man."

Sullivan watched the eyes of the guard turn toward his commander. A bead of sweat trickled down the sentry's dirty cheek as he leaned slightly forward, the tip of the weapon indenting his skin. A few onlookers gathered near the carriage with their interest piqued by the spectacle. Sullivan went speechless as the commander allowed several seconds to pass by.

"Just as I thought," mocked Arnold from behind. "A craven. Drop your weapon."

The soldier suddenly frowned as if disappointed and pulled the musket back. He retreated two paces and returned to a stance of attention.

"Be gone with yourself," ordered the commander. "And watch your tongue."

"Very well," exclaimed Franklin. He yanked Sullivan out of the mix. "Thank you, Benedict. Thank you for your understanding." Ben bowed and doffed his cap. "Again, congratulations on your commission." His body continued to push Sullivan away as he walked backwards. "I look forward to meeting Mrs. Arnold upon her arrival to town." Franklin returned the hat to his head. "Yes, indeed. She comes from a most admirable family." He fumbled for the latch and opened the door. "I insist on hosting a dinner in your honor." He went to close the door. "Godspeed, old friend."

The door closed and Franklin spun back at Sullivan. "Are you insane?" whispered the founding father in an incredulous tone. "He could have given the order to eviscerate you right on the spot. Kill you… without any recourse! Gather yourself together, John! You're talking to a Major General in the Continental Army. A warmonger! This isn't 2020!"

Sullivan's heart beat wildly in his chest, his emotions not allowing a verbal reply. He put a hand on his stomach and felt nauseous. The hallway began to spin.

"Get upstairs," barked Franklin. He pushed John up the stairwell. "I'm surprised you're still alive! You publicly questioned the man's integrity. How dare you!"

Sullivan collapsed into a chair and fell into a sweaty daze, the face of the young girl unable to be erased from his mind.

"The grandfather paradox!" howled Franklin. "We must never intervene. First, do no harm! Never directly accuse someone in public… certainly not in today's day and age!"

As the lecture continued Sullivan drew the blanket back over his shoulders. He stood up and walked over to the busybody mirror to view Major General Benedict Arnold's carriage pull away from the sidewalk. He waved to the adoring crowd as he rode away. Behind him stood the servant girl alone on the sidewalk. She turned away, glanced up at the window and walked back into the Arnold homestead.

"I'm sorry," said Sullivan as he watched her disappear. "It's just that I've never seen a slave before." A chill ran through his body.

# CHAPTER SEVEN
## JOIN, OR DIE
## 2020

"I'm moving to Florida," stated Barry Zuckerman as he stood outside of his home on Elfreth's Alley. "My lumbago can't take these goddamn winters anymore." While speaking he hammered a sign into a patch of grass just outside his front door. "This house is officially for sale by owner as of…" He delivered a final blow from the mallet. "Now!" Zuckerman wore baggy trousers, a button shirt and grey sweater that sagged below his waistline. He was eighty-one years old and his entire body habitus sagged in unison with his attire. "Let the bidding begin… caveat emptor!"

"Yes, indeed," huffed Attorney Fred Mills as he held a hand to his chest, a bit out of breath, the alley being five blocks from the nearest bus stop. "Exactly how long have you lived here, sir?"

"Who are you guys again?" asked Zuckerman. He put a hand on his lower back and arched it in pain.

"We're from the West Philadelphia Historical Society," proclaimed Mills. "You may have heard about us during the recent Franklin Wing demolition." Behind him stood Wally and Burt. "We made national headlines."

"Nah. Never heard of you guys."

"Well, regardless," continued Mills. "We're here today at your home to carry out some research of historical significance."

"Research on my home?" laughed the owner. "Historical? Hell, you can have it if you like." He dangled a set of keys in the air. "It comes with a parking spot in the rear and everything inside. I just put on a new roof, too."

"It's a beautiful home," commented Wally. "I like the red shutters."

"Red was my wife's favorite color," stated Zuckerman. "But she's long gone. In fact, everyone's gone. That's the problem." He scanned the trio. "Do you gentlemen want to come inside for a private tour?"

Mills looked at his comrades as they nodded in unison. "Sure," said the president. "That would be wonderful, that is if you don't mind."

"Nah. Come on in. You guys don't look that hostile." He started to walk toward the front door. "Hell, I could probably whip all three of you at once. Do you guys ever go to the gym?"

No one answered as the historical troop entered the home.

"Wow!" exclaimed the guests as they scanned the first floor.

Scattered everywhere were artifacts from colonial America with an obvious emphasis on the Revolutionary War. Paintings of George Washington and Charles Cornwallis faced each other on opposing walls, and a stack of three rifles were held together by a swivel in a classic upright pose. Flags of all shapes and sizes adorned the walls and a hallway leading to a back stairwell. A framed copy of the Declaration of Independence hung next to a portrait of King Louis XVI of France. A cannon complete with wheels dominated half of the room, along its side a pyramid of black cannonballs.

"Holy smokes!" declared Wally. "This place is like a museum."

"Are those Pennsylvania rifles?" asked Burt in amazement as he stepped up to the weapons.

"Ah, a keen eye," said Zuckerman. "Yes they are… the preferred weapon of the Continental Army sharpshooter. They're originals, made by a German gunsmith down near Chadds Ford. Only a few select soldiers carried a Pennsylvania rifle during the war."

"Why is that?"

"It took twice as long to reload than the standard issue Brown Bess musket," stated Zuckerman as he pointed to another firearm on the wall. "And the elongated stock and barrel was delicate, so no good for melee combat. But the Pennsylvania rifle could hit a target much farther away."

"How far?"

"Up to 250 yards," answered Zuckerman. "With accuracy. Many a British officer sitting smugly behind the lines took a bullet from the long barrel. In fact the Brits referred to the gun as a "widow maker". The Pennsylvania rifle changed the course of many a battle."

"What about the cannon?" asked Wally.

"Another original. I had to get the flooring reinforced for that baby to roll in. It's a three pound galloper, the preferred weapon of the artillery." He patted the gun's muzzle as he spoke. "Smaller than you would expect… right?"

"Yes," answered Burt.

"It was easy to transport, hence its popularity," said the homeowner. "I got this from a gun enthusiast up in Wilkes-Barre."

"Real cannonballs, too?"

"Absolutely. They're held in place by a brass monkey so they all don't roll around." He pointed to a square base beneath the stack of ordinance. "There were many types of cannonballs used in the war. These balls are standard issue cast iron, shot parallel and ultimately across the ground like a skipping stone, its aim to dismember any human in its path." He handed a ball to Burt. "They each weight about three pounds and a skilled crew could fire off three or four rounds per minute."

"An absolutely fascinating collection of artifacts," said Mills as he continued to survey the room.

"A treasure trove," added Wally.

"What's your occupation?" asked Mills. "If you don't mind me asking."

"You just did and no… I don't mind. I'm a retired elementary school teacher. I taught history and geography in Philadelphia public schools for oh… let's say about forty-five years." He pointed to a framed picture on the wall. "Here I am during the nation's bicentennial at Valley Forge with my class." He reminisced while lifting the photo. "Time sure does fly by. These kids here are probably all retired now and scattered around the world."

"So, how did all of this come about?" asked Burt as he inspected a Moultrie flag on the wall. "You're obviously a collector."

"My wife's great grandfather was the original collector," replied the host. "He secured the bulk of the items. According to her memory, he was the third person to own the home, the previous two owners from Barbados. The house has been in the family for generations, well back to the early 1800s. Each generation added to the historical array, so it naturally grew over time. I've since become the curator of the collection by default, except for the cannon, which I purchased on a whim. It actually still works."

"And you're selling it all?"

"Yes. I'm the end of the line. No children unfortunately. All my nieces and nephews consider it junk. They won't even take a cannonball off my hand." He led the visitors down the hallway to a basement stairwell. "I tried to sell it to the city, but they weren't interested… apparently Philadelphia already has enough antiquity when it comes to the War of Independence."

"Is the entire house loaded with artifacts?"

"No. Just the first floor and basement." He opened the door to the cellar. "Below are the servant quarters." He took a step downward. "Would you like to take a peek? They're relatively well preserved."

"Absolutely," came the unanimous reply.

The rickety stairs creaked as the tour descended into a subterranean chamber that mimicked a primitive confine aboard a ship. A single rectangular window measuring one foot high by two feet wide allowed some rays of sunlight to enter the cellar which was damp and cool.

"I usually run a dehumidifier down here," grumbled Zuckerman. "But the hose keeps getting clogged." He turned on a light.

The walls of the entire basement were constructed of red colonial brick with light grey mortar. A set of plain, wooden bunk beds ran adjacent to a wall and a few chairs next to a spinning wheel occupied the far corner of the room. Near the stairwell sat a wicker laundry basket and some buckets and opposite the bunk beds rose a small, square fireplace with a wooden mantle. A black pot hung inside the fireplace over dry pieces of firewood. Two glass bottles and some scattered plates occupied the mantle. The flooring consisted of tightly packed bricks in no particular order.

A moment of silent retrospect ensued.

"This is the original layout," said Zuckerman. "It's been untouched… at least to my knowledge. Those beds are over 200 years old."

"This is where the servants stayed?" asked Wally as he ran a hand over the wooden post of the bed. Several names were carved into the wood.

"Yes," replied the owner. "They were responsible for the daily operation of the home to include laundry, cleaning, maintaining all the fireplaces and of course the preparation of meals."

"Were they free men and women?" asked Mills tentatively. "Or were they…"

"That all depends, Attorney Mills," interrupted Zuckerman.

"On what?"

"Their skin color," came the blunt reply. "In colonial times a white man or woman was surely an indentured servant. Nearly a third of all immigrants in the 1700s arrived as an indentured servant, someone agreeable to work for several years in exchange for passage, room and board."

"What about someone of color?"

Zuckerman took a deep breath before continuing. "Unfortunately, a Black man or woman living in this room was surely enslaved, that being the property of the homeowner… indefinitely I may add, with no hope of freedom." He ran his hand slowly along the spinning wheel. "So this is rather sacred ground my friends. A snippet of history that no Zuckerman could bear to destroy."

"And rightfully so," added Burt. "It should be preserved as a reminder of such a dark time in our nation's history."

Each man continued to inspect the room.

"I've got a feeling of remorse in my soul," muttered Wally as he picked up a rag doll. "It's hard to imagine such a time existed here in Philadelphia."

"We used to bring school classes through on tour, but all that has gone by the wayside," continued Zuckerman. "The kids loved it, but now they have an Independence Visitor Center and the new Museum of the American Revolution. Hopefully the next owner will respect the history."

"I can't imagine the City wouldn't be interested in this," stated Mills as he reached up to the mantle and brought down a coin. "These artifacts looked as if they've been left behind in 1776 and never touched again."

"Look at the floor inlay," said Wally. He pointed to an area of flooring beneath the stairwell where the image of a serpent appeared to be hiding beneath the grime.

Zuckerman walked over and began to clear the dirt away with his foot, his actions revealing the curvilinear body of a snake inset along the cellar floor, with a tongue sticking out of its mouth. The snakes body was sliced multiple times, resulting in a total of eight segments, each situated beneath either one or two letters. The serpentine display ran across the floor for at least ten feet.

"Anyone recognize that symbol?" asked Zuckerman.

"I've seen it around town," replied Mills with a hand on his chin. "It's a Revolutionary War symbol, that much I know."

Zuckerman allowed some time to pass before answering. "It's the legendary *'Join, or Die'* logo… made famous by none other than Mister Benjamin Franklin." His declaration stunned the guests. "Franklin printed it in his *Pennsylvania Gazette* just before the war, in hopes of uniting the colonies. It's widely considered to be the first political cartoon in America." He pulled a cell phone out from his pocket. "Let me turn on the flashlight from this device. My family showed me how to do it." He began to unsuccessfully fumble with the phone's keyboard. "My nephew's son just gave me this phone… said I can't live without it." After some effort, he looked up at his guests. "Do anyone of you gentlemen happen to have a cell phone?"

"No," came the combined reply.

"Consider yourselves lucky," quipped Zuckerman as he continued to mishandle the cellular device, his actions prompting a soothing vibratory tone along with the appearance of a young boy's face on the screen.

"Hey, Grand Uncle Z," said the boy with a grin. "What's happening?"

Zuckerman gawked at the phone. "Tommy. What are you doing on my phone?"

"You Facetimed me," said the boy.

"I what?"

"You Facetimed me." Some laughter was heard in the background.

"No I didn't."

"Yes you did."

"No I didn't," argued Zuckerman as he stared in awe. "I don't even know what Facetime is, so how could I have done it?"

"Grand Uncle Z, I'm at practice now." He laughed. "I'll call you back tonight." He waved good-bye before another soothing zoom occurred. His face vanished.

"What in the hell?"

"Here, I've got a penlight on my keychain," said Wally as he stepped forward. He shined the light upon the ground.

"Back in the day there was a common myth that a severed snake would come back to life if all of its pieces were put together before sunset," stated Zuckerman. "So Franklin put out this cartoon, in hopes of uniting the colonies. They had to join together… or die. Each letter represents a colony."

"But there are only eight segments," said Mills as he counted each with a pointed finger.

"Yea. There were thirteen colonies," added Burt.

"Look over the head of the snake where it says 'NE,'" said Zuckerman. "Ben lumped all the New England colonies into one."

"And the 'P' segment is for Pennsylvania?" asked Wally.

"Yes. He put the Pennsylvania segment on the top of the curve and along the midportion of the snake. Ben considered Pennsylvania critical to unification, hence the term 'keystone state.'"

"Fascinating."

"The symbol was eventually put on a flag and served as a rally cry for the Continental Army," continued Zuckerman. "It represented unity and a resistance to British oppression." He kicked some dirt off the tail. "Hell, it was even used in the Civil War… by both sides! You'll still see it flying around town nowadays. It's recently experienced somewhat of a renaissance."

"What craftsmanship," said Wally as he bent down on one knee. "It's made out of granite." He stroked the artifact.

"This is original to the home," stated Zuckerman. "It's been down here forever and I've never let anyone touch it." He pointed back toward the room. "We've had contractors dig trenches here and there but I always had them avoid old Snaky. A city inspector once told me I had to dig it up in order to run a new sewer line out to the street. He mentioned something about a city code violation."

"So, what did you do?"

"I told him to take a hike."

"And it worked?"

"Yea. Along with a handful of cash." Zuckerman chuckled. "Nobody touches Snaky."

"How can you possibly give all this up?" asked Wally as he stood erect.

"I don't want to… but there's no next generation," came the somber reply. He looked at the historians in a canny way. "But, for the rock bottom price of 2.7 million dollars, it can all be yours, gentlemen." He winked and grinned. "Snaky included. Think about it."

"Mr. Zuckerman," said Attorney Mills. "Who was the original owner of your home?"

"Good question."

"Because that's why we're here," continued Mills. "To determine if Mr. Benjamin Franklin resided at this address. Certainly, this remnant may strongly suggest so."

"It was always assumed that he lived here," stated Zuckerman. "For generations… until the guy moved in next door."

The guests looked at Zuckerman a bit confused.

"My neighbor is a historian from the University," continued Zuckerman with a role of his eyes. "The department chairman to be exact."

"And he refutes that Franklin lived in your home?"

"Absolutely. Over the past ten years he's written a series of scholarly articles proving beyond a doubt that Ben Franklin lived on Elfreth's Alley… but not in this exact house. I tried to discuss it with him but heaven forbid a retired grade school history teacher question his authority."

"So where did he say Ben lived?"

"The home next door," came the reply. "His home. The one with the black shutters. The esteemed professor is in the process of having his residence recognized by the National Register of Historical Places." Zuckerman frowned. "The guy stole my family's thunder."

Mills furrowed his forehead. "But, there must be a deed. I specialize in real estate law and can certainly help…"

"There's no original deed with Franklin's name on it," said Zuckerman. "I've searched over and over. But what does it matter, gentlemen? I'll be on a beach down in Florida by this time next year."

The story silently riled the historical cadre as Zuckerman led them back upstairs. It was directly in front of the cannon that Fred Mills stopped to talk.

"Mr. Zuckerman," declared Mills. "As president of the West Philadelphia Historical Society, I beg of you to allow us to investigate this matter further. We would consider it an honor and a privilege to accurately determine whether or not Mr. Franklin owned your home."

"For what purpose? The house is for sale."

"We're historians!" howled Mills with a raised index finger. "It's our responsibility to accurately record events of the past for the benefit of future generations. That's what we do!"

"Hear, hear," said Wally.

"There is history in all men's lives!" roared Mills, his cheeks now red.

"Was that a Ben Franklin quote?" asked Zuckerman.

"No. William Shakespeare."

Zuckerman grinned while considering the proposal. He looked at Mills and his historical cronies, considering them men of his ilk.

"Well…" said the owner.

"You owe it to old Snaky," pleaded Wally.

"Yea," added Burt. "Some millennial is going to jackhammer that snake out of its nest and throw it right into a dumpster. They don't care about history."

Zuckerman scowled at the possibility. "Not on my watch! Nobody touches Snaky." He shook Mills' hand. "Let's do it, gentlemen. I'm in. Join, or die."

## CHAPTER EIGHT
### VARIOLA MAJOR
### 1779

"A gentleman recently asked me a most interesting question," stated Franklin as he walked down Spruce Street beside Sullivan. The two men had just visited Ben's daughter across town. "One that has generated immense reflection on my behalf."

"What was the question?" asked Sullivan as he wiped some sweat off his forehead. "Boy is it hot." A man carrying some chickens in a crate passed by.

"It was during a recent tour I gave on Elfreth's Alley in 2020," continued Ben. "The chap asked me what I would do differently if given the opportunity to travel back in time, that being to the 1700s and the birth of our nation. A question I had never before pondered."

"So, what did you tell him?"

"I incorrectly told him that backwards time travel was impossible," answered Franklin with a shake of his head. "In retrospect a gross miscalculation."

"You can't be right all the time," chuckled Sullivan as he side stepped a load of horse manure in his path. "Curb your horse," he mumbled to himself.

"Regardless, for some reason, God has delivered me back in time," continued Franklin. "And in doing so has granted me an opportunity of significant magnitude to have a second go at it." He grinned. "A proverbial second bite of the apple."

"What do you mean, Ben... a second bite of the apple? Don't forget the grandfather paradox. You're the one who lectured to me about it. We can't do anything significant to change the future... especially you! Your actions are already etched in the annals of time... in stone I may add."

The two men continued forward as they pondered the question at hand.

"Well, for one thing," said Franklin. "Despite all my accomplishments, I'll never be voted 'Husband or Father of the Year'. That much I'm sure of."

"How so?"

"I'm traveling all the time, usually wandering around in Europe. I once set sail for England to take care of some matters for the Penn family, and told Deborah I'd be back in six months."

"And?"

"I came back seven years later! Oh, the woman is a saint. She welcomed me with open arms." Franklin hung his head in shame. "For heaven's sake, I didn't even attend the weddings of my only two children. Imagine that? How dreadful in retrospect." He sighed. "The great Benjamin Franklin... a no show."

"So you're saying there's room for improvement in regard to your role as a husband and father?"

"Absolutely. Thus our visit to Sarah and tonight I'm taking Mrs. Franklin on invite to the Washington's home for dinner. She at first refused, but I insisted she accompany me. I plan to make amends for prior indiscretions on my behalf." He thrust an index finger in the air. "This time around its family first."

"What's going on up ahead?"

"Now, wait until you hear my second resolution," continued Franklin, deep in thought. "It's both ingenious and dastardly at the same time. A real game changer in my humble opinion." He smiled in a self-satisfactory way. "I was thinking, what would happen if I just..."

Two men on horseback suddenly galloped past the duo, both wearing the uniform of the Continental Army. They headed directly toward a boisterous crowd outside the State House. Several people on foot ran past Sullivan and Franklin in pursuit.

"What's all the commotion about?" asked Franklin to a middle aged man huffing and puffing his way by.

"A hanging!" gasped the man, short of breath. "A Loyalist to the Crown just convicted of spying." He pushed forward while hollering. "Hang 'em high!"

Franklin and Sullivan picked up their pace as several women, children and a dog sped by. Some hollering could be heard as they arrived at the State House where a man was being escorted outside by armed guards. His hands were tied behind his back as an angry crowd rained profanities upon him. A few waved sticks as they hollered.

"Traitor!" shouted one.

"God save your King!" heckled another.

"Oh my," said Sullivan as he scanned the swarm of Philadelphians. He peered at a makeshift, wooden gallows, with a single transverse beam and rope attached. "I don't believe it… a lynch mob!"

"No," said Franklin as he was pushed about by the angry horde. "It can't be a mob… a mob has a leader." He steadied his frame from a blindside shove. "I don't see any leader here."

The soldiers nudged and pushed the condemned up a set of steps that led to the back of a horse-drawn wagon, situated beneath the rope. At one point the man fell to his knees in a fit of hysteria, only to be dragged forward.

"You're a spy!" screeched an elderly woman wearing a white bonnet next to Franklin. She waved a clenched fist in the air. "Turncoat!"

As the shouting continued, the doomed man was positioned beneath a hangman's noose. Three burly guards held him at attention as the surrounding madness intensified. The two men on horseback appeared to the left of the gallows and one rider dismounted with scroll in hand. He walked over to a podium of equal height to the wagon as the bell tower in the State House chimed three times. It was then that Benedict Arnold appeared on horseback, his gallantry in full display. He wore a majestic red hat and rode a sleek, black stallion. He nodded for the soldier to proceed.

"Hear ye, Hear ye!" shouted the crier. "Before thee stands the condemned, one Jonathan "Shep" Shepford, tried and convicted for the crime of treason."

"I'm innocent!" screamed the man, tears streaking down his face. "Innocent! You have to believe me!"

"Silence, sot!" shouted a guard as he drove a fist into Shepford's back.

The crowd cheered at the strike.

The proclaimer continued. "The condemned colluded with British forces in an attempt to destroy the gunpowder supply stored in Christ Church, his plan intercepted by a local..."

"Gunpowder is in very short supply in the colonies," said Ben as he leaned near Sullivan. "It's a critical ingredient to the success of our fighting minutemen. Without gunpowder we cannot wage war. Towns typically store them in their church for safe keeping."

The crier slowly rolled up his scroll and looked at the man. "Do you have any last words?"

"I didn't do it!" screamed the man. "It was the Pagano brothers... Mario and Antonio. They're the guilty ones! God is my witness!"

"The Pagano brothers!" repeated Sullivan. He glanced at Franklin. "Did he just say the Pagano brothers?"

"Yes. You met them when we first arrived. The brothers tend to the gunpowder supply at the church. They're drunkards with expertise in explosives, a rather risky combination indeed. But they're passionate when it comes to blowing things up."

"What?" exclaimed Sullivan. "How can that be?"

"The Pagano boys are the village idiots," proclaimed a man as he turned back to face Sullivan. The right side of the man's forehead was covered by an ulcerated skin cancer exposing a portion of his skull. "Mario is the taller of the two and the stupidest." He grinned. "Antonio only has three fingers on his left hand." He pointed back at the gallows. "Shep is one of their drinking buddies." The informant snickered and turned his attention back to the stage.

"Sarah, never forget me," shouted the man as a blindfold was placed across his face. "I will always love you!"

Sarah Shepford collapsed to the ground near the wagon wheel as family members tended to her side.

The hangman's noose was forcefully placed around the man's neck as he continued to struggle. He gasped loudly as the rope was snugged in place.

The three men vacated his side as Major General Arnold slowly trotted aside the horse-drawn wagon. The commander raised his hand and the crowd became instantly quiet.

"There is no greater shame… than the shame of a betrayal!" bellowed Arnold as he looked out over the crowd. He peered back at the man with disdain. "And there is no greater betrayal… than that of a traitor to our noble cause." Arnold's horse temporarily bucked as the man's wife desperately shrieked. He looked down at her and smirked. "Therefore, by the powers invested in me, I hereby condemn this man to hang until dead. May God have mercy on his soul… proceed."

A set of two drummers began a rapid drum roll. Arnold held his hand high for five seconds and then quickly dropped it, his action prompting the horseman to crack the reins on his steed. The wagon burst forward and the rope snapped taut. The body of the condemned contorting violently for a brief second as the drum roll stopped.

A collective gasp emanated from the crowd, followed by absolute silence. The dead man's body slowly rotated to the left and right as a crow in an adjacent tree began to caw, the sound muffling the wail of his widow at his side.

"Leave him hang until sunset," ordered Arnold. "Then cut him down." The military governor rode slowly through the crowd, the adoring throng parting way. He disappeared behind the State House.

"Oh my God," stammered Sullivan. "How barbaric."

"It's an insult to be hanged," stated Franklin.

"What?"

"The honorable way to be executed is by firing squad," explained Franklin. "I'm sure that's what the dead man requested, but Arnold probably ordered him hanged, as further punishment."

"He got what he deserved," declared the woman in the bonnet with a shake of her gnarled index finger. "The man didn't deserve a firing squad." She walked away as the crowd slowly dispersed. "Traitor."

"Blaah," moaned Sullivan as he vomited onto the ground. "Blaah!"

"John, are you alright?" asked Franklin as he grabbed hold of Sullivan's forearm.

Sullivan wiped his mouth with his sleeve and looked upward, his face pasty white. His body shivered intensely as he leaned forward. "Oh my, I suddenly don't feel well." He got down on one knee and then rolled onto the ground. "I've got a terrible headache." He held his stomach while continuing to groan. "We better get home."

"You're burning up with fever," commented Ben as he held his arm. Franklin rolled up Sullivan's sleeve with a look on concern. "Ah, John... how long have you had this rash?"

Scattered across Sullivan's forearm were tightly packed pustules, having the appearance of peas beneath his skin. A few of the firm nodules were beginning to scab over.

Sullivan began to hyperventilate as he looked upward, the concerned crowd strangely moving away. He noticed Franklin motion to a passerby pushing a cart for assistance. The physician next felt his body being hoisted upward onto the cart into the supine position. Sweat poured down his forehead as the makeshift ambulance began to move forward.

"John!" shouted Franklin as he leaned forward. "What year were you born in?"

"1977," moaned Sullivan. "Why?"

"Oh boy," whispered Franklin.

"Pennsylvania Hospital I presume?" asked the cart owner.

"No," replied Franklin. "He won't be permitted through the gate. Take him to my home… on Elfreth's Alley."

"Yes, Mr. Franklin."

The ride to Elfreth's was a bumpy blur to Sullivan, his mind drifting in and out of consciousness. He recalls several men struggling to carry his frame up to the second floor of Franklin's address and being placed on a sofa. He also remembers a cold washcloth being placed on his forehead along with encouragement to drink water. Afterwards he drifted into a state of delirium from the fever.

Sullivan dreamed of traveling out of control through the time tunnel, his arms and legs spread wide and his body slowly rotating like a pinwheel. To his right was Ben Franklin and to his left Vince Pagano. Blue and white sparkles emanated from their frames as they cartwheeled through the ages, their destination unknown. There was no sound, concern or worries, only a soothing solace in the journey to wherever. The serenity continued indefinitely until a disturbance in the distance could be felt, prompting Sullivan to look forward, into the dark abyss of the portal. There appeared a man rapidly approaching with arms wrapped around his flexed hips and knees as if shot from a cannon. He ricocheted off the sides of the rotating tunnel like a pinball and screamed wildly. The man collided directly into the midsection of Sullivan, driving him backward as Franklin and Pagano continued out of sight. Sullivan tried to break free, but he could not, the grip of the interceptor too tight. He opened his eyes and stared into the maniacal face of Mingo, his tongue flapping in the void of the vacuum. They clutched onto each for the duration of the dream.

The following day Sullivan awoke to the morning sunlight, his body still spread prostrate across the sofa. He could hear the hoof beats of a lone horse slowly making its way down the cobblestone lane and the coo of a mourning dove on the windowsill. He ran a sore, bumpy tongue across his front teeth and looked down at his arms and legs. A hideous rash covered his body, with some of the raised areas now thick with an opaque fluid inside, ready to burst. He felt warm and reached for a glass of water on a side table, his strength noticeably diminished. He then heard a soft voice singing.

The song itself was gentle and soothing, although somewhat mournful in tone. It came through the wall and perhaps via a shared chimney space with the Arnold residence.

> "As I went down to the river to pray
> Studying about that good old way
> And who shall wear the starry crown
> Good Lord show me the way"

Sullivan closed his eyes and continued to listen, the melody pleasing to his infirmed state.

> "Oh sisters let's go down
> Let's go down come on down
> Oh sisters let's go down
> Down to the river to pray"

The voice repeated the lyrics several times.
"Hello?" shouted Sullivan.
The singing stopped.
"That's a beautiful song. What's your name?"
No one answered.
Sullivan tried to stand but he couldn't. He heard the sound of footsteps coming down from the third floor. At his side appeared Franklin and Dr. Casey with looks of concern. Franklin spoke first.
"How are you feeling, John?"

"Weak. What's going on? What's with this rash?"

"You're a very sick man," stated Casey. "Dr. Sullivan, I regret to inform you that you have been stricken by the most dreaded disease of our time."

"Alright," followed up Sullivan uneasily. "What disease are we talking about?"

"Smallpox," came the blunt reply.

Sullivan scanned the eyes of both men before speaking. "Smallpox… variola major? That's impossible, gentlemen. Smallpox has been eradicated from the face of the earth. I may have even been vaccinated as a…"

"It was eradicated as of 1980," interrupted Franklin. "It's 1779, John. Smallpox is running rampant through the colonies."

"We're in a bit of an epidemic at the current time," added Casey. "The port of Philadelphia is an unfortunate gateway for the disease. Despite our best efforts, it continues to spread."

Franklin leaned forward to roll up Sullivan's sleeve. He inspected the upper portion of his arm, near the shoulder. "John, I don't see the characteristic smallpox vaccine scar on your arm." He stepped back. "And, you were born in 1977."

"Which means?"

"Routine vaccination of the American population stopped in 1972, after the disease was eliminated from the United States."

"So… I wasn't vaccinated?"

"I'm afraid not," replied Franklin.

"Forgive me for my ignorance of this disease," bemoaned Sullivan as he scanned his arm. "But we didn't receive much training on smallpox in medical school… because it didn't exist on the face of the earth." He sighed. "Are you sure it's smallpox?"

"John, my beloved son Francis died of smallpox at age four," lamented Franklin. "I know the disease when I see it. Trust me… you *have* smallpox."

"I'm sorry," said Sullivan. "I didn't know that." He tried to formulate a treatment plan in his head while looking up at Casey. "So what do we do now and more importantly, why are you standing next to me? Aren't I contagious?"

"You're highly contagious," stated Dr. Casey. "Especially when those vesicles scab or burst. You're considered contagious until the last scab falls off. That's why you weren't taken to the hospital. Smallpox patients are not permitted inside."

"We're immune," proclaimed Franklin.

"Excuse me?" countered Sullivan. "That's impossible. You have no vaccine."

"Don't you remember the story of the milk maiden, John? They must have mentioned it in medical school. If not, I'd say your professors were a bit remiss."

"It rings a bell," stated Sullivan as he rubbed his head. "Boy, what a headache."

"Just recently a dairymaid in England boasted that she and her coworkers were immune from smallpox due to their daily contact with cows," professed Dr. Casey. "During their handling of infected utters, most milk maidens eventually contract a disease known as cowpox. Cowpox is a much milder relative of smallpox that affects bovine cattle and can be transmitted from animal to human. In other words… a zoonotic disease."

"Cowpox presents in humans in a similar way to your appearance," added Franklin. "With raised rashes and vesicles, but it's not a lethal disease. Therefore, all milkmaids that are affected, ultimately survive."

"So an astute English physician named Edward Jenner took heed to their story and postulated that exposure to cowpox somehow protects an individual against the more dreaded smallpox," continued Casey. "He tested his hypothesis by taking some pus of a cowpox lesion from the arm of a dairymaid named Sarah Nelms. He then introduced the extracted fluid into the body of an eight-year-old boy named James Phipps via an arm scratch. Phipps was a healthy lad who subsequently developed a mild case of cowpox and fully recovered. Dr. Jenner then boldly continued his experimentation by taking pus from a fresh smallpox lesion and again introducing it into the body of little James."

"And?" asked Sullivan, amazed by the lack of modern day ethics on Dr. Jenner's behalf.

"James Phipps never developed any symptoms of smallpox, hence confirming Jenner's theory and sealing the milkmaid story into medical folklore."

"A brilliant physician," declared Franklin. "Considered by many to be the Father of Immunology."

"I'd consider the boy a hero," remarked Sullivan as he sat up more erect on the sofa. "So you two have inoculated yourselves with cowpox?"

"No, we've actually used live smallpox," quipped Franklin proudly. "There simply aren't enough cowpox cases around and I've always been a proponent of what we call variation, which is the introduction of pus extracted from a smallpox lesion into the arm of a healthy individual, in order to immunize that person. It's done by dipping a lancet into the ripe pustule of a person suffering from smallpox and then subcutaneously introducing the material into the arm or leg of the nonimmune person."

"What… you used a live virus? That's dangerous!" declared Sullivan.

"Variolation is fatal 2% of the time," stated Dr. Casey. "That is, compared to a 30% fatality rate from smallpox in general. So most people take the odds during an epidemic."

"We just treated General Washington in such a manner," continued Franklin. "With great success I may add."

"So, I have a 30% chance of dying?" asked Sullivan.

"No, you have a 70% chance of living," countered Casey. "We'll take good care of you, John."

"I've got to get out of here," declared Sullivan as he tried to stand. "Back to 2020 is where I'm headed. I've got to get back to the Philadelphia General Hospital."

"I don't recommend that," said Franklin with a raised hand.

"Why not?"

"If you show up in Philadelphia in the year 2020 suffering from smallpox, they'll instantly declare you a bioterrorist. Remember John, in the future only two specimens of smallpox exist, that being in a United States and Russian laboratory, where they're under heavy guard. You'd be immediately arrested and grace the front page of every newspaper in the world."

Sullivan realized Franklin was right. He couldn't go back while contagious. It would also put the entire populace of Philadelphia at risk. "How long will I be contagious?" he asked.

"About three weeks," answered Casey. "You are hereby quarantined to this home until then. Understand? No one is permitted in or out... especially you."

"John, remember the twenty to one ratio," added Franklin. "Three weeks of our time equals just over a day in the future. We'll get you back soon enough."

"I'm not worried about time," groaned Sullivan as he dropped back into a supine position. "I'm worried about surviving." He put the washcloth back on his head.

"Very well," said Casey as he put on his derby hat. "I'll be back shortly."

"Where are you headed?" asked Franklin. "We haven't finished breakfast yet."

"To the bog," said the physician energetically. "To gather some mud for a salve and some leeches. I believe a controlled bloodletting is in order here. Some well-placed leeches on his toes and fingers will help draw out the bad humors. Trust me, I've seen it work." He exited down the stairwell. "I'll be right back!"

"Ben..." stammered Sullivan with wide eyes. "Promise me that no blood will be sucked or drained out of my body... no matter what my condition."

"I promise," chuckled Franklin as he poured some water from a pitcher into the glass. "Drink up and get some rest, John. Three weeks will go by fast." He walked away. "I'll be upstairs if you need me."

Sullivan drifted back into a fitful sleep. He dreamt of his concerned mother caring for him during a late childhood case of chickenpox. She dabbed calamine lotion on his body and fretted over a pitted pox mark on his forehead. It was sometime during the dream that he heard a voice.

"My name is Sary."

# CHAPTER NINE
## MUNCHAUSEN SYNDROME
## 2065

"We have no other choice," apologized the policeman as he helped stand Vince up. "Let's go, we have a patrol car waiting outside."
Vince stood up from the chair, his pleas for clemency denied. The lawmen were right; he technically was an undocumented and therefore had to be detained. He held no driver's license, passport or explanation to justify his presence in the United States. He deferred on his right to an attorney.
"Where am I going again?" asked Vince.
"Downtown Philly," said the corporal holding his right arm. "Immigration and Customs Enforcement."
"ICE?"
"Yea... ICE."
Pagano sighed as he hobbled out of the building and into a patrol car. Dr. Schmidt's warning about the Internet of Things certainly proved correct. He ducked into the back seat and started to formulate an escape plan as soon as the vehicle lurched into motion. He couldn't let them take him to a lock down unit, otherwise he may never make it home. He hatched his plan as soon as the vehicle got on the Schuylkill Expressway. The two officers were seated in the front seat.

Pagano lowered his head between his knees and began to rapidly hyperventilate through his mouth. After about fifteen seconds the policeman in the passenger seat looked back through the metal screen.

"Hey, what's going on back there?" asked the officer.

Pagano didn't reply but kept inhaling and exhaling like a dog choking on a bone.

"What's happening?" asked the driver as he glanced backward.

"I don't know," said his partner with concern. "He won't answer!"

Pagano felt extremely dizzy and sat erect. He placed a thumb in his mouth and forcefully tried to blow outward, his face turning beat red in the process.

"What in the hell?" shouted the driver.

Vince Pagano passed out, his head striking the back of the center console. The impact cut open his forehead.

"Pull over!" shouted the front seat passenger. "He's bleeding!"

"I can't pull over," said the corporal as he looked into the rear view mirror. He reached for the radio receiver and brought the microphone to his face as they passed an exit sign for the Philadelphia Zoo. "2A45 requesting a rescue ambulance unit at the Philadelphia Zoo entrance gate for male suspect, middle aged, unconscious and bleeding from the forehead."

"2A45 roger."

Pagano felt himself slowly coming back to consciousness as blood trickled down his nose. He voluntarily rolled his eyes backwards and started to violently contort his body. He gurgled some saliva in his mouth.

"He's seizing!" shouted the officer. "Divert! We've got to get him to the hospital."

The driver quickly spoke over the radio a second time. "2A45 show us transporting our suspect from Schuylkill Expressway to Philadelphia General Hospital. Suspect remains unconscious and now suffering from seizure."

"2A45, roger," crackled the response from the dispatcher. "Will alert the Philadelphia General of your arrival."

The police car pulled up just outside the Philadelphia General emergency room. Two attendants rushed out with a gurney and loaded the still trembling body of Vince Pagano onto the stretcher. They wheeled him inside.

"He's a John Doe," said a nurse as he wrapped a blood pressure cuff around Vince's arm. The gurney rolled into an exam room. A nurse's aide waiting inside slapped some EKG pads on Vince's chest as a medical resident walked in.

"What's up, Nurse Mike?" asked the doctor as he stuffed the stub of a Philadelphia pretzel into his pocket. Along the lapel of his white coat ran the lettering 'Richard Polk IV, MD' next to a red ketchup stain.

"A gentleman in... I'd say his mid 30s, brought in by the police with a reported seizure," replied the nurse. "No other info."

"Any family with him?"

"No. The police claim he's an illegal."

"Undocumented," said the nurse's aide. "I learned that in a sensitivity training class. You can't say 'illegal' anymore."

"Really?" mumbled Polk as he approached Pagano. "He's got a visitor's pass around his neck from the Pagano Institute." He lifted up a sheet covering Vince's lower torso. "And a cast on his leg. So, he must have a local physician taking care of him."

"Nobody knows," countered the nurse as he looked up at the monitor. "His vital signs are normal, except for a rapid heart rate."

"He's got a nasty gash on his noggin," declared Polk as he leaned over the bed, his protruding stomach contacting a side rail. "Get a cat scan of his head ASAP. Let's make sure he doesn't have a bleed."

"Will do."

"Run all the labs, including a toxicology profile," added Polk. "If the head scan is negative get a CT angiogram to make sure he didn't have a pulmonary embolus... especially with the cast on. He may have flipped a blood clot."

"Good thinking."

"Hey, I'm the pro from Dover," boasted Polk as he patted himself on the chest, the self-adulation adding some yellow mustard to his ensemble. "Consult the ortho boys to look at his leg and I'll send in a medical student to suture up his dome."

"Got it."

"I'll be down in the cafeteria," said Polk as he walked out. "It's free French fry Friday… call if you need me."

Vince kept his eyes closed as a pressure dressing was applied to his forehead. He barely flinched as multiple vials of blood were taken from his left arm. Next he was whisked off to the cat scan suite, where studies of his head and pulmonary cavity were read as negative. He dozed off a bit beneath a sterile drape as a medical student fumbled his way through a suture repair of the forehead laceration. About five hours passed before Dr. Polk ambled back into the darkened room.

Pagano raised his head and squinted his eyes as the resident flipped on the overhead light.

"Good evening, my friend," said Polk as he grasped the bed rail. "How's your head?" He leaned forward to inspect the suture line. "Yikes!"

"Where am I?" stammered Vince. He fanned a hand in front of his face to vent away Polk's oniony breath.

"The Philadelphia General," came the response. "But I'm not here to answer your questions." Polk grinned. "Now tell me, sir. Who are you and where are you from?"

"My last name is Pagano."

"Very good. That's a start. And you're from…"

"The year 2020," said Pagano with complete clarity. "I'm a time traveler."

"Alright," stated Polk as he cautiously leaned back a bit. "That's interesting, but your name tag claims you're a guest at the Pagano Institute. What's up with that?"

"The Pagano Institute is actually named after me."

Polk chuckled. "So, you're the Pagano whose name is written in big letters outside, on top of the building?"

"In the flesh. Dad wanted everyone in New Jersey to see our name."

Polk just stared at the patient, fully aware that his blood and urine toxicology came back negative for any illicit drugs.

"Everyone thought I died during the construction of the building," continued Pagano. "Back in 2020 that is."

"The construction?" chuckled Polk. "You died during the construction of the orthopedic center? Is that what you're telling me?"

"That's right, but I didn't really die… I just transported forward in time, through a wormhole in the basement. I kind of snuck out."

"How'd you break your ankle?" asked Polk, unfazed by the dialogue.

"It happened when I rocketed out of the time tunnel. The speed of light can be a dangerous thing. One must tuck and roll during re-entry."

"OK," said Polk as he grinned. "Well, Mr. Pagano. Welcome to the future. You just won an overnight stay in our little hotel here. I hope you didn't double park your time machine outside."

"You have to believe me," pleaded Vince. "I'm not crazy."

"Well, how about we let the experts decide?"

Nurse Mike walked back in. "All his labs are normal."

"Yea," said Polk. "I know. But he's out in la-la land." Polk walked past the nurse and slapped him on the shoulder. "Get him a room up on the Psych floor and consult the shrinks. They'll have a field day with this crank."

"Why?" asked the bemused nurse. "Everything is coming back normal."

"He's a time traveler," laughed Polk as he departed. "Go ahead… ask him."

Vince Pagano was admitted to the PGH psychiatry unit, a desolate and dilapidated floor within the hospital complex. He spent the night alone, in a stark room with overhead lights on and a video camera at the foot of his bed. A cafeteria worker brought him a baloney sandwich with fries, chicken soup and a stale brownie square. At around midnight a nurse with skull bone tattoos and the smell of alcohol on his breath performed a shoddy history and physical exam.

Vince woke the following morning to find two physicians standing at the foot of his bed. One was Dr. Schmidt and the other a thin, bespectacled man in a white coat with a goatee. A rectangular window high on the wall with security bars allowed some light to filter into the room. The bearded man stared down at a chart as Schmidt spoke.

"He's visiting the country on invite from the Pagano Orthopedic Institute," declared Schmidt. "My personal invite. I'm not sure what happened to his passport." Schmidt glanced at Pagano as he continued to fabricate. "Perhaps that hit on the head played a role in it?"

"The man stated to an emergency room physician that he is a time traveler," stated the psychiatrist. "From the year 2020 to be precise."

"I have no explanation for that," countered Schmidt. "However I can vouch for his surname. It is Pagano."

"And his first name?"

"Vito. He's from a town to the west of Florence, Italy. Lucca to be exact."

"Very well. I surely trust you, Dr. Schmidt." He stepped forward to the right side of Vince's bed. "Hello, Mr. Pagano. My name is Dr. Franz Wolfgang. I'm am an attending physician in the psychiatry department here at the PGH. A pleasure to meet you."

"Hello, Dr. Wolfgang. I'm Vito Pagano."

"How is your head?"

"Fine," replied Vince as he dabbed the dressing with his forefinger. "A little sore."

"Why don't you tell me a little bit about yourself," continued Wolfgang.

"I have a nasty headache," whined Vince. "And I feel nauseous."

"The man surely had a concussion," stated Wolfgang as he stepped back. "I'll order a stat MRI of the head just to make sure we're not missing anything. Let's get that first before we dig any deeper."

"Thank you, Franz," said Schmidt. "I appreciate anything you can do to take care of my friend."

"We'll take good care of him, Dr. Schmidt. I can assure you of that." Wolfgang looked back at Vince. "We'll talk a bit later. OK, Vito?"

"Sure," said Vince. "Thank you."

Wolfgang left the room. Before speaking, Zachary turned back to espy the overhead camera and cautiously approached Vince. He waited a bit before whispering.

"Very nice, Vincent. Very nice. It's been a long time since I've seen a patient display a factitious disorder to trick a physician into believing they have a true medical emergency." He smiled. "A classic case of Munchausen Syndrome. Baron von Munchausen would be so proud of you."

"What did you want me to do?" said Vince. "They were about to take me downtown to an Immigration and Customs office. I'd be locked up there for years." He pushed himself up in bed. "I had to do something."

"I warned you. Remember? So much for the surgeon's mentality."

"Well, it wasn't hard to trick that resident downstairs with all the condiments on his coat. He was more interested in food. Residents nowadays are soft. There was no 'French fry Friday' when I trained. We had to pilfer food off patient's trays to survive."

"Perhaps," said Schmidt as he brought a hand to his chin as if trying to generate a plan. "But how do we get out of this current predicament?"

"I don't know, but I'm just glad a policeman isn't sitting outside the door."

"You're the least of the Philadelphia Police Department's worries. But I'm sure a social worker will contact the proper authorities prior to your discharge. You're not out of the woods yet."

"Well, what's your plan?" grinned Pagano. "I've gotten us this far."

"I recommend you stay put, here in the PGH. I'm good friends with Dr. Wolfgang, so we have some leeway in that regard." Schmidt looked down at Pagano with some trepidation. "All I ask is that you carefully play the Munchausen card for the next 24 hours until I come up with a more definite plan. Alright? Just try and keep the cost down for the hospital, you're already racking up quite a bill."

Pagano laughed. Despite only knowing Schmidt for a short time, he found the man to be both savvy and trustworthy. "Sounds good," said Vince. "Thanks."

"I'll be in touch. I hope you're up to speed on your Italian," quipped Schmidt as he left the room. "Ciao."

The remainder of Vince's day proved unremarkable. He ate breakfast and went downstairs for an MRI of his head. After lunch a nurse came into the room to take his vital signs and offer two Tylenol tablets for a headache. He watched an afternoon baseball game on TV and just before dinner time, took a thirty minute nap. In the evening he strolled down to the day room to work on a puzzle with a fellow inpatient, the man claiming to be the second coming of Jesus Christ. Together they completed a puzzle of the Philadelphia skyline. The entire floor then sat through a Hollywood award ceremony on television, where over a three hour period, beautiful people gave awards to other beautiful people. Afterwards, Vince went to bed. It was then the nurse with skull bone tattoos walked in.

"Any problems?" asked the nurse, his breath 100 proof alcohol.

"Nah," said Vince.

"I hear you're a time traveler."

"That's right… from the past. The year 2020 to be exact."

"We occasionally get another patient on the floor claiming to be a time traveler," declared the nurse. "The guy's a regular… a real screwball."

"There are a few of us in town," said Vince. "Two time tunnels exist in the city."

"His name is Mingo," continued the nurse. He put the bag down. "He thinks he's from the 1700s, a personal acquaintance of Benjamin Franklin."

"Oh really?"

"Yea. Is he your friend?"

"There are but three faithful friends," answered Vince. "An old wife, an old dog, and ready money."

The nurse burst out in laughter, his sinister laugh echoing in the hallway. "Good one, man. Did you just make that up?"

"Nah. It's a well-known Ben Franklin quote. You never heard of it?"

"No." The nurse fixed his gaze on Pagano. "Are you sure you're crazy?" he asked. "Because you seem too smart to be on this floor. The Messiah was working on that puzzle for weeks, and you finished it off in two hours."

"Beginner's luck," laughed Vince as he pulled the sheet up to his chin. "Can you turn off the light, please?"

"Nope. The overheads stay on for new patients. Nice try. Good night."

"Good night."

Vince put his hands behind his head and stared out the lone window, the brick wall of a higher building in view. He thought of Jordan Ally and their plans for matrimony as the low, energetic hum of the surrounding medical center brought a sense of calm to his soul. Just outside the whir of an approaching helicopter could be heard along with the trailing sound of a street siren. Before dozing off he thought of John Sullivan, wondering if he would ever return. The faint voice of an overhead operator could barely be perceived down the hallway… paging a Dr. Pagano.

# CHAPTER TEN
## SARY
## 1779

Nearly 300 years earlier, John Sullivan drifted in and out of consciousness, his battle with smallpox in its closing stages. Over the past two weeks a high fever blunted his sensorium and stubbornly refused to recede. The ongoing struggle between life and death cost Sullivan thirty pounds and peppered his body with gruesome pox marks from head to toe. At one point, he vomited so violently that gobs of bright red blood accompanied his emesis. Franklin even had a cleric visit Sullivan's bedside two days earlier to perform last rites. Yet by the grace of God, the fever began to slowly abate and the majority of lesions shed their scabs. Throughout all of the turmoil and suffering, Sullivan perceived one constant: the sense of an angelic presence at his side. It was late in the evening when he heard a voice.

"The Syrup of Buckthorn really helped," boasted Dr. Casey. "It really cleaned him out."

"A cathartic unlike any other," added Ben. "Liquid dynamite." Ben chuckled. "And the Spirits of Ammonia opened up his lungs."

Sullivan inhaled, the pungent fumes from the nitrogen-based brew stinging his sinuses. He batted his eyes as they burned and watered.

"Here, put this on him," ordered Casey. "Lather it all over his skin. It's a soothing agent."

Sullivan felt a calloused set of hands gently begin to apply the ointment to his arms, the firm and circular hand motion providing instant relief.

"What's that, doc?" asked Ben. "I've never seen it before."

"Basilicon ointment," answered Casey. "A balm made out of hog's lard, pine resin and yellow wax. I even added a little olive oil to take it up a notch. I just got the recipe from Washington's doctor. Martha uses it on her boils."

Sullivan briefly opened his eyes and saw her again, kneeling at his side while applying the salve. She smiled. He tried to speak but his lips were parched and stuck together. She continued to apply the ointment.

"Thank you, Sary," said Franklin. "You've been a real lifesaver."

"Oh, you're welcome, Mr. Franklin," came the respectful reply, her voice young and energetic. "He's going to make it. I said a prayer last night." She squeezed Sullivan's forearm tight.

"The next 24 hours will be crucial," cautioned Casey. "But I agree, he's trending in the right direction. Get a washcloth on his forehead."

"Yes, doctor."

Sullivan felt safe and at peace. He closed his eyes and drifted back into a deep sleep, not waking until the following morning. At his side sat Franklin, fast asleep in a wing-back chair. The founding father's head was tilted hard to the left and drool ran down his check. To his right stood an empty wine glass next to an open and turned over book. A set of bifocals remained in Franklin's left hand.

"Ben," said Sullivan, his voice weak. "Ben Franklin. Wake up."

Franklin stirred and mumbled. "Judas sold only one man, but Benedict Arnold… three million."

"Ben… wake up!"

Franklin roused and opened his eyes. He looked around to gather his bearings while wiping away the saliva. "What's going on here?"

"You were dreaming," said Sullivan. "About Arnold."

Franklin blinked his eyes multiple times before putting on his glasses. He forced his eyes wide open, yawned and stretched his arms high into the air. "Well, well… look who's rejoined the human race. Welcome back, John."

"I'm alive!"

"It was certainly touch and go over the past several days," declared Franklin. "I'll admit that." He stood up and arched his back. "But you made it old chap. You've survived smallpox. Congratulations."

"I had my doubts," said Sullivan. "Must have been all the ammonia I inhaled. Thanks." He looked around. "Where is she?"

"Who?"

"The woman, or girl, that took care of me… from next door?"

"Sary?"

"Is that her name?"

"Yes, it is," answered Franklin. "Commander Arnold left town for a few weeks and offered me the use of his house servant."

"His slave?"

"Yes. So, I accepted. It was perfect timing. Oh, she was absolutely magnificent in caring for you. Perhaps it had to do with the concern you showed her the other day. Remember… with the overhead luggage, when you almost got yourself impaled by Arnold?"

"Yea. I remember," retorted Sullivan. "Where is she now?"

"Asleep downstairs… in my servant's quarters," came the reply. "I relieved her of her duties late last night. The girl is exhausted."

"Did I expose her to smallpox?"

"No. She had it as a child."

Sullivan struggled to sit up on the sofa. "Wow. I am weak." He scanned his extremities. "Look at all these scars!"

"You're lucky to be alive my friend. Dr. Casey lost five patients just yesterday to smallpox. The recent epidemic has been more deadly than usual."

"How long have I been out of it?"

"Just over two weeks."

"I still have some scabs."

"Doc said it will take about another five days for all the scabs to fall off. Until then, I'm afraid you are still quarantined to my home."

"Another five days! Ben, I've got to get out of here. They must be worried sick about me back home."

"Understood," said Franklin. "But remember, only about two days have passed in 2020 and you can't leave until all the scabs are gone. Technically, you're still contagious."

Sullivan was too tired to argue. He ate a light breakfast and drank a tremendous amount of liquid, his body in a dangerous state of dehydration. By mid-morning he felt strong enough to pay a visit to the privy, an elegant outhouse in the rear of Franklin's home, complete with lightning rod. It was during afternoon teatime that Franklin spoke of some necessary travel plans.

"I'll be out of town for the next five days," stated Franklin as he took a bite of butter cookie. "I've some important business up in Bethlehem."

"I'm not going anywhere," replied Sullivan as he blew across his tea. "Doctor's orders."

Franklin chomped on his cookie in regal fashion before cautiously continuing. "I've asked Sary to care for you in my absence."

"No," came the stern rebuttal. "Never."

"Consider her my servant, John. At your disposal. You're a weak man and will be in need of assistance."

"I'll get by... I am *not* using a slave."

"But John, how are you going to cook for yourself, go to the market or haul water into the kitchen? You're ailing, man. Sary can and will assist..."

"Forget about it."

"She specifically offered her services to help in your recovery." Ben took another thoughtful sip of tea. "The military governor won't be home for another few days."

"What about Mrs. Arnold?"

"She's still in Virginia. Won't be back for another month."

"I'll get by," declared Sullivan.

"But, John…"

Just then some footsteps were heard rapidly coming up the basement steps. Sary darted through the room holding a basket full of laundry, heading toward a rear door. "Good morning Mr. Franklin… good morning Dr. Sullivan!"

"Morning, Sary," said Ben.

Sullivan felt too ashamed to even speak.

"She used to be Tom Jefferson's slave," stated Ben. "One of his favorites among the house staff. However, there was a recent breach between Mrs. Jefferson and Sary." Ben raised an eyebrow before continuing. "So, to my understanding, she had to leave his home… immediately."

"What do you mean by a 'breach'?"

"A breach… an issue, a clash, perhaps of a personal nature."

"So, that's how the poor girl ended up with the demon next door?"

"The timing could not have been better," continued Franklin. "Benedict suddenly dropped into town and the two men came to terms."

"In other words, Jefferson *sold* her to Arnold. Is that what you're saying?"

"Absolutely. Remember, it's 1779, John. The Emancipation Proclamation is about 80 years away. So please, bear with the times."

Sullivan momentarily sulked, the slightest suggestion of accepting such an offer unimaginable. He glared at Franklin. "What's your position on slavery?"

"Evolving rapidly," answered Ben. "John, I set my servants free years ago, realizing what's ahead of the curve. However, about 30 percent of Philadelphians currently own slaves. I can't fast forward history."

Some tense silence passed between the two.

"You have the power to make a difference," continued Sullivan. "You're Ben Franklin. You just spoke of such a great opportunity at hand, a second bite of the apple… remember? The beneficiary of a twist of time? So why not become an activist?"

"Yes. I'm Ben Franklin, currently dealing with a Revolutionary War and the birth of a nation, wanted for high treason by the British Crown and in failing health. So please, don't lecture me on the morality of slavery. I abhor the institution, yet I cannot magically ratify the abolishment of such a heinous entity. I'm sorry, John. First things first."

Sullivan sighed. "I'm sorry, Ben. It's just that I can't get the cries of that poor woman out of my mind. She's being abused next door."

"Nor can I," said Ben. "So, allow her to spend some time with you. Bring a ray of sunshine into her life. She's an intelligent and engaging woman. Just think of what it would mean to her." Ben took another sip of tea. "If not, she'll have to return next door and sit alone in Arnold's basement, darning his socks and underwear." While reaching for another cookie he grinned and looked over his bifocals. "Now, I *know* you don't want her doing that."

Sullivan frowned, the object of a schmooze job by the master of the art. He heard the backdoor open again and Sary walked in. She wore a simple blue skirt and white blouse, threadbare along the sleeves. A red cloth covered her hair.

"The laundry is hanging outside," proclaimed Sary. "What would you like for dinner, Mr. Franklin?"

"Sary, I'm going to be out of town by dinner time… for a few days." Franklin looked at Sullivan. "Perhaps Dr. Sullivan can tell you what he'd like for dinner?"

Sullivan pursed his lips defiantly.

"I still have some left over chicken bones," stated Sary with a warm smile. "And this morning at the market I got some fresh fish. Perhaps I can make a fish stew?" She grinned. "There are some fresh carrots and onions next door and well, nobody will know if they're missing."

"John?" asked Franklin. "Would you like some fish stew for dinner?"

Sullivan didn't speak.

"A ray of sunshine," whispered Franklin. "You can make a difference, too. Not just me." He tilted his head to encourage a response. "Please, John."

"Sure," capitulated Sullivan. He looked at Sary. "That would be nice. Thank you, Sary. Fish stew sounds perfect. Thank you very much."

"Sure, Dr. Sullivan! I'm glad you're feeling better. You had me worried." She bolted down the stairwell while talking to herself aloud. "I'll get the onions and carrots, and maybe go back to the market for a potato. For dessert I can pick up some apples..."

"Thank you, John. It will mean a lot to Sary."

Sullivan took a defiant bite of a cookie, his mind in sudden disarray.

"A servant," said Franklin in a reassuring tone as he finished his tea. "She's a servant, John. Keep repeating that."

The dinner turned out to be delicious, savory but not too heavy, and stoked with nutrients. The warmth of the meal expelled the final chill of smallpox from Sullivan's frame. Surprisingly, his stomach handled it well.

"Thank you, Sary," said Sullivan as his spoon rattled in an empty bowl. "That hit the spot." The physician sat alone at a dinner table lit by two candles. A window at his side looked over the back yard. A quarter loaf of bread still remained.

"You're welcome," said Sary as she took away the empty bowl. "Do you need more water?"

"No. I'm fine." Sullivan cleared his voice. "What did you have for dinner?"

"Me? I had some corn meal with lard, mixed up with some snap beans from Mr. Franklin's garden." She wiped the tabletop with a rag. "I hope you saved room for dessert."

"I did." He smiled. "But, when did you eat?"

"About two hours ago… downstairs." She went back into the kitchen and returned with some freshly sliced apples. "Here, I put some cinnamon over them. I hope you like apples."

"I do."

As Sullivan ate a few apple wedges, he wondered about appropriate etiquette. Sary certainly didn't seem uncomfortable working around a complete stranger, that much he sensed. She appeared relaxed and focused on her chores. He decided to continue the conversation on a bit more personal level.

"Sary, may I ask how old you are?"

"Oh, I don't really know," came the carefree reply. "Maybe eighteen."

"You don't know what year you were born?"

"No. I don't." She began to softly sing a hymn while scrubbing some dishes in a basin, trying to deflect the discussion.

"I heard you singing through the wall the other night. You have a nice voice."

"Singing is praying twice."

Sullivan allowed the serenade to continue, the tune solemn yet uplifting.

"Where are you originally from?"

"Barbados."

"I hear it's nice there. Warm all the time."

She didn't answer but continued singing.

"Do you have any family in Philadelphia? Brothers or sisters perhaps?"

The scrubbing stopped and Sary looked directly at Sullivan. "Dr. Sullivan, please don't ask me about my family. It will make me sad." She frowned and waited for a reply.

"I'm sorry," came the immediately response. "I'm so sorry. It's just that…"

"Where are you from?"

"Me?" smiled Sullivan, impressed by her tact. "Philadelphia originally… West Philadelphia to be exact."

"Where's that... West Philadelphia?" I've never heard of it."
"Oh, right. Well, on the other side of the Schuylkill River," came the clarification. "Toward the direction of the setting sun."
"People live over there... with all the Indians?"
"Yes they do, or should I say, will."
"Amazing." She walked over to pick up the empty apple bowl and returned it to the wash basin. "Now, Dr. Casey told me that you should rest. So go now. Go rest for a bit. I washed all your bed linens earlier today."

Sullivan smiled, amazed by the grace and maturity of the young woman in command. She seemed unfazed by her lot in life, perhaps a necessary coping mechanism to withstand such hardship. She also projected an inner strength and genuine dignity that was palpable.

"Go on! There's a pitcher of water on the night table. It's fresh and I boiled it too."

Sullivan rose, gratified by the dinner and conversation. "Thank you, Sary. The dinner was absolutely splendid. You're a wonderful cook."

"Just wait until you see what I make for you tomorrow, Dr. Sullivan. I'm going to make some pop-robins for breakfast and broiled dumplings for lunch. For dinner I'll whip up a pot pudding made from some meat scraps and grain. It's so good. People around here like to call it scrapple."

As Sullivan walked away he listened to Sary ramble on about her plan to get started on the following day's menu. He noticed that she commonly sang or spoke aloud to herself, each mode of personal expression soothing to the bystander. For several minutes he sat on the side of the bed listening to her rattle off one anticipated chore after another, as if nothing else mattered. He slid under the fresh sheets and quickly fell asleep.

A fierce knocking on the door awoke Sullivan several hours later. He stumbled down the steps in darkness. Sary appeared at the top of the basement steps with a candle in hand as the pounding became louder.

"What's the matter, Dr. Sullivan?"

Sullivan opened the door and before him stood Dr. Casey with a look of concern.

"John, Ben's ill. We need your help."

"What?" said Sullivan, still trying to orient himself. "What time is it?"

"Two o'clock in the morning."

"What's wrong?"

"He took ill just a few miles outside of the city. They rushed him back to Pennsylvania Hospital." Behind the doctor stood a horseman with carriage. "An acute case of dropsy."

"Dropsy?"

"Yes… dropsy. His legs are swollen up like a pumpkin," continued Casey. "As bad a case as I've ever seen."

"Probably CHF," said Sullivan. "Ben mentioned that his heart was acting up. In fact, he had a follow-up appointment scheduled with his cardiologist… but we missed it."

"CHF?"

"Congestive heart failure," clarified Sullivan. "His heart is getting too weak. It's like a pump that can't generate enough pressure to keep the blood and humors flowing, so the fluid pools up in his legs."

"I've already administered some mercury and applied leeches to his toes."

"Oh boy," stammered Sullivan. "We have to get moving." He turned backward to see Sary handing him his clothes. She lit two more candles in the room. "But what about my skin lesions?" asked Sullivan as he slid into his trousers. "I'm still contagious."

"Barely," came the reply. "I've quarantined Ben off in the basement of the hospital. So, we'll be fine, but I suggest you hurry. He kept mumbling something about 'having unfinished work to do.'"

"Let's go!"

"Good luck!" shouted Sary.

The ride across town was exhilarating to Sullivan as the sound of galloping hoofbeats echoed through the empty streets. The passing landscape was illuminated by a full moon in a serene yet sensational fashion. As the driver approached the front gate of the hospital, he pulled up on the horse's reins.

"Whoa, Ellie! Whoa, old girl."

The mare came to a controlled halt at the front gate and the two physicians rushed inside. They found Franklin in the basement with a hospital attendant, a single lantern burning at his side. Sullivan immediately noted his shortness of breath.

"Ben! What's going on?" asked Sullivan.

"The old ticker acting up again," came the labored reply. Franklin took several quick breaths before continuing. "I seemed to have lost my medications in transport." He sat up in bed. "I can't seem to lay flat."

"He passed out just North of Manayunk," stated Casey.

Sullivan leaned forward and put his ear onto Franklin's chest. In doing so he observed Franklin's swollen legs and leeches clinging to his toes. "Take a few deep breaths in and out, Ben. Nice and easy."

Franklin complied and began to cough after the third deep inspiration. Frothy saliva with a spot of blood appeared on his blue-tinged, lower lip.

"He's in acute pulmonary edema," declared Sullivan as he stood up. "His lungs are filling up with fluid!"

"What should we do?"

"First off, please remove those leeches. They serve no purpose."

Casey motioned to an aide at the foot of the bed to comply. The assistant carefully plucked each engorged parasite from Franklin's lower extremities. He dropped them into a bowl of water.

"What else?" asked Casey.

"Well, an EKG, some blood work, a pulse oximetry and chest x-ray would be in order. Perhaps even an emergent cardiac catherization."

Casey and his aide could not understand the medical jargon.

"Sit him up in bed erect," ordered Sullivan. "And open up all the windows. He needs some oxygen."

The aide bolted into action.

"Do you have any morphine?" asked Sullivan.

"Morphine?" asked Casey, a bit bemused.

"Yes. Morphine. A common pain killer. It's from the poppy seed of an opium plant."

"Oh… opium! Yes, we have opium."

"In what form?"

"Laudanum, which is tincture of opium," stated Casey. "We're well stocked."

"Get some down here immediately," ordered Sullivan. "It will ease his pain and anxiety."

Without being told, the orderly ran out of the room in search of laudanum.

"Let's elevate his legs," continued Sullivan as he lifted Ben's lower limbs into the air. Casey shoved a pillow beneath them.

"What else?" mumbled Sullivan to himself. "We need a diuretic and some sort of medication for blood pressure support."

"Perhaps another dose of mercury?" suggested Casey.

"No. He's had enough."

The orderly returned to the room with a dark glass bottle and eye dropper. He handed the medication to Dr. Casey.

"Ah, the laudanum." He took hold of the eye dropper and drew some liquid into its reservoir. "How much should I administer?"

"What's the usual dose?" asked Sullivan.

"Four drops every four hours."

"Hit him with four drops."

Casey leaned forward. "Ben, open wide and stick out your tongue."

Franklin obliged and stuck out his pale tongue. Casey began to drip the reddish-brown mixture into Franklin's mouth.

"Yuck!" winced Franklin.

"It's extremely bitter," said Casey. "C'mon Ben… two more drops."

Franklin opened wide to complete the dose. After swallowing it he leaned back with a grimace and gasped. "Absolutely horrid."

"What next?" asked Casey.

Sullivan paused while trying to formulate a treatment plan. Franklin needed a diuretic, a medication to help his body rid itself of extra fluid. He looked at Casey. "How's your garden been growing?"

"Excuse me?"

"Your medicinal garden on the hospital grounds? Are most of the plants in bloom?"

"Why, yes. I just inspected the garden yesterday. The growing season has been fabulous so far. Plenty of sunshine and rain."

"Great. Do you mind if we take a look at some of the plants?"

"Now? Visit the garden in the middle of the night? Why?"

"Why?" said Sullivan as he picked up the lantern. "So we can save Ben Franklin's life."

The two physicians hurried outside.

# CHAPTER ELEVEN
## PINKY PROMISE
### 1779

Sullivan and Casey were joined by two hospital orderlies as they approached the medicinal garden in the hospital courtyard.

"You mentioned foxglove during my tour," stated Sullivan. "Can you show me that plant?"

"Sure," replied Casey as he instructed his assistants to veer left. "Right over here. They're just about ready to bloom." He pointed to several plant stems, each about two feet high. "There you go... *Digitalis purpurea*."

Sullivan knelt down to feel the seed buds. "Digitalis is a byproduct of foxglove. It's used to make digoxin."

"Digoxin? I'm unfamiliar with that term."

"It's a drug used to treat congestive heart failure," stated Sullivan as he plucked a bud off the plant. He brought the seedpod close to a lantern and peeled it open. "It inhibits a cardiac enzyme and in the process increases the heart's ability to contract."

"So it makes the heart stronger?"

"Yes, which is what Ben emergently needs. But unfortunately these seeds are weeks away from maturity." Sullivan looked up in dismay.

"I have a stockpile of dried seeds from last year's harvest," boasted Casey. "It was a bumper crop. We use them to make medicinal teas."

"You have a supply of dry foxglove seeds?"

"Absolutely! Doctor, may I remind you we're the bellwether for all apothecaries in town. Our collection is vast and well organized."

"Excellent!" declared Sullivan. "Can you get a few teabags stoked with digitalis seeds to Ben's side as soon as possible? That will help him the most."

"I'll personally tend to it at once," answered Casey as he stepped away.

"And throw in some hibiscus petals, too," added Sullivan. "That's a potent diuretic."

"A diuretic?" asked Casey as he turned back toward Sullivan. "You used this term earlier yet I'm still unfamiliar with it. I'm sorry."

"A diuretic is a drug that helps your kidneys release more sodium into your urine. The sodium pulls more water from your blood and therefore reduces the amount of fluid flowing through your veins and arteries. It helps ease the heart's workload."

Casey cocked an eyebrow. "In layman's terms, please."

"It's a water pill," continued Sullivan. "It makes you pee." He smiled. "Ben Franklin is going to pee like a racehorse after drinking that tea."

"Got it!" said Casey as he again turned away.

Sullivan scanned the remainder of the garden. "Gentlemen," he said to the orderlies. "Can you please gather up some fresh parsley, ginger and oregano if you have it?"

"Yes, doctor."

"And over there." He pointed to a patch of lawn with yellow flowers glowing in the moonlight. "See all those dandelion flowers. Bring me as many as you can." Sullivan grinned. "We're going to make Ben a diuretic salad that's not only therapeutic, but savory and delicious too."

The two orderlies obliged and went about their task.

Within twenty minutes, a therapeutic cup of tea was steeping at Franklin's side as he munched on a salad.

"I'll admit, those rancid drops of laudanum helped ease my cough," declared Franklin as he plucked a beetle from the salad bowl. "And this salad is heavenly… *sans* the infestation."

"How do you know so much about plants?" asked Casey to Sullivan.

"Well, the combination of a water pill and heart stimulant are standard protocol for treating dropsy," professed Sullivan. "All those greens and herbs are well-known diuretics. I teach an herbal medicine class at my institute."

"Fascinating," said Casey as he reached forward with the tea. "Here you go, Benjamin. Drink up."

"Wow. That's a big mug," commented Sullivan.

"Doctor," quipped Franklin. "The correct verbiage is 'cup'. It's a *cup* of tea… not a mug. Please abide by the King's English."

"What! You're worried about the King's English when you're leading a revolution against the man?" laughed Sullivan. "Please, spare me the lecture on what may soon be your ex-King's English."

The exchange brought some much needed levity to the room. Ben finished his salad and tea, the combination immediately bringing some color to his skin. The medical team monitored his progress over the next hour.

"I'm not that short-winded anymore," declared Ben as he took a few deep breaths. "Thank you, John. I owe you one."

Sullivan reached forward and felt Franklin's pulse. He then put the back of his hand on his forehead. "You're looking much better, my friend. I think you're out of the woods." He looked at Casey. "I recommend you keep him on a regular schedule of laudanum every four hours along with a cup of foxglove tea and hibiscus every six."

"Certainly! We'll monitor him through the night."

"I've got to urinate," announced Ben as he tried to get up. "Real bad."

"Stay down," ordered Dr. Casey. "We'll get you the honey bucket."

"Make it quick," said Franklin as he squirmed in bed.

"Ben, I'm heading home for some rest. Sary's probably wondering what's going on."

"How did it go?" asked Franklin as an orderly handed him a wooden bucket. "With Sary?"

"Great," said Sullivan. "You were right… she's an articulate and bright woman. I'm glad I met her. Thank you."

"You're very welcome, John. Thank you."

"The carriage man will be waiting outside," said Casey. "He may be asleep, so just rouse him."

"Thanks, Edward. We'll touch base later today. Good night."

Sullivan took a flight of stairs up to the main hospital floor, his exit route taking him directly through the psychiatric wing. While walking by he peered into each cell room through its door slot, only to see motionless bodies curled up on each floor. However, in the last room stood a man perfectly erect and staring up at a high window, his frame aglow in the moonlight. He stood motionless, as if in a trance.

"Mingo?" whispered Sullivan as he continued to gaze into the room. "Mingo, is that you?"

The inmate slowly rotated his head to the right and made eye contact with Sullivan. He then turned his attention back skyward.

"Mingo. Listen to me… I know you're a time traveler. I need to talk to you."

Mingo didn't budge.

"I'm a time traveler, too." Sullivan paused and looked up and down the dark corridor. "Please, talk to me. I'm from the future."

Mingo held still.

"The ring. I know it's the ring that opens the portal. Walt took it from you."

Mingo turned back toward Sullivan and squinted his eyes as if trying to focus.

"That's right. You know what I'm talking about. The ring opens the time portal… but now you don't have it."

Mingo slowly nodded his head in agreement.

"Walt has it. So we need to get it back. I can help you."

Mingo began to walk toward Sullivan, his footsteps bare and deathly quiet. To his right a moon shadow mirrored his every pace. He stopped directly in front of the door and glared into the slot. A black horsefly landed on his left forehead.

"I'm Dr. Sullivan, from the year 2020."

"We need to drain the swamp," muttered Mingo as his eyes bore down on the physician.

"Exactly," replied Sullivan. "Mingo, where's your time tunnel in town?"

"I need my ring back."

"I know," said Sullivan. "We'll get it, but first tell me, where's the tunnel?"

"No. Get me the ring… then I'll show you the tunnel."

"Sounds fair." Sullivan glanced over his left shoulder as the sound of a wooden board creaking echoed down the hall. He turned back. "Where does Walt keep the ring?"

Mingo held up his thumb.

"On his hand?"

"His thumb. He keeps it there. Walt's an a-hole."

"Yes. So it seems. Alright my friend. That's all the information I need tonight. We'll get you out of here… I promise. I'll work on getting the ring and once you're feeling better, we'll take a little trip together to the future. Deal?"

Mingo smiled. He held up his pinky finger to the slot.

"What? I thought you said it was on his thumb?"

"Pinky promise?" asked Mingo.

Sullivan laughed and held his arm high. He passed his hand through the slot and locked his fifth finger onto Mingo's. They both pulled tight.

"Pinky promise," grinned Sullivan.

Mingo held tight and vibrated his hand fiercely before letting go. He then walked back to his original position and stared back up at the moon.

"Good night, Mingo."

Sullivan turned to his right and walked out of the psychiatric wing through the foyer just inside the hospital's main entrance. He was halfway across the lobby when a large mass from the right violently crashed into his frame. The unexpected hit knocked some wind and saliva out of Sullivan's mouth as he spiraled across the marble floor. He ended up on his back with a hairy forearm forcefully pushing down across his throat, the force nearly crushing his windpipe.

"Where the hell do you think you're going?" growled the assailant.

"Ahhh… you're choking me," gasped Sullivan, his body paralyzed beneath the bulk.

The behemoth leaned his face forward as if trying to identify his prey. He gently eased back from Sullivan's throat.

"Who are you?" asked Walt.

"Dr. John Sullivan. A friend of Dr. Casey."

"Who?"

"John Sullivan. A personal friend of Benjamin Franklin."

Walt cautiously leaned backward and then slowly stood up. He held out a hand to help Sullivan stand. "Sorry about that doctor. You looked like Mingo from behind. I heard some noise from the psych wing and thought he was trying to escape."

Sullivan groaned and rubbed his neck. "Oh my God. What are you doing here in the middle of the night?"

"I live here. Just down the hall."

"You live in the hospital?"

"Yep. I've no other home."

"You almost killed me!"

"Sorry. But I'm not going to let that crazy Mingo slip out again. The guy is a thorn in my side. He's like a cat." Walt furrowed his forehead. "But… why are you here?"

Sullivan shook his head as if trying to clear a concussion. "I was just downstairs with Dr. Casey. He admitted Mr. Franklin to the hospital a few hours ago. I helped care for him."

"Is Benjamin alright?"

"Yes. He's fine."

"I'm sorry," repeated Walt. As he spoke he brought his left hand to his chin. He was missing the tips of his index, long and ring finger. On his thumb gleamed a ring with a dark gem, the moonlight reflecting off the jewel. "I hope I didn't hurt you."

"I don't think so," said Sullivan as he moved his arms and legs. "Everything seems to be working alright."

"Mingo is a menace to society… always squawking about being a time traveler. He's escaped three times already. It's not going to happen again."

"Where did you get that ring?" asked Sullivan.

"My ring? What does it matter to you?"

"Ah… nothing in particular. It just glistened a bit in the darkness and caught my attention."

"Never mind about my ring," came the gruff reply. "Let's get you home."

"Sure," said Sullivan. "There's a carriage waiting for me outside."

Walt escorted the unexpected guest out to the courtyard and woke the carriage driver. Sullivan boarded the transport.

"Sorry to wake you," apologized Sullivan as he pulled away. "Good night."

The security officer didn't respond as he watched the carriage pass through the front gate and down Pine Street. He looked down at his hand and pushed the ring tighter onto his thumb.

The return trip to Elfreth's Alley was just the opposite of the mad dash to the hospital, the streets of Philadelphia fast asleep. Sullivan estimated the time to be about five o'clock in the morning. Some daylight was starting to filter over the eastern horizon and a few birds chirped in the stillness of dawn. As the carriage turned onto Elfreth's Alley, Sullivan immediately noticed a more ornate two-horse transport parked in front of General Arnold's house. A valet slowly unloaded several crates from the rear of the carriage, placing the luggage on the sidewalk.

"Whoa, Ellie," said the driver, his voice echoing in the narrow lane.

"Thank you," said Sullivan as he hopped off, his eyes fixated on the other buggy. He noticed a lamp lit in front of Arnold's home and an illuminated second floor window. His driver pulled away.

Sullivan entered Franklin's home and immediately sensed unease. He heard Sary noisily cleaning up the kitchen, moving pots and pans in rapid fashion.

"Hello?" he said. "Sary?"

She didn't respond as Sullivan approached the kitchen. As he turned the corner their bodies collided.

"Aaaah!" screamed Sary as two pewter plates flew out of her hands. The unexpected impact tossed her body to the floor.

"Sary!" shrieked Sullivan. "I'm so sorry!" He reflexively reached down to help pick her up, in the process grasping her forearm with his hand and placing an opposite hand across her shoulder. "Are you OK?"

"Yes," came the rapid reply. "I'm…. fine." She wiped a tear from her eye.

"Sary, are you crying?"

"No, I'm fine." She ran a blouse sleeve across her face. "I'm not crying." She picked up the plates, placed them on a shelf and made her way downstairs.

Sullivan followed.

"Sary, what's wrong?"

She didn't reply while nervously gathering her clothing and personal belongings, placing them in a wide, wicker basket.

"He's home, right?" asked Sullivan. "Major General Arnold is home?"

She frowned and kept moving, her silence a positive reply.

"Oh, Sary."

She scanned the room, her safe harbor for the past several weeks, and took a deep breath as if saying goodbye. She spotted a coin on the fireplace mantle and stepped forward to retrieve it, passing in front of Sullivan. He reached out an arm and stopped her progress. She looked up at him in terror, her cheeks red and her eyes moist. Sullivan estimated her age to be fifteen or sixteen years at best.

"Sary, I want to intervene, but I can't," confessed Sullivan. "I just can't. You have to understand."

Her body began to physically tremble.

"I'm sorry."

She burst into tears and drove her face into Sullivan's chest, her body convulsing with rapid sobs. Sullivan held her tight, wondering when the last time someone had done so in a caring way. A terrifying pang took hold of the physician's heart. He had no ability to protect her from the savage next door.

"How could such a horror exist?" mumbled Sullivan as he consoled her. "How is it possible?"

Sary pushed back from Sullivan and looked up. "Thank you, Dr. Sullivan." Her body jerked as a knock on the front door echoed through the home. "I have to leave you. Thank you for being so nice to me." She stiffened her upper lip and picked up the wicker basket. Sullivan followed her up the stairwell, her gait self-assured and defiant. She turned into the kitchen, allowing Sullivan to reach the front door first.

"Oh," frowned Benedict Arnold. "It's you." He wore black britches, riding boots and a white shirt with no jacket.

"Can I help you?"

"Where's Mr. Franklin?"

"He's been admitted to Pennsylvania Hospital. I just spent the night caring for him."

"Is he alright?"

"He's going to be fine," answered the physician. "An acute case of dropsy. Dr. Casey is currently at his bedside."

"Ben preaches moderation but his appetite does not," opined Arnold. "The man's a sot." He looked past Sullivan. "Where's Sary? I've come to get her."

An anger roiled inside Sullivan like he never felt before, his visual field suddenly razor sharp. His heart began to rapidly beat as he tried to control his breathing. "She's gathering her things."

"I'm tired," stated Arnold as he took a step inward to brush by the house guest. "I've no time to wait."

Sullivan spontaneously placed his body in a protective position between Arnold and the foyer, the maneuver creating contact between the two men.

"That won't be necessary," said Sullivan in a bold tone. "I'll go get…"

Arnold took hold of the doctor's shirt with both hands and drove his body to the ground, his brute force equal to that of Walt's. A vein across his forehead swelled as he declared, "Don't ever touch me again!" He picked up Sullivan like a rag doll and shoved his body into a wall. "Understand?" He continued to lean on the physician, his breath hot and foul.

"I'm ready," stated Sary as she appeared behind the beatdown. "Sorry it took me so long." Her face was dry and she smiled while stepping forward, her body driving a wedge between the men, forcing Arnold to let go. "Let's get you home, General Arnold. You must be hungry. I've got some pop-robins already made and I'll boil some eggs." Sary exited the building and turned left. "I'll make dumplings for lunch and some scrapple for dinner. I just have to get to the market for some more onions…" Her voice trailed away.

Arnold straightened his shirt out and glared at Sullivan. "I don't know where you're from," snarled Arnold. "But you've worn out your welcome on my street. Understand?"

Sullivan pointed a trembling index finger defiantly at the military leader. "If you ever lay a finger on that girl, so help me God… I'll report you to the authorities."

Sullivan never saw or expected the vicious right cross that landed squarely on his jaw. He tumbled to the ground in a heap only to have Arnold kick him directly in the groin, twice. The war hero then spit on him. "I *am* the authority!" growled the autocrat.

"So go ahead and try!" He stomped on Sullivan's abdomen with a black boot. "You're lucky Mr. Franklin considers you a friend, or else I'd have killed you by now." He placed his boot on Sullivan's bloodied face and pressed down hard. "Don't *ever* speak to me again!"

General Benedict Arnold turned and walked away, not bothering to close the front door. Dr. Sullivan groveled on the floor as the morning sun began to light the lane. His beaten body lay prostrate on the wooden floor as blood trickled down his chin.

## CHAPTER TWELVE
### THE ALPHABET
### 2020

Professor Alabaster Bookman stood at a makeshift podium in his living room. Before him sat a collection of dignitaries to include fellow faculty members from the University, the deputy mayor of Philadelphia, a local news team and some close relatives. They gathered in four rows of perfectly placed folding chairs with their backs to Elfreth's Alley. Behind the professor hung a massive reproduction of Robert Feke's 1746 painting of Benjamin Franklin. The grandfather clock in the foyer chimed twice as Bookman began to speak.

"Good afternoon, everyone. Thank you for all coming out today for this special occasion. As you all know, I've committed a significant amount of my time, energy and resources into researching the history of this residence which dates back to the early 1700s. In fact, this very home was built in the year 1729, when the Port of Philadelphia was a bustling metropolis of 35,000 strong."

"Wow!" exclaimed the deputy mayor in the front row. "Only 35K… poor tax base."

Bookman ignored the comment and continued.

"Of course, everyone is aware of Benjamin Franklin's residence in West Philadelphia and his main domicile over on Franklin Court. Yet Benjamin often spoke in his writings of a 'special place' away from Deborah and the children, where he could meet with his Junto and other scholars to create and foster the intellectual fabric that led to the birth of this great nation." Bookman took a deep inspiration, the air whistling through his capacious nostrils.

"Until recently, the location of this academic sanctuary was a point of conjecture, prompting wild and unfounded proclamations as to the exact whereabouts of Ben's so-called "man cave."" He air-quoted the term "man cave". "However, I'm proud to say that with the help of my colleagues present today, we have beyond a doubt..."

Just then a disturbing thud hit the base of the wall behind Bookman, causing Franklin's portrait to tilt askew. The sudden impact startled several guests in their seats. A faint voice could then be heard through the wall.

"No... we're alright. Wally just dropped a cannonball!"

Some laughter filtered through the room.

"Don't shoot until you see the whites of their eyes!" followed the next muted cry from next door.

Some more laughter.

"Yes... well," muttered Bookman. "I apologize... remember, this house was built in 1729. The walls are a bit thin." He cleared his throat to recalibrate. "Now, as I was saying. After years of scholarly work, I've proven beyond a doubt where Franklin's mysterious 'third address' was located in the city of Philadelphia." Bookman grinned and looked to his left directly into a television camera. "Ladies and Gentlemen, it gives me great pleasure to officially announce that the very home you are sitting in, *my* home... was indeed the mysterious third address of Mister Benjamin Franklin!"

A round of applause followed Bookman's absolutism.

"That's right, you are all seated in Mr. Franklin's personal oasis, his think tank. A sacred inner sanctum that spawned the Declaration of Independence and the Constitution of this great land we call America!"

More enthusiastic applause ensued.

"Now, it gives me great pleasure to introduce Mr. Winston Williamson, a representative of the National Register of Historic Places." Bookman looked to his right. "Mr. Williamson."

A portly man with a mustache and bad comb-over approached the podium amid cordial applause. He held a bronze plaque in his left hand.

"Thank you, Professor Bookman. Ladies and Gentlemen, it's an honor to be here in this fascinating home. As President of the Northeast Region for Historic Places, it gives me great pleasure..."

The sudden sound of muffled music interrupted the presentation.

*"Come, join hand in hand,*
*Brave Americans all,*
*And rouse your bold hearts at*
*Fair Liberty's call;*

Williamson paused as the first stanza played out. He tried to continue.

*No tyrannous acts shall*
*Suppress your just claim,*
*Or stain with dishonor*
*America's name.*

Bookman stood up and stormed over to the wall. He banged on it several times. "Quiet with that music!"

*In Freedom we're born and in Freedom we'll live.*
*Our purses are ready.*
*Steady, boys, steady.*

"Idiots!" shouted Bookman as his face turned red. He bolted toward the front door. "I'll be right back." The music continued unabated.

Bookman charged outside and veered right to his neighbor's front door. After several unanswered raps he turned the doorknob and stepped inside. A bizarre scene played out in front of the historian as the music continued.

> *Then join hand in hand,*
> *Brave Americans all,*
> *By uniting we stand,*
> *By dividing we fall;*

Burt and Wally were marching in unison down a hallway with their backs to Bookman. Each man held a Pennsylvania rifle over their right shoulder. In the front parlor to Bookman's right stood Attorney Mills, energetically waving a Betsy Ross flag back and forth. He wore a white handkerchief around his head as if the victim of a battle wound. The three men were oblivious to Bookman.

"What's going on here?" shouted Bookman.

> *In Freedom we're born and in Freedom we'll live.*
> *Our purses are ready.*
> *Steady, boys, steady!*

It was Mills who spotted Bookman first. He put down the flag and rushed over to a record player near the cannon.

"Company... halt!" bellowed Wally as he and Burt circled back through the front room via a separate hallway.

"Frrrip!" screeched the vinyl record as Mill's dragged the needle across its surface.

Bookman stepped into the front parlor, a scowl across his face. His sudden appearance surprised Wally and Burt.

"What in the hell are you three gentlemen doing?" snarled Bookman. "We're in the midst of a formal ceremony next door!"

"Ah, yes," stammered Attorney Mills. He went to step forward but tripped over a cannonball on the floor, sending his body to the ground.

"Good God, man!" wailed Bookman as he stepped aside.

Mills quickly stood up and extended his right hand. "Yes. I'm sorry. Allow me to introduce myself. Attorney Frederick Mills here… from the West Philadelphia Historical Society."

Bookman cocked an eyelid and stared down the attorney.

"These are my two associates," jabbered Mills. "Mr. Wally Roberts and Mr. Burt Bilkins."

Burt and Wally nodded, a sheepish look across their faces. They each lowered their weapons.

"What exactly are you doing?" asked Bookman.

"Well, um," stuttered Mills.

"A re-enactment," interrupted Wally. "The Battle of Bunker Hill."

"A re-enactment? And you men are from where?"

"The West Philadelphia Historical Society," said Mills proudly. "I'm the president of the society. Perhaps you've heard of us?"

"No. I haven't." Bookman looked back toward the foyer. "Where's Mr. Zuckerman?" While waiting for a response he scanned the room, astonished by the deluge of Revolutionary War artifacts.

"I'm not sure," stated Mills with a hunch of his shoulders. "He seems to have broken rank."

"Mr. Zuckerman knows you're here?" queried Bookman. "Inside his home… having a military parade?"

Before Mills could answer, Zuckerman appeared from behind.

"Ah, Professor Bookman. Good to see you," said Zuckerman as he extended his hand. "I'm so glad you finally stopped by. Welcome to my home!"

"Barry!" bemoaned Bookman. "I'm in the middle of an important ceremony next door and this so-called battle re-enactment has disrupted the process." He sneered at Wally and Burt. "May I ask that you please keep the noise to a minimum for the next hour or so?"

"Oh, I'm sorry," stated Zuckerman. "Sure. No problem."

"Thank you."

Bookman went to step away.

"So, you've met my colleagues?" asked Zuckerman.

"Yes. I have."

"They're doing some on site research for the West Philadelphia Historical Society."

"Really. On what?" asked Bookman with one foot out the door.

"On the original owner of this home," stated Mills.

Bookman stepped back inside and sent a laser stare through the skull of Attorney Mills. "Continue," ordered the university professor.

"Yes," garbled Mills as he raised his index finger. "Our society has recently received credible information that a Mister Benjamin Franklin resided in this very house." He bobbed up and down on his toes excitedly. "So we've taken it upon ourselves to investigate the matter more thoroughly... hence our appearance here this afternoon. We're on a fact-finding mission, that is of course, with permission from Mr. Zuckerman."

Bookman's eyes rapidly blinked as if peering into a sandstorm. His lips trembled as he tried to formulate a rebuttal.

"Yea," added Wally. "This is Mr. Franklin's mysterious 'third address'. Have you ever heard of that term?"

Bookman's head began to gyrate back and forth as his body quivered. "Do you know who you're talking to?" he huffed.

The historical society officers stared forward in blank fashion. Zuckerman went to speak, but Bookman cut him off.

"Professor Alabaster Bookman... acting Chairman of the Department of History at the University." He pointed directly at the historical society members. "How dare you insult my intelligence!" He stepped backward, visibly agitated. "How dare you!" he gasped before slamming the door.

"What's his problem?" asked Burt as he returned the rifle to its stand.

"What a crab apple," added Wally. "He's your neighbor?"

"Yes," replied Zuckerman. "The man I spoke of trying to steal my family's historic thunder. There's some sort of an award ceremony going on next door."

"And he didn't invite his next door neighbor?" asked Mills as he removed his head bandage. "How rude."

"No. He didn't," answered Zuckerman. "Believe it or not, that was the first time he ever stepped foot into my house. I've invited him over multiple times to inspect my collection, but he never accepted the offer."

"The guy's a crank," interjected Burt.

"He did seem pretty impressed by your display," declared Mills. "Did you see his eyes as he scanned the room?"

"Really?" asked Zuckerman.

"He looked like a kid in a candy shop," stated Wally.

"Yea," added Attorney Mills. "I bet dollars to doughnuts he'll be knocking on your door as soon as his so called 'important ceremony next door' is over. All this stuff is like crack cocaine to a guy like that. Trust me."

The president of the West Philadelphia Historical Society was indeed correct in his psychological assessment of Bookman. At approximately seven o'clock that very evening, the professor politely knocked on his neighbor's door. Barry Zuckerman answered.

"Professor! So good to see you again," declared Zuckerman. "Do come in."

Bookman tentatively stepped inside the residence, his eyes looking left to right for any members of the historical society.

"They're gone," declared the host.

"Great. I was expecting a volley of cannon fire across the foyer."

Zuckerman laughed. "They're quite the collection of historians. Great guys. Passionate about their field."

Bookman held his tongue in regard to the irreverent usage of the term 'historian'.

"How did the ceremony go?" asked Zuckerman.

"Fantastic! My house has finally been registered with the National Register of Historic Places. I can't believe it took so long. But that's what happens when you're dealing with a government bureaucracy."

"Congratulations. I'm sure…"

"Is all this Revolutionary War antiquity included in the sale price of your home?"

"Why, yes. Yes it is," replied Zuckerman. "It was recommended by my estate attorney to lump it all together. It makes the transaction a heck of a lot easier. Otherwise I'd have to individually dole out all of this junk. It's common practice here on Elfreth's Alley for homes to be sold fully furnished. Did your home come with everything included?"

"Where did you get it all?" asked Bookman as he started a self-guided tour into the front room. "I mean, this is an amazing collection."

"The family… over time. It certainly didn't happen overnight. The cannon is my favorite."

Bookman drifted through the room in awe of the artifacts. One by one, he inspected each item and gave a brief synopsis of its role in the American Revolution. He was particularly enthralled by a powder horn sitting on a windowsill next to the rifle stack. The horn had ornate carvings on it to include the engraved slogan 'Liberty or Death' along with the soldier's name: 'James Cluebeck'. Beside the name were a total of thirteen short slants whittled into the dried bone.

"How beautiful," commented Bookman as he uncorked the cap. He held it up and looked down the funnel. "It's made of ox horn." He pointed to the thirteen slants.

"Thirteen colonies," declared Zuckerman.

"No… thirteen kills," grinned Bookman. "It was common practice for a soldier to etch his powder horn after killing a redcoat." He ran his finger over the original owner's name. "James must have been quite the shot, a real sharpshooter."

To the right of the powder horn sat a printed copy of Thomas Paine's *Common Sense*. Bookman picked it up, his mouth agape as he opened the front cover. "Oh my, this is an original copy of *Common Sense*." He turned to the second page. "Printed by Ben Franklin's very own press."

"It wouldn't surprise me," quipped Zuckerman. "According to the experts, Ben did live nearby."

Bookman didn't process the sarcastic comment as his expedition continued. He paged through a King James Bible, handled a wooden canteen and carefully inspected a framed muster roll. The professor was speechless by the time he finished the first floor tour.

"Wait until you see the basement," announced Zuckerman as he led his guest downstairs.

"Barry, why didn't you ever alert me of your collection?" asked the professor as he carefully descended the stairwell.

"I actually did, several times." Zuckerman held out his hand expansively as his neighbor entered the room.

"Oh Lord," gasped Bookman. He stepped forward, his gait solemn and pious. "Oh, Barry. This is truly amazing."

As the professor scanned the room he went silent, as if transcended to another place and time. Slowly he studied some personal artifacts including several coins, a set of earrings and some drinking vessels. However, it was a paper notebook on a wooden shelf that captured his full attention. He lifted up the journal and caressed it carefully with both hands. After blowing some dust off the front jacket, he opened the cover.

"Oh my," he muttered. "Barry, this is a personal diary written by…"

"Sary. At least that's what it says on the first couple of pages."

"Sary is indeed correct," stated Bookman. "A common name given to a slave girl during colonial times." He respectfully turned a few more pages.

"She spells her name several times, but then it turns into gibberish," stated Zuckerman. "Someone must have been trying to teach her to read and write."

Bookman's body froze as he held the ledger in hand, his eyes moving in a rapid left to right direction.

"Professor, are you OK?" asked the host. "You look as if you've just seen a ghost."

Bookman held the journal in one hand and turned the open pages to face Zuckerman.

"Yea. Like I said... gibberish."

Across the page appeared a mishmash of vowels and consonants, occasionally interrupted by some unidentifiable marks. Just over each entry stood some recognizable dates from the year 1779. "I once took it to a linguistic expert," continued Zuckerman. "But even they couldn't translate it. It's written in some sort of unrecognizable code."

"Do you know what this is?" stammered Bookman excitedly.

"Nope."

"These are journal entries from the year 1779, written by a slave named Sary..." The professor turned the book back toward himself. "... in a phonetic alphabet created by none other than... Benjamin Franklin!"

"Really?"

"Yes!"

"That wouldn't surprise me. According to a local expert, Ben did live nearby."

The pun again failed to hit its mark as Bookman carefully ran an index finger across each line.

"So, Ben wrote his own alphabet? Is that what you're telling me?" asked Zuckerman.

"Absolutely. A phonetic alphabet. He tried to reform the English language." While speaking the professor continued to read the diary. "He omitted the letters c, j, w, x and y and added a bunch of new vowels and consonants."

"Wow, Ben's mortal," chuckled Zuckerman. "One of his ideas bombed. I've never heard of the Franklin Alphabet."

"Not many people have. Franklin invented it in the mid-1760's but it didn't appear in print until around 1779. Franklin subsequently presented his work to Noah Webster, hoping that Webster would validate his proposal, in which letters were organized by the way the corresponding sounds were formed in the mouth." He paused while finishing an entry. "But it failed miserably and was soon forgotten."

"But it appears to me that you can understand it?" stated Zuckerman as he watched Bookman devour the entries. "Is that true? Can you read the Franklin Alphabet?"

"Absolutely. I know everything about Benjamin Franklin. I actually wrote my doctoral thesis in this language."

"Wow. So… what does it say?"

"The entries are indeed from a woman named Sary. Apparently a close friend of Franklin. She writes of her daily activities here in this home." He looked around. "She briefly lived in these quarters."

"I would assume she knew Mr. Franklin. Who else could have taught her his alphabet?"

"Her entries speak of mundane tasks, such as going to the market and tending to chores. She speaks of a man named Sullivan, a friend of Mr. Franklin's from the North." He slowly closed the journal. "But she also speaks of a horrible beast who lived next door. A tormentor in her dreams."

"An animal, perhaps a dog?"

"No… a man. But she doesn't refer to him by name."

"Next door… in your home?"

"Perhaps," stated Bookman with a faraway stare. "It's unclear which neighbor, but she referred to him several times as the 'serpent from next door.'"

"Interesting."

"Ah, Barry. Do you mind if I borrow this diary? I believe it warrants a detailed examination at the University."

Zuckerman considered the direct request before replying. "Well, professor… it's just that I promised the West Philadelphia Historical Society first crack at all the artifacts in my home. They're a bunch of real enthusiastic guys who are passionate about history. Perhaps once they're done with their research I can loan it out?"

Bookman kept his emotions in check. "I completely understand." He politely set down the journal. "All I ask is that you keep me in mind. I have all the resources available to analyze this notebook in a manner deserving its significance."

"Absolutely," replied Zuckerman. "Now, come on over here. Let me show you something special." He led Bookman across the room. "Over here is this crazy inlay on the floor I call 'Snaky'. It's carved out of pure granite and I'm sure you'll recognize…

Sleep did not come easy for Professor Bookman that night. He lay awake repeating the lines written over 200 years ago by a slave girl named Sary. He failed to divulge to Zuckerman the complete translation of Sary's text, especially the part about her daily life "in the basement of Benjamin Franklin's home".

## CHAPTER THIRTEEN
### A SECRET BIN
### 1779

"*You lost the keys!*" screeched Sullivan with both hands on his head. "Ben! Please, tell me you didn't!"

"Ah, unfortunately I have," cringed Franklin as he sat in his home, having been discharged earlier in the day from the hospital. "A rather regrettable action on my behalf."

"Regrettable! That's an understatement! I'm trapped in the past!" Sullivan frantically paced back and forth. "I can't believe it! I just cannot believe it!"

"Well, when you took ill I confiscated your key… just in case," muttered Franklin. "You were a very sick man, John."

Sullivan was too distraught to reply.

"So, I had both keys in my possession when I collapsed up in Manayunk."

"And then what? What happened next, Ben?"

"Well, everything is a bit fuzzy from that point forward." Franklin took a sip of tea. "I do recall them tossing my body onto the back of a flat carriage like a sack of potatoes. A bystander prematurely proclaimed, 'Ben Franklin's goose is cooked.'"

"And?"

"Well, the next thing I remember is waking up in the basement of Pennsylvania Hospital, under the expert care of a Drs. Casey and Sullivan."

"So, they could be anywhere between here and Manayunk?"

"I suppose."

Sullivan took a deep sigh. "Who drove you back to Philadelphia?"

"Oh, I remember that. The Pagano brothers, Mario and Anthony."

"So, maybe the Pagano brothers have them? But why did they drive you home? Don't they live in Philadelphia?"

"They're personal friends of mine," continued Franklin as he chomped on a cookie. "They used to work in my print shop before I sold out. I subsequently secured a job for them over at Christ Church. They're always available to do odd jobs for me. I'm sure someone sent for them."

"So we have to find the Pagano brothers and ask them."

"Or, maybe I hid the keys here somewhere prior to departure? Let me think now." He held an index finger to his forehead.

"Ben! Concentrate. My life depends on it!"

"Ah John, the memory banks aren't what they used to be." Franklin pushed himself up and out of the chair with a moan. "If I did hide them, they'll be downstairs in the secret bin. That's where I stash anything of importance." He slowly walked to the top of the steps leading to the basement.

"The secret bin? You have a secret bin in the house?"

"Yes. You never know when the tax collector or British are going to storm in." He took a step downward. "When in doubt, check my secret bin."

Sullivan shook his head in disbelief. He had finally been cleared to time travel by Dr. Casey earlier in the day. He followed Franklin into the cellar where Ben led him to the 'Join, or Die' inlay on the floor.

"Snaky," stated Ben as he leaned downward. "The world's first political cartoon. I had a German mason set the stones into the foundation." He grasped the hunk of granite adorned by the letter

'P' and began to wobble it back and forth. As he struggled to dislodge the stone he declared, "Pennsylvania is the Keystone State, John. Never forget that. The key."

"Here, let me help," said Sullivan as he knelt down.

Together both men lifted the boulder and placed it aside. Beneath the rock was a hidden chamber honed out of granite, three feet wide and three feet deep. Franklin stuck his hand into the dark cavity.

"Let's see what we've got," stated Ben as he moved his arm in a circular fashion. "It's been a while. Ah… here we go."

Franklin served up a racoon hat.

"Oh boy! My favorite cap!" He put the hat on his head and smiled. "The French took quite the liking to this piece of fur." He chuckled and looked at Sullivan. "It became quite the rage across Europe. What do you think?"

"Ben," steamed Sullivan. "The keys… I need the keys."

"Oh, yes. Forgive me… for I digress." He placed the hat aside and reached back into the hollow.

"Do you feel them? Please tell me you do."

Franklin again withdrew his hand, this time with a diary. He looked at Sullivan sheepishly. "I've been teaching Sary how to write." He held his finger up to his lips and whispered. "Don't tell the neighbors. It's shunned upon but she's such an intelligent girl. A quick learner."

Sullivan slapped his forehead with the palm of his hand, prompting Franklin to return the notebook into the chamber. He continued to fumble. "Nah. There are no keys in here." He pulled up a handful of gold coins. "Only some souvenirs from France. I'm sorry, John."

"Ah, Ben. With all due respect, how could you? I'm sunk." Sullivan stepped back and sat down on a bunk bed. He leaned forward and put both hands on his head. "I'll never make it back to the future. How could this have happened? I should have immediately returned. What were we thinking?"

"John, oh ye of little faith!" countered Franklin as he shoved the boulder back into place. "Remember the immortal words just spoken by my good friend, John Paul Jones… 'don't give up the ship!'" He stood up with a raised fist.

Sullivan gawked at Franklin.

"What? You've never heard of that one?"

"Ben. Captain Jones said, 'I have not yet begun to fight.'"

"Oh," said Franklin with a bemused look. "So who said, 'don't give up the ship'?"

"Commander James Lawrence… the War of 1812," said Sullivan. He dropped his head back into his hands. "You're dating yourself."

"In a forward sense," chuckled Ben. He began to walk toward the stairs.

"Where are you going?"

"To see the Pagano brothers over at Christ Church. Maybe they'll know where the keys are."

The two men exited the home and turned left, their path coursing directly in front of the Arnold residence. As they passed the front door the booming voice of General Arnold could be heard deriding Sary, his potato soup too thin and cold. Franklin clutched Sullivan's forearm and steered him farther down the lane. To their right rose the spire of Christ Church. In the basement of the house of worship, they found the Pagano brothers fast asleep.

"Ah, always on guard," stated Franklin proudly. He pointed to several wooden kegs surrounding the sentries. "Gunpowder."

"In the church?"

"Yes. Mario and Antonio are sentinels for the Continental Army. Most towns protect their gunpowder supply inside the church, even in Europe. That's why I invented the lightning rod."

"You lost me on that one." Sullivan walked past the snoring brothers laid out flat on some flour sacks. Their airspace reeked of body odor and alcohol.

"A church steeple is the highest point of elevation in every town," explained Franklin. "Whenever a lightning storm approaches, the city crier climbs the church steeple to ring the bell and alert the populace."

Sullivan continued to listen as he picked up and sniffed an empty bottle of moonshine.

"Unfortunately, lightning strikes the highest object, the end result being a rash of bellman fatalities across Europe and the colonies."

"So you invented the lightning rod to save the criers?"

"Yes." Franklin kicked the skinnier Pagano brother in the leg. "And the gunpowder." The guard didn't budge. Ben jabbed him in the stomach with his cane. "Mario, wake up. The British are coming!"

The sentry jumped to his feet as if defending himself. He nearly lunged at Sullivan before the familiar face of Franklin caught his eye. He rapidly blinked his eyes and shoved his brother's shoulder.

"Ben Franklin, what brings you here?"

Before Ben could reply Antonio spoke.

"Shep was planning to blow the gunpowder supply," declared Antonio. "We had nothing to do with it, Ben. So help me God!" He raised his right hand into the air.

"Yea," agreed Mario. "We're innocent. You have to believe us."

"Gentlemen. Gentlemen. I come as a friend." He patted Antonio on the shoulder. "To thank both of you for transporting me back from the outskirts of town. You saved my life."

The Pagano brothers looked at each other and grinned.

"You remember Dr. Sullivan," continued Franklin. "You both met him late the other night just outside the graveyard. He's in town from the North woods."

The Pagano boys respectfully nodded to the physician.

"Gentlemen," countered Sullivan, unimpressed by their physical presence. They wore ragged clothing and black soot covered their hands and faces. He noticed the taller man's left eye to blink in an uncontrolled fashion. Sullivan estimated their ages to both be in the late twenties.

"Thank you so very much for the ride home," continued Ben. "Like I've always said, I can count on the Pagano boys."

"It was an honor and a pleasure," stated Mario. "Anything for our friend."

"Yea," continued Antonio. "We heard you were in trouble and immediately hitched the horses to the wagon. There was never a doubt."

"Yes," said Franklin. "Now, about my ride home. It seems that I lost a set of keys in transport. A set of rather important keys. Is there any chance that you've come upon them?" He anxiously held eye contact with Mario in anticipation of a positive reply.

Mario looked at his brother and hunched his shoulders. "No, I'm sorry, Ben. We have no such set of keys. Isn't that right, Antonio?" He stared at his brother who pulled a black keyring from his pocket. The ring had three large keys attached.

"No," stammered Antonio as he counted the rings. "I mean, yes… you are right. We don't have them. We only have the keys to the church." He held the larger of the three in hand. "Here's the one to the basement and the other two are for the front doors."

"Are you absolutely sure?" pleaded Ben.

"Yes."

"Maybe they can check the wagon," suggested Sullivan. "They may have fallen out of your pocket in transport."

"Good idea," said Mario. "The wagon is out back. Keys can certainly get stuck between the wooden slats."

The men quickly turned toward a rear exit before Ben stopped the group. "Ah, Antonio… why don't you give the good doctor here a little tour of the basement. Show him how we make and store gunpowder."

"Sure," replied Antonio as he picked his nose. He vigorously rotated a finger in his nostril as he turned back to Sullivan.

"John, you'll enjoy this," declared Ben. "Like I've told you before, gunpowder is the sine qua non for any successful revolution. My recent diplomatic mission to France in large part centered upon securing a French agreement to supply the colonies with black powder." Franklin then turned and followed Mario outside.

"I thought it was to caress all the French women," cackled Mario. "Ain't that right, Ben?"

"Ah Blinky, you're incorrigible."

Their voices trailed away, leaving Sullivan with the stouter of the two brothers, still with his finger up his nose. Sullivan noted an oddity to the man's hand, as if he had too many digits.

"The French make the best gunpowder," stated Antonio, his voice muffled by his hand. He brought his finger out of his nose and pressed it against the opposite nostril. The guard forcefully snorted, his effort sending a wad of snot to the ground. He wiped his nose in his sleeve. "See this emblem?" He pointed to a red coat of arms emblazoned onto a wooden barrel. "That's French. We just got it through the blockade."

"I see," said Sullivan.

"There's no better gunpowder on earth. Just ask any dead Brit who thought they were outside of shooting range." The sentry spit on the ground. "It packs a lot of punch."

Sullivan nodded in agreement.

"Gunpowder is made of three ingredients. Do you know what they are?"

"Ah… no I don't."

"Charcoal, sulfur and saltpeter. Saltpeter is the most important of the three." While talking he wedged open the top of a barrel, exposing a fine, black powdery content filled to the brim. He ran his hand through the powder. "This my friend, is gunpowder."

Sullivan dipped his fingers into the mixture, it's consistency similar to that of sifted flour.

"We get the charcoal from burning wood," continued the tour guide. "Alder, buckthorn and cottonwood burn the best."

"So charcoal is basically carbon," stated Sullivan as he dusted off his fingertips.

"No. It's charcoal. I never heard of carbon."

Pagano slapped the lid back onto the barrel and pounded it shut with a rubber mallet. He continued walking down the barrel line.

"How about the sulfur?" asked Sullivan. "Where does that come from?"

"Do you know another name for sulfur?"

"No."

"It's also called brimstone or burning stone," grinned Pagano. "We get if from the West Indies. A ship brings it into harbor every few days."

"And the saltpeter?"

"That's from the West Indies, too. It's the hardest and most important ingredient to get."

Pagano led Sullivan to a back room anchored by a central table. Mounds of raw charcoal, sulfur and saltpeter stood in separate corners of the room. On the floor lay a dead mouse next to a black cat curled behind a broomstick. On top of the table stood a large mortar and pestle next to a balance scale.

"This is where Mario and I grind," professed Antonio. "We make the private gunpowder supply for all the officers and General Washington himself." He sat down in front of the scale. "Gunpowder is 75% saltpeter, 15% charcoal and 10% sulfur." He looked up at Sullivan. "Never forget that ratio."

"I won't," winced Sullivan from the smell of sulfur. There were no windows in the room. "Isn't this kind of dangerous? It smells like rotten eggs." He waved a hand in front of his nose. "There's no ventilation in here."

"All of these ingredients are safe on their own," replied Antonio as he sat down at the table and dusted some yellowish powder onto the scale. It was then that Sullivan confirmed an extra finger on his right hand, a bizarre genetic anomaly that he had never seen in an adult. "But once you mix the three together… be careful!" He placed a weight opposite the sulfur and carefully adjusted its dose. "Mario and I won't even fart in this room for fear of an explosion." He scooped the sulfur off the scale and rapidly mixed it into a bowl with the other ingredients. "Here you go, doctor," said Antonio as he held up the final product. "Fresh gunpowder. Let's go test it out!" He stood up and walked down a hallway to the base of a short stairwell that led outdoors. The black cat hissed as they passed by.

Just behind the basement exit stood a narrow, makeshift rifle range. Antonio picked up a rifle. "Have you ever shot a rifle before?"

"Ah, yes. In Boy Scout camp… a BB gun that is. I got a badge for it."

"I'll take that as a 'no,'" smirked the sentry. "Let me show you how this works. Step one is to level the firearm." He held the weapon parallel to the ground. "Next, half cock the trigger." He pulled the trigger half-way back. "Now take out a cartridge filled with gunpowder." He reached into his pocket and delivered a rolled piece of paper approximately four inches long and a half-inch wide. "I just made this batch last night." He raised the cartridge of black powder to his teeth and bit off the top, spitting the paper onto the ground. "Next, pour a portion of the powder into the pan." He drizzled some fresh gunpowder onto a metal plate just below the trigger head. "Pour the remaining powder down the barrel." He steadied the gun butt onto the ground with the nozzle pointing skyward and dropped the remaining paper cartridge into the muzzle end. "Next, drop your iron ball." He took a round musket ball from his other pocket and dropped it down the shaft of the rifle. "Get your ramrod and pack it all down." He delivered a long, narrow metal rod from just below the gun barrel and drove it into the barrel itself, compacting the bullet and the powder. After several downward tamps, he returned the ramrod to its slot. "Now fully cock the trigger." He pulled the trigger backwards and handed the firearm to Sullivan. "There you go, mate. Let's see what you got." He pointed down the firing line to a wooden silhouette in the shape of a British shoulder.

"Ah… I'm alright," stammered Sullivan. He handed the rifle back. "You can shoot it."

"What are you, a chickenshit? Fire the weapon." Pagano spit on the ground and stepped backward. "Go on. Fire it." He snorted and pointed down the range.

Sullivan ran his hand up and down the long, sleek barrel of the weapon, surprised at its perfect balance. He was a bona fide pacifist and abhorred guns of all caliber. He strangely recalled his childhood during each hunting season, aghast by dead deer roped to the hoods of passing cars, their tongues sticking out in grisly fashion. He went to lower the weapon.

"Hey! Don't point that barrel at me!" shouted Pagano as he jumped to the side. "Are you stupid or something? Man up!"

The derogatory comment angered Sullivan. He sneered at Pagano, turned about and brought the rifle parallel to the ground, snugging the butt of the weapon into his shoulder. He lowered his eye and took aim.

"Well, look at you," chuckled Pagano. "A real Timothy Murphy."

Sullivan's left arm began to quiver as he tried to steady the barrel in relation to the target. He had no idea who Timothy Murphy was. He placed his hand on the trigger.

"Squeeze it like it's your girlfriend," snickered Pagano.

Sullivan pulled the trigger, the ensuing explosion driving the trigger lock backward into his face. His ears rang out as the stench of sulfur filled his nose. He stumbled over a log and fell backwards to the ground, the rifle still clenched in his right arm.

"Aha, ha, ha!" laughed Pagano. "Nice shot! Aha, ha, ha. You just killed the neighbor's cat!"

Sullivan wiped some blood off his cheek and stood up. He peered down the rifle range hoping to see a hole in the target. There was none. Pagano then pushed him aside.

"Here's how you drop a redcoat," boasted Pagano as he pulled a pistol out of his waist area. He raised the weapon and fired. A hole ripped through the torso of the target. "And if he's still moving… finish him off." Pagano pulled a second pistol out of his waistline and squeezed off a second round, the target now with a hole in its head. "Bingo!" hollered Pagano. He turned and spit. "Any questions?"

"What's all the racket?" asked Ben as he turned the corner with Mario. "Are we under attack?"

"Nah," laughed Antonio. "I was just showing this greenhorn how to shoot."

"How did he do?"

"Well, if he was aiming for the target, rotten. If he was aiming for the neighbor's cat… he's a dead-eye."

"I was aiming for the cat," retorted Sullivan with a bruised ego, his ears still a buzz. He handed the rifle to Pagano and looked at Ben. "Did you find the keys?"

"No. I'm sorry, John. We did not."

"We'll find them," stated Mario. "Tomorrow we're going to retrace our steps from here to Manayunk. Ain't that right, Antonio?"

"You bet. You can count on the Pagano brothers." He patted Sullivan on the shoulder. "Trust me when I say that."

Sullivan left the church emotionally dejected, his fate seemingly sealed by a Benjamin Franklin lapse. He turned right but Ben turned left.

"Where are you headed now?"

"To the graveyard. Please, join me."

The two men walked into a small burial ground adjacent to the church, surrounded by a low stone wall. Ben slowly knelt down in front of a tombstone. The engraving on the stone read:

Francis Folger Franklin
Son of Benjamin and Deborah Franklin
Aged 4y 1mo 1d
The Delight of All Who Knew Him

"My biggest regret in life was not having him inoculated against smallpox," whispered Ben as he pulled some weeds out from in front of the tomb. "I thought about it, but hesitated." He sighed deeply. "I miss him dearly."

Sullivan remained quiet as several seconds passed. Franklin stood up and looked around the graveyard as if trying to orient himself. "Let's see," he pondered while pointing to his left. "My final resting place sits over here and the sun rises over there." He pointed toward the western horizon. "So the tree belongs… right there." He pointed to a patch of grass.

"What tree?" asked Sullivan as he stared toward the back of the graveyard. "There's not a tree in sight."

Franklin pulled an acorn out of his pocket and held it up in his hand. "Our acorn, John. Remember? From the lightning strike?"

"Oh, right. I forgot."

Franklin walked over to the corner of the yard and kicked up some dirt with his heel. He carefully placed the acorn into the hole and covered it with soil. "There. I'll have the Pagano brothers water it daily. Little Frankie loved climbing trees." He glanced up at Sullivan. "You would have liked him, John. He was a wonderful lad… with a bright future."

The two men walked home in silence.

## CHAPTER FOURTEEN
### AN AFFAIR OF HONOR
### 1779

Dr. John Sullivan tried to gather his composure as he approached the main entrance of Pennsylvania Hospital. He remained hopelessly trapped in the past, his fate in the hands of two men searching for lost keys in the Philadelphia area. Equally concerning were the cries of Sary that penetrated the walls of Franklin's home last night, a result of her ruthless tyrant. Sullivan dare not look at his reflection that day, utterly ashamed of his inaction. His stomach churned in despair as he met Dr. Casey just inside the hospital gate.

"Good morning, John. Thank you for coming by," said Casey, immediately recognizing Sullivan's drained presentation. "Are you alright?"

"No. Ben lost the keys to the future."

"*What?*" shrieked Casey as the two men walked toward the hospital. "Are you sure?"

"Yes, I'm sure. The Pagano brothers are on a search mission somewhere up in Manayunk."

"Good luck with that," quipped Casey. "They're boozehounds, probably sleeping one off as we speak."

"And the great Benedict Arnold is abusing his servant again."

"Excuse me?" asked Casey. "What did you just say?"

Sullivan explained in vivid detail the pattern of abuse within the confines of Arnold's home, including his physical confrontation with Arnold himself. His body trembled as he spoke.

"John, you're lucky to still be alive!" declared Casey after listening to Sullivan's words. "You have to understand, Sary is his property... period! There is absolutely nothing you can do about it."

"I wish he had killed me. At least I would have died with honor."

"You're alive because of Ben Franklin. He would have killed anyone else."

"The man's a monster... and a traitor."

"A traitor? Why would you call him a traitor? The man is a war hero, a confidant of General Washington himself."

Sullivan held his tongue as the two physicians entered the hospital foyer. They were immediately greeted by echoing howls of insanity.

"I do appreciate you coming by," said Casey in an attempt to divert the narrative. They walked down a short hallway. "I'd like you to examine a soldier brought in yesterday with a bayonet wound..."

"Hey, doc!" came the cry from a side room.

Both physicians stopped and turned to the right, staring into Walt's personal quarters. The giant sat at a table leaning over a mound of food.

"Sorry about the other night!" garbled Walt with a mouthful of meat. "I thought you were Mingo."

"Oh yes, I heard about your little engagement," chuckled Casey as he walked into Walt's room. "I should have warned you, John."

"I knocked the snot out of him," added Walt, some saliva on his chin. He wiped his mouth with a sleeve and took a hearty chug of liquid from a mug. Dense hair covered his arms.

"No problem," stated Sullivan. "So you actually do live in this hospital?" He scanned the room, which contained a small table, a bed and one chair.

"I sure do," replied the sentry. "Home sweet home."

"Walt's been living here full time for about three years now," added Casey. "Now that's loyalty."

"Plus I get three square meals a day," laughed Walt while picking his teeth with a dirty thumbnail. He leaned to his right and spit a piece of gristle into a bucket.

Sullivan didn't respond as the guard resumed his assault on the mountain of foodstuff before him, a concoction of meat, potatoes and bread. Large black flies hovered both above and atop the grub stack, the scene reminding Sullivan of a pig at a trough. The sentry even snorted as he masticated.

"Ah, good old Walt," quipped Casey as he turned and continued down the hall. "What would we do without him?"

Sullivan felt it a good time to make a personal request.

"Dr. Casey, would you mind if I spent a little one on one time with Mingo today?"

"Mingo suffers from classic madness. He's hopeless. I'm just thankful we can keep him off the streets, for the safety of everyone."

"Understood," continued Sullivan. "But his ramblings about the future, along with some hand carvings on the wall, fascinate me."

"What, you think he's another time traveler?"

"No. I do not. But he does drop an occasional buzzword that hints of things to come. I find that intriguing. Some individual therapy is warranted, in my humble opinion."

"Be my guest," said Casey. "But don't let Walt catch wind of it. Those two are mortal enemies. If he sees you trying to rehabilitate Mingo, Major General Arnold will no longer be your biggest worry." Casey grinned at Sullivan as they entered an open ward. "Here we are." He pointed to the corner of the room. "Over there is the young man I'd like your impression on. He was impaled in battle just the other day, a stab to the upper arm, yet his main problem is wrist function."

The two physicians approached the soldier, a man of twenty years old. A bloodied bandage covered his right shoulder and upper arm. He sat on a cot pushed against the wall.

"Private Smith, this is the doctor I was talking about. He's here to look at your arm."

The soldier nervously looked up at Sullivan.

"Let's take a look young man," said Sullivan as he scanned the walls.

"What do you need, John?"

"Gloves. I'd like to remove the bandage."

"We have no gloves. Why would you want to put on a pair of gloves?"

Sullivan grinned and shook his head. "Right, I'm sorry." He sat down on the side of the bed. "You've never heard of rubber or latex."

"I have not."

The two physicians stripped down the dressing, exposing a two inch laceration from a bayonet along the back of his upper arm. The wound itself although oozing some blood, was overall clean and dry. The remainder of the patient's right upper extremity was unremarkable. Sullivan gently placed two fingers along the palm side of the patient's wrist.

"He has a strong pulse," stated Sullivan. "His fingertips have excellent capillary refill and his hand is warm and well perfused."

"Private Smith, straighten out your fingers," ordered Casey.

The two physicians looked at his hand, fully expecting the patient's fingers to straighten. They did not.

"How about your wrist? Can you straighten it out?"

The patient was unable to actively extend his wrist.

"He has a wrist drop," muttered Sullivan as he looked back at the bayonet wound. "A radial nerve injury."

"Excuse me, John."

"The stab wound must have injured his radial nerve, which wraps tightly around his upper arm bone, or humerus. The radial nerve provides motor function to the finger and wrist extensors."

"A palsy?"

"Yes. A palsy," agreed Sullivan as he stood up.

"The prognosis?"

"Well, if the nerve was cut… poor for any recovery of hand function. However if it was just contused, then wrist and finger function may return, but it can take weeks or months."

"I see," said Casey as he reapplied a wrap on the wound.

"I suggest you maintain your finger and wrist range of motion," instructed Sullivan to the soldier. He began to show him a hand exercise. "You have to keep the fingers limber in case the nerve starts working again. Do you understand?"

The wounded soldier nodded his head.

Just then, a commotion occurred at the opposite end of the ward. Before Sullivan and Casey were able to turn, their patient jumped out of bed and stood erect.

"Attention!" shouted a burly man from behind. "General George Washington on the floor!"

Sullivan turned about to see an entourage of military personal slowly walking in orderly fashion down the aisle. In the middle of the company stood a distinguished gentleman dressed in impeccable military garb, standing at the foot of a patient's bed. He stood lithe and toned at least three inches taller than his contemporaries and wore a blue wool coat with broad tail that ran to the back of his knees. A waistcoat and knee breeches complemented the outfit along with matching rows of yellow metallic buttons. Black, well-polished boots covered his lower legs up to knee level.

"General Washington!" stated Dr. Casey as he moved toward the leader. "What a surprise." As he approached two guards crossed their weapons to halt his progress. After a brief exchange of words, Casey was allowed within the inner circle of the cadre. He stood next to Washington as the commander leaned forward and placed a hand on a wounded soldier. He appeared to speak a few words of compassion.

The procession continued down the ward, with Washington stopping at each bed and Dr. Casey providing a brief synopsis of the patient's medical condition. As they neared, Sullivan's heart began to pound rapidly, the iconic historical figure moving closer with each step. He estimated the future president's age to be around fifty, his facial features certainly more youthful than future portraits would capture.

"Thank you for your brave service," said Washington to a young soldier. The patient stood proudly next to his bed with his head wrapped by bloody gauze.

"Thank you General Washington."

"Dr. Casey will get you home soon," continued Washington, his voice clear and firm. "Do you have any children?"

"Yes. I have five young girls at home."

"You're a lucky man," quipped Washington as he placed a hand on the soldier's shoulder. "Get well soon, son."

"Yes, sir."

It was when Washington approached the adjacent bed that Sullivan had a flashback to his early grade school days, his memory banks trying to recall some historical facts. He first thought of Washington's teeth... were they wooden? Did he really chop down a cherry tree as a child or throw a silver dollar across the Potomac River? How difficult was the winter at Valley Forge or the crossing of the icy Delaware River? How could he ask him?

"I hope you feel better," said Washington as he shook the patient's hand. He then slowly turned toward Private Smith and Sullivan, first making eye contact with the injured soldier.

"Private Smith," said Casey in a low, calm tone. "Admitted yesterday with a bayonet wound to the upper arm, resulting in a nerve palsy."

"What battle were you injured in?" asked Washington.

Sullivan counted a total of six sentries surrounding the leader, all shorter in stature. Two of the guards centered their eyes upon him.

"A skirmish just north of Philadelphia," answered the private. "Some redcoats were trying to capture a mill. We held them off."

"Very good," continued Washington as he scanned the man's upper arm. "I'm glad to hear that. Are you in pain?"

"No sir."

"Where are you from, private?"

"Coopersburg, Pennsylvania, sir."

"Near Allentown?"

"Yes sir."

"I stayed over in that area just after the Battle of Trenton," stated Washington as he kept his gaze locked on Smith. "A beautiful valley indeed. I believe there's a factory in town that manufactures musket cartridges. True?"

"Yes, sir. Next to Lehigh Creek. My father works there… along with my two younger brothers."

"How's the fishing in Lehigh Creek?"

"Fantastic," came the reply through a broad smile. "It's filled with trout. They love corn floated without a bobber."

"Very good. I'll remember that the next time I'm up there," declared Washington. "Private Smith, consider yourself a sergeant in the Continental Army."

"Pardon me, sir?"

"You've just been promoted," grinned Washington as he put a hand on Smith's left shoulder. "Congratulations, son. Your father will be proud of you."

"Thank you, Mr. Washington… I mean General Washington! Thank you very much!"

"Thank you, Sergeant Smith," countered Washington as he turned his attention to Sullivan.

It was the color of Washington's eyes that immediately struck Sullivan, a deep blue with a whisper of slate grey. His physical presentation was exact and authoritative, not a hair or piece of clothing out of place. Sullivan noticed his lips and gums to be a bit prominent in relation to his facial features.

"Here we have Dr. John Sullivan, from the North of Pennsylvania," announced Casey. "He's volunteering his time here at the hospital."

"Very nice. Thank you, doctor," said Washington. "What kind of doctor are you?"

"A geriatrician," blurted Sullivan, his thought process askew. He suddenly recalled a lecture in medical school discussing a medical bloodletting that led to Washington's death.

Washington cocked an eyebrow.

"A general practitioner," intervened Casey with a smile. "With a specialty in herbal medicine."

"I see," said Washington as he slightly squinted his eyes. "So, what do you recommend I eat to stay healthy, Dr. Sullivan?"

"Well, I recommend a well-balanced diet with plenty of fish, vegetables and whole grain. I would avoid red meats, sugar additives and of course, limit your alcohol consumption to two drinks a day and stay away from all tobacco products."

Some light-hearted laughter broke out in the ranks.

"If that's the case… I haven't long to live," mused Washington. "But then again, I've already survived malaria, smallpox, diphtheria, tuberculosis and dysentery. I'm running out of lives, doctor."

"Dr. Sullivan is staying at Ben Franklin's flat on Elfreth's Alley," interjected Casey. "Right next to General Arnold's new home."

"Ah, Benedict… a trusted friend of mine," declared Washington. He stood still in anticipation of a response. "A proven leader."

Sullivan didn't reply.

"Have you met the general?"

"Yes. I have," came the terse response. Despite talking to perhaps the most famous American of all time, Sullivan could not repress his contempt for Arnold.

"And…?" asked Washington with a piqued interest. "What do you think of the general?"

Sullivan noticed Dr. Casey beginning to shift uneasily next to the military leader.

"I cannot comment on his military prowess," answered Sullivan. "Except for the fact that his record speaks for itself."

"What about Benedict as a fellow Pennsylvanian?" continued Washington, not in a rush to end the impromptu inquiry. "Can you speak in that regard?"

Sullivan went to reply but held his tongue.

"Go ahead, doctor. Speak your mind."

"Well… I've only met him once or twice, and it would be premature…"

"Doctor," commanded Washington. "Do not dodge my question. What do you think of General Arnold as a man?"

Sullivan nervously glanced at Washington's entourage.

"Perhaps a moment alone?" suggested Washington as he walked toward an exit unaccompanied by his guard. He put his hand out, permitting Sullivan to go first.

The two men disappeared through a doorway, only to reappear several minutes later. A frown ran across Sullivan's face and upon Washington's, a look of genuine concern.

"Well, thank you, Dr. Casey," stated Washington. "All of us appreciate the work you are doing here at Pennsylvania Hospital. Your commitment to the war is admirable and never hesitate to call upon me for assistance. I am at your disposal."

"Thank you, General Washington," said Casey with a bow. "We all thank you."

Washington then departed with his contingent, amid the applause and cheers of the soldiers and staff.

"Oh my God," gasped Casey. "John, what an honor. A private audience!"

Sullivan leaned forward and put both hands on his knees, feeling a bit faint. "Wow!" He stood erect and took a deep breath in and out. "I just spoke to George Washington!"

"What did you tell him?"

Sullivan just smiled and slowly nodded his head up and down, as if relieved.

"I hope you didn't mention…"

"He asked that we keep our conversation confidential," interrupted Sullivan. "What a gentleman... a man of true principle. An amazing human being."

"You're a lucky man," said Casey. "Wait until Ben hears about this!"

The two physicians left the ward and as promised, Sullivan was allotted a private examination room on the third floor. There he met Mingo, accompanied by a guard much younger and thinner than Walt. The guard offered to remain in the room for protection, but Sullivan asked that he speak to the patient alone. Mingo sat down across a bare table from Sullivan, his appearance disheveled.

"Where's the ring?" whispered Mingo, his eyes and tongue flickering.

"Walt still has it. I saw it on his thumb earlier today."

"It's tough to get off."

"How did you do it?"

"He was drunk on the floor. I almost had to chew it off... but ended up using the slime from his hair. When are we leaving?"

"Soon," replied Sullivan. "I just have to figure out a way to get possession of that ring. Then it will all happen quickly. You have to be ready on a moment's notice. Are you sure you know where the tunnel is?"

"Yes."

"Where is it?"

"The ring first. I need to see the ring."

Sullivan stared at the inmate, impressed by his savvy. Mingo remained his only viable ticket home. He had to trust him. "Is the wormhole nearby? Can we walk to it?"

"Yes." Mingo turned his attention to a black beetle crawling out from beneath the table. He quickly reached down and snatched up the insect, bringing it up to his face. He squinted at the bug, turned it side to side, and ate it.

"I'm counting on you, Mingo. I get the ring and you show me the tunnel."

Mingo swallowed the bug and scanned the floor for any others.

"Do you understand my plan?"

"Yes."

Sullivan held out his hand and extended his pinky finger. Both men locked fifth digits and held firm, their covert mission intact.

"Don't tell anyone," whispered Mingo. "I'll be ready. Keep America great. Stay well, my friend."

Later that evening, Ben Franklin was utterly enthralled by Sullivan's description of his chance encounter with General Washington. The two men sat across each other at the dinner table, enjoying a meal delivered earlier by Betsy Ross.

"You're a very lucky fellow," declared Ben. "Washington is a stickler for protocol, he usually doesn't partake in unscripted chit-chat. What did you two talk about?"

"Oh, the war effort," came the muted reply. "He had some personal medical questions." Sullivan attempted to change the subject. "This pork is tremendous."

"Being a bachelor has its pork… or should I say perks," laughed Ben as he dabbed his mouth with a napkin. "Every woman on the block thinks I'm starving."

"I knew Betsy Ross could sew," said Sullivan. "But I didn't know she was such a good cook. You just don't learn that kind of stuff in the history books."

A knock on the door interrupted their conversation.

"Who can that be at the dinner hour?" asked Franklin as he stood up and checked the busybody mirror. "A stranger. Oh, I love meeting new people." He enthusiastically walked down the stairwell to answer the front door.

As Sullivan finished his dinner, he could hear bits and pieces of a conversation occurring between Franklin and another man. The stranger's voice was unfamiliar but the surnames of Arnold and Sullivan could occasionally be overheard in the discussion. Franklin returned several minutes later with a look of concern.

"Who was that?" asked Sullivan.

"Ah, John. Did you happen to discuss anything else with General Washington that you would like to tell me about?"

Sullivan's stomach began to churn.

"Perhaps a comment or two about my neighbor, Benedict? Did you happen to mention his name to the general?"

"Why? Who wants to know?" asked Sullivan. He stood up.

"That was General Arnold's 'second'. Do you know the role of a person called a 'second' in colonial times?"

"No. I do not."

"His role is to convey a rather serious message to another so-called 'second', which by default is me."

Sullivan felt nauseous as Ben's face turned grim.

"John, it appears that you've besmirched the Arnold name in public. A rather unacceptable practice in the upper echelon of today's society."

"And..."

"Your spoken words have turned into an affair of honor."

"So, what are you telling me?"

"I'm telling you that the great Major General Benedict Arnold, a seasoned warrior, has challenged you to a duel."

"WHAT!" screeched Sullivan.

"You heard me... a duel. But fortunately, you get to pick the weapon."

# CHAPTER FIFTEEN
## THE MEDICAL EXAM
## 2065

"Good morning… my name is Tyrone B. Brown and I am your president. This meeting shall come to order!" Brown stood in the day room of the Philadelphia General's psychiatric ward, dressed in a hospital gown and slippers, his gaunt frame well over six feet tall. "Today is June 6$^{th}$, 2065," bellowed Brown. He looked to a fellow inpatient to his left. "And now a word from our vice president."

"A younger man with bedraggled hair quickly stood. "I am Clifford James, your vice president." He stroked his beard as he spoke, a tattoo of two hands clasped together in prayer on his forearm. "Tonight's movie will be the 1957 movie of the year, *The Bridge on the River Kwai*. It will start at exactly 1900 hours. Popcorn and soda will be served. See you then." James sat down.

"Thank you, Vice President James," howled Brown. He looked farther to his left. "And now a word from our treasurer."

A morbidly obese man with a red face pushed himself up from a chair. He held out a small piece of crumpled paper in front of a set of reading glasses. Yellow tobacco stains covered the tips of his fingers. "I am Stanley Rutkowski, your treasurer." He coughed to clear his throat. "We currently have $45.36 in the treasury."

Rutkowski looked over his reading glasses a bit short of breath. "Any questions?"

The fifteen male patients sitting in front of their elected officers remained silent, except for Vince Pagano. He raised a hand.

"Yes," said Rutkowski.

"Where do you keep the money?"

Rutkowski looked back at President Brown.

"In the bank!" spouted the president.

"In the bank," resounded Rutkowski.

"Thank you," countered Pagano. "I have no further questions."

"Thank you, Treasurer Rutkowski," barked Brown. "Is there any old business?"

No response.

"Is there any new business?"

No response.

"Are there any announcements?"

"I have an announcement," declared Dr. Wolfgang with a raised hand. The physician sat to the right of Brown with an entourage of medical providers including residents in training, medical students and therapists. They all wore white coats and sat on folding chairs in an orderly fashion, monitoring the ward's morning assembly. "I'd like to introduce the newest member to our floor, a Mr. Vito Pagano, originally from Italy. He was admitted last night and will be spending some extended time with us." Wolfgang and the medical team offered some light applause. "Vito, can you tell the group a little bit about yourself?"

Pagano stood up. "Sure, my name is Vito Pagano and I'm a time traveler. I arrived in the year 2065 via a wormhole located in the basement of this hospital. A driverless vehicle immediately tagged me as an undocumented citizen and I was arrested by the Crankyville Police Department. I fabricated a seizure in their patrol car and they emergently transported me to the Philadelphia General." Pagano looked around at his brethren. "The Pagano Orthopedic Institute is named after me and I finished a puzzle last night with the Messiah. Thank you." He sat down.

The brash introduction failed to generate any response from the gathering. All eyes returned back to Dr. Wolfgang.

"Very nice, Vito," followed up Wolfgang. "And welcome to 2065. We hope your stay here is productive." He turned his gaze to a paper in hand.

"Just a few housekeeping details," continued Wolfgang. "All residents on the floor must participate in the upcoming 2065 census. Representatives from the Census Bureau will be here tomorrow to take a head count. Remember, the census results determine how billions of dollars in federal funding flow into your home communities each year. Numbers also determine how many seats in Congress each state gets. The United States has counted its population every decade or so since 1790."

Blank faces stared back at the psychiatrist.

"And don't forget," said Wolfgang with a smile. "Two weeks from now is our annual March for Mental Health in Fairmount Park. This is always an exciting day for us." He looked back at an administrator who nodded in agreement. "Our bus will leave the hospital at nine o'clock sharp and I'm hoping that each one of you can walk a mile or so to help support the cause."

No response.

"And remember, inappropriate behavior will not be tolerated during the march. It's an honor to be invited to this event and I know I can count on each of you." He slowly scanned the room.

"Are we provided sunscreen for the event?" asked Pagano.

"Ah, I'm not sure," stammered Wolfgang as he looked back at his team. Several members of the group began to rapidly shuffle through papers in search of a reply. "We'll get back to you on that, Vito. But I see no reason why some sunscreen can't be provided. Thank you."

Vince nodded his head up and down in a satisfactory manner.

"That's all I have," said Wolfgang. "Thank you, President Brown."

Tyrone Brown stood back up. "This meeting has come to an end. Everyone is dismissed!"

The entire assembly stood up and collectively stampeded toward an outlet on the wall. One by one they leaned forward and lit a cigarette inside the electronic lighter, taking a few puffs in the process. Each resident subsequently stepped to their right and walked into an open air atrium screened in by steel mesh. Within a minute, Vince Pagano was the only inpatient left in the room.

"You don't smoke, Vito?" asked Wolfgang. Behind him was a third year medical student wearing a short white coat. She wore her hair in a ponytail and her nametag read, 'Olivia Parker'.

"I used to vape."

"What's vaping?" asked Olivia.

"Vaping was a rage about forty or fifty years ago," answered Wolfgang as he intently eyed Pagano. "It lasted about a decade but fell into disfavor… due to an astonishing rash of lawsuits and premature pulmonary fibrosis."

"You're kidding me," grimaced Vince. "Just when you think it's safe."

"Medical Student Parker is going to perform a history and physical examination on you today," stated Wolfgang. "Is that alright with you? She just started her psychiatric rotation today."

"Sure," said Vince. "Let's see if she can figure me out. I'm an enigma, wrapped in a shroud, surrounded by a mystery."

"Fantastic," replied Wolfgang as he signaled to a male orderly dressed in white. The aide was past his chronologic prime yet physically fit, a bulldog tattoo above the words 'USMC' on his arm. "Chester will stay in the room with you two during the examination. Thank you, Chet." The attending then stepped away.

The trio returned to Vince's room where the history portion of the examination began. Vince began by happily recalling his childhood days growing up in South Philadelphia and attending school at St. Joe's Prep. He boasted of his years as a collegiate quarterback including the details of a game winning touchdown pass thrown on homecoming day. He passionately talked about his own surgical training at the Philadelphia General, a puppy called Barnyard and his fiancée Jordan. The student listened carefully as

Pagano reiterated his current occupation as that of a time traveler, in desperate search of a path back home.

"So, who has the key?" asked Olivia.

"Dr. John Sullivan, the founder of the Sullivan Institute. He jettisoned me into the future to save my life during a hospital demolition. I couldn't run because of a broken ankle." He pointed to his cast. "He wears the key on a necklace made of wolfram. The key has the initials 'R.S.' on it."

"Who's R.S.?"

"I don't know, but that key is the proverbial key to the future. Without it I cannot get back… I'm stuck in the future."

The medical student listened to the conviction of Pagano's spoken words in amazement, his outlandish story strangely believable.

"Now I'm going to perform a physical examination," announced Parker as she stood up tentatively. "Just relax now, I'm going to begin by checking your reflexes."

It was during the physical examination that Vince began to turn the tables.

"Do you know a common mnemonic to remember the names of the twelve cranial nerves?" asked Pagano as Parker tapped his biceps tendon with a rubber, wedged shaped hammer.

"On old Olympus Towering Tops, a Finn and German viewed some hops."

"Very nice," replied Pagano. "That is correct."

"That's the clean version."

"I know," chuckled Vince.

She next brought a stethoscope to his chest. "Take a slow deep breath, in and out. Again." She intently listened to his breath and heart sounds.

"Do you know why orthopedic surgeons never listen to their patient's heart?"

"No," said Parker as she took the stethoscope out of her ears and folded it into her jacket pocket.

"An orthopedic surgeon can mend a broken bone, but not a broken heart."

"Hah!" laughed Parker. "I'm going to remember that one."

"It's true."

"Now, can you please lay down on your back? I'm going to examine your stomach."

"Sure." Vince dropped back on the bed.

She began to slowly palpate his abdomen. "Tell me if you have any pain."

"No. But that tickles."

The student grinned.

"What's the name of rumbling or gurgling sounds made by the movement of fluid and gases in your stomach?" asked Vince.

As Parker percussed her patient's liver, she hunched her shoulders. " I don't know. What?"

"Borborygmi," stated Pagano. "Borborygmi. That's Italian for I shouldn't have had that second bowl of spaghetti!" Vince burst out laughing.

"You're pretty funny," grinned Parker. "And you have a good knowledge base."

She then examined his axial spine and extremities.

"Last one," quipped Vince as he sat down. "What do you call two orthopedic surgeons looking at an EKG?"

"I don't know. What?"

"A double blind study!"

The orderly in the room began to snicker. "Good one, Vito."

"You should be a stand-up comic," suggested Olivia as she stood in front of Vince. A tentative but serious look appeared on her face. "Now, Mr. Pagano. I'm going to have to … "

"No. I defer."

"On what?"

"The rectal exam. Put that on my chart… the patient deferred on a rectal exam."

"Alright," smiled Olivia with relief. "Understood. But remember, the physician who treats himself has a fool for a patient."

"Bravo!" shouted Vince with hands in the air. "A-plus on your examination, Medical Student Parker. Very thorough. I'm going to give you my highest recommendation. You have a very bright future ahead of you."

"Wow. That's quite a compliment," said Olivia as she gathered some items and placed them in her backpack. "Especially from a time traveler. Thank you, Mr. Pagano." She zipped the backpack and slung it over her shoulder. "By the way, I'm actually engaged to a medical resident whose last name is Pagano."

Vince froze.

"His first name is Anthony… Anthony Pagano."

"Where's Anthony from?" he asked.

"South Philadelphia… Wharton section of town."

"And what's his father's name?"

"Anthony. I think every first born male in the family is named Anthony or Antonio." She smiled. "At least that's what he tells me. In fact, he kind of looks like you. My fiancé has cousins all across town."

Vince's older brother was named Anthony. In 2020 his brother had three teenage boys, the first named Anthony, too. It had to be his grandson, he thought.

"Thank you, again," said Parker. "I hope you go back in time soon. Enjoy your visit to 2065 and stop vaping. It's bad for your health." She began to walk out of the room.

"Olivia, wait! Don't go," pleaded Vince with an outstretched hand. "I need to talk to Anthony!"

The student stared back with hesitation. "Well, he's working long hours and currently on a rotation in center city. I don't think…"

Vince stood up, his action prompting Chet to step forward. "Don't leave. We have to talk."

Chet grabbed his forearm. "Easy now, Vito. She has to go," said the orderly. "Stand down."

"I'm sorry," said Olivia nervously. "The examination is over. Thank you, Mr. Pagano." She walked out.

"Wait!" howled Vince as he tried to shake off Chet's grip. "I may be Anthony's uncle, or great uncle!" Chet locked both arms around his upper torso, incapacitating him. "Ask him if he knows my father, Winky Pagano... or if he had an uncle killed in an explosion! Don't go. You have to help me!" He continued to shout as the student vanished down the hall. "We owned Pagano Destruction Company! You have to believe me! Please, come back!"

Chet held tight until Vince stopped ranting. "Relax, dude. Take it easy. I'm going to let go. Let's not cause a scene." He slowly released his grip. "We don't want any drama this early in the morning."

"Olivia Parker," enunciated Pagano slowly as he sat down on the bed. "I have to remember her name. Anthony, too. Dr. Anthony Pagano." He looked for a pen and paper, but there was none.

"It's just a coincidence," said Chet as he headed toward the door. "I'm sure there are a lot of people named Pagano in this city."

"Maybe it's my grandson?" whispered Pagano to himself. "She said he looked like me. I should have asked for the name of his mother. Or maybe..."

"Small group therapy is going to start in thirty minutes," interrupted Chet while rapping his knuckles on the door jamb. "Go wash and brush your teeth. You even have time for a sitting head call, but remember, if you're late, you get a demerit point. You don't want that." The orderly left the room.

Vince pondered the multitude of possibilities as to who Dr. Anthony Pagano could possibly be. He was unaware of Dr. Wolfgang suddenly standing in front of him.

"Vito. How did it go?" asked Wolfgang.

Vince looked up. "Fine. Medical Student Parker is one smart cookie. Give her high honors."

"I heard you shout something about the Pagano Destruction Company."

"Yea. My father owned it. His name was Tommie, but everybody called him Winky."

"I actually worked for the Pagano Destruction Company one summer," declared Wolfgang. "When I was in my junior year of high school. My father got me the job. What a disaster."

"You're kidding me?" said Vince as he stood up. "We may have worked together. What year where you there?"

"Well, let me think. I graduated high school in 2022, so 2020 or 2021… somewhere around there."

"What! I disappeared in 2020! Who did you work with? Do you remember any of their names?"

"I remember a few of them," grinned Wolfgang. "Quite a cast of characters… especially a guy named Big Bart and their foreman, Rocco. I have nightmares about that brute."

"Oh my God."

"I didn't last long," smiled Wolfgang. "As you might guess, I'm more brain than brawn."

"Do you remember what they were blowing up?"

"They were getting ready to implode a section of the Philadelphia General," said Wolfgang. "I forget the exact name…"

"The old Franklin Wing?" asked Vince. "And technically it's not an implosion."

"Yes!" Wolfgang snapped his fingers and pointed at Vince. "Now that you mention it. It was the Franklin Wing."

"So you were there when it happened?" asked Vince. "Right? You witnessed the whole thing? What a tragedy."

"Well, actually no," confessed the physician. "That Rocco guy leaned on me a bit too much, calling me all sorts of names… like candy ass and egghead. So I quit the job pretty quick. I only lasted about two weeks." He sighed. "Looking back I probably had a nervous breakdown. They certainly didn't offer any sensitivity classes in that company. Rocco was a bully."

"So what happened after that?"

"My dad sent me over to Germany for the rest of the summer, to visit family. I think he felt bad."

"So you missed the mishap… and my death?"

"I'm afraid so. Sorry, but I've blocked Pagano Destruction out of my mind for the past forty years, a classic self-protective mechanism of the subconscious. Your shout of the company name brought it all back to life."

"I'm sorry. I guess."

"No. That's alright. I'm a big boy now."

"So you believe me? Right? I'm a time traveler. There's no other explanation. I died in the explosion."

"No. You are Vito Pagano, from Italy," stated Wolfgang in a calm and reassuring tone. "A visiting professor at the Pagano Institute." He clasped his hands together. "I consider it a mere coincidence in regard to your surname being Pagano. Now get ready for group session, Vito. I've teamed you up with the Messiah. You two seemed to have hit it off well together." He turned away.

Vince couldn't believe it, so many parallels running across his path in so little time. He had to keep pushing the envelope while sticking with the Munchausen plan.

"Wait! Dr. Wolfgang!"

The attending turned back. "Yes."

"Do you think we can get an orthopedic surgeon up here to take a look at my ankle? It probably needs a follow-up x-ray."

"Sure, Vito. I'll put in a consult for ortho."

"And I suffer from hypertension and prediabetes," continued Vince. "Can we have a medical man see me, too?"

"Absolutely. I'll consult the house internist to swing by and address your concerns. Anything else?"

"No. Thank you, Dr. Wolfgang."

"You're welcome, Vito."

Later that evening, Dr. Wolfgang drained the internet for information regarding the 2020 destruction of the Philadelphia General's Franklin Wing. He read in horror the description of the blast, which claimed the life of Dr. Vincent Pagano, an orthopedic attending on staff and the namesake of the future Pagano Orthopedic Institute. In the midst of the article stood snapshots of the Pagano Destruction Company kingpin, Tommy Pagano,

Jr. and his dead son. Wolfgang tilted the glasses on his nose and leaned forward to focus on the photograph of Vincent Pagano, the resemblance of the deceased striking in relation to Vito.

"Fascinating," mumbled Wolfgang to himself. "A classic case of dissociative identity disorder." There could be no other explanation thought the psychiatrist. His patient, Vito Pagano, had taken on the identity of a locally deceased physician with the same last name. "Absolutely fascinating," muttered Wolfgang as he placed his glasses down on the table. He leaned back in the chair and began to formulate a psychiatric treatment plan. While deep in thought, a single line at the bottom of the article captured his eye. He put on his glasses and again leaned forward.

"*The remains of the deceased were never found.*"

## CHAPTER SIXTEEN
### CAVEAT VENDITOR
### 2020

"You sold the house!" wailed Frederick Mills as he stood up at his desk. "But... I don't understand. The historical society was just starting to make headway and now the project is over? Everyone is going to be so disappointed."

"Well," replied Barry Zuckerman. "I'm sorry, but yesterday this guy appears at my doorstep asking to buy the home. I just couldn't believe it. Up until then the house was dead on the market."

Mills stood speechless.

"It was a fantastic offer," continued Zuckerman.

"Did he offer you list price?"

"Way over list!" proclaimed Zuckerman with a wave of his hand. "I couldn't pass it up."

"I suppose," groused Mills as he lowered his frame back into a creaky chair. The two were seated at his home office in West Philadelphia. "And now you want me to oversee the transaction? Is that my understanding?"

"Yes," replied Zuckerman. "I've kind of grown accustomed to you and the historical society and in a way feel bad about selling the place. So I thought steering the business in your direction would be appropriate. You do deal in real estate, right?"

"Absolutely," huffed Mills. "That's my specialty. Real estate is what I do." He pointed to a plaque on the wall. "You're looking at the West Philadelphia Real Estate Attorney of the Year… 1998. Caveat emptor."

"I'm the seller, not the buyer."

"Well then… caveat venditor! Let the seller beware! I can't begin to tell you the horrors I've incurred in the simple process of a house transaction." He leaned back, placing both hands atop his protruding stomach. "I've seen it all over the past forty years. Trust me. Emotions can run wild."

Zuckerman scanned the office, a musty front room on the ground floor of Mills' home. Scattered across the floor were stacks of folders held together by rubber bands covered in dust. A hodgepodge of knickknacks littered the desktop, including a baseball, one photograph, some denture adhesive and a bottle of stool softener. Zuckerman went to speak but the noise from a passing trolley outside shook the windows of the home.

"Ah, the old Baltimore Ave streetcar," mused the attorney as he looked at his watch. "Right on time." He looked up with a grin. "One of the perks of living here."

"Yes. I see," said Zuckerman as he repositioned himself in his chair. "So what's our next step? Believe it or not, I've never sold a home."

"That depends."

"On what?"

"On what's been done so far. Was it a handshake, a signature, a contract? What's transpired between you and the buyer?"

"Well, he insisted that we sign a home purchase agreement," stated Zuckerman.

"Did you sign it?"

"You bet I did! The man offered me way above market value. I wasn't going to let him get away."

Mills pursed his lips and nodded. "Very well."

"What? What's wrong? Why do you look so distraught?"

"Well, in essence, you've sold your home," declared Mills. "A purchase agreement is a legally binding contract between two parties, which by designs protects the buyer."

"Oh. So I shouldn't have signed it?"

"No. That's not what I'm saying. But understand this... if you ever try to back out of the deal for reasons other than those outlined in the purchase agreement, the buyer may be able to recover damages in court."

"I see no reason for that to happen," countered Zuckerman. "I'm comfortable in my decision. It's time to move on."

"Very well. But as your counsel, I had to clarify your legal obligation."

"I will admit. He seemed a bit pushy about signing the document. Maybe I should have spoken to you first?"

"Perhaps," replied Mills. "What's done is done. Ipso facto is a term we commonly use in the profession. That means 'after the fact.'"

"Really? Is that what that means? I thought the phrase ipso facto..."

"Let's start with *his* name?" interrupted Mills as he took a pen from a drawer. "Let's begin there... with the identification of the parties." He clicked the pen emphatically. "That's step one in any real estate transaction. What is the buyer's full name?"

"Bookman," came the somewhat muted reply. Zuckerman cleared his throat. "Mr. Bookman."

Mills excitedly wrote the name down without any sign of recognition. "And his first name, please."

"Alabaster."

"Alabass... Ala-bastard? Say that again," requested Mills.

"Alabaster," enunciated Zuckerman slowly. He spelled out the name.

"That's a real tongue twister," chuckled Mills. His pen ran out of ink, prompting him to rummage through another desk drawer.

"I believe it's an old English name."

"I don't care about the man's heritage. As long as his money is green." The attorney looked up and smiled but Zuckerman did not. "That's a joke, Barry. An attorney joke. Relax. You're in good hands. This isn't my first rodeo."

Zuckerman suddenly began to have some serious second thoughts about hiring Mills. Several millions of dollars were at stake. Just then a self-propelled vacuum cleaner rattled into the room, the circular disc grinding its way along the hardwood floor in between the two men.

"Oh, sorry about that," muttered Mills. "My sister got that contraption for me as a gift. She's always worried about her little brother." The cleaner hit Zuckerman's foot and redirected itself between his chair legs. "It's good for the hallways but no good in tight corners. Whoever designed it should be fired. I mean, how can a round object clean a corner? The cat hates it, too."

As the discussion continued, the sweeper rattled back and forth beneath Zuckerman's chair, beeping madly.

"Now, where were we?" asked Mills.

The phone on the attorney's desk rang, an older model with a rotary dial. Mills let it ring four times before answering.

"Attorney Mills' office," he said in an odd, high-pitched voice. "How can I direct your call?" He stared forward while listening. "Hold please... I'll see if the attorney is available to speak to you." Mills pressed the receiver against his shirt and winked at Zuckerman. "And old trick my dad taught me," he whispered. "Keeps the overhead down." After ten seconds he brought the receiver off his chest and spoke. "The attorney will speak to you now, hold while I transfer the call." He reached for the dial on the phone face and rotated it from the number three position twice. "Yes. Attorney Mills' here... how can I help you?"

Zuckerman had seen enough. He stood and lifted his chair upward, the action liberating the angry vacuum. As he repositioned the chair, Mills began to speak.

"Of course, of course," rambled Mills as he peered at Zuckerman. "In fact I have the owner of the clock sitting right in front of me."

# A TWIST OF TIME

He continued to listen enthusiastically. "Fascinating! Let me check, hold on." He brought the receiver to his chest. "Barry, exciting news. This is the horologist on the line, he's asking if we can come over to take a look at your clock."

"What clock are you talking about?"

"The one from your home. Do you have a few minutes? We can run over right now. He only lives a few blocks away."

"I don't know what you're talking about, but sure. What the hell."

Mills spoke back into the phone. "We'll be over in a few minutes. Right. See you then. Thank you, Aloysius." He hung up.

"What clock are you talking about?" asked Zuckerman. "And what's a horologist?"

"A clockmaker," answered Mills. "A horologist is a clockmaker. You've never heard that term?"

"No. And how could he possibly have one of my clocks?"

"Ahem," started Mills as he stood. "Well, you see, we borrowed an old clock from your basement and took it over to Aloysius for repair. The plan was to surprise you with it in the near future, as a token of our appreciation. We found it buried in a closet next to some contraption that looked like a bazooka."

"The glass harmonica? It was next to the glass harmonica?"

"If that's what you call it," replied Mills as he stepped toward the front door. "But why would someone make a bazooka out of glass?"

"That's a musical instrument that Ben Franklin invented," clarified Zuckerman as he stood. "Franklin gave one to Mozart as a gift. It's made of glass."

"Mozart owned a bazooka?" asked Mills as he pointed toward the approaching sweeper on an intercept course with Zuckerman. "I didn't know they existed back then."

"They didn't exist back then! He owned a glass harmonica. Not a goddamn bazooka!" exclaimed Zuckerman as stepped over the vacuum and followed his attorney out the front door. "It's a musical instrument."

179

"Oh. Why didn't you just tell me so?"

Fifteen minutes later, both men walked into the clock shop of Aloysius Mahler, located near the corner of 43$^{rd}$ and Spruce Street. Once inside the door they were greeted by a deluge of timepieces crammed into the first floor showroom. Grandfather clocks stood next to mantle pieces surrounded by cuckoo clocks from the Black Forest of Germany. The methodical din of advancing cogwheels filled the air.

"Hello?" said Mills as he glanced past the display. "Mr. Mahler?"

His call went unanswered, the clickety-click of hundreds of timepieces muffling his call.

"He must be in the back," stated Mills. "That's where he works."

Both men began a circuitous route through the gauntlet of time, twisting and turning their frames in the process. Suddenly a large farmer's clock on the wall began to clang. It was eleven o'clock in the morning.

"Oh no," muttered Mills.

All at once every timepiece in the shop began to proclaim the time, the combined racket a disturbing cacophony of dings, bongs, chirps and chimes.

"Sweet Jesus," howled Zuckerman over the clamor. He held both hands to his ears.

The barrage continued for several seconds and then abruptly stopped, except for the whistle of a teapot deeper inside the shop. Both men continued forward, their path now progressing beneath a massive clock over a narrow doorway, its ornate vines of gold spreading across the wall.

"It's like we're in a time tunnel," joked Zuckerman as he passed beneath the display.

The serpentine route took them through yet another room clogged with timepieces. It was in the back room that they came upon Aloysius Mahler, his back to the visitors with a teapot in hand. Slowly the horologist poured hot water over a teabag in a cup. He wore saggy pants with suspender belts over his shoulders. A white hanky protruded from his back pocket. To his right and left stood workbenches cluttered with instruments and dissembled timepieces.

"Mr. Mahler," said Mills.

The owner didn't respond.

"Mr. Mahler," repeated Mills loudly. "Sir! Hello!"

Aloysius slowly turned about as if caught off guard. "Oh, Attorney Mills. You surprised me." He slowly shuffled over to a small stove to place the teapot down. "How dare you sneak up on an old man." He chortled. "Hey, hey, hey."

Mills grinned. "I'd like you to meet Barry Zuckerman. He owns the clock we brought over for repair."

"Ah, a pleasure," said Aloysius as he extended a handshake. Mahler stood only five foot, four inches tall with slightly hunched shoulders and a fragile frame. Some fluffs of white hair stood above two very large ears that flanked a broad nose with large nares. A set of black framed glasses with enormously thick lenses immediately caught Zuckerman's attention, the prescription eyewear magnifying his eyes in dramatic fashion. "Welcome to my shop. Just in time for tea."

"No. That's quite alright," stated Mills. "We're fine."

"Don't be ridiculous," said Mahler as he pulled down a metal tin from a high shelf. He opened the lid, took out two teabags and poured each man a cup. He next reached for a white egg timer on his workbench and set the dial for five minutes.

"Thank you," said each guest.

"Now, you're interested in purchasing a clock?" asked Mahler. "You've come to the right man. I've got over 500 pieces in stock ready to go."

"No. No, Mr. Mahler," replied Mills. "You just invited me over."

"I did?"

"Yes. By phone. You had some important information about Mr. Zuckerman's timepiece. Remember?"

"Yes. Yes. Of course!" He tapped his index finger on his forehead and turned toward the workstation to his left. "Come over here." He reached down and slowly pushed an orange cat off his stool. "Move along now, Milo." He stood in front of the stool and carefully lowered his frame downward. "It's this three wheel clock that you brought in. There's something very special about it."

Mills and Zuckerman approached the bench, their eyes immediately fixating on a three foot tall wooden timepiece with two circular dials. The smaller circle stood over the larger face of the timepiece which displayed a distorted alignment of Roman numerals around its perimeter. Only one hand jutted out from a central attachment.

"There it is," declared Mills to Zuckerman. "That's the clock from your basement." He looked back at Mahler. "Did you get it working?"

"No. Not yet. This is an amazing find, gentlemen. Believe me when I say that. I've been in the clock business for over seventy years."

"How so?" queried Zuckerman as he sat down next to the watchman.

"Well, it's a Benjamin Franklin three wheel clock. Ben designed this model along with the bizarre alignment of the hourly markings."

"It only has one hand," followed up Zuckerman. "Where's the other?"

"There is no other," countered Mahler. "It's classic Ben Franklin. He devised the clock as a much more efficient and cheaper alternative to other clocks of the Colonial era. The man was always tinkering."

"I've never heard of it," stated Mills.

"Not many people have… for two good reasons," continued Mahler as he took his glasses off and donned a professional set of eyewear complete with magnification loops. "First of all, nobody could tell what time it was!" He laughed. "The clock's face has a four hour dial as compared to the conventional twelve. Only Ben was smart enough to decipher the time."

"It certainly is distorted," said Zuckerman. "I mean, what time is it now?"

"Who knows? That was the main problem."

"What was the second reason?"

"Well, that's the odd part," quipped Mahler as he lifted up a miniature screwdriver. He unscrewed the side panel of the clock and began to toil inside, as if correcting a problem.

"Mr. Mahler, the second problem?" asked Mills. "You were saying?"

"Oh yes… problem number two." He put down the screwdriver and turned slowly toward the visitors. "The second problem is that no three wheel clocks were ever made during Ben Franklin's lifetime."

"Excuse me?"

"Ben put the concept on paper sometime around 1760, but the three wheel clock was never produced until sometime later, over in France in the 1800s."

"So, this clock is from France?"

"No. That's the odd part." Mahler picked up a slender probe with a sharp tip and pointed it inside the gear box. "See here, we have three wheels, two weights and a pendulum. Pretty simple."

"If you say so," said Zuckerman.

"Now look here," continued Mahler as he turned the clock a bit toward its owner. "Engraved in the cherry wood panel. Read that."

Zuckerman leaned in and squinted. "B. Franklin, Philadelphia… 1770."

Mahler leaned back and took off his magnifying glasses. "Gentlemen, what we have here is perhaps the original three wheel clock prototype, constructed under the supervision of Mr. Franklin himself, in the year 1770. There's no other reason why Ben would have etched his name inside. This is a historical find of immense importance in my humble opinion."

"Ben probably owned it," added Zuckerman. "He lived in my house."

"That's certainly possible," continued Mahler as the egg timer went off. The clock master stood up and shuffled over to silence the timepiece. He took a sip of warm tea and reached for a carton of cookies. "Cookie anyone?"

The discussion paused as Mahler and his guests snacked, time ticking by serenely. Once teatime ended, the horologist stood back up. "Now, let me show you the real reason why I called you over." He held a finger in the air while walking back to his workstation. "Wait until you see this. Move along, Milo." He again coaxed the cat off her perch and sat down. Slowly he rotated the clock to expose a rear panel, which he removed. "There, see that? The rectangular box?" He pointed into the depths of the gearbox. "Attached to the rear crank mechanism?"

Mills and Zuckerman simultaneously leaned forward, their heads colliding.

"Go ahead," ordered Mills as he slowly backed off and rubbed his noggin. "It's your clock."

Barry leaned forward. "Yea, I see it."

"Reach inside that box and carefully pull out its content," stated Mahler. "Careful now, it's over 200 years old."

Zuckerman reached inside the box and placed his fingers on a rolled up piece of paper, carefully tucked between several strips of wood, as if in a crate. He delivered the relic outside the box, its size about four inches long. Slowly and carefully he unrolled the scroll.

"What does it say?" asked Mills as he leaned forward.

Zuckerman began to slowly read the note.

*"In this world nothing can be said to be certain, except death and taxes. When I'm food for worms, check the secret hiding spot in this home, for it contains all my personal treasures and remember… lost time is never found again. - B. Franklin, printer."*

Each man fell silent for several seconds as the words of Franklin echoed aloud.

"Holy smokes!" said Mills. "That's an original note written by Ben Franklin himself! He's describing a secret hiding spot in your home."

"Yes. Indeed," followed up Mahler. He exchanged the magnifying loops for his own eyewear. "I couldn't believe it. That note has been hiding inside this timepiece for over 250 years. That's why I called you over."

"What should we do with it?" exclaimed Mills. "I mean, we need to have an expert take a look at it." He looked at Zuckerman. "Barry, can you believe it? That's undeniable evidence that Benjamin Franklin lived in your house. We proved it beyond a doubt. The West Philadelphia Historical Society strikes again!" He thrust a fist high into the air. "Wait until that snooty neighbor hears about this. He'll be in shock!"

"You're right about that," replied Zuckerman. "He'll definitely be in shock, because per my attorney, he currently owns the place. Caveat venditor."

## CHAPTER SEVENTEEN
### CODE DUELLO
### 1779

"When I'm food for worms, check the secret hiding spot in this home," mumbled Franklin as he ran a quill pen across the paper. "For it contains all my personal treasures and remember… lost time is never found again." He signed his name and leaned backward. "Hah! There we have it. A mystery note for someone in the future." A devilish grin appeared across his face as he rolled up the scrap of paper and reached into the back of the clock. "Long live my racoon hat."

"Who drew that clock face?" asked Sullivan. "It's completely out of whack." He sat opposite Ben on a sofa. "Someone with a right parietal brain lesion?"

"What do you mean?"

"Never mind," came the morose reply. "I'm worried about a duel with an expert marksman and you're hiding notes in a clock. What's wrong with this picture?"

Two days had passed since Arnold's demand for a duel and since then, Sullivan had not ventured outside. He sulked inside Franklin's home in a state of terminal despair.

"I'm going to die," moaned Sullivan. "I've only shot a gun once before and in the process, accidently killed the neighbor's cat."

Ben didn't respond as he carefully reattached the rear panel on the clock. "This is the original prototype of my three wheel clock," stated Franklin. "A horologist in town just finished it. What do you think?"

"It's missing a hand. Send it back."

"Time will tell if it catches on," continued Franklin. "No pun intended." He wiped a fingerprint smudge off the clockface. "That's the key to becoming a member of the avant-garde, doctor. Always have a lot of pots on the stove and do not fear failure."

"Bury me next to your gravesite. Can you do that for me, Ben? I'd consider it an honor to be at your side for all eternity."

"You're getting ahead of yourself, John. Neither one of us are dead."

"At least Sary is safe. That brings me tremendous solace."

"Yes. I fully agree. I too was pleased to see Mrs. Arnold arrive back home from Virginia. Her physical presence certainly shields Sary from her husband."

"Have you ever killed a man, Ben?"

"With words yes, but with a weapon… no."

Sullivan chuckled at the witty reply. He quickly learned that living with a sage wasn't easy, as most answers were rendered to provoke more reflection. "Wow. Death by newsprint," countered Sullivan. "Ben Franklin, the scholarly assassin."

"You can't kill Arnold," cautioned Franklin. "I'm sure you're acutely aware of that."

"I know," agreed Sullivan. "The grandfather paradox. Benedict Arnold must live in order to betray our country and go down in infamy."

"Exactly."

"But why can't I run away? Isn't that an option?"

"No," countered Franklin. "He would hunt you down like a dog. Remember, we're at war and military checkpoints exist along all the roadways. You wouldn't have a chance."

"So I'm going to die?"

"Not if I can help it. I have discussed your current predicament with General Washington."

"And…?"

"He dare not intervene. Washington noted that over the years Benedict has been a bit of a thorn in his side, always playing the martyr. He hopes the military governorship post appeases his massive ego. Time will tell."

"So General Washington isn't going to intercede on my behalf?"

"No. He's not. But he sends his best wishes."

"Great. That's just great." Sullivan sighed deeply. "Ben. Why did you have to lose those keys?" To date the Pagano brothers had failed in their quest to locate the keys.

"I have another plan," said Ben. "I've asked a neighbor and good friend of mine to stop by and offer some advice. He's a man that's already been involved in several duels to date, all with positive outcomes. A real veteran. I trust his opinion in this matter."

"What's his name… Lucky?"

"John, contrary to popular belief, most combatants do not die in a duel. Think of it as an acceptable way to regain one's honor via a willingness to risk one's life. A duel is typically reserved for nobility or members of the upper class. You have a multitude of options on the dueling field."

"Like what?"

A series of wraps on the door interrupted the exchange.

Franklin stood and checked the busybody mirror. "Oh good. He's here, the gentleman I just spoke of. John, can you please go down and let him in?"

Sullivan walked down the stairwell and opened the door, fully expecting to see an old Western gunslinger with spurs and a scar across his cheek. Instead, before him appeared a handsome man in his early twenties about five feet, seven inches tall with a crop of reddish brown hair. He wore an orderly military uniform that flattered his trim torso and broad shoulders. A warm smile came across the visitor's face.

"You must be Benjamin's friend in need," stated the man with an extended hand.

"Yes. Yes, I am," replied Sullivan with a handshake. He appreciated the firmness of the gentleman's grip. "My name is Dr. John Sullivan. And you are?"

"Alexander." He released his grip and doffed his hat. "Lieutenant Colonel Alexander Hamilton, from just down the lane. A pleasure to make your acquaintance."

Sullivan went to speak but began to stutter after hearing the name Alexander Hamilton. He froze and gawked into the deep brown eyes of the future founding father and author of the Federalist Papers.

"Are you alright?" asked Hamilton. "You look a tad pale."

"Yes. I'm fine." Sullivan rapidly blinked his eyes to recalibrate. "Do come in, Lieutenant Colonel Hamilton. Mr. Franklin is waiting upstairs."

"Thank you," grinned Hamilton as he patted Sullivan on the shoulder. He held a wooden box in his left hand. "Relax, doctor. I'm here to help you."

Sullivan slowly stepped back, allowing the honored guest inside.

"Ah, Alexander!" exclaimed Ben as his guest arrived upstairs. "Thank you for coming over on such short notice. You've met John already." Ben shook hands and walked over to a side table. "A nip of rum to get things going?"

"Sure," replied Hamilton. He placed the wooden box down.

"There you go, Alex," said Ben as he handed the guest a cordial. He poured another round for Sullivan. Franklin then hoisted his glass high. "E pluribus unum!"

"Hear, hear!" shouted Hamilton.

The three men tossed down their drinks.

"Do you like it?" asked Franklin.

"Yes," answered Hamilton. "Ben Franklin serves good rum."

"No. Not the rum. The saying… e pluribus unum? It's Latin for 'out of many, one'. I've spoken to Washington today about possibly adopting it as a motto for the colonies. It has a stately ring to it. Don't you think?"

"I do like it," countered Hamilton as he extended his glass back to Ben. "Along with the rum."

"Spoken like a true native of the Caribbean," said Franklin as he poured another glass of the sugary brew.

"E pluribus unum!" shouted the three men.

They then took a seat at a small roundtable, Sullivan sitting in between the two historical demigods. Franklin began the discussion.

"Let's start with the code," suggested Ben.

"Yes. I have it here." Hamilton unlatched the wooden box and opened its lid. He took out a piece of paper and slid it on the table toward Sullivan. Inside the box were two pistols of identical caliber. "Here you are, doctor."

Sullivan gazed uneasily at the weaponry and then the paper. Across its top ran the words: *Code Duello*. He began to scan the document.

"The *Code Duello* is a standard set of rules for one-to-one combat," stated Hamilton. He repeatedly tapped his finger on the tabletop. "There are twenty-five rules in total. I suggest you familiarize yourself with all of them."

Sullivan began to read the code, a surprisingly verbose and complex set of instructions governing a duel.

"The code just came out in 1777," stated Ben. "From Ireland. It's currently the accepted standard in Europe and the colonies." He inhaled defiantly. "I respectfully disagree with several of the regulations, but who am I to question the Irish?"

Sullivan continued to read the instruction manual, a mishmash of terms written in older English that began to muddy his mind.

"You get to choose the weapons," interjected Hamilton. "But Arnold gets to pick the field of honor." He looked at Ben. "I bet he drags everyone up to that field near the Schuylkill River, just in spite."

"This is getting very confusing," muttered Sullivan as he brought a palm to his forehead. "I mean just listen to these words... honor, first offense, apologize, must proceed to two shots or a hit, begging pardon, both men disabled, exchanging three shots, any insult to a lady, challenger chooses his distance, a miss-fire is equivalent to a shot and of course... everyone's favorite, any wound sufficient to agitate the nerves and necessarily make the hand shake, must end the business of the day." He looked up at Franklin. "Are you kidding me?"

"I've strongly disagreed with Rule #13 since first reading the *Code Duello*," barked Franklin. "It makes no sense." He looked at Hamilton. "Your thoughts on that one, Alexander?"

"Dr. Sullivan, please read aloud Rule #13," requested Hamilton.

"Sure. Rule #13 reads: *No dumb shooting or firing in the air is admissible in any case. The challenger ought not to have challenged without receiving offense; and the challenged ought, if he gave offense, to have made an apology before he came on the ground; therefore, children's play must be dishonorable on one side or the other, and is accordingly prohibited.*"

"Do you wish to apologize?" asked Hamilton after listening to the reading.

"For what?" snapped back Sullivan, the rum tweaking his bravado. "I didn't do anything wrong. He should apologize to me."

"You sullied his name, John," interjected Ben. "We've been through this before."

Sullivan thought of Sary and her screams of horror. "No. I refuse to apologize. He's in the wrong."

"Then, I too disagree with Rule #13," followed-up Hamilton.

"I don't even understand what the rule is saying!" whined Sullivan.

"It's not allowing what's called a '*delope*', which is French for 'throwing away' or wasting a shot," explained Hamilton. "I've wasted a shot on the duel field many a time and so have honorable men fifteen paces my opposite." He stood up and pretended to be at attention on the duel field. "If you immediately discharge your first fire into the ground or overhead, then you've apologized with action as opposed to word." He held a cocked finger to the sky. "The duel should immediately cease at that point." He lowered his arm.

"Is that what you recommend, Alexander?" asked Franklin.

Hamilton sat back down and looked into Sullivan's eyes. "What are your pistol skills, doctor?"

"I've never shot one in my life."

"Then I strongly recommend you waste a shot. Your opponent is obviously a man of superior skill, so it's morally acceptable. It's your only option."

"I agree," said Ben. "Ignore Rule #13. There's no governing body to enforce the rules anyway. How ridiculous is that? I'm going to author a revision to the *Code Duello* for the sake of future combatants."

Sullivan stared in awe at Hamilton as a surreal sense of euphoria overtook his thought process, thanks in part to Hamilton's engaging persona and the alcohol in his veins. He couldn't disagree with the man whose name was synonymous with the most famous duel in American history, despite the grim outcome. It appeared that he had no other option to free himself of the mess.

"Lieutenant Colonel Hamilton, I accept your advice," declared Sullivan. "I'll waste a shot."

"Good," came the combined reply.

"Now. How exactly does one go about wasting a shot?"

Hamilton quickly stood and took hold of both pistols. "Stand up, doctor and take hold of this pistol." After checking that the weapons were unloaded, he handed Sullivan a firearm. "These smooth bore flintlocks have been in my family for several generations. They've always brought me good luck in a duel and I insist that you use them."

Sullivan awkwardly took hold of the handgun. "Wow, it's heavy."

"Now, head over across the room. Ben will serve as our second."

Sullivan walked to the edge of the room, as did Hamilton to the other. Franklin positioned himself between the two and took a handkerchief from his coat pocket. Fifteen to twenty feet stood between the two armed men.

"The duel starts when Ben drops his kerchief," said Hamilton loudly. "First, both combatants must lower their weapon toward the ground."

Sullivan obliged.

"Now wasting a shot can be a bit risky," declared Hamilton. "Most duelers will waste a shot by firing directly into the ground, but I don't recommend that."

"Why not?"

"First of all, you can blow your foot off," chuckled Hamilton. "That's considered bad form."

"And the second reason?"

"You don't want to insult your opponent."

"The man that's trying to kill me?" asked Sullivan incredulously. "I don't want to insult him… is that what you're telling me?"

"That's right," continued Hamilton. "He may consider a shot into the dirt a sign that he's an unworthy opponent. In other words, a man not honorable enough to shoot."

"This whole thing is crazy," responded Sullivan.

"Remember, John. This is an affair of honor," interjected Ben.

"I recommend a shot high into the air," said Hamilton.

Sullivan raised his pistol straight up to the ceiling.

"No. Not that high. Only about half-way to the sky," instructed Hamilton.

Ben turned his head toward Sullivan and whispered. "About 45 degrees high, John."

"Perfect," said Hamilton. "Now, drop your arm back to a starting position. Let's give it a go. On Ben's signal, immediately waste a shot into the air. You must do it quickly!" He looked at Franklin. "Benjamin my dear friend, commence the duel."

Franklin cleared his throat and slowly raised his hand parallel to the floor. He looked at Hamilton. "Are you ready, sir?"

"Yes."

He looked at Sullivan. "Are you ready, sir?"

"Yes."

"I shall say 'present', afterwards you may fire," bellowed Franklin. He paused.

Sullivan looked down the firing line at the young and proud soldier staring him down. He visualized the exact scene scheduled to play out some twenty years later on a deserted plot of land in New Jersey. His heart began to pound fiercely in his chest. Did Hamilton waste his first shot on Burr as he just recommended? How could Burr have taken the life of such a noble man? Perhaps he misunderstood Hamilton's *delope*, thinking it was an actual attempt on his life. If so, Hamilton should have shot into the ground instead of overhead.

"Present!" shouted Franklin as he dropped his handkerchief.

Sullivan snapped out of his dream only to see Hamilton aiming a weapon directly between his eyes.

"Click," said Hamilton. "You're dead." He lowered his weapon.

"John, what happened?" asked Ben. "Wake up!"

"Doctor," stated Hamilton firmly. "You must stay alert. You've only one chance in this game. Your life depends on it."

"I'm sorry," whimpered Sullivan. "It's just that, perhaps I should just shoot into the dirt. This does seem a bit risky especially if my opponent…"

"John," warned Franklin with an extended pause for effect. "Let's try this again. Pay attention to my signal and listen to Alexander's instructions, he's the dueling expert."

"I'm sorry," replied Sullivan. "Let's run through it again."

The second practice round went off without a hitch, as did the third and fourth.

"Fantastic," said Hamilton as he tucked the family weaponry back into the box. "You're going to do fine. Just get that shot off quickly."

"But, what if Arnold fires back anyway? What happens then?"

"Benedict is a hothead," replied Hamilton. He closed a latch on the box. "But he's also a man of honor. He will return the wasted shot with a waste of his own. Then the duel is over and both men walk away in honor."

"For an opponent to then insist upon a second shot is considered bloodthirsty and improper," added Franklin.

"But isn't Benedict Arnold bloodthirsty and improper?" asked Sullivan.

"Yes, but honorable," reassured Hamilton. "This is foremost an affair of honor. If he breaks protocol, his name would be tarnished forever. Benedict is too proud to allow that to happen."

Sullivan nodded his head in ironic agreement. "I'll take your word for it, gentlemen." He looked at Ben. "When you write that critique on the *Code Duello*, add an option of dropping your weapon and running off the duel field like a scared jackrabbit. I think that's still the safest alternative. Feel free to use my name… call it the *Code of Sullivan*."

"Doctor," stated Hamilton firmly. "Those who stand for nothing, fall for everything." He grinned. "So take your stand. Always remember that!"

Sullivan stared back in awe.

"Godspeed, my friend," continued Hamilton. "I'll be out of town this Saturday and unable to attend."

"Thank you," said Sullivan as he shook his hand. "Thank you so much."

Hamilton turned toward Ben and bowed. "Mr. Franklin. Thank you for your hospitality. You're a very gracious host. Good day." He placed his hat atop his head.

"Good-bye, Alexander. All the best to Eliza and the children." Hamilton departed.

Sullivan stepped back and collapsed into a chair. "Wow!" he exclaimed. Meeting George Washington was fascinating but discussing the art of a duel with Alexander Hamilton was beyond his comprehension. "That was amazing." His whole body trembled.

"I knew you would enjoy it," said Ben as he took another nip of rum. "So it's settled. You'll waste your first shot and we'll be done with this whole matter."

"Absolutely," said Sullivan as he took in a deep breath. "I'm going to waste a shot."

In the adjacent row home stood Benedict Arnold and his wife, silent with their ears pressed up against the wall. A sordid grin came across Benedict's face as he stepped back and slowly clenched his fist.

"He's going to waste his shot," snickered Peggy. "What a fool."

Benedict nodded his head in agreement.

"So what's your plan?" whispered his wife.

"My plan? It's simple. I'll let him shoot overhead and then place a bullet directly into his heart."

She smiled. "That's my Benedict."

"Doctor John Sullivan is going to die this Saturday at high noon, on the banks of the Schuylkill River," declared the military governor of Philadelphia. "Not even the great Benjamin Franklin can save his life now."

One story above the Arnolds lay Sary on the floor, her ear pressed to the hardwood. She closed her eyes and recited a prayer for John Sullivan.

## CHAPTER EIGHTEEN
### THE FRANKLIN PLAN
### 1779

Sary gazed out onto the windowsill while scrubbing a frying pan. Earlier in the day she placed a few breadcrumbs on the ledge in hopes of attracting her favorite songbird. The plan worked. A black-capped chickadee suddenly swooped down on the perch, its inquisitive face staring back inside.

"Fee-bee. Fee-bee," went the bird's cry.

The small bird moved its compact frame deftly over the meal, occasionally shifting from side to side. Sary always found its black cap face and bib striking in relation to two chubby, white cheeks.

"Fee-bee. Fee-bee."

She stopped scrubbing and listened carefully, the song taking her back to her earliest childhood memory.

She first heard the call of a chickadee while disembarking in Charleston, South Carolina, along with her older brother and mother. Carefully her mother guided her two children down a wooden gangplank into a swarm of inhumane transactions. Men shouted and dogs barked as the new arrivals were separated in a haphazard fashion, too barbaric for any child to comprehend. Only women and children exited the ship that fateful morning, the men having been removed the prior day under much duress. The sun and fresh air felt divine on her skin after fifteen days in the dark, musty hull of a cargo ship. While walking beneath a blooming magnolia she gazed up to see the songbird on a branch, singing so merrily. It made her smile.

Untold horror soon followed to include an auctioneer's block, haggling, jeers and the terror of a pitted faced man with saggy, white skin dragging her brother away. His screams haunted her that night as she held tight to her mother's arms in the back of a rickety wagon. Seven days later she arrived scared and hungry in a land called Virginia, where she took up residence in a crowded field house on a sprawling plantation. Her mother died the following spring of smallpox.

Her biological mother named her Kiabree, but her new owner dubbed her Sary. A community of equally oppressed human chattel raised her over the next six years by default, their byproduct a precocious girl with a steely personality that quickly outpaced her peers. Sary sewed the fastest, learned the quickest and worked the hardest. She possessed a keen wit and captivating smile that generated a unique personal charm. Yet what truly separated her from the others was a remarkable resiliency; an inner grit that absorbed indignity on a daily basis yet generated genuine concern and compassion in return. Whatever the situation, Sary exuded a palpable zest for life in a terminally hopeless world.

Puberty as always brought about change. By age fourteen she incurred an intense and unsolicited amount of interest from males on both sides of the human bondage abyss, the end result a hysterical directive from the plantation owner's wife for her to be banished. She arrived in Philadelphia five days later at the age of fifteen. Within a week she took up residence on Elfreth's Alley under the reign of her current owner.

She made eye contact with the bird and thought of her brother, having never seen him again.

"Sary!" screamed Major General Arnold. "Where's our dessert?"

Her body jolted from the harshness of the cry. The bird flew away.

"Coming!" she hollered while quickly placing the frying pan down. She reached back to pick up two plates of sliced fruit and walked into the dining area. "Fresh pears and blueberries! I picked them this morning."

Sitting opposite one another were Major General Arnold and his wife, each with a bloated and pompous look across their face. Mrs. Arnold picked her teeth with a fingertip as she spoke.

"Did you sprinkle sugar on mine like I told you?" she asked.

"Oh no. I forgot," replied Sary as she placed the bowls on the table. "I'll be right back." She darted into the kitchen while ignoring a comment chiding her intelligence. "Here you are, Mrs. Arnold." She carefully sprinkled some raw sugar over the fruit.

"Use a spoon next time!" barked Mrs. Arnold. "Not your stinky fingers!"

"Yes, ma'am. Would you like some cinnamon too?"

"Sary," ordered Arnold with a mouthful of fruit. "I'll need my finest uniform ready to go tomorrow, with boots and buckles shined. Have them ready outside my door by sunrise. I've got some important business to tend to at noontime."

"Yes, sir."

"Remember that tear in my trouser leg? Sew that up too."

"Yes, sir."

"And make that breakfast you served me the other day," continued Arnold. "The one with some sort of sauce over the eggs. I do my best shooting on a full stomach."

The comment disturbed Sary. "Yes, sir."

"You put sauce on eggs? laughed Mrs. Arnold. "I've never heard of such a ridiculous thing. What kind of sauce?"

"Tell her, Sary."

"Well, Mrs. Arnold," explained Sary excitedly. "I make the sauce from the yoke of some eggs. I beat the eggs *really* good and add some lemon juice and spicy mustard with a dash of hot pepper." She grinned. "Only a dash of the cayenne pepper now. Then I steam in some hot butter." She moved her hand as if making the concoction. "That's the sauce part."

"Sounds horrible," opined Mrs. Arnold with a piece of blueberry skin stuck on her front tooth. While finishing a glass of wine she spilled some on her blouse.

"Then I toast two muffins and place some bacon and poached eggs over each one."

"Yummy," interjected Arnold. "Dear, you have something on your front tooth." He reached across the table.

"And that's what you pour the sauce over?" asked Mrs. Arnold as she pushed away her husband's hand.

"Yes, ma'am. I lather it up good with sauce."

"Hah, I'd be out in the outhouse in a flash if I ate that," scoffed Mrs. Arnold. "No thank you." She rubbed her blouse and front teeth with a napkin.

"It's fantastic," countered the major general. "Does the dish have a name, Sary?"

"No, sir. It has no name. I learned that recipe from the cook down in Virginia. She just called it eggs and sauce." Her eyes widened as if struck by an idea. "Major General Arnold! Maybe we should name it after you? Especially since you like it so much."

"Yes! A grand idea," huffed Arnold proudly. "Let's say we call it 'Eggs Benedict'. After yours truly, the military commander of the City of Philadelphia."

"Hah! Like anything you recommend ever catches on," sniped his wife. "Nobody listens to what you think, dear. That's the problem. We're like two nobodies around here. The Washingtons live in a mansion and we get stuck in a rowhome next to a guy that likes to fly kites in the rain." She poured herself another glass of wine.

"Well, I still think it's a good idea," retorted the major general.

Sary stood at attention, awaiting further instruction.

"Don't just stand there like a statue!" snapped Mrs. Arnold. "It's impolite!"

"Yes, ma'am." She turned away.

"Didn't they teach her anything in Virginia?" snarled Mrs. Arnold. "How rude."

"She's from the fields. Give her some time. I've had worse."

Sary began to hum a tune as she quickly resumed her kitchen chores. While sweeping the floor she overhead Mrs. Arnold ranting about the war and raving about an old friend called Major John André. The general's response triggered a heated barrage from his wife over money and debts followed by a series of blunt, female forewarnings in regard to their marital relationship. In the end, General Arnold surrendered, his tone of voice apologetic as he begrudgingly agreed to secretly meet the British soldier named André. The couple then left the house for a walk, an uncommon event for both of them.

Sary cleaned up their plates and hurried upstairs. She tiptoed into their front bedroom which was opposite that of Franklin's study. Rapidly she began to tap on the wall, three quick raps followed by two heavier thuds. After each signal she stopped and listened while occasionally glancing at the busybody mirror. While waiting for a response she scanned the bedroom. The place was a mess with clothes and underwear strewn all over the floor. After the fifth set of taps, Franklin returned his end of the secret code. She then heard his muffled voice.

"Sary. What's wrong?"

She cupped her hands to her mouth and brought them to the wall. "I need to talk to you. It's an emergency."

"This evening," came the quick reply. "After they're asleep. The back door."

"Got it." She tapped twice and bolted out of the room.

Later that evening Sary dutifully prepared Arnold's military uniform and spit shined his boots. She readied his breakfast ingredients and waited patiently in the basement for the Arnolds to fall asleep. In the process she entered a few more lines into a diary provided to her by Franklin. She wrote of Sullivan's bravery and the peril he would face the following day. She dare not mention the Arnolds by name. At around eleven o'clock she tiptoed out a back entrance as if heading to the privy. After waiting five minutes to assure stealth, she snuck into the unlocked door of the Franklin residence. There she found Ben fast asleep on a sofa with both legs elevated on some pillows. To his right burned a candle next to an empty teacup. On his chest teetered a half opened pamphlet titled *The American Crisis* by Thomas Paine. She gently shook his shoulder.

"Mr. Franklin. Mr. Franklin," she whispered. "Wake up."

Ben roused and babbled. "These are the times that try men's souls."

"Mr. Franklin. Please, wake up." She repeatedly jabbed his shoulder.

Franklin's eyes popped wide open. He scanned the room to get his bearings and then focused on Sary. After clearing his throat he swung to a seated position with much effort. "My dear Sary. What's the matter?"

"Mr. Franklin, they're going to kill Dr. Sullivan! They overheard your conversation with Mr. Hamilton. Something about a wasted shot and the doctor being a fool. Oh it's horrible! General Arnold shoots best on a full stomach and tomorrow morning I'm making him Eggs Benedict. I just shined his boots and he talked about Dr. Sullivan dying at noon and putting a bullet in … "

"Sary. Sary. *Slow down* my child," whispered Franklin as he patted her on the hand. "No one is going to kill Dr. Sullivan. Now, take a few slow, deep breaths and try to relax." Franklin put on his bifocals and arched his back. "There you go. Now, slowly Sary… from the beginning, tell me exactly what you heard."

Sary divulged Arnold's conversation with his wife in full detail, including the major general's plans to ignore the wasted shot and execute Sullivan. Her lips trembled as she spoke. "Oh Mr. Franklin, you have to warn him. Don't let him go! I wanted to warn you earlier, but Mrs. Arnold never leaves the house. She doesn't like the sun spoiling her skin."

A look of disgust overcame Franklin's face as he digested the news. "What a shameless miscreant," he muttered. Slowly he stood up with a menacing frown. "A skunk of a man." He wiggled his arthritic index finger back and forth. "An inglorious knave if there ever was one."

"What are you going to do, Mr. Franklin?"

Franklin took a deep breath as his thought process began to churn. "First of all, we must alert John. Let me wake him." He stepped forward and headed into Sullivan's bedroom. "We can't let this happen."

Sullivan was pleasantly surprised to find Sary sitting in the parlor. He hadn't seen her since Arnold's dismantling of his physical and mental wellbeing in the entrance foyer. The three gathered around a single candle, plotting their next steps. Franklin spoke first.

"John, much to my chagrin, the Pagano boys have failed in their assigned task of recovering those lost rings."

"That's no surprise to me," retorted Sullivan. "I had my doubts."

"So let's consider our remaining options," continued Ben. "By my observations, you haven't the heart nor the skill to square up with Arnold on the duel field. True?"

"Yes and yes," agreed Sullivan. "No heart. No skill."

Franklin grimaced.

"Oh, it's all my fault," interrupted Sary. "General Arnold wants to kill you because of me."

"No, Sary. That's not the reason," implored Sullivan.

"Yes it is! You let me talk to him," said Sary boldly. "I'll talk him out of it." The pupils in her eyes grew larger in the candlelight as she spoke. "I can do it. I've dealt with men like him before."

"No, Sary," stated Ben respectfully. "We appreciate your enthusiasm and I'm sure you can do it, but any further involvement on your behalf may infuriate the incorrigible Mr. Arnold even more. This issue is spring loaded."

"Yes, Mr. Franklin," said Sary respectfully. "I understand."

Franklin slowly brought a hand to his chin and sighed. He then looked Sullivan square in the eye. "Well John, I didn't want to do it, but it may be time to initiate the Franklin Plan."

"Franklin Plan? What are you talking about, Ben?" asked Sullivan. He flipped his palms up toward the ceiling. "I never heard of the Franklin Plan."

"John, in life one must always be prepared for the unexpected. Remember, the person who fails to plan, plans to fail."

"But we had a plan."

"And it failed," countered Ben slowly with a tilt of his head. "Hence the need for another plan."

Sullivan just shook his head, well aware of his inferior debating skills in the presence of the master himself. "Go on," he said. "What's your plan?"

Franklin leaned forward as if letting out a secret. He looked over his right and left shoulder for added effect. "John, believe it or not," he whispered. "There's another trinket in town that can open a time portal to the future. It's been so long that I completely forgot about it. I had it on during the lightning strike and well, it was lost in a somewhat testy card game with John Adams and subsequently stolen. You see…"

"Mingo's ring!" broke in Sullivan. "The one on Walt's thumb! Is that what you're talking about?"

Franklin fluttered his eyebrows in surprise. "Why, yes. Yes it is. So you know about it?"

"I had my suspicions. Especially after seeing Walt manhandle the ring away from Mingo when he was admitted to the hospital. Mingo also likes to drop a lot of buzzwords from the future."

"And you figured it out solely upon that?"

"Not really. Mingo's shirt gave it away?"

"His shirt?"

"Yea. The one that says, 'Schmidt's of Philadelphia'. A dead giveaway to the trained eye."

"Hah!" exclaimed Franklin. "Too funny. Schmidt's… one beautiful beer."

Sullivan grinned. "Now, let's hear it, Ben. Tell us about your plan."

Franklin went to speak.

"Wait," snapped Sullivan with an extended hand. "Before you go on, please tell me it involves liberating Sary from the torture chamber next door."

Franklin paused to choose his words carefully. "John, we've had this discussion before. I have no magical wand to wave against the injustice of human enslavement. So my plan *does not* ... "

"But, we can't leave her behind," argued the physician. "I can't leave her behind. I won't allow it."

"John, first things first," countered Ben firmly. "Our number one priority is saving your life, which may I remind you, is in significant peril at the moment. Hence this clandestine meeting."

Sullivan remained silent.

"The plan I'm about to tell you is a longshot at best. It involves multiple moving parts, the recovery of a stolen ring from a brute, and the cooperation of an insane man. I'm putting my reputation and life on the line here." He paused to let the magnitude of his comments take effect. "I don't think we need to include Sary in that regard."

"Well, it's just that ... "

"John, do you know what the penalty is for abetting the escape of a slave?"

"No. No I don't," came Sullivan's timid reply. "I can only imagine."

"Hanging until dead. For both the accomplice and the slave. So you can forget about Sary being included in my plan. We can't jeopardize her life in an attempt to set you free."

Sullivan didn't reply.

"Thank you, Dr. Sullivan," said Sary. "Thank you for caring about me. I'll be fine. Don't worry about me."

"You're welcome, Sary. I'm sorry." He looked back at Ben. "Go ahead, Mr. Franklin. Tell us about your plan."

"Well," whispered Franklin. "Earlier in the week I contacted Dr. Casey to uproot one of his mandrake plants in the garden. Then I spoke to the Pagano brothers who per my charge, hid a few kegs of gunpowder ... "

# CHAPTER NINETEEN
## JUICE OF THE MANDRAKE
## 1779

A tremendous explosion at three o'clock in the morning marked the commencement of the Franklin Plan. The blast occurred in an empty field along the banks of the Delaware River, just east of Elfreth's Alley. The ensuing concussion immediately woke Arnold from a sound sleep.

"What the hell was that?" muttered the military governor as he listened to some dogs howling outside. He turned toward his wife who remained sound asleep with earplugs and a sleep mask in place. A second detonation followed, bringing Arnold to his feet. He stumbled out of the bedroom.

"General Arnold! General Arnold!" cried out Sary from downstairs. "Did you hear that?"

"Yes. Of course I heard it," stammered Arnold as he quickly dressed into his military garb. "An explosion of some nature."

"It sounded like cannon fire!" continued Sary. "Oh Lord! The British are coming!"

"Don't be silly," barked Arnold as he made his way half-dressed down the stairwell. "They're fifty miles due east of the Delaware River." He brushed past Sary. "Where are my boots?"

A knock on the door prompted Sary to open it. Standing before her were two military guards from a checkpoint at the end of the alley. Behind them stood a concerned set of neighbors in their nightgowns, including Franklin. One of the soldiers pushed past Sary.

"Sir," said the sentry. "Two explosions just east of here. Near the river."

"Any word from our forward scouts?" asked the commander while buttoning his shirt.

"No sir."

"Sary! Where are my..."

"Here are your boots, General Arnold," said Sary as she handed him the footwear.

A third explosion suddenly echoed through the lane.

A concerned Benedict Arnold hopped on one leg as he shoved an opposite foot into a boot. "Sound the alarm," ordered Arnold. "Get a platoon down to the river immediately."

"Yes, sir!" The sentry pivoted and hustled away.

"Get me my horse," snapped Arnold to the other soldier. "Quick!"

"Benedict. What's going on?" asked Franklin as he stood in front of some townsfolk.

"How should I know?" snapped Arnold at his neighbor. A church bell in the distance began to ring. "Tell everyone to get back inside." Arnold swung a strap holding a black powder horn across his neck as Sary handed him his pistol belt. He donned the weaponry, shoved Franklin aside and hobbled outside. "Where's my horse?"

Approaching hoofbeats were heard along the cobblestone as a sentry delivered Arnold's stallion to the front door. The military governor mounted the black steed and looked down at his subjects. "Go back to your homes! Everything is under control." He kicked the horse and snapped its reins. "Ride Raven... ride!" He galloped away down the lane.

Franklin looked at Sary and slowly nodded his head. She ran to the back of the house and quietly tapped on the wall three times. John Sullivan bolted out the back door. He began to run opposite the approaching platoon, toward Pennsylvania Hospital. His progress went unchecked in the chaos of the moment.

Once inside the walls of the hospital, Sullivan spotted a single lantern being swung by Dr. Casey. He entered the hospital through a side entrance.

"You made it!" exclaimed Casey. "Good job."

"Did he take the bait?" asked Sullivan, a bit out of breath.

"Like a thirsty camel," replied Casey with a smile. The two physicians headed to the first floor, toward Walt's quarters. "I offered him a fresh bottle of rum at around midnight and he started to guzzle it down. The man is a drunkard."

"What about the opium?"

"I laced the spirits with a load of laudanum. He should be out cold by now."

They turned the corner into Walt's room only to see the behemoth wobbling his way toward the door.

"I've going to take a leak," stammered Walt as he waved a near empty bottle of booze in his right hand. He tapped the bottle on Dr. Casey's shoulder. "Great rum, doc. Thanks."

"What?" cried out Casey as Walt disappeared toward the outhouse. "I gave him enough opium to put down a horse! I even mixed in some jimsonweed."

"Oh, boy," declared Sullivan. "What now? We've got to get that ring… or else."

"To the garden!" ordered Casey firmly. "Let's initiate Ben's back up plan."

"What back up plan?" shouted Sullivan as he quickly followed. "Why am I always the last to know about Ben's plans?"

He followed Casey out to the medicinal garden with a shovel in hand. Some church bells in the distance could still be heard clanging along with an occasional shout from the street.

"Luckily it's a Friday night with a clear sky," stated Casey as he approached a plot in the center of the garden. "This is my last mandrake. I hate to dig it up."

"What are you talking about?" asked Sullivan.

"The root of the mandrake plant. It's one of our mainstay treatments for madness. In fact, Mingo has been on it for several days now with good results." He looked up to the sky. "Ah, there's the moon. Perfect. Now, we need to determine the wind direction." As he spoke he positioned himself between the moon and the mandrake.

Sullivan looked over his shoulder to see the massive shadow of Walt staggering back toward the hospital. "Hurry!" he said. "I don't know what you're doing, but please hurry."

Casey took out a wad of wax and stuffed a piece into each ear. "A mandrake root can only be harvested by moonlight on a Friday or in the month of May," he shouted. "With the wind at the gatherer's back and ears stuffed with wax."

"Why?"

Casey began to loosen the soil around the plant with the spade. "So you don't go deaf from the scream of its root! The scream can also cause insanity or worse yet… death."

"Excuse me?"

"The juice of a mandrake root is packed full of potent compounds," hollered Casey. "It's used as a pain reliever, an aphrodisiac and a cure for everything from hemorrhoids to memory loss. It's also a potent sedative when mixed with alcohol." He continued to circumferentially work loose the root. "It's been around since the ancient Egyptians and goes by a variety of names such as love apple, crazy apple, mad apple and the devil's testicles."

"Wow, that's quite the visual."

Casey cast the shovel aside and reached down to take hold of the green and leafy plant. "It's loose. We're ready to go."

"It looks like a head of iceberg lettuce."

"Cover your ears!" ordered Casey. He vigorously yanked the plant upward with both hands, delivering the swollen, forked root ball to the horizon.

"Yikes!" said Sullivan as he winced at the root system. "It looks like a voodoo doll!"

Casey tentatively opened his eyes while still holding the root at arm's length. "Are you alright?"

"Yes. I'm fine."

"You can still hear me?"

"Yes! I can hear you!" shouted Sullivan. He pointed to his ears. "You can take your ear plugs out. I'm still alive."

Casey obliged and proudly proclaimed, "What a fantastic specimen of mandrake root!"

"It does look like an angry little human being," laughed Sullivan. "But I didn't hear a scream and I don't see any testicles."

"Mandrake is short for the Latin term 'mandragora', or 'human dragon,'" professed Casey. "Come on. Let's get this inside and into Walt's system. We've no time to spare!"

Sullivan followed Casey back into the basement of the hospital. There Casey placed the mandrake root between the jaws of a wooden vice and cranked down on the lever.

"Juice from the root is much more potent than from the leaves," stated the physician. As the vice began to crush the root, orange tinged liquid began to drip into a bucket below.

"How much do you use?"

"That's a good question," replied Casey as he continued to pulverize the root. "In a normal person, perhaps a half of fluid dram."

"What's a fluid dram?"

"A measurement of volume. It's the amount of whiskey that you can swallow in one mouthful."

"That's a lot for Walt compared to the average man. Hit him hard. We need that ring."

"That's easy to say, Dr. Sullivan. But please understand, when using the juice of a mandrake plant, the difference between a cure and a kill is just a few drops. We don't want a fatality on our hands."

As the final few drops of juice dripped from the root, Casey opened another bottle of rum and filled a tin cup half full. The physician then reached down into the bucket with an empty shot glass and dunked it into the mandrake juice. He brought the glass to eye level and studied it in the lantern light.

"Pure root of mandrake," he whispered proudly. "Nectar of the gods."

"It looks like carrot juice."

"Perhaps we'll start with a half a dram," suggested Casey.

"Remember, Walt already has alcohol, opium and jimsonweed on board."

"Give it all to him and then some," countered Sullivan. "We've only one chance here. Walt can take it. He's the size of a moose."

"I concur." Casey dumped the full amount of juice into the drink.

"How fast does it work?"

"Within minutes. Let's go!"

Upstairs they found Walt slumped in a chair, his words slurred and movements slow.

"Oh, what's the occasion?" smiled Walt. "More rum?"

"More rum, Walt!" shouted Casey. "A toast." He handed the glass to Walt and poured a drink for himself and Sullivan. "To the future!"

The drunk sentry tossed the fluid back in a single gulp. "To the future!"

"Walt, I need your keyring," requested Casey.

The giant slowly reached his hand to belt level and fumbled loose the ring full of skeleton keys. He babbled incoherently while handing over the keys.

"Now the ring on your thumb, Walt. Give it to me."

"Never," jabbered Walt. "Mingo."

Casey reached down and lifted the guard's hand.

"Hey, go away," slurred Walt. He slowly swatted at Casey. "Leave me alone."

"Walt. I need your ring," ordered Casey firmly. "Hand it over."

The brute's eyes slowly closed shut and he fell still. Casey again reached for his thumb.

"Stop it!" barked Walt. He staggered to his feet, his frame towering over the medical doctors. "What do you think you're doing?" He swayed back and forth. "Nobody gets the ring!"

Casey handed the set of keys to Sullivan. "Go get Mingo. Walt's fading fast. We'll have the ring shortly."

"Right," said Sullivan. He took the keys and ran down to the psychiatric ward. There, through the door slot, he spotted Mingo standing at attention. "Mingo," whispered Sullivan. "It's time."

"Open the door," ordered the patient.

Sullivan complied and Mingo immediately darted out like a wild animal.

"Mingo!" shouted Sullivan.

Mingo rushed down the hallway and into Walt's quarters. Casey immediately spotted him approaching Walt from behind.

"Mingo!" shouted Casey with a raised hand. "NO!"

Mingo vaulted onto Walt's back and placed a choke hold around his neck. The sentry reflexively charged forward and into a wall, the impact failing to dislodge the assailant from his upper torso.

"Mingo, let go!" screamed Casey.

Walt roared like a lion and spun his frame violently in circles while attempting to unsaddle the madman on his back. His arms flailed up and down as he pirouetted across the room. The mortal enemies crashed into tables, smashed chairs and rolled across the ground as Mingo howled like a werewolf, his death grip unbreakable.

"He's choking him!" shouted Sullivan.

Both physicians tried to intervene but bounced off the duo under the demonic spell of the mandrake root. They watched helplessly as Walt and Mingo continued to thrash about the room as if in a bull riding contest to the death. Then suddenly Walt let out a guttural moan while arching his back; he lunged forward and crashed face first into the ground. The impact failed to dislodge Mingo. Both men lay absolutely still.

"He's dead!" screamed Casey while shoving Mingo. "Get off of him!"

Mingo held firm for several more seconds, his ear cocked to the side of Walt's face. He grunted and slowly let go.

The combined effort of Casey and Sullivan rolled Walt supine, his face a peculiar combination of red and blue. Some blood trickled from a gash across his forehead. Sullivan reached for his wrist as Casey put an ear to his chest.

"He's got a pulse," said Sullivan.

"And he's breathing," added Casey. "Thank heavens."

Mingo grabbed the ring on Walt's thumb and starting yanking forcefully. It refused to come off.

"Get away!" ordered Casey but Mingo refused to let go. He pulled so hard that it appeared Walt's thumb would disengage from his hand.

"Put some liquid on it," suggested Sullivan as he poured some rum onto Walt's hand.

"Mingo, let go!" shouted Casey. "You're going to hurt him."

Mingo leaned forward and started gnawing on Walt's thumb. He snarled and growled as he chomped down on the digit like a dog with a bone.

"Mingo!" screamed Sullivan to no avail. "He's biting it off!"

Casey hit Mingo over the back with the poker from a firepit, the unexpected strike causing him to squeal and disengage. "Stop it!" screeched Casey. He held the pointed metal rod forward to keep Mingo at bay.

"It's absolutely stuck," bemoaned Sullivan as he too tried to pull off the ring. "His finger is so swollen it will never come off."

Casey looked at Sullivan in dismay. "John, that ring has to come off… one way or the other."

Mingo began to wail and run in circles around the two physicians.

"What? You want me to cut his finger off?" asked Sullivan. "Is that what you're suggesting?"

"How else are we going to get it?"

Sullivan sighed, sensing the Franklin Plan on the verge of failure. He couldn't let Ben down. There was no other option.

"Wait!" blurted Dr. Casey. "I've got an idea. Take him with you."

"Take who?"

"Walt. Take the ring *and* Walt. Nobody will miss him."

"What? What about his family?"

"Walt has no family. He's a squatter here at the hospital. His only two friends are the bottle and the baton."

Mingo leaped over the two physicians as they remained crouched at Walt's side.

"If you don't take him… we cut the thumb off," proclaimed Casey. "You make the call, John."

"Alright. Let's take him," decided Sullivan. "Mingo. Walt's coming with us."

Mingo violently shook his head in disagreement.

"Pick him up!" ordered Casey with a wave of the poker. "Or I'll lock you up for good. *Do it!*"

Mingo lunged down at the sentry. He slid both hands beneath his body and heaved him off the ground in a feat of superhuman strength. In one quick motion he hoisted Walt into the air and onto his shoulders, the end result a classic fireman's carry. He ran toward the exit.

"To the carriage!" directed Casey. "Place him in the back."

Once outside, Mingo obliged by casting Walt's lifeless body into the rear of a four-wheel, wooden buckboard wagon. A horse stood hitched to the front of the carriage.

"Get going," shouted Casey to Sullivan. Some shouts could be heard just outside the front gate. "Take the rear entrance."

"But where's the driver?" asked Sullivan as he watched Mingo scale the wagon.

"There is no driver, John," said Casey. "This is a one way ticket out of town."

"What? A suicide mission?"

"I sure hope not. Get on, quick! It's up to you and Mingo now."

Sullivan barely made it into the rear of the flatbed wagon before Mingo cracked the reins, his action lurching the transport forward. He grasped both hands onto Walt's torso.

"Godspeed, my friends," yelled Casey. "No. Mingo! Take the rear entrance! Not the front!"

Mingo stood tall on the driver's box as he drove the coach directly out the main gate. He kept one foot on the forward buckboard as he lashed the leather straps wildly. "Aaah-oooh!" screeched the bedlamite. Sullivan looked up to see the silhouette of the crazed driver illuminated by a full moon. "Where are you going?" he yelled. Mingo ducked his head beneath the passing archway of the hospital entrance gate. He swung the vehicle hard left and in the process almost ejected Sullivan and Walt onto the street. "Slow down!" screamed Sullivan as he pushed Walt's frame off his body.

The escape transport ran amok for several blocks with an occasional passerby shouting, *"look out!"* or *"slow down!"*. Each bump in the road violently tossed Walt and Sullivan up and down on the wooden plank cargo bed. Sullivan estimated Mingo to be about six blocks from the hospital when he made another sharp turn, the maneuver almost capsizing the wagon.

"You're going to kill us!" shrieked Sullivan. He struggled to push up and look forward, the steeple of the Christ Church in sight. Suddenly Walt's body began to stir, the wounded guard coming to life. "Mingo, he's waking up!" Sullivan grasped the ring and pulled tight, the maneuver further arousing Walt, causing his opposite arm to rise up and crash down on the physician. "He's alive!" shouted Sullivan as he rolled away. In panic he looked over the wagon side.

At that instant, Sullivan viewed several soldiers on foot staring back at the passing carriage. In the midst of the cadre appeared a figure in full military garb on the back of a stallion. Sullivan made direct eye contact with Major General Benedict Arnold. Reflexively, he ducked his head back down.

"Yaw!" screamed Mingo as he flicked the reins. "Yaw!"

Walt tried to stand but the forward momentum tossed him back to the deck. He grabbed Sullivan's upper leg and pulled firmly.

"Let go!" shouted Sullivan as he repeatedly kicked Walt in the face with his opposite leg. "Let me go!" The physician grabbed the side rail and elevated his body, only to see Benedict Arnold in full gallop pursuit about sixty yards back. "Mingo!" hollered Sullivan. "Hurry!"

"Whoa!" bawled out Mingo as he pulled hard on the reins and turned the speeding wagon sharply.

His maneuver capsized the wagon and catapulted the three occupants forward, their bodies tumbling to a halt in the Christ Church graveyard. Mingo rose and started to drag Walt toward the rear of the yard. Sullivan joined in but after about fifteen yards stumbled over a grave marker. He looked back to see Arnold and two other soldiers pull up beside the overturned wagon blocking the graveyard entrance. They quickly dismounted.

"Mingo! Where are we going?" shouted Sullivan as he latched back onto Walt's leg. "Where's the tunnel?"

Mingo didn't reply as he pulled Walt's opposite leg, their combined effort dragging the unconscious victim over the ground on his back. As they passed the small grave of Francis Franklin, Sullivan looked back up. He saw Arnold extend an arm and take hold of a rifle from an aide. He slowly brought the firearm level to his eye and took aim.

"He's got a gun!" screamed Sullivan.

Mingo lunged forward and took hold of Walt's hand. He yanked it back and in doing so brought Walt into a seated position.

Sullivan peered back at Major General Arnold as he held the gun barrel steady. The military governor slowly raised his eye from the gunsight and grinned. He retook aim and squeezed the trigger.

Sullivan first saw the flintlock flash, followed by the crack of the Pennsylvania rifle. Everything then went black.

## CHAPTER TWENTY
### FATHER JOE
### 2065

Sullivan winced from the pain. His eyes remained shut but his ears registered the sound of a passing car. A painful groan emanated to his right.

"Vagrants," complained a passerby to his left. "They ought to clear them out of here."

"I agree," said another voice as it trailed away. "A real shame."

Sullivan forced his eyes open, the morning sun just beginning to light the eastern sky. "Where am I?" mumbled the physician. He ran a hand over his chest and felt some warm liquid. "What the hell?" said Sullivan as he pushed his torso perpendicular to the ground. He looked down to see his hand covered with blood. "Oh, no." He suddenly recalled Arnold's sinister smile and pull of the trigger. He scanned his body for a bullet wound.

Mingo began coughing to his right in a spasmodic fashion similar to a child suffering from whooping cough. Sullivan turned to see him on all fours and foaming from the mouth. The hulking frame of Walt separated the two, his body facing the opposite direction. A city bus rumbled in front of Sullivan.

"Ah, Mingo," said Sullivan, his voice weak. "You forgot to tell me what year your ring transports a person to." As Sullivan spoke he squinted at an advertisement on the bus touting an upcoming performance of the Philadelphia Opera. Opening night was July 15, but the exact year had some graffiti written over it. "Please tell me it's the year 2020."

"Ahh!" moaned Walt. "My arm!"

"Mingo," pressed Sullivan. "The year, please."

Mingo forced himself upright and gathered his wits by looking left to right. He scratched his buttocks, arched his back and readjusted his tattered hospital gown. A diabolical grin appeared on his face.

"Mingo," repeated Sullivan slowly. "Talk to me. What *year* is it?"

Mingo ignored the request and sprinted away in a crazed fashion. Within ten seconds he turned a corner and vanished.

"Mingo!" hollered Sullivan to no avail. "Don't leave me here!"

"You son of a bitch!" wailed Walt as he tilted his head toward Sullivan. "I'll kill you!" He went to grab Sullivan with his right hand but the gunshot wound to his midshaft humerus wouldn't allow it. The sentry and Sullivan both gazed down at a ghastly open fracture along Walt's upper arm, the bone sticking out of the skin with several fragments on the pavement. Pulsatile blood squirted out from the blast zone with each contraction of his heart.

Sullivan jumped to his feet realizing the blood over his body was from Walt. The bullet fired by Arnold had hit the sentry directly between the shoulder and elbow. "Oh Walt, you've been shot!"

The guard went to stand but collapsed in painful shock, the impact further distorting the already grotesque angulation of his arm.

Sullivan knelt at his side and surveyed his remaining extremities and torso. The gunshot was isolated to his right upper extremity. He tore a strip of fabric from Walt's trousers and quickly wrapped it around his upper arm just below the armpit. As he finished tying a tourniquet knot Walt reached across his body with his opposite hand and took hold of Sullivan's neck.

"Bastard," snarled Walt as he slammed Sullivan's face into his broad chest. "You dirty bastard!" He repeatedly smashed Sullivan's face up and down while screaming. "I'll kill you!"

"Let me go!" screeched Sullivan as his head bobbed up and down. "I'm trying to help you."

Walt let go with a terrible cry. "The pain!"

Sullivan rolled away from the wounded man and stood up. "Stay here, Walt." He pointed directly at him. "Do not move. I'm going to get help."

"What have you done to me?" pleaded Walt. "Why? Why? Why did you do this?"

Sullivan reached down and tried one last time to remove the ring from the sentry's finger. He yanked on the keepsake but in the process almost amputated his damaged arm. The ring didn't budge.

"Bloody bugger!"

"Don't move, Walt. Keep that tourniquet on!" Sullivan turned and ran in the same direction as Mingo. Halfway down the block a drone buzzed directly over his head. "Oh, no. Please," begged Sullivan. "No, it can't be…" He came to an abrupt halt at the street corner, his eyes shifting to a large granite cornerstone on a skyscraper. It read, ANNO DOMINI 2060. He began to wail while leaning forward and placing both arms on the marker. "No! Not 2065!"

"Excuse me. Are you alright?" asked a woman passing by. Before Sullivan could reply she recoiled and screeched. "You're covered in blood!"

"Get help," demanded Sullivan. "I'm alright but a man's been shot a block away." He pointed in Walt's direction. "Call an ambulance. He needs immediate care."

The woman stepped back while activating her watch to alert emergency services. A voice over the wristband confirmed the pending arrival of a medical technician in exactly three minutes. Sullivan turned right and ran again in the direction of Mingo. He had no plan in mind. "Thank you," he shouted. "His name is Walt!"

The city streets were still somewhat desolate at half past five o'clock in the morning. Sullivan rinsed the fresh blood off his body via a sprint through a city water fountain. He ran another block before turning into a small church sandwiched between two high-rise buildings. A sign above the wooden doorway proclaimed, "Father Joseph's Mission – Joy in the Journey".

The rear vestibule of the church was dark, except for a few lit candles with yellow flames flickering in red glass holders. A large statue of the Blessed Mary holding baby Jesus stood to his left. The blue eyes of Mother Mary appeared strangely real as she gazed down upon the visitor. Sullivan stepped forward and peered through some stained glass along the upper half of two inner doors. Inside was a small chapel with approximately fifteen rows of pews along each side of the main aisle. A statue of Jesus Christ nailed to the cross hung behind a bare altar. Along a rail set low and parallel to the altar knelt a man wearing a black cassock, his hands clasped and head bowed in prayer. Sullivan opened the door and stepped inside. To his left towered another statue of the Virgin Mary and to his right Saint Joseph wearing a brown robe. He began to slowly walk down the aisle. The holy man made the sign of a cross, stood and turned as he approached.

"Ah, a stranger," said the man in black with open arms. He stood wiry at six foot tall with a bald head and keen eyes. "Welcome, friend. Joy in the journey." He made the sign of the cross over Sullivan.

"Hello," said the physician tentatively. He bowed respectfully.

"I am Father Joe," continued the clergyman with clasped hands. He scanned Sullivan's shoddy appearance including the occasional stain of blood. "You are in need?"

"Yes. Yes, I am."

"Do you wish to be redeemed by the word of God?"

"I do."

"Then come. Come inside. Breakfast is about to be served." He extended an arm to invite Sullivan into a side sacristy. "Every morning we are born again," proclaimed the priest. "What we do today is what matters most."

"Thank you," said a relieved Sullivan as he walked by the priest. "Thank you very much."

"Are you a Philadelphian?" asked Father Joe.

"Yes."

"From whereabouts may I ask?"

"West Philadelphia, up near 43$^{rd}$ Street."

"Ah, a wonderful neighborhood. I taught for many years at West Catholic High."

"I know the school well."

They walked through a dressing room just to the left of the main altar. A few liturgical gowns hung from a metal coat rack along a side wall.

"By what first name shall I call you?" asked Father Joe.

"John," replied Sullivan as they walked down a narrow corridor behind the altar.

"Very well, John." The two men entered a stark room with a bench and open shower. On the bench were separately sealed, clear plastic bags each containing a pair of cotton pants and a button down short sleeve shirt. "You have no material goods?"

"No."

"Excellent. A good start. You can only lose what you cling to," said the priest. He pointed to the plastic bags. "I ask that you take a shower, be rid of your worldly clothing and fit yourself with one of our outfits. There are a wide range of sizes to choose from."

"Thank you, Father Joseph," said Sullivan as he began to unbutton his shirt.

"Are you a period actor?"

"No," laughed Sullivan as he removed his garb from colonial times. "It's a long story."

"No doubt. Just as a snake sheds its skin, we must shed our past over and over again." He smiled. "I'll see you in the main dining hall. It's through the door to your left and down the hall. Breakfast begins at six o'clock sharp." He looked at a wall clock. "You have twenty minutes."

"Thank you, Father."

Sullivan showered and dressed into a light grey pair of pants and shirt. His care packet also contained a pair of white socks, clean underwear, a toothbrush and an oval medal of the church's outer facade with the words, *"Joy in the Journey"* along its rim. He placed the medal around his neck and carefully wiped away any remaining drops of blood from his shoes. After tossing his old clothes into a garbage bucket, he joined the rest of the congregation for breakfast. The aroma of black coffee and eggs filtered through the air as he entered the main dining room.

Sullivan walked into a gathering of men of similar ilk. A few stood in line while others sat at one of two rectangular tables with food trays before them. Two teenage girls wearing plastic gloves served him breakfast from behind a cafeteria counter, each with a 'Volunteer' nametag on their chest. Sullivan sat down as more men wandered up from a basement stairwell. No one seemed to recognize him as a stranger. Father Joe then appeared in their midst.

"Be present at our table Lord," said the holy man with his head piously bowed. "Be here and everywhere adored. These mercies bless and grant that we may feast in fellowship with thee."

"Amen," said the congregation.

Sullivan glanced at the middle-aged man to his left, a cachectic man with yellow-tinged eyes and hypodermic needle scars up and down his arms. A tattoo of two teardrops adorned his left cheek as did the word *'Atone'* written in cursive across his forehead. Sullivan began to introduce himself just as two city policemen entered the room. His heart began to rapidly pound as Father Joe stood to greet the officers.

No one else in the room seemed concerned, so Sullivan kept his eyes trained on the breakfast before him. He would occasionally glance up with a mouth of food only to see Father Joseph talking with his hands moving in a slow and reassuring fashion. As he spoke the officers listened while scanning the assembly of identically clad men. After several tense minutes one of the policemen shook Father Joe's hand, gave him some contact information, and departed. The priest sat back down at his table without making eye contact with Sullivan.

Mass in the chapel followed breakfast. During his homily, Father Joe spoke of the need for suffering in order to obtain redemption. He cited the devastating financial collapse and ruin of the church from the great viral pandemic of 2020 as an example, a pox upon the church and in hindsight, a blessing to begin anew. He spoke of crossover points in life, the role of hardship and the need for humility and compassion in today's world. Lastly he spoke of the need for dutiful prayer in every man's life, while imploring all present to seek out their own personal joy in the journey toward redemption. After communion everyone solemnly sang *Shall We Gather at the River.*

The congregation spent the bulk of the day cleaning up two neighborhood parks, their collective act of service unnoticed by the passing flock of Philadelphians. It was during dinner time that Father Joseph sat down next to Sullivan to break bread.

"Are you at peace?" asked the priest. "The first day can be the hardest."

"Actually I am, Father. It's impossible for me to tell you what I've been through in the past few days."

"Do not dwell on the past or dream of the future, my friend. Let's focus on the present moment." He smiled. "You've no need to mention my discussion with the police earlier today. You are among sinners here."

Sullivan peered into the cleric's eyes as he took a deep breath. Twenty-hours ago he was seated at a table with Benjamin Franklin plotting out a plan to save his life, and now here he sat, out of danger in a mission for lost souls.

"Thank you, Father."

"You're welcome, John." The cleric looked at the bowl set before the physician. "I hope you like pea soup. Our cook is from Amsterdam."

Their conversation dovetailed into sports and the need to bring back live umpires to call balls and strikes behind the plate in baseball. Father Joe spoke of his minor league career as a second baseman cut short by a call from God, while Sullivan talked of his championship Little League team that played in Williamsport. Group prayer followed dinner as did an hour of silent meditation. Lights out at the mission occurred at exactly ten o'clock, with seventeen men sleeping side by side on cots in the basement. Sullivan stared at the flat ceiling above as he tried to sleep.

"Hey, are you new here?" whispered a morbidly obese man in the cot to his left. His white underwear, socks and t-shirt illuminated the darkness.

"Yes. My first day."

"Keep it tight. You'll do fine." He extended a mammoth hand toward Sullivan. "My name is Diesel."

"I'm John," said Sullivan as he shook hands. "A pleasure to meet you, Diesel."

"My advice is to take it one hour at a time. Enjoy sixty minutes of life and thank God, then do it again. Don't look any further than that."

"Thanks, Diesel. I appreciate the advice."

"Good night, John." Diesel's cot creaked and moaned as he rolled over.

Sullivan tried to sleep but could not. With two lost keys he was terminally trapped in the future, his goal to return Vince back to 2020 now impossible. Walt's ring only transported a time traveler between progressive colonial time and 2065, so trying to recoup it didn't address the current dilemma. He sighed deeply, realizing that although the Pagano brothers aided his escape, they would never find the lost keys. How ironic he thought, Ben Franklin's biggest gaffe would never be known by anyone else except him.

A meaningless footnote in the historical life of the Philadelphia legend.

Diesel began to snore, the drone prompting Sullivan to turn in the opposite direction. He thought of Sary. Franklin was right, it being too risky to have rescued her from beneath the eye of her evil owner. In the silence of the mission he recalled her nursing him through smallpox and volunteering to stand up to Arnold in defiance, in order to protect him. His last contact with her involved three soft taps on the wall, which set him free. In essence she saved his life twice, yet he left her behind in the clutches of a wretched abuser. A disturbing pang took hold of his stomach. He curled into the fetal position and began to doze but the screams of Sary echoed inside his head. John Sullivan had hit a dead end with no escape in sight.

A flashlight in the distance slowly began to approach his cot. He immediately thought of the police, prompting the physician to sit upright. His heart raced as the spotlight on the floor came nearer. Father Joe knelt at his side in the darkness.

"Father, what's wrong?" whispered Sullivan.

"Brother John. I just tried to make that emergent medical appointment that you requested with a Dr. Zachary Schmidt."

"Yes," replied Sullivan.

"Well, I just spoke over the phone with another physician on call," said the cleric quietly. "And ... "

"And what?" asked Sullivan, sensing angst.

"Well, unfortunately he informed me that Dr. Schmidt had recently passed away. I'm sorry to tell you that."

Sullivan's mind went blank, the news derailing his thought process. He stared into the darkness.

"Brother John, are you alright?" He put a hand on his forearm. "Shall we take you to the local emergency room?"

"No," muttered Sullivan in disbelief. "It can wait."

Sullivan looked directly into Father Joe's concerned face.

"Did you know Dr. Schmidt well, my son?"

"Sadly, I did not," whispered Sullivan. "He was my father."

Father Joseph paused out of respect. He made the sign of a cross over Sullivan's head and recited a prayer. The mission man then departed, leaving the doctor alone with his thoughts.

# CHAPTER TWENTY-ONE
## ZACHARY'S NOTE
## 2065

"He asked that I give you this envelope upon your return," stated Allister Brooks. He handed the sealed packet to Sullivan. "He knew you would make it back."

Sullivan took hold of the parcel and carefully inspected it. Across the front of the envelope ran his name written in pencil with no other markings. He slowly placed it down on a desk. The two men were seated together in the former office of Dr. Zachary Schmidt. Father Joe had arranged Sullivan's transport to the Philadelphia General campus earlier in the day.

"Allister, you were his friend and time travel co-pilot. What happened? Why so fast? I mean he appeared healthy and robust to me."

"Zachary hid his disease well," explained Brooks. "He was a very sick man. As time progressed the targeting infusions became less and less effective. Zachary knew his ultimate fate and accepted it. Near the end he stopped all medical care and let the disease process run its course. He died in peace, John."

Sullivan didn't respond as he looked around the basement office, the reality of the situation sinking in. He glanced at some photos atop a desk marking the milestones of Dr. Schmidt's medical career, his engaging smile and handlebar mustache the common theme throughout. Schmidt died just four days earlier, his remains subsequently cremated.

"You have to realize that Zachary Schmidt was born in 1930," continued Brooks. "So in reality, his physical composition was over 130 years old. He squeezed every last ounce of spirit from that slight frame. The man had incredible energy."

Sullivan nodded.

"A real Renaissance man if there ever was one."

"I agree."

"He lived life to the fullest, John. Trust me when I say that."

"What about family? Did he have any on this side of the tunnel?"

"He had a significant other," answered Allister. "Her name was Lucy. They enjoyed a wonderful relationship but lived apart."

"Any children?"

"No."

The answer surprised and saddened Sullivan, making him the only living offspring of Zachary Schmidt.

"Did he speak much of his relationship with me?" asked Sullivan tactfully. He was unaware as to Allister being privy to their exact biological connection.

"John, Dr. Schmidt and I were inseparable. I heard and listened to his every word. You saved his life with a targeting agent transfusion because of your kinship to him. The facts are undeniable." Brooks paused as he chose the next words carefully. "He spoke of you often."

"As his son?"

Brooks held eye contact with the physician for several seconds before answering. "The envelope, John." He pointed at it. "Check the envelope. I'm sure it's all in there."

Sullivan sighed. "It's just that I never got to truly know the man. I wanted to ask him so many questions."

"He was trapped in the future for over forty years, John… not by his design. Your actions brought him back. Seeing you was the happiest moment of his life. I can assure you of that. You made his life complete. He departed this world with no regrets."

The words brought much needed solace to Sullivan. He picked up the envelope, smiled and tapped it several times on the desk. "Thank you, Allister. Thank you for the kind words. I feel much better." Sullivan stood and folded the letter. He tried to place it in a pocket, but there was none.

"Where did you get that outfit?" chuckled Brooks. "It has no pockets."

"From a good Samaritan. Now, let's find some real clothes and go get Vince. Does he know about Dr. Schmidt?"

"Yes. He does. He was just as surprised as you. However, getting him may be a problem."

"How so?"

"He's locked down on the psychiatric unit of the Philadelphia General, claiming to be a time traveler."

"What?" exclaimed Sullivan with a slap to his forehead. "How in the world did that happen?"

Allister spent the next several minutes disclosing the scheme hatched by Vince and Dr. Schmidt.

"It's actually the safest place for him to be," declared Allister near the end of the discussion. "To my understanding once he's discharged from the hospital, U.S. Immigration and Custom agents will take him into custody. You're lucky they haven't tagged you yet."

"I owe it all to Father Joe."

"So what's the plan?" asked Allister. "Visiting hours on the psychiatry floor don't start for a few hours."

"Well then, I may take a little rest," said Sullivan while stretching his arms. "I didn't sleep very well last night. Afterwards we can visit Vince. Without any keys, there's no hurry to do anything. We're both trapped… indefinitely."

"Sounds like a plan," agreed Brooks. "I'll dig you up some clothes in the meantime. I recommend you stay right here."

"I will. Thank you, Allister."

Brooks left the office.

Sullivan slowly gazed around and respectfully began to walk through Dr. Schmidt's office, the surreal tour a tribute to the life of a well-respected physician. There were thank you cards from patients, a few framed honorary degrees and the occasional letter of gratitude from a medical colleague. One note just to the right of Schmidt's desk caught Sullivan's particular attention. It was written by Schmidt and titled: *"How to Stay Resilient"*. A series of bullets points followed to include: *"use your sense of humor, dwell on what is going right with your day, go for a daily walk, no junk food and avoid sugar, fill your surroundings with light and pleasurable sounds"*. The bottom of the list contained two underlined recommendations: *"savor interactions and moments with others"* and *"always believe in something bigger than yourself"*. Sullivan paused to digest the fatherly advice. He leaned back in the chair and unfolded the envelope with his name on it. He opened it and began to read.

Dear Son,

If you are reading this letter, I am gone. I beg pardon for the early departure but I gave it my best. I lived a long and joyful life. Do not anguish over my demise for I am at peace.

John, our lives are full of twists and turns and no one knows that better than you and me. I crossed paths with your mother during a vulnerable time in both our careers, our actions certainly reprehensible, yet the end result truly exceptional. The beauty of time travel is the ability to witness the consequences of one's actions via the retrospectoscope. With that in mind, I could not be more satisfied with the outcome. Regardless, I do apologize for my indiscretion.

George W. Sullivan raised you in a manner befitting his honorable name. So George W. Sullivan will always be your 'father', that much is true. So forever refer to his name as such. However, I did contribute to half of your genome, which qualifies me as your 'founding father'. Think of me as that.

So in reality you have the best of both worlds. A rather distinguished pedigree in my humble opinion. Congratulations.

I've donated a significant portion of my life savings to the Philadelphia General Hospital School of Nursing. Next September a scholarship will be available to an incoming student that exhibits the qualities of Martha Sullivan, that being empathy, attention to detail, respect and a continual desire to learn. The four-year grant will be known as 'The Martha Sullivan Scholarship for Excellence in Nursing'. Mom would be proud. It was so good to catch up with her during my brief return to 2020. I have you to thank for that.

John, cherish every moment of your life on earth. My final hope is that you return to your loved ones without delay. That is where you belong. 2065 is a nice place to visit, but there's no time like your biological clock time. So 'gluckliche Reise' my time travel friend. I look forward to the day when we shall meet again.

Sincerely,<br>Zachary

P.S. Enclosed is the only known photograph of your mother and me together. It was a group picture taken on the third floor nursing station of the Franklin Wing. Mom is seated in front of me to the left. If my calculations are correct, you were also present in the photo. You can find it in 2020 within the Philadelphia General Hospital archives.

P.S.S. I almost forgot. In case you didn't figure it out, the initials 'R.S.' stand for Richard Saunders which of course was Benjamin Franklin's second favorite pseudonym. So 'R.S.' is Ben Franklin! (The original I may add!) There's a second time portal in Philadelphia near his grave. Seek him out in times of need. He occasionally returns for medical care. The man is a real gem.

Sullivan took hold of the grainy photograph, a two row, group shot of health care workers on the Franklin Wing floor. Standing in the center was Dr. Schmidt with his trademark grin. Seated in front of him were a total of eight nurses, including Nurse Martha Sullivan. Everyone looked so energetic, young and happy, especially his mom. He sighed deeply and closed his eyes. His parents were gone.

Sullivan woke up some time later. Next to the desk sat a set of clothes in a laundry bin. He looked to his right to see Allister napping on an examination table, his hands folded across his chest. He showered, got dressed and woke Allister.

"Allister. Let's go."

"Do you feel better?" asked Allister as he sat up. He noticed the opened envelope and letter on the desk.

"Actually, I do," answered Sullivan in a reflective tone.

"What? What's the matter? There's something on your mind."

"Nothing. It's just that I had a most peculiar dream." He picked up Schmidt's letter and slid it into his rear pocket. "I was back in colonial times with Benjamin Franklin and he gave me some good advice."

"On what?"

"On what to do if there's ever a crisis."

"Crisis? What kind of crisis?"

"Oh, you know. Like when the tax collector shows up unexpectedly or the British troops storm in," clarified Sullivan with a smile. "Ben's full of good advice and anecdotes."

Allister stood and straightened out his shirt. "You lost me on that one, John." He checked his watch. "Perfect timing though, visiting hours just started on the psychiatric ward. Let's go see Vince."

"No," stated Sullivan firmly. "There's been a change in plan."

Allister stared back.

"Allister. Can you safely get me downtown without being tagged by the ubiquitous Internet of Things?"

"Maybe? Why? What's downtown? That's quite a mischievous grin across your face, John. Now you're starting to look like your father."

"Well. Can you?"

"Sure I can. But where are we going?"

"Zachary told me to seek out Benjamin Franklin in times of need," said Sullivan as he finished buttoning his shirt. "He may be right." He stepped toward the door and put on a hat. "C'mon. We're heading down to Elfreth's Alley. I've got a crazy hunch about something."

"Oh no, here we go again," declared Brooks as he followed. "You time travelers are all alike. Wait, John." He grabbed a pair of sunglasses from a side table. "Put these on. This is a covert operation."

"Roger, Allister. Thanks."

Allister drove Sullivan downtown, their parking spot just a block away from Elfreth's Alley. They turned the corner onto the historical lane at approximately two o'clock in the afternoon.

"Wow, this alley looks exactly the same," declared Sullivan. "It's probably one of the few constants in America since its inception."

Patriotic flags continued to furl from the majority of historic homes as did some busybody mirrors. Nothing much had changed throughout the lane since the year 2020, except for some odd appearing electric vehicles parked along the curb. Sullivan's heart surged as he approached Major General Arnold's front door, his mind expecting the military governor to defiantly step outside in full military garb. He glanced up at a second floor window, hoping to see Sary.

The two men stopped in front of Franklin's home, its shutters still red.

"What the heck," muttered Sullivan as he read a metal plaque set to the left of the front door. The following words were embossed on the marker:

## THE BENJAMIN FRANKLIN HOME

~~~

Benjamin Franklin resided at this address during the late 1700s. Here he met with the Junto and entertained dignitaries while helping to forge our nation's destiny. Documents discovered inside this home forever changed the course of life for all Americans.

~~~

The West Philadelphia Historical Society
Frederick Mills, President

"Open daily from 10 A.M. to 4 P.M.," read Allister from a small placard above the historical plate. He looked up at the building.

"They've turned it into a museum," stated Sullivan in awe. "Oh my God, Attorney Mills and his gang did it!"

"Did what?" asked Brooks. "This has been a museum for decades."

Sullivan slowly reached forward and opened the door. Just inside the foyer dozed an elderly man seated behind a wooden desk. He wore a United States National Park Service uniform.

"Oh no," gasped Sullivan. "I think I know that man," he whispered. "You better pay." He slid past the desk into a room to his right, immediately enthralled by the treasure trove of Revolutionary War artifacts to include a cannon, Pennsylvania rifles and framed historical documents. As Sullivan continued to meander, he heard the voice of the elderly gentleman collecting payment from Brooks.

"That will be five dollars, young man. Would you like a map?"

"No, thank you," answered Brooks.

"You can take as many photographs as you like, but please don't touch any of the exhibits. The museum is limited to the first and second floor only. They're remodeling the basement. We apologize for this inconvenience."

Brooks joined Sullivan as their self-guided tour progressed through the first floor.

"Allister, this is where I stayed with Ben!" exclaimed Sullivan. "Of course, none of this stuff was here. Over there was the kitchen and down these steps is where the servants lived."

"John, the basement is closed for renovations," whispered Brooks.

"I don't think so," came Sullivan's rebuttal as he detached a crowd control red velvet rope from an upright stanchion. He stepped across the barrier and reattached the rope.

"John, what are you doing?"

Sullivan smiled. "Cover me while I'm downstairs. This is a covert operation. Remember?"

Brooks shook his head in disapproval and looked back down the hallway at the guard, shuffling through some papers.

The basement stood void of any workers and appeared to Sullivan as it did back in 1779. He immediately walked toward a glass covered display full of artifacts including Sary's diary, some dining utensils and her rag doll. The diary was opened to a page from June 5, 1779, the note written in Ben Franklin alphabet. He tried to decipher the entry but could not. Sullivan ran his fingers along the glass edge in search of a latch, but it was secure. He turned toward the bunk beds which were pulled away from the wall. The renovation itself appeared to be centered on the wall behind the beds, where large openings in the foundation were being reinforced. He turned right and headed to the rear of the room. At that point some voices could be heard at the top of the stairwell.

"If he went down there, why can't I?" squealed the high pitch voice of a man. "That's not fair. I paid the same to get in!"

"Nobody is down there," countered the guard. "The basement is closed."

"I saw him go down!"

Sullivan quickly glanced at Snaky, the inlay still visible but covered by a large sheet of thick, laminated safety glass. Heavy bolts in each corner anchored the glass to the floor. A marker to the right of the glass titled the exhibit 'Our Nation's First Political Cartoon'.

"Hello!" shouted the guard from atop the steps. "Is anybody down there? This section is closed."

"I'm going to file a complaint!" howled the unhappy guest.

Sullivan quickly knelt and inspected Snaky. The granite inlay appeared well preserved beneath the glass.

"Hello! If you don't come up I'm calling the police," threatened the sentry. "This section is closed to the general public."

Sullivan stood and walked back up the stairwell. "Oh, I'm sorry," he stated. "I thought the second floor was closed. My apologies."

"I told you he was down there!" whined the man with a house map in hand.

"Sir, this section is closed off!" grumbled the octogenarian as he unlatched the rope barrier. "Didn't you see this rope?"

Sullivan apologized again as he tilted his head downward and sidestepped the government employee.

"I demand access to the basement!" ordered the guest. "I've driven all the way down from Rochester to see this exhibit and your website said nothing about the basement being closed! That's unacceptable."

"Sir, I can only do what I'm told."

"I demand a refund! For Pete's sake there isn't even any parking around this place. I had to walk ten blocks to get here!"

"Sir, I'm sorry," replied the now flustered sentry. "I'm not permitted to give out any refunds."

As the standoff between the guard and ill-tempered guest continued, Sullivan and Brooks slipped out the front door. They turned left and hustled down the lane.

"Are you happy now?" asked Brooks. "You got that old timer in trouble."

Sullivan didn't answer as they approached the parked car.

"You're darn lucky there weren't any security cameras in that house," continued Brooks. "You don't want to end up like Vince. Do you?"

Sullivan remained quiet during the ride back to the Philadelphia General, his mind churning out a plan. Later that evening he sat in Dr. Schmidt's office with Brooks, both men huddled beneath an overhead light.

"Allister, the situation is grim," declared Sullivan. "Think about it. Ben is trapped in the past and we're stuck in the future."

"So the original two keys are lost," recapped Allister. "But, what about Walt's ring? I mean, that can at least jettison you back to colonial times. At least it's a way out."

"Perhaps, but that's no guarantee of a way back to 2020, and it leaves Vince trapped here. My first priority is getting Vince Pagano out of this mess. The only way to get him back home is through the time tunnel in this very office. He has to transport back from this very spot."

"Which requires the key with the R.S. initials."

"Exactly."

"But that key is lost somewhere back in the 1700s."

"Exactly."

"So you're stuck."

"Not exactly."

Allister raised an eyebrow. "Alright then," he said slowly. "Why don't you tell me a way out of this pickle. I don't see any other options."

Sullivan leaned forward as if divulging a secret. "It's a longshot, but here's my plan. Tomorrow, during the March for Mental Health parade in Fairmount Park, we separate Vince from the crowd. Then, all three of us immediately head downtown and hide..."

## CHAPTER TWENTY-TWO
### THE SULLIVAN PLAN
### 2065

The Sullivan Plan commenced the following day at approximately two o'clock in the afternoon. The troupe of psychiatric patients marching in the parade under the charge of Dr. Wolfgang had just passed Boathouse Row, when Vince asked to use the bathroom. Earlier in the day his walking cast was changed to a much lighter ankle brace. An orderly escorted him off the parade route to a row of portable potties lined up in a parking lot behind the Art Museum. Sullivan approached the two as they entered the parking lot.

"Vince Pagano!" shouted Sullivan with his arms spread wide as if surprised to see him.

"Doctor!" shouted Vince in return. "I knew you would come back."

They hugged each other.

"What's going on?" asked the orderly. "Who are you?"

"I'm a time traveler from the future," answered Sullivan. "I've come to take Vincent home."

The orderly laughed. "No way, man. This guy isn't going anywhere." He grabbed Vince by the arm and pulled him forward. "C'mon Vince."

"Wait, sir," continued Sullivan as he stepped up alongside the moving hospital employee. "You don't understand. He's my…"

The aide reflexively held out his arm to keep Sullivan at bay. When their bodies touched, Sullivan stumbled to the ground.

"Oh! My ankle!"

The orderly instinctively released Vince and took a step toward Sullivan.

"Oh, sir. I'm sorry."

Pagano hobbled to his right down a grassy knoll.

"Hey!" shouted the confused orderly as he turned back toward Vince. "Where do you think you're going!"

He began to run after Pagano only to see him hop into a waiting car on the museum roadway. The door shut and the car pulled away. "Vince!" screamed the orderly as the car vanished around a corner. He turned back toward Sullivan only to see him disappear around the row of toilets. "Oh no, man. What the hell?"

Sullivan hopped into the getaway car on the other side of the museum complex. Within a few minutes, Allister dropped both men off at the corner of 2$^{nd}$ Street and Elfreth's Alley.

"Well, good luck you two," said Allister as the two undocumented men bailed out. "My role in this felony is now complete." He handed Sullivan an I.D. card from the Philadelphia General with Dr. Schmidt's face on it.

"Thanks again, Allister," replied Sullivan with a firm handshake. "No offense, but I hope to never see you again."

"No offense taken," countered Brooks with a grin. "But you know where to find me if your plan fails. Tally-ho!"

The car drove away.

Sullivan and Vince hustled to the Benjamin Franklin House. There, at the front door, sat the aged guard. Sullivan stood a bit behind Vince's frame as he paid the entrance fees. For the next hour the two men would occasionally exit and reenter the facility, at times confusing the guard as to their exact whereabouts. Only three other elderly visitors were inside the estate. At ten minutes to four, Sullivan dove underneath an upstairs bed next to a wall and curled up in a ball. Vince exited but then slid back in the front entrance as the guard took a picture with a guest. He too rolled beneath an upstairs bed. At four o'clock an intercom system politely asked all guests to please leave the facility. The sentry then took a final walk through the building before leaving. He dutifully locked the front door with both men inside.

"Mission accomplished," declared Sullivan as he slid out from beneath the bed. "That wasn't too difficult."

"Well, they don't have the cream of the crop guarding this place," laughed Vince. He brushed some dust off his frame. "Now, where's this snake you were talking about?"

Sullivan led Pagano into the basement.

"Here. Beneath the glass," said Sullivan while pointing at Snaky.

"This is it, John? Our ticket back to 2020?"

"Perhaps," replied Sullivan as he knelt down. "Help me get this glass off."

Both men pulled, kicked and yanked the glass cover to no avail.

"It won't budge," gasped Vince as he looked around the room. "We're going to have to smash it with something."

"But what?"

Each man began to search the subterranean confines for an appropriate weapon. Pagano inspected the tools used by the remodeling team as Sullivan explored an unfinished portion of the basement used by a handyman and groundskeeping team.

"I've got a shovel!" hollered Sullivan.

"I've got a sledgehammer," shouted Pagano.

"Oh," said Sullivan as he circled back. "You win."

"Back away from the glass," warned Vince as he spit into both hands and rubbed them together. He took hold of the sledgehammer and raised it over his right shoulder.

"Careful now."

Pagano drove the head of the mallet into the center of the protective glass. The impact shattered the shield into hundreds of pieces but a safety layer of plastic film did not allow any shards to fly away.

"Bullseye," quipped Sullivan.

"Nice," quipped Vince as he leaned the hammer head on the cracked glass. "Now what?"

Sullivan stepped forward with his spade and began to split the glass into several quadrants. The vandals carefully lifted off each sheet of broken glass. Sullivan leaned down and wiped away some dirt from the historic artifact.

"It's perfectly preserved," he whispered.

"Alright. What next?" asked Vince.

"Back in that rough basement, get me a trowel."

"Right."

Sullivan blew away some remaining dirt lodged between each granite slab. Slowly he ran his fingers across the block beneath the letter 'P', recalling the voice of Franklin saying, "Pennsylvania is the Keystone State, John. Never forget that. The key." He tried to wedge his fingernails between the segments of snake.

"Here you go," said Vince as he returned with the trowel. "That little nook back there is packed with just about everything."

"It smells from fertilizer," added Sullivan as he took hold of the tool. The physician carefully began to scrape away the dirt surrounding the Pennsylvania block. "There," he said after creating a circumferential trough. "Let's lift this up."

With Pagano's help they were able to rock the boulder back and forth and lift it to one side.

"That stone is heavy," moaned Vince as he wiped the dirt from his hand.

Sullivan looked at his partner in crime. He took a deep breath before saying, "This is it, Vince. Say your prayers." He placed his hand down the dark hole.

"What?" said Vince as Sullivan slowly moved his hand around in the chamber. "Is it in there? Please tell me it is."

"Ahhh!" screamed Sullivan as he quickly brought up a hunk of fur up from the trench. "A raccoon!" He wiggled the brown pelt in front of Pagano's face.

Pagano screeched and rolled on his back away from the dig site. He grabbed the shovel as Sullivan began to laugh. "What?" asked the surgeon in a defensive posture. "What is it?"

"It's a hat!"

"A hat?"

"Yea. A hat."

"Are you crazy?" laughed Vince. "You scared the hell out of me." He put the spade down.

Sullivan placed the cover atop his head. "It was Ben's favorite. He wore it over in France to impress all the women."

"I wonder how that went?"

"Pretty well, I think." Sullivan took off the aged headpiece and brushed flat some of its hairs with a hand. "It held up well over the years."

"C'mon, keep digging," ordered Pagano. "This is serious stuff."

Sullivan again reached in and brought out a handful of coins. Next followed a few medals, a gaudy medallion and a somewhat dry rotted book that he brought into the light.

"*Poor Richard's Almanac, Special Collector's Edition*," he read.

"1780. Is that what it says beneath the title?" asked Vince.

"Yes." Sullivan slowly fanned through the aged pages as if expecting something to drop out. "But unfortunately there's nothing inside."

"That's it?" whined Vince as he sat onto the ground. "There's nothing else in that chamber?"

Sullivan lowered his hand back in. Slowly he ran his fingertips through and around all the edges of the granite vault. It was empty. He dropped his head down to the basement floor and remained silent.

"It's over," whimpered Pagano. "We're burnt toast."

"It was only a hunch," replied Sullivan as he brought his reddened face upright. He sighed. "Only a hunch."

Both men sat in silence for some time until Vince spoke.

"Let's get out of this rathole, John. Readmit me to the psych floor. I'll be happy there."

# A TWIST OF TIME

Slowly the distraught physicians began to return the artifacts back to the cavity. They then took hold of the granite cover block and began to hoist it into the air.

"Hey, what's that?" asked Vince.

"What?" groaned Sullivan as he held his portion of the rock in midair.

"That!" exclaimed Pagano with his eyes locked to the ground. "Something fell off from beneath this hunk of stone! It was stuck to the bottom."

Sullivan looked over to see a brown envelope on the ground. "Put the granite down," he ordered. Quickly he grasped the envelope.

"What in the world?" muttered Sullivan as he brought it into the light. Across the outside of the packet ran the writing, *"The Used Key is Always Bright"*. Sullivan's heart began to pound.

"Open it!" ordered Vince. "Open it and let's go home!"

Sullivan carefully ripped open the narrow side of the envelope and pulled out a folded piece of paper. In Ben's characteristic handwriting it read, "J.S. I hope this note finds you well. Anthony and Mario located the keys! I pray they come in handy. Do stop by if you have time. Bon voyage old friend. B. Franklin, printer." Sullivan tilted the envelope to one side and out slid two skeleton keys.

"Yes!" screamed Sullivan as his hands trembled. He looked to the sky. "Yes! *Thank you, Ben Franklin!*"

Pagano dropped his head into his hands and began to sob. "I don't believe it. Thank you, Jesus. Thank you!"

"We're going home, Vince!" exclaimed Sullivan as he hugged Vince. "We're going home."

They stood up, high fived each other and walked beneath the main overhead light.

"Which one is it?" asked Vince.

Sullivan studied the two trinkets. "Here, the one with R.S. on it." He held the key to Pagano. "See it?"

"I see it."

Sullivan placed the other key back in the envelope along with the note.

"What are you doing, John? Take both of them."

"No. Two keys will twist time and transport us back to 1779. You do not want to go there. I learned that the hard way. It's loaded with disease and despots. Trust me." He folded the envelope to close the top. "Let's get this back in the bin and seal it up."

They returned the second key and the Pennsylvania block to its original position and carefully tried to reconstruct the segments of glass over the snake inlay. Pagano then leaned the sledgehammer on the glass as if it were an accident.

"There, do you think they'll notice?" he laughed.

"It looks like an obvious industrial mishap to me," quipped Sullivan. "Let's go my friend."

They walked upstairs and peered out a front window.

"Ah John, there are a lot of people out there. We may want to wait a bit."

"I agree. We've come too far to blow it now. Let's stay put until after sunset."

"Roger."

Both men began to wander about the home, Vince ultimately taking a nap and Sullivan mulling over Ben's invitation to return. He calculated the 20:1 ratio in terms of years, realizing that Franklin passed away in the spring of 1790. When basing the computation on a 2020 time schedule, that left him with just over six months to return in time to revisit Ben. If he failed to arrive back in colonial times by then, Ben Franklin would die of natural causes and be placed in his tomb. Yet the problem was, he needed two keys to travel back to the 1700s.

"One step at a time," muttered Sullivan to himself. "Let's get back to 2020 first. Then we'll figure out how to recover the second key again."

The hours passed slowly.

"Let's go," said Vince at about 11 P.M. This place is starting to give me the creeps. It's haunted if you ask me."

They headed to the front door while checking outside for any foot traffic.

"Good to go," said Vince.

Sullivan turned the doorknob but it didn't rotate. He tried again.

"It's locked."

"Well, unlock it," said Vince.

Sullivan inspected the doorknob. There was no inside bolt latch. He scanned the perimeter of the door for any possible locking mechanism.

"Move away. Let me try," snapped Vince. "This isn't rocket science."

The orthopedic surgeon forcefully tried to rotate the knob to no avail. He then began to drive his shoulder into the front door in an attempt to dislodge it.

"I can tell you're an orthopedic surgeon," laughed Sullivan. "I'll check the rear exit."

"This door is like a vault," growled Vince. "I'll tear it off its hinges!"

Sullivan checked the door that led to the backyard, its locking mechanism identical to the front.

"Take it easy, Vince. The neighbors will think there are burglars inside and call the police."

"There are burglars inside!" He let go of the doorknob. "What's going on here, John? We're trapped inside."

Sullivan pointed to a keypad along the side wall. "There must be a code. I saw a similar pad outside."

"The windows," said Vince. "How stupid are we? Let's open a window."

Fine metal security bars covered all the windows on the first and second floor.

"We're in goddamn Fort Knox!" bellowed Pagano. "Trapped like two rats."

"Alright, take it easy, Vince. The place is obviously very secure to protect its contents. Let's think this through."

The doors were locked tight. No basement exit existed and the windows were impenetrable. They checked the third floor for a roof exit but there was none.

"Get me the sledgehammer," ordered Vince. "I'll knock a hole through the wall."

"Are you crazy? The neighbors will hear you." Sullivan walked over to a wall and inspected a fire alarm.

"Are you crazy?" countered Vince. "If you pull that alarm this place will be swarming with firemen and police in an instant. We'll be arrested and incarcerated."

"But it might emergently open the doors," postulated Sullivan as he read the standard written instructions around the alarm.

"Too risky. Don't do it. *Do not* pull the alarm."

"So we're stuck?" asked Sullivan. "At the mercy of a guard or park employee that opens the door tomorrow morning? Who knows what they'll do when they see two transients in their museum."

They sat down in the room adjacent the entrance foyer, dejected.

"So much for the Sullivan plan," scoffed Vince.

"Wait a minute," said Sullivan slowly as he looked around the room. "Wait a minute!"

"What?"

"I've got an idea. If only I could find..." He stood up and hurried down the basement stairwell while talking to himself. Several minutes later he reappeared with a green plastic bag in one hand and a box in the other.

"What's going on?" asked Vince.

"Vince. Have you ever fired a cannon before?"

"What?"

"A cannon? Like this bad boy to your right?" He pointed to the howitzer next to Pagano.

Pagano stood in disbelief. "You've lost your marbles, John."

"No I haven't." He placed the material goods down and defiantly walked behind the three pound galloper parked in the back corner of the room on a slant. Sullivan lowered his head behind the barrel sight. "It's taking aim right at the front door. How convenient is that?"

"John. You're going to fire a cannon to get us out of here? Are you insane?"

"Nope. We blow the door open and run. It couldn't be easier. Ten minutes later the police arrive trying to figure out why an antique cannon discharged in the middle of the night."

"That thing isn't loaded," argued Pagano. "I'm sure of that."

Sullivan pointed to the pyramid of cannonballs to the left of the artillery.

"What about the dynamite or whatever you need to fire it?"

"Gunpowder, Vince. Gunpowder fires a cannon." He walked over to a fireplace in the room. "Do you know how important gunpowder was to the Continental Army during the Revolutionary War?"

"No. I don't. I'm not a history buff."

"They stored it in the churches for protection," continued Sullivan. "The French made the best gunpowder, too."

"Well, I don't see any church nearby... or Frenchmen."

"Black powder is composed of three simple elements, Vince. Do you know what they are?"

"Uh, no... I'm not a gunpowder expert."

"True... but your ancestors were and they taught me well." Sullivan knelt in front of the fireplace. He took hold of a hearth shovel and scooped some residue out from beneath a metal log grate. "The first ingredient is charcoal." He dumped the black ash into a pewter bowl to the right of the fire pit.

Pagano sat in silence, still in utter disbelief of the plan.

"The second is sulfur," continued Sullivan as he lifted the bowl of ash off the hearth. "Fortunately that rough basement downstairs is chock-full of gardening supplies for the backyard. "I found some sulfur fertilizer and the most important ingredient of all." He lifted up the carboard box.

"Stump remover," laughed Pagano. "You're going to fire the cannon with stump remover? Hah!"

"No. Saltpeter or potassium nitrate. It's what stump remover is made of." Sullivan kicked the pewter bowl toward Pagano. "Start grinding that charcoal down, Vince. I need some fine powder."

Pagano complied and the two physicians went to work.

"The ratio is 75% saltpeter, 15% charcoal and 10% sulfur," instructed Sullivan as he mixed the two fertilizers. Vince handed him the ground down charcoal. "It's absolutely safe until I mix in this charcoal." After measuring out an approximate 15% load of charcoal dust, he carefully combined it with the other ingredients. "There," he whispered. "Ready to go. Do not sneeze." He stood and poured the powdery mixture into the open end of the cannon's muzzle.

"I still think you're nuts," opined Pagano.

Sullivan took a wooden rammer and gently coaxed the gunpowder down the barrel.

"Vince. Load a cannonball."

Pagano lifted one of the black orbs from the stack and rolled it down the cannon bore. Sullivan again jammed it down to the base.

"Now what?"

"Well, we don't have a fuse so I guess I'll just pour the black powder down the priming hole." Sullivan began to gently sprinkle some gunpowder down a primer hole at the base of the cannon. He reached back and peeled a strip of birch bark off a log and stuffed it into the hole. "This will have to do."

"Are you sure you know what you're doing?"

"An old orthopedic friend of mine once said, 'this isn't rocket science'. Now stand back," ordered Sullivan. He reached for a box of matches on the fireplace mantle.

"God save us all," announced Pagano as he took several steps back and placed a finger in each ear.

Sullivan lit the wooden match, lifted his opposite hand straight in the air. "Ready to fire," he declared. Slowly he brought the match to the wood shaving and lit it. "*Fire!*" he yelled while covering his ears.

The flame struggled and then went out.

"Hah," laughed Pagano.

Sullivan lit another match and repeated the sequence. "*Fire!*" This time the birch bark smoked and glowed fire red before going out.

"Well, you're certainly no Frenchman," scoffed Pagano. "It's a good thing the British aren't … "

"*KABOOM!*" roared the cannon with a fiery muzzle blast.

The ensuing concussion knocked Sullivan to the ground and blew the front door completely off its hinges, the projectile embedding itself in a parked car just outside. Whitish smoke and the smell of sulfur filled the room as did a cacophony of car alarms and barking dogs outside.

Pagano hoisted Sullivan to his feet. "Are you alright?" he yelled.

"Yea! But my ears are ringing!" Sullivan looked ahead. "We did it!"

"Let's get out of here!"

Both men charged out the front door and turned right, their escape route silhouetted by household lights switching on in the alley. After turning the corner the sound of sirens could be heard in the distance.

The following morning the Internet of Things mapped out the bizarre trek of two undocumented vandals roaming the streets of Philadelphia. They ran down a subway entrance and took the Market Street Line to 34th Street. There they disembarked and subsequently entered the Pagano Orthopedic Institute via a side entrance by using a deceased physician's swipe card. The two fugitives worked their way into to the basement office of Dr. Zachary Schmidt, never to be seen again.

## CHAPTER TWENTY-THREE
### FUGUE STATE
### 2020

"So, in summary, from a cognitive standpoint, Dr. Vincent Pagano suffered from a classic dissociative disorder called a fugue state," professed Dr. Sullivan. He paused to allow time for the crowd to digest the medical jargon. Before him stood a slew of family members, colleagues, reporters and cameras. They were gathered together in a meeting room located within the Sullivan Institute. The words 'Recall, Respect and Rejuvenate' were emblazoned across the front of his podium. "Are there any questions at this point?"

A reporter in the third row raised her hand. "So, if I understand this correctly, a fugue state is some sort of a concussion? True?"

"The etiology of a fugue state can be varied," replied the physician. "With a concussion being one of the reasons. So, in this specific case, yes. Dr. Pagano sustained a definite closed head injury during the explosion that brought down the Franklin Wing. This head trauma immediately flipped his brain into a state of fugue."

"And that's what caused his memory loss?"

"Absolutely. Dr. Pagano has no recall of the event. He subsequently suffered retrograde amnesia for several months after the blast."

"But how did he make it out of the basement undetected?"

"I can't answer that. We know that he must have been thrown to the ground. Remember, the man suffered a broken ankle during the event. Otherwise, the cameras inside the Franklin Wing basement failed to provide any additional details regarding his escape route."

"And then he decided to travel to the West coast under a fictitious name?" asked another reporter in a somewhat incredulous tone. "To the town of…" He looked at a paper in his hand. "Livermore, California. Is that what you're asking us to believe?"

"Yes. When a patient's brain is affected by a fugue, three things commonly occur. The first is significant distress or impairment. The second is confusion about your own identity or, which happened in this case, the assumption of a new identity. And the last believe it or not, is sudden, unexpected travel away from home or one's customary place of work. These three components are contained within the strict definition of a fugue state per the Diagnostic and Statistical Manual of Mental Disorders." Sullivan smiled as he glanced at Vince seated by his side. "It's a rather bizarre but well recognized psychiatric diagnosis."

"So, how did you become aware of Dr. Pagano living under an alias in California?"

"That's a good question," said Sullivan. "Out in the Silicon Valley they're starting to perfect the so-called Internet of Things or IoT, which as you know assimilates a multitude of data from inanimate objects. The IoT also utilizes facial recognition and that's what picked up a Dr. Vincent Pagano living in Livermore. The authorities out West contacted me and I immediately flew out to investigate."

"Why did it take you so long to bring him back?"

"I had to let the disease run its course," replied Sullivan. "A fugue can last for a few days or several months. During this time period a practitioner must be careful not to retraumatize the patient. I cautiously monitored his progress from afar under the premise that a full and rapid recovery is the norm."

"Can it happen again?" asked the reporter while looking at Vince. "Is Dr. Pagano at risk of vanishing in the future?"

"Fortunately, it's rare for the disease to recur. An individual usually has only one lifetime episode." Sullivan paused and scanned the crowd. "Are there any other questions? If not, I'm going to turn the podium over to Dr. Pagano." He stepped back and looked at the surgeon. "Vince, it's all yours. Welcome home. We missed you."

As Pagano stepped to the podium a round of spontaneous applause filled the theatre. He waved in appreciation and pointed at his family and fiancée seated in the front row, having personally reunited with them several days earlier. The devilish Pagano grin flashed across his face.

"Boy, it's darn good to be back home," started off Vince. His opening remark sparked another round of applause. Over the next few minutes he thanked everyone involved with his mental rescue effort, including Dr. Sullivan and the entire staff at the Sullivan Institute. He spoke of how puzzling it felt to emerge from a fugue state. "I took a job at a winery out in Livermore," he recounted. "One of the worker's broke his wrist and everyone was amazed as to my knowledge of the injury. That's what triggered the beginning of my recovery process." He spoke of second chances in life and the absolute joy of being able to see his family again. Lastly, he spoke of the emotional reconnect with his father, who up until that point was haunted by the death of his son.

"Are they going to take down your memorial plaque in the Pagano Institute lobby?" asked another reporter.

"No," replied Vince. "I've requested to keep it there as a constant reminder. From this point forward I'm going to live each day as if it's my last. In the immortal words of a famous Philadelphian, 'lost time is never found again.'" He raised a hand again to the crowd. "Thank you everyone and thank you Dr. John Sullivan for bringing me back home where I belong. God bless you all."

A final round of applause erupted as Vince left the stage. A wine and cheese social followed in the lobby. During the reception, Dr.

Sullivan met with members of the Historical Society for the first time since his return.

"We thought you were dead," declared Burt with a wad of cheese in his mouth. "You missed three meetings. That's grounds for membership suspension."

"I'm sorry, Burt. I got the call and immediately headed out West. My number one priority was Dr. Pagano." Sullivan turned toward Attorney Mills. "How's it going with the research project on Elfreth's Alley?"

"Rotten," snapped Mills. "Zuckerman sold the place."

"He what?"

"He sold the place, but the transaction is hung up in red tape," clarified Mills as he swiped some hors d'oeuvres from a passing waiter. "Hey, salami on a cracker!"

"Wait a minute. Back up," ordered Sullivan. "Barry Zuckerman sold his house. To who?"

"Ah, I can't recall his name. But the guy turned out to be a real horse's ass." He paused to swallow the cracker. "Sad though. We were just starting to gain traction on the project. Wally and I found this goofy clock in the house containing a note written by Ben Franklin himself. In the memo he spoke of a secret hiding spot in the home." Mills took a slug of wine. "Can you imagine that?"

Sullivan's mind seized up.

"Zuckerman is absolutely distraught over the whole event," continued the attorney. "A classic case of seller's remorse. In fact, the worst I've ever seen. Can you envision a new owner finding some sort of secret bin jammed with Ben Franklin artifacts? It's like hitting a jackpot of historical proportions."

"So, let's go search the house," recommended Sullivan. "We'll find whatever hiding spot Franklin was talking about before the keys change hands."

"We did. Multiple times. We combed the place high and low but couldn't find anything."

"So, let's do it again," pleaded Sullivan. "*Right now*. Today."

"No can do. Zuckerman is out of the country and the place is locked tight."

Sullivan paused to reset his thought process. "Fred, what do you mean by the transaction getting hung up in red tape? Is the house officially sold from a strict legal standpoint?"

"Well, no. The deed hasn't been transferred but both parties signed a home purchase agreement, John. Which in legalese is just as good as being sold. That's the kicker. Once Zuckerman changed his mind I tried every trick in the book to put the kibosh on the transaction."

"And?"

"It's hard for a seller to renege on a purchase agreement without significant repercussions. First I respectfully asked the buyer that we mutually nullify the deal on an amicable basis, but that failed. We then offered a rather generous cancellation fee, to no avail. Then I tried a bit of legal maneuvering with regards to the purchase price involving historical artifacts of previously unrecognized value. I demanded that two separate appraisers chime in on the sale price."

"Did that work?"

"Legally, no. But it did infuriate the buyer. He ended up suing us in court. So the whole mess is tied up in litigation for who knows how long." He wiped some mustard off his lapel. "It's turning into a legal fistfight, John. I'm thinking of getting my litigator friend from Scranton involved. The guy's a bulldog."

A combination of shock and disbelief struck Sullivan silent.

Attorney Mills craned his neck over the crowd. "Where's the waiter with the shrimp tray?"

"He's been ignoring us all afternoon," chimed in Burt. "Just like the wine guy. What kind of a food service did you hire here, John?"

Mills waved his hand in the air to signal a waiter. He stood on his toes and snapped his fingers in the process.

"Fred. Listen to me. Where's Zuckerman?"

"Italy for a week. On vacation." He continued to wave. "He sees me. I know it."

"So, who has the keys to his house?"

"They're in a legal escrow box at a neutral party's office, along with the deed. The place is locked up tight per a district judge. The case is in legal no-man's land until further notice."

"So, the house is empty?"

"Of people, yes. Zuckerman flew out of town this morning. Of revolutionary war artifacts, no. Nothing has been moved out of the house."

Sullivan's mind began to churn.

"Here he comes!" announced Burt. "Finally."

Sullivan stood silent as his colleagues swarmed the waiter and gorged themselves on shrimp cocktail. He restarted the conversation only after they began to lick their fingertips clean.

"Gentlemen, I need to get in that house before it changes hands," pleaded Sullivan. "Please understand. You have to help me."

"Bookman!" exclaimed Mills suddenly. "That's the buyers name." He hoisted a finger in the air. "Albatross Bookman." He grinned.

"Bookman?" asked Sullivan aghast. "Did you just say, *Bookman*?"

"You bet. It took a while to come to the surface. Must be the wine."

"Alabaster Bookman?"

"Alabama... Alabaster," muttered Mills. "Whatever. That first name is a real doozy. I spelled it wrong on a few forms already."

"Alabaster Bookman is Barry Zuckerman's neighbor," declared Sullivan. "The professor who smokes the pipe. The guy who refused to come and talk to the society."

"The highfalutin guy that interrupted our parade in Zuckerman's home?" asked Mills.

"Yea. That's him. Why would Barry want to sell his house to his smug neighbor? He certainly didn't speak highly of the man."

"John, if there's one thing I've learned in the legal profession it's that money talks. Bookman's money is green, just like everyone else's. He offered Zuckerman a pretty penny for that place, way over market value according to everyone involved in the matter. He really wants all that Civil War stuff if you ask me."

"Revolutionary War," corrected Sullivan as his innards began to stew. "Something's not right", he whispered to himself. "Bookman knows something that we don't." Paranoia began to set in. "Why does he want his neighbor's house bad enough to sue him?"

"Hey, they're bringing out more shrimp!" blurted out Burt. "I promised Wally I'd bring him home a goody bag."

"We better track that guy down," announced Mills with a check of his watch. "This shindig is over in twenty minutes. That might be the last tray."

"Where's Wally?" asked Sullivan.

"Home. His prostate is acting up."

"Fred, you grab the shrimp and I'll swipe a few blocks of cheese," ordered Burt. "We can't let old Wally down."

The two members of the historical society quickly set out on their mission.

Sullivan spoke to a few more guests but really didn't hear what they had to say. With attorneys involved he knew the Zuckerman affair could easily take upwards of a year to resolve. Ben would certainly be dead by then. He had to get back into the house as soon as possible. He needed the second key to transport back in time. Somehow, he had to take charge of the impasse.

That night, just before sunset, Sullivan decided to take a walk down to Elfreth's Alley. Humid July air hung heavy over the lane as did the faint bouquet of Cavendish pipe tobacco. Sullivan looked for Bookman amid the occasional tourist and street inhabitant but failed to spot his towering frame. After several strolls up and down the alley he stopped in front of Franklin's home. A 'For Sale' sign out front had the words 'Sale Pending' across it. Slowly he tried to rotate the locked doorknob. He stepped to the right and peered into a front window, thinking of Ben in the past and the cannon blast in the future. He smiled while picturing Pagano's face after they blew the front door off its hinges. Suddenly something moved inside, nothing major, just a subtle stir among still shadows. He brought both hands up to the glass and cupped them to block out the ambient streetlight. The physician continued to stare. Nothing else moved. He reflexively looked up at the busybody mirror upon which the front door of the adjacent Bookman residence opened. Out stepped the academician.

"Good day, sir," bellowed Bookman as he stepped toward Sullivan. "What's brings you out this fine evening?"

"Oh nothing, just getting some fresh air."

The professor stepped closer and squinted downward. "Ah, Dr. Sullivan. Is that you? Fancy seeing you here after so much time."

"Hello, professor. Going for a walk?"

"Ah, yes. I thought it a grand night to take a stroll. Care to join me?"

Sullivan noticed no pipe in the professor's hand. "Sure. Where to?"

"Ah, perhaps to Mr. Franklin's grave? I've been watching the progress on the oak tree stump removal. It's a shame a storm brought that tree down. Those roots are wrapped around little Franky's vault. They're trying desperately not to disturb it."

"Yes. A real shame."

"Shall we go?"

Sullivan peered back into Franklin's home. "Is Mr. Zuckerman home?"

"I don't know," came the terse reply. "Perhaps."

"I see. Someone said he may be over in Italy."

Bookman didn't reply but rocked anxiously back and forth on his toes.

"Do you know if he was planning to travel to Europe?"

"No. I'm unaware of Mr. Zuckerman's travel plans. I do know he is planning to relocate permanently to Florida." He gasped. "What a dreadful state, full of reptiles and ghastly mosquitos."

Sullivan smelled a rat. No pipe. No knowledge of Zuckerman being out of town and some movement inside. He decided to take the bait. "Sure. I'll go for a walk. Thanks for the offer."

Both men began a slow and congenial stroll away from Franklin's home.

"Congratulations on your home being recognized as the official Benjamin Franklin residence," said Sullivan as he glanced at the plaque mounted on the exterior wall. "That's quite an honor."

"Thank you, doctor. Being recognized by the National Register of Historic Places is a once in a lifetime event. When I purchased the homestead I had no idea Mr. Franklin lived there."

"What a coincidence. I mean you being an authority on his life. Talk about luck."

Bookman inhaled regally. "I am a strong believer in luck and I find the harder I work the more I have of it."

"Ben Franklin quote?"

"Indubitably. Benjamin at his best."

They neared the end of the lane. Sullivan decided to push the envelope further.

"I hear you're buying the Zuckerman home. Is that true?"

"Yes. Common knowledge."

"Why two homes?"

"There's a treasure trove of historical artifacts in that estate," replied the professor. "As a historian, it's too rich to pass up."

"Another once in a lifetime event?"

"Perhaps," replied Bookman, sensing a touch of sarcasm. "Time will tell."

They turned the corner onto North 2$^{nd}$ Street, heading south.

"Speaking of time. Are you aware the West Philadelphia Historical Society discovered a clock inside Zuckerman's home that contained a hidden note from Ben Franklin himself?"

The revelation stopped Bookman in his tracks. "No. I'm unaware of such a find." Out of habit he brought his right hand toward his mouth as if it held a pipe. He stroked his jaw. "Interesting. May I ask what the note said?"

"Ben spoke of a hidden chamber inside the home. A secret bin."

Bookman remained silent, yet broke eye contact with the physician. The musculature just below his right eye began to flicker.

"Are you aware of such a possibility?" continued Sullivan.

Bookman went to speak but hesitated.

"Because for some strange reason, I think you are aware of such a hidden chamber."

"Well, um..."

"Why would I think such a thing, professor?"

"I have no idea," stammered the educator. He nervously cleared his throat. "Perhaps..."

"Is there someone in Mr. Zuckerman's home?"

Bookman froze.

"Because I could have sworn I just saw some movement inside."

The educator's lips began to quiver as his face turned red. His eyes began to blink rapidly. "Look here, man," stated Bookman. "Are you suggesting some sort of impropriety on my behalf? Because if you are..."

"Answer me," interrupted Sullivan. "Is somebody in Zuckerman's home *right now*?"

"How dare you sully my name?" huffed Bookman as he reached for a cellphone in his pocket. "The audacity!" He tapped the cell screen.

"Oh no you don't!"

The professor brought the phone to his ear.

Sullivan bolted to his left, down a narrow access lane running parallel and behind Elfreth's Alley. He turned left into Zuckerman's backyard, noticing the rear door slightly ajar. Quickly he peered back at Bookman who stood at the corner talking into his cellphone. Sullivan rushed into Zuckerman's home only to encounter a portly man with a cherubic face and bowtie frantically working his way up the basement stairwell. He held the handrail tightly as his frame wobbled right to left in the process. Sweat marks drenched his armpits.

"Hey. What's going on?" shouted Sullivan as the man reached the top of the stairwell. "Who are you?"

The intruder pushed past Sullivan while dropping a narrow chisel on the floor. "Don't touch me!"

"Stop!" shouted Sullivan as the stranger burst out the back door. The thief stumbled to the ground and tore his pants. He quickly got up and scampered in the direction of Bookman.

Sullivan hustled down the stairwell to see a light on and a mallet atop Snaky. Several bricks were lifted off the home's foundation just below the granite inlay, but no granite blocks were removed. Sullivan mustered all of his energy to hoist the Pennsylvania block upward, quickly recovering the necessary key. He shoved the block back in place and ran up the steps. There he met Bookman at the rear entrance.

"What's going on?" shrieked Bookman. "A burglary!"

"You know what's going on!" retorted Sullivan. "I'm calling the police!"

"Wait one minute, doctor! Let's not get hasty!"

Sullivan ignored the educator's pleas and called the Philadelphia police. Upon their arrival at the scene, he recounted the exact sequence of events, sans the recovery of the skeleton key.

The following morning Calvin Stottlemyre and his father, along with an attorney, appeared at the local police precinct. Calvin identified himself as a post-doctorate student at the University under the tutelage of Professor Alabaster Bookman. He confessed to the unlawful breaking and entry that occurred the prior evening on Elfreth's Alley. During his tearful confession he fingered Professor Bookman as the mastermind of the botched burglary, declaring his mentor had personal knowledge of a "once in a lifetime historical find" beneath the basement foundation. Bookman claimed to have learned of the secret bin while reading the diary of a slave girl named Sary.

# CHAPTER TWENTY-FOUR
## THE CONVENTION
## 1787

The first thing Sullivan noticed was the size of the oak tree in the graveyard, now nearly fifteen feet high. Quickly he scanned the burial ground for fresh dirt and new headstones. There were a few but none with the words 'B. Franklin' etched upon them. Looking to his left he spotted the spire of Christ's Church and took several steps in that direction, only to trip and fall over a pair of feet jutting out from behind a grave marker.

"Hey, watch it!" said a man dozing on the ground, his back up against a tombstone.

Sullivan turned back, immediately recognizing the man. "Mario? Mario Pagano? Is that you?"

The man blinked his eyes in an attempt to focus on Sullivan. "Dr. Sullivan? Where did you come from?" He stood up and looked over his shoulder as if to find the answer. "Holy smokes! Where have you been?"

Sullivan stood and shook Pagano's hand. "It's good to see you my friend."

"How long has it been?" asked Pagano. "And what kind of outfit are you wearing? Those aren't breeches."

"Mario. What year is it?"

"Oh, no. Here we go again with the year." He began to concentrate. "Let's see…" He looked up to the sky while extending the digits in his right hand one finger at a time. "I was never good at math." He furrowed his brow. "Why, it's 1787… yep, that's the year." He smiled broadly. "1787."

"Eight years! It's been eight years?"

"You got me and Antonio in a heap of trouble with that little gunpowder caper in the middle of the night. General Arnold tossed both our behinds in prison. He was hopping mad!"

"I want to personally thank you for saving my life."

"Ben dragged out our trial but ultimately accepted a date for us to hang!"

"And… what happened?"

"Arnold all of a sudden turned on General Washington and the colonies. Haven't you heard? The man turned out to be a traitor. A yellow-belly turncoat!" He dipped his face to the right and spit on the ground. "I never liked him. Nobody did."

"So, Ben got the charges dropped?"

"Yes indeed. Good old Mr. Franklin. And we got our jobs back at the church, too."

"Good for you," declared Sullivan emphatically as he put both hands on Mario's shoulders. "I'm happy it turned out well."

"Are you in town for long?"

"Hopefully not this time. I've learned not to overstay my welcome in the 18th century."

Pagano stared back blankly.

"Can you get me to Ben's house?"

"Sure."

Sullivan accompanied Pagano to a horse and wagon hitched at the rear of the church. After snapping the transport forward, Pagano reached over and felt the material of Sullivan's pants.

"Denim jeans," quipped Sullivan. "Mid wash. Slim fit."

The neighborhood looked the same to Sullivan, brimming with patriotic flags furling in front of the tightly packed homes. Horses passed by as did the occasional dog and chicken. Some children played hopscotch in front of a butcher shop hanging cured meats.

"So the war's over?" asked the physician as he took in the surroundings.

Pagano turned to his rider with a cocked eyebrow. "Ah, yea. The war's over. It's been over for a few years." He spit again. "Guess who won?"

Sullivan began to laugh aloud.

"What kind of question is that?" chuckled Pagano. "Where have you been? Outer space?"

Sullivan grinned as he looked down a side street. "Not exactly, but close." The physician turned back to get his bearings. "Hey. Where are you going? Isn't Elfreth's Alley in the opposite direction?"

"Yep."

"So, where are you going?"

Pagano didn't reply as he carefully turned the wagon onto a much larger street. He doffed his hat at two young women standing on the corner.

"Mario. You're going in the wrong direction."

"No, I'm not," came the retort as the wagon turned left beneath a majestic carriage archway. Beyond the arch ran a narrow cobblestone lane toward a large home. "Mr. Franklin moved. He's in the process of selling the old home."

"He what?"

"He built this new home for his whole family. Ben's been living here since coming back from Europe, about two years ago."

As the wagon approached the front entrance, Sullivan took in all the grandeur of the Franklin estate. It stood easily ten times the size of his Elfreth's flat with two large chimneys jutting through the slate roof.

"Whoa, Sammy!" ordered Pagano as the wagon came to a stop. "Here you go, Dr. Sullivan… 322 Market Street. The new home of Mr. Benjamin Franklin."

Sullivan hopped off and bid farewell. He slowly walked up to the front door as two small children burst out into the open air court.

"Grandpa! Grandpa!" one of them yelled. They stopped short upon seeing Sullivan.

A woman appeared at the front door holding an infant. "Yes? May I help you?"

"Hello. Forgive me for the intrusion. I'm looking for Benjamin Franklin. My name is Dr. John Sullivan."

"Hello, doctor," replied the woman with a step forward. She held her child with two hands. "Forgive me for not shaking. I'm Sally Bache, Ben's daughter."

"Ah, a pleasure Mrs. Bache. I'm a friend of your father."

"So is the world, it seems."

"Is he home at the moment?"

"Not yet." She looked over his shoulder. "But here he comes."

Sullivan turned and peered back down the lane. There in the distance rode a figure sitting in an ornate chair perched atop two rows of moving men. Wooden rails running parallel along the inside shoulder of each man held the throne high. Alongside the footmen jogged young boys and girls cheering and waving wildly. As the procession neared, Sullivan easily recognized the stout frame of Franklin.

"Grandpa!" yelled the child again.

"He can't walk very far," explained Sally with a sympathetic smile. "So they carry him back and forth from the state house."

As the troupe neared, Franklin recognized Sullivan. He let out a broad grin and held both hands high in the air. "Hello, John!" he bellowed. "Welcome back to Philadelphia!"

Three burly men stood along each side of Franklin's elevated roost, all wearing identical orange uniforms with the wording 'Walnut Street Prison' stitched upon them. The work gang of incarcerated Philadelphians stopped in front of the home and gently set Franklin down. Several prison guards trailed closely behind.

"My new sedan," boasted Ben as he pushed himself out of the chair. One of the prisoners handed him a cane. He groaned and wobbled forward. "Thank you very much, gentlemen. See you tomorrow morning." He then stepped toward Sullivan. "John, you made it back! Fantastic."

"All because of you," said Sullivan, noting how much Franklin had aged. Both men embraced.

"Grandpa! Grandpa!"

"Hello, my little ones!" shouted Ben as he patted their heads. "John, this is my granddaughter Deborah and she is…"

"Six!" shouted the freckled faced girl, her grin absent two front teeth.

"And this is my grandson Richard who is…"

"Twee," declared the little boy proudly with three fingers in the air.

"And it looks like you already met my Sally."

"And this is little Sarah," added Sally as she tilted the infant toward Sullivan. "She's nine months old."

Franklin beamed with joy as two more children ran out the front door.

"Oh, now there's Louis, he's eight and my darling Eliza. Keep your eye on her, John. She's…" Franklin looked up in the air.

"Ten, father. Eliza is ten."

"Ten. How could I forget?" exclaimed Franklin as he tapped his forehead. "Let's all go inside! You must be exhausted from your travels." He pointed his cane at the house. "Do you like the new home?"

"I love it," replied Sullivan as he stepped inside with the entire Franklin Bache clan. Sally helped her father to the parlor where both men sat down.

"Oh," moaned Franklin as he plopped down into a chair. He wiped beads of sweat from his forehead with a handkerchief. "I'm unfortunately fighting two undefeated enemies, John."

"And who may they be?"

"Father Time and gravity," chuckled Ben. "A lethal one-two punch."

"We all are," echoed the physician as he accepted a glass of iced tea from Sally.

"The Pagano brothers found the keys just after you left," continued Franklin as he took a sip of the icy brew. "Both keys fell out of my pocket and through the slats of their wagon. Fortunately an underboard caught them. They had to dissemble the wagon bed to find them."

"Oh Ben, if only we had them before the duel date. It could have saved all of us a lot of trouble."

"Indeed."

Sullivan explained in full detail his harrowing escape with Mingo and Walt, followed by a recap of events in 2020 and 2065. "How did you know I'd check Snaky in the future?"

"A shot in the dark. It was our only hope of seeing each other again. However, I must admit, I am appalled by the actions of Professor Bookman. We had our differences, but I considered him an honorable academician. It goes to show you that many foxes grow gray, but few grow good."

"And General Arnold? He met his ultimate fate?"

"Right on schedule," reported Franklin. "Our actions failed to alter his deplorable act of treason and ultimate place in history. To my understanding he is living in disgrace somewhere in England. General Washington took it the hardest. He fully trusted the man."

"And what about…"

"We have another guest," announced Sally as she entered the room.

Behind her strolled Dr. Casey. "Hello! Hello!" He glanced at Sullivan. "Dr. Sullivan! A pleasure to see you again! When did you arrive back in town?"

"Just about an hour ago." Sullivan held up both keys attached to a tungsten steel chain welded tight. "They're not leaving my body this time."

"No doubt." Casey stepped up to his patient. "And how are you, Benjamin? How's the breathing?"

"Not bad for a man of eighty-one years," boasted Franklin. He cleared his throat. "Considering how many terrible diseases the human body is susceptible to, I find comfort that only three incurable ones have fallen upon me… that being the gout, bladder stones and old age."

"Very well said," replied Casey as he placed the palm of his hand on Franklin's chest. "Now, take a deep breath."

Franklin did and began to cough.

"Have you been using the milk of sow thistle that I brought over?"

"Sure I have. The cat really likes it," chuckled Franklin. "Her fur never looked better."

Casey smirked and reached down to press a thumb into Franklin's calf. Upon lifting his finger a deep indentation remained in the skin. "Your dropsy is returning again, Ben. What's going on?"

"I'm dying, gentlemen. It's been a good run considering the average male in the colonies lives to the age of forty-four."

"That's why I returned," interrupted Sullivan. "Let's get you back to 2065 for a medical tune up. Remember, this all started when we tried to go see your cardiologist?"

"No!" replied the octogenarian with a defiant shake of his cane. "There's too much going on in town right now! I've unfinished work to accomplish. Remember John, this is my second bite at the apple."

"Your health is your number one priority," declared Sullivan. "We'll get you back soon."

"I can't let the people down! Not now."

Both physicians stared back at the luminary, realizing they were powerless to change his decision.

"Let me explain the current situation," requested Ben. "Please, listen."

Over the next several minutes Franklin enthusiastically described a convention currently underway in the city, its goal to modify the Articles of Confederation previously adopted in 1777. The meeting began on May 25$^{th}$ when enough delegates arrived in Philadelphia to reach a quorum of seven states. The problem at hand centered upon a bankrupt central government lacking the necessary coercive powers to regulate commerce, levy taxes and fund the military. No monies were available to pay soldiers or repay foreign loans granted to support the war effort.

"We won the war but the European nations consider us a 'second-rate' republic," bemoaned Franklin. "So we elected George Washington as president of the convention and our first rule of business was to make all deliberations secretive."

He then spoke of strong willed men such as Hamilton, Madison and Morris debating a multitude of issues and proposed remedies including the Virginia and New Jersey Plans, along with the Connecticut Compromise.

"We're trying to strike a delicate balance between liberty and authority," added Franklin with a raised finger. "A very fine line indeed. Not everyone is happy we're here. Rhode Island boycotted the event, fearful of a powerful federal government, and even Patrick Henry snubbed us by stating he "smelt a rat in Philadelphia, tending toward the monarchy.'" He leaned forward and whispered. "But most of us are glad John Adams didn't show. The man can be a bit of a prig."

Both physicians smiled at the declaration.

Franklin finished up by disclosing a myriad of additional matters on the table to include congressional representation, executive power, the Bill of Rights and how to elect a president. He took a deep breath. "So you see, gentlemen. There's a lot at stake here in Philadelphia. It would be remiss of me to leave 1787 at the current time. One might even say… unpatriotic. I can't let that happen." Franklin leaned back in the chair. "Any comments?"

"He's staying," declared Dr. Casey to Sullivan.

"Yes. I concur with your assessment," added Sullivan as he stood. "But Ben, you need to restart the digitalis tea and salad that I recommended. Your heart needs a boost to keep the good humors flowing. Especially in this hot, humid weather. And stay away from the salt and dessert cookies. Understand?"

"Surely I do. I'll start your recommended regimen tomorrow." He stood up. "Now if you'll excuse me, it's time for my nap. I'll see you two for dinner this evening." He stepped away but turned back. "Gentlemen, what I just told you stays within the four corners of this room. Let's not spoil the future."

Later that evening Sullivan sat alone with Franklin in an open air atrium outside his home, beneath a mulberry tree. Some tree crickets chirped overhead as an oppressive heat bore down on the men below. A cat curled up in a ball sat to the right of Franklin's feet.

"Emotions are running high in the state house," declared Ben. "This wretched heat is starting to wear everyone down. I fear a perfect solution will never be reached."

Sullivan sat silent.

"Time is running out, John. Mason drew up a Bill of Rights to safeguard individual liberty, but it will never be adopted. Our failure to do so will be the biggest criticism of this convention. Everyone is exhausted. Discourse has been going on for three months." He sighed. "It's due time to compromise."

Some prolonged silence ensued before Sullivan spoke.

"Ben. Where's Sary?"

Franklin paused for some time before answering. "Slavery is the proverbial elephant in the Pennsylvania State House, John. It's driving a stake between the North and South. For everything that Washington and I agree upon, we couldn't disagree more than on the issue of slavery." A look of forlorn appeared on his face as he continued. "There are about 300 slaves working at his Mount Vernon estate. George is known to be a fair but demanding owner." He sighed. "Thomas Jefferson has over 600 under his charge and agriculture in the South is about to boom with the production of cotton." Franklin paused to ponder the impasse. "Washington and I are going to miss a golden opportunity here, John. It appears that the word "slave" won't even be mentioned in the final draft of our nation's most seminal document… the Constitution of the United States."

"Sad," replied Sullivan. "Perhaps you need to take the point?"

"On the slavery issue, I cannot. At least on the national stage. It's too hot a topic. I'm going to have to leave that up to a man named Lincoln, but he has yet to be born."

"But what about your self-proclaimed second chance, Ben? Your second bite at the apple? Remember, the twist of time that brought you back?"

"A tricky subject with the grandfather paradox in play. I cannot change what's about to happen from now until modern times. The Civil War must take place, John. I cannot remedy the slavery issue. I'm sorry."

"Ben. Where's Sary?"

Franklin didn't answer.

"Please tell me."

"After Benedict Arnold's diabolical plot was uncovered, Washington took immediate custody of all his possessions."

"Including Sary?"

"Yes. Including Sary. She moved to his Philadelphia estate on Sixth and Market Street."

"Is she there now?"

"I don't know, John."

"Why not?"

"For years I kept track of her but Washington has recently recognized that slavery is becoming unpopular in Philadelphia. So he started rotating his slaves back and forth from Virginia in order to abide by state laws on the subject. He changes his staff every six months."

Sullivan stared downward.

"Sary disappeared about two years ago. I have to assume to his Mount Vernon estate." Franklin looked at his friend. "I'm sorry,

John. I tried my best. Unfortunately, all of my connections in Virginia are dying off."

Sullivan inhaled deeply and let out a slow gasp.

"I have failed you, my friend. There is nothing more that can be done."

Sullivan took some time to gather his emotions as a bitter distaste brewed in his soul. "No, Ben. For once you may be wrong. There is one final option."

Ben looked at him but remained silent.

"I'll ask General Washington himself," spouted Sullivan. "He must know where Sary is."

"John, I don't recommend that," shot back Franklin. "George is at his wit's end. All this haggling has worn the man down. I've never seen him so petulant. Bad idea, John. Forget about it."

"Nope," countered Sullivan boldly. "Washington owes me one. The man spun my private comments about Arnold back at me. It could have cost me my life."

"John, he may not even remember that discussion."

"I'll remind him of our conversation in the hospital. He asked for my opinion of the man, which in hindsight was spot on."

"John, bringing up the words 'Benedict Arnold' in George Washington's presence would be tantamount to social suicide. Don't do it. Please," pleaded Franklin. "I'm sure Sary is fine. She's a very resilient young woman."

"Can you get me a private audience with the man?"

"No. I won't be a part of this." Franklin stood up to leave.

"Ben! You have to do it! Sary's counting on us."

Franklin scowled.

"She saved my life, Ben!"

Franklin still wouldn't agree.

"Very well, I'll get to Washington one way or the other, with or without your help. I hope you understand."

"You won't get near him without my help."

"So help me, Ben. I just need to know that she's OK. Once I hear that, my heart will be at rest. Until then, I'll be in turmoil. I couldn't bear leaving without knowing she's safe, especially after we failed to protect her from Arnold."

Franklin was tired and the hour late. He shook his head in disgust. "Well," he moaned. "I do appreciate your enthusiasm. A right heart exceeds all."

"So, you'll do it?"

"Yes. I'll do it, John. Under two conditions."

"What's that?"

"Don't mention the name Benedict Arnold."

"Easy enough. What's the other?"

"Do not mention the word slavery."

# CHAPTER TWENTY-FIVE
## MASON'S DISSENT
### 1787

The signing of the United States Constitution occurred inside the Pennsylvania State House on September 17, 1787. Just prior to the event, Franklin stood to address his peers.

"I confess that there are several parts of the Constitution which I do not at present approve, but I am not sure I shall never approve them: For having lived long, I have experienced many instances of being obliged by better information or fuller consideration, to change opinions even on important subjects, which I once thought right, but found to be otherwise. It is therefore that the older I grow, the more apt I am to doubt my own judgement, and to pay more respect to the judgement of others."

Applause interrupted the words of the sage, nearly twice the age of the average delegate. Franklin raised his hand forward and continued to speak.

"Thus I consent, Sir, to this Constitution because I expect no better, and because I am not sure, that it is not the best. The opinions I have had of its errors, I sacrifice to the public good. I have never whispered a syllable of them abroad. Within these walls they were born, and here they shall die."

More applause.

He slowly scanned the faces in the room before finishing. "On the whole, Sir, I cannot help expressing a wish that every member of the Convention who may still have objections to it, would with me, on this occasion doubt a little of his own infallibility – and to make manifest our unanimity, put his name to this instrument!"

A standing ovation followed the speech as George Washington first stepped forward to sign the historic document, followed by Franklin with tears in his eyes. The infirmed octogenarian needed help to steady his hand in the process. Thirty-seven additional delegates followed suit to ink their signatures on the four most powerful pages of America's history.

"We did it!" howled Franklin as he entered his Market Street home. "We the People of the United States, in Order to form a more perfect Union, establish Justice, ensure domestic Tranquility, provide for common defense, promote the general Welfare, and secure the Blessings of Liberty…"

Before he could finish a seismic wave of grandchildren crashed into his frame.

"Hurray!" went the unified cry.

"…do ordain and establish this Constitution for the United States of America!" bellowed Franklin. He bent down to hug the brood.

Sally gave her father a kiss and led him to the parlor.

"Oh Sally, we finally got it done! The art of compromise at its finest. I couldn't be happier."

"Congratulations."

"A woman just outside the State House just asked me, 'What have you given us, Mr. Franklin?'. I said… A republic, Madam, if you can keep it!" He laughed heartily. "What a memorable reply. How glorious!"

"I'm so proud of you. Now you can rest. Let me get you some tea and a biscuit."

"Where's John?" asked Franklin. "I've something marvelous to tell him."

"He's out for a walk, but I'm sure the news will spread quickly. He'll be back soon." Sally left to prepare his tea.

Sullivan found Franklin sitting out back beneath the mulberry tree, sipping his brew. He peacefully stared up at some clouds in the sky as a bird in a hedgerow sang a song. The physician paused for several seconds before interrupting the tranquil moment.

"Ben. Congratulations!"

"Ah, John. Come sit here my friend. I've some fabulous news for you."

"What can be grander than the news I've just heard? The nation has a new government! They're celebrating in the streets." Sullivan sat at his side.

"First off, I apologize for not arranging your meeting with Washington earlier. I hope you understand. More pressing issues dominated our collective thought process."

"I fully understand."

"Two nights from now, George and Martha Washington are hosting a gala dinner in celebration of the convention coming to a close." Franklin glowed as he broke the news.

"And?"

"And you, Dr. Sullivan… are invited!"

"Oh, Ben! Thank you. I knew you'd come through. Did General Washington remember me?"

"Well. Ahem. I actually didn't mention your name."

"But… how am I invited then?"

"Washington gave me carte blanche to bring whomever I wish. And you my friend, are therefore on the guest list."

A rush of emotions ran through Sullivan, not only at the opportunity to meet the founding fathers of the nation, but a chance to bring closure to Sary's whereabouts. Everything was falling into place. He wanted to reach out and hug Ben.

"You know what?" asked Franklin as if suddenly struck by an idea. "I've a hankering for a pint of beer. How strange is that?"

"Ben, your gout. Let's not flare it."

"I'm glad you agree," said Franklin with a spry step away from the house. "Let's scoot out the back alley before Sally catches wind of it. Come along John, we'll celebrate at my favorite watering hole, the most noble tavern in America."

Sullivan had trouble keeping pace with Franklin as he beelined down a well-worn path heading west. Two blocks later they strolled into the Town Tavern, amid a boisterous round of hoopla.

"Three cheers for Benjamin Franklin!" screamed a local denizen as the two men entered. "Hip, hip… hooray! Hip, hip… hooray! Hip, hip… hooray!"

Franklin doffed his cap while working his way through a deluge of adoration. A tidal wave of back slaps, hugs and handshakes slowly spun both men to the center of a long bar made of mahogany.

"How about a Schmidt's?" asked Ben to his guest. "One beautiful beer."

"Sure!" answered Sullivan over the din.

"Hah! Got you!" laughed Franklin. "Over a century too early!" Franklin looked at the bartender. "Two pints of harvest ale, Barney."

Sullivan surveyed the crowd, the majority of patrons with a beer in hand. There were no women in the room and the place was dark and a bit musty. Along the perimeter of the establishment ran a series of booths each with a wooden table.

"Here you go Ben," said the bartender. "On the house."

"Thank you, Barney."

"Mr. Franklin," added the barkeep. "Let me tell you, I'm 67 years old and I've never seen the likes of what happened today. Thank you, sir."

"You're welcome my friend." Franklin hoisted his mug into the air. "Gentlemen, a long life may not be good enough, but a good life is long enough! Cheers!" He took a mighty gulp of the spicy brew.

"Hear, hear," shouted the chorus.

Ben wiped some suds off his top lip as he looked over Sullivan's shoulder. "Ah, Roger! A grand celebration indeed."

Sullivan turned to his right to see an elderly and distinguished man standing beside him. He wore a tailored suit and had deep set eyes over a rectangular jaw.

"John, I'd like you to meet the author of the Connecticut Compromise, Mr. Roger Sherman from New Haven," stated Franklin. "The second most-eldest delegate at the convention."

"Mr. Franklin still has me by 15 years," laughed the gentlemen as he shook Sullivan's hand. "And he dozed through all the afternoon meetings."

"A pleasure to meet you. Dr. John Sullivan here."

"This is good beer, Ben," declared Sherman. "I hear it's your secret recipe."

"Yes indeed. I learned it from a brew master in the south of England. The key is to go light on the molasses and not add the malt to the mash until you see your reflection."

"Interesting."

Franklin turned back toward Sullivan. "John, Richard also signed the Declaration of Independence. He's yet another signer of that document with the initials 'R.S.'"

"I see," said Sullivan as he touched the keys around his neck.

"Ben. Which way to the privy?" asked Sherman. "The bladder isn't what it used to be."

"Out the back door to the right. Beware of the dog."

"Thanks." Sherman patted Franklin on the shoulder and walked away. "Good job, Ben."

Another man immediately stepped in between Franklin and Sullivan, his hairline a widow's peak and his age perhaps forty. A Roman nose stood haughty above a cleft chin as he held a dainty glass of alcohol in hand.

"Ah, Jimmy Madison!" wailed Franklin. "My second most favorite Virginian!"

"Funny finding you bellied up to the bar," quipped Madison. He looked at Sullivan.

"James, I'd like you to meet a fellow Pennsylvanian and good friend of mine, Dr. John Sullivan."

Sullivan extended a hand in awe of the future fourth president of the United States.

"A pleasure," stated Madison in a formal tone. He quickly turned his attention back to Ben. "Ben, I have signer's remorse. We dropped the ball on the Bill of Rights."

"It's certainly bittersweet," countered Franklin. "But certainly more sweet than bitter. The people will get their Bill of Rights in due time."

"Perhaps," mused Madison as he sipped the flavored drink.

"James was pivotal in drafting the Constitution," declared Ben in an attempt to change the subject. "I've therefore dubbed him the 'Father of the Constitution.'"

"Why thank you, Ben. You're too kind."

Sullivan stood quiet as his memory banks tried to recall any other facts about Madison. He could only remember a university named after him in Virginia.

"I'm just glad it's over," continued Madison with a sigh. "But I feel sorry for George over there." He tilted his head to the right. "I tried to cheer him up, but the man is distraught."

Franklin peered to his left. There, over the crowd sat a man alone in a booth, staring into his beer.

"Go cheer him up, Ben," recommended Madison. "He had already written the first four or five amendments for the Bill of Rights. Hell, some of us even signed his rough draft just to make him feel better." He smirked. "Kind of like a take home souvenir from the convention." Madison scanned the room. "By the way, where's the loo in this place?"

"Out the back door to the right. Beware of the dog and knock first, Sherman's in there."

"Thank you, Benjamin."

Madison turned to Sullivan and bowed. "A pleasure, doctor."

"Thank you," stammered Sullivan.

Madison walked away.

"Wow. That's the second future president I've met so far."

"Becoming President of the United States is a risk we all take in life," stated Ben as he kept his gaze upon the lone man in the booth. "We both know that."

"Who's George?"

"George is George Mason, another delegate from Virginia. He refused to sign the Constitution."

"What? Why?"

"Two reasons. The first being no comment on the slavery issue. George wanted it abolished." Ben took a slow sip of beer. "The second being his demand to attach a Bill of Rights... which ultimately failed."

"Oh," replied Sullivan sheepishly, the brew starting to muddle his thought process. "I apologize Ben, but the Bill of Rights, can you give me a short overview again?"

"We're talking liberty versus authority again, John. Mason is part of the anti-federalist camp, who prefer a weak central government. Simply put, they fear we've just sown the seeds for another monarchy. So in order to protect the rights of the individual, a Bill of Rights has been proposed to address their concerns."

"So the Bill of Rights limits government power?"

"Exactly, and in so doing guarantees personal freedom." Ben finished off his beer and motioned to Barney for another. "You know... freedom of speech, freedom to assemble, the right to bear arms, all that good stuff."

"Important stuff."

"No doubt. We planned to come up with five or ten amendments during the convention and sign them as the Bill of Rights."

"So what happened?"

"We ran out of gas, John. I mean we kicked around some ideas but everyone is exhausted and wants to go home. We've been at it six days a week for four months now. Enough is enough."

Sullivan finished his beer. "Wow, this is some heady stuff."

"On the house again," stated Barney as he placed two more drafts on the bar.

"I better go talk to him," said Franklin as he grasped his mug. "The man looks absolutely despondent. Will you be alright here alone?"

"Sure. I guess so. Hey look, George Washington!"

Franklin didn't flinch. "Don't make me laugh. George wouldn't be caught dead in a rathole like this. I'll keep it short and whatever you do… don't lose our spot at the bar!" He pointed to the floor. "This is a prime spot." He stepped away toward Mason.

"George! May I join you?" shouted Ben.

"Be my guest," answered Mason with a carefree wave of his hand. The Virginian wore long brown hair to shoulder length behind a receding hairline, his age twenty years shy of Franklin. "Misery loves company."

"How do you like the beer?" asked Franklin as he shoehorned his frame into the booth.

"I've had better."

"Yes. Of course."

"This whole convention was one colossal waste of time," whined Mason. "I should have listened to my Sarah and stayed home."

"That was quite a statement you made during the signing ceremony, George. Sitting on your hands in protest will be remembered forever."

"As it well should be!" growled the delegate. "No mention of the word 'slave' in the Constitution of the United States! How lame is that?" His lips quivered as he continued. "Slavery will bring the judgement of heaven on the country if not ended soon."

"Perhaps."

"And no Bill of Rights! You may as well put a crown on Washington's head already. The revolution was all in vain."

"Now George, may I suggest…"

"I would sooner chop off my right hand than sign the Constitution of the United States without a Bill of Rights attached!" He angrily tapped his forefingers on the table. "You just watch, Ben. This new government will soon start meddling in our affairs… telling us this and telling us that." He shook his head.

"Mark my words… today is the beginning of the end of liberty in the United States."

"George, please… calm down," urged Franklin. "We've accomplished a lot of good here in Philadelphia. This is a process… trust the process."

Mason took a deep breath and slowly exhaled. He reached into his front coat pocket and pulled out a sheet of paper. "Here it is Ben, my place in history, now a worthless piece of paper." He tossed it on the table.

"May I?" asked Franklin as he picked up the paper. "Madison apprised me that you've drawn up a few proposed amendments."

"Go ahead, read them. They've no use before the new throne."

Franklin began to read the hand-written note simply titled 'The Bill of Rights'. Below it ran a total of five amendments. The document was dated September 17$^{th}$, 1787.

"I wrote Virginia's Bill of Rights, so it's nearly the same language."

Franklin carefully studied the document, its verbiage eerily similar to the future Bill of Rights authored by James Madison in 1789 and ratified into law by 1791. In fact, the wording was identical.

"Did you show this to Madison?" asked Ben as he lowered the paper.

"Sure. He liked it and made a copy."

"What's with all the signatures?"

"Madison thinks he's funny. After making a copy he had just about everyone sign it after the convention was over. He called it my consolation prize."

The wheels in Franklin's head began to turn as he motioned to Barney for two more beers. He rescanned the paper before speaking.

"Listen, George. What you have here is good stuff. I like it."

"Thanks."

"Now listen, I have an idea." Franklin leaned in close. "Let's say I publish this list of proposed amendments in the next issue of the *Pennsylvania Gazette*."

"Why would you do that?"

"Get it out there for public consumption… a trial balloon. I've learned from experience that when you're testing to see how deep the water is, never use two feet."

Barney dropped two beers on the table. "On the house."

"That way we can gauge public reaction from afar and," said Franklin as he took hold of his beer. "… solidify your thoughts in the annals of history." He gently clinked his mug against Mason's. "What do you think?"

The Virginian took a chug of beer, his demeanor suddenly improved.

"I don't see why not," mused Mason. "Deep down, I think Madison is going to take credit for my idea."

Franklin skillfully paused, letting the oil of alcohol lubricate the machinery inside Mason's mind.

"Who knows, maybe I'll be famous some day?"

"Could be," continued Franklin. "The only way to know is by getting this paper into the light of day. What good is a sundial in the shade?"

Mason giggled. "You're a good man, Ben. Funny, too."

"So you'll do it?"

"Sure. What the heck? Go ahead. What have I got to lose?"

"Marvelous!" said Ben with a raised mug. "You won't regret it."

"Cheers!" bellowed Mason with a wide grin.

Ben took a celebratory sip of brew while looking down at the document. He reached out, slowly turned the paper around, and slid it toward Mason. "George, may I make one little suggestion here?"

"Sure, Ben. Go ahead."

"Everything reads well except for this one amendment." He pointed at the list of five.

Mason read the article of concern. "Hmm. Pretty straight forward to me. What don't you like about it?"

"Well, may I suggest perhaps a few more words to tighten it up... you can easily tack them on at the end."

Mason began to squirm and looked around the room.

"You may want to add..." Franklin offered his suggestion as Mason continued to fidget in his seat.

"Sure Ben. Go ahead and plug it in."

Franklin stood, walked over to a waiter's station and brought back a quill and ink. He winked at Sullivan in the process.

"Let's say we use your own handwriting, George." He dipped the quill into the inkwell. "We don't want anyone to suggest impropriety on our behalf."

"Hurry up, Ben. I've got to pee."

Franklin reached the quill across the table. "Here you go, my friend." He repeated the suggested redact. "Just cover the period at the end of the sentence with the letter 'e' in the word 'except.'"

Mason quickly obliged, the recommended addition only six words in length.

"There... done!" Mason set down the quill. "Ben, where's the outhouse? I've really got to go!"

"Out the back door to the right," said Franklin as he spun the paper back around. "Beware of the dog and knock first, Madison's in there." He slowly blew across the fresh ink, allowing it to dry.

# CHAPTER TWENTY-SIX
## THE BIRTHDAY GIFT
## 1787

As Sullivan struggled to tie the white kerchief around his neck he heard Franklin holler from downstairs.

"C'mon John, we don't want to be late… Washington will have a bird."

"Be right there!" replied Sullivan as he put on a blue, silk waistcoat with ornate buttons. Quickly he pulled a pair of white stockings to knee level and adjusted the bottom of his breeches. He stepped into a pair of leather shoes with brightly polished metal buckles.

"The man will be late for his own funeral," he heard Franklin lament.

Sullivan hustled down the stairs to meet Franklin and his daughter in the foyer with multiple grandchildren at their side.

"Where's your powdered wig?" asked Ben.

"Nope. Sorry, Ben. That's where I draw the line."

"Let me fix your cravat," said Sally. She stepped up to Sullivan and quickly adjusted the silk cloth around his neck. "There, perfect."

"How do we look?" asked Franklin as he proudly stepped next to the physician. The founding father wore his Sunday best with cane in hand.

"Absolutely dashing," declared Sally.

"Do we have time for a photo?" asked Sullivan.

"Let's go, John. Photography is forty years away." He handed Sullivan a tricorn hat. "Goodbye everyone. Don't wait up."

"Have a wonderful time!" said Sally.

Just outside the home waited an ornate carriage with an enclosed passenger coach. A man in a top hat sat in the driver's seat, as a valet opened the door. Two chestnut brown horses stood before the transport with blinders on.

"Hey, Antonio!" exclaimed Sullivan as he recognized one of the Pagano brothers. He looked up at the driver. "Mario!"

"Good evening," said Antonio with a bow and tip of the hat. "Watch your step please."

Both men helped Franklin up the carriage step and into the coach.

"Get along," ordered Mario as the carriage lurched forward and down the lane. Once past the gate, the transit turned west onto Market Street.

"Oh, how grand," declared Franklin as he peered out the window. "I just love a good soirée. Everyone is going to be here."

"I must admit, I'm a bit nervous," declared Sullivan.

"There's going to be a formal receiving line and per etiquette, George and Martha will be first."

"And then their children?"

"They have no children," said Franklin. "At least of their own. They raised two previous children from Martha's first marriage, but both have passed away."

"Oh."

"There will be some local dignitaries in line, perhaps a foreign diplomate or maybe a few delegates from the convention. Basically, anyone staying in the estate at the current time. The place is quite large."

"How about the house staff? Will any of them be in line?"

"No. Not directly, but perhaps a few steps behind Washington."

The rhythmic clip-clop of horse hooves resonated beneath the coach.

"I do know Washington's cook quite well," declared Franklin. "A solid built man named Hercules. George brought him up from Virginia. His bouillabaisse is to die for."

Sullivan didn't reply.

"And I do know Martha's personal attendant. Her name is Oney Judge. She's been with Martha for years now and travels everywhere with her. A spirited young woman, perhaps in her mid-twenties."

"So, the same age as Sary?"

"Yes. In fact she reminds me of Sary. They kind of look alike."

Sullivan pictured Sary in his mind. "I hope I see her tonight."

"Whoa, Sophie! Whoa, Ellie!" cried out Mario.

The carriage came to a stop at the corner of 6th and Market Street. Antonio opened the door.

"We've arrived, gentlemen. Watch your step."

Sullivan exited after Franklin onto the street, directly in front of a majestic brick estate with dormers on top. Two large chimneys jutted from each side of the home and a long brick wall ran along its side parallel to Market Street. Before them stood a slow moving line of about ten couples waiting to enter the front door. A Betsy Ross flag stood still above the entryway.

"Wow," said the physician. "Nice place."

"It was originally built by a wealthy widow named Mary Masters," stated Franklin as they took their place in line. "Then the Penn family lived here until General Howe made it his headquarters during the British occupation of the city."

"Then the Washingtons moved in?"

"Well, not exactly," replied Franklin. "Benedict Arnold briefly resided here with his wife, Peggy."

The Arnold name dampened Sullivan's enthusiasm just as another horse and carriage pulled up behind them. Out stepped a rather striking young couple.

"Ah, Elizabeth and my dear Alex!" hailed Franklin with both arms raised in the air.

Sullivan immediately recognized Alexander Hamilton beside his wife, a petit woman wearing an elegant gold gown to ankle level. The couple exchanged niceties with Ben and stepped forward. Hamilton looked upon the physician.

"Dr. Sullivan!" stated Hamilton in slow and dramatic fashion. "My waste a shot protégé!" He stepped forward and placed both hands firmly on Sullivan's shoulders. "So good to see you! Where have you been my friend?"

"Oh, up North a bit."

"It must have been way, way up North," chuckled Hamilton. "Because old Benedict turned the colonies upside down looking for you. He was mad as a hornet."

Sullivan just smiled as the line moved closer to the door.

"Elizabeth, this is Dr. John Sullivan," continued Hamilton. "Doctor... my wife, Elizabeth."

"A pleasure," said the woman with a slight curtsy.

"John was all set to duel General Arnold until some sort of an explosion in the middle of the night upset the whole apple cart," continued Hamilton with a glance toward Franklin.

"Oh, you men and your duels," scoffed Elizabeth. "Don't you ever get involved in those silly things, Alexander." She squeezed his forearm.

"Rumor has it that Benedict was never the same after that morning," stated Hamilton. "Maybe that caused him to flip?"

"I heard it was his wife, Peggy," whispered Elizabeth as she leaned in closer. "They were apparently living too high on the hog and ran into debt. At least that's what Mrs. Madison told me... and she's very good friends with Martha Washington. Peggy introduced Benedict to Major Andre."

"Very interesting," said Ben as they stepped up to the door.

"You're better off the whole thing fell apart," interjected Hamilton. "Who knows what that madman would have done? He may have ignored the wasted shot and killed you."

A pang of sorrow struck Sullivan as he looked at Mrs. Hamilton's face. He went to speak.

"John," interrupted Ben firmly with an extended hand into the foyer. "Our time has arrived."

Sullivan stepped inside where a doorman took hold of his hat. Large vases full of colorful asters and chrysanthemums anchored each side of the entrance hall. General and Mrs. George Washington stood just ten feet inside.

"I'll go first," said Franklin as he fixed his hair. "Stand up straight and follow my lead."

Sullivan began to hyperventilate as he trailed behind Franklin. Above him soared a rotunda with spiral staircases flanking the side walls. Beyond the antechamber came the pleasing sound of a string quartet playing chamber music.

"My dear Benjamin," stated George Washington warmly. The two men shook hands. "So glad you could join us tonight."

"General Washington, it's an honor to be here."

As they continued their conversation, Sullivan briefly looked past Washington, only to see Martha staring back blankly as if trying to recall his name.

Franklin stepped slightly to his left while saying, "And perhaps you remember my friend from up North, Dr. John Sullivan?" Franklin gently pulled Sullivan in front of the leader. "He's been instrumental in keeping me above ground and above room temperature," chuckled Ben.

Sullivan stepped before Washington and looked him directly in the eye.

"Doctor," said Washington with a firm shake of the hand. "Welcome."

"It's a pleasure to be here, sir" replied Sullivan. "Thank you." Sullivan noticed out of the corner of his eye Franklin already hobnobbing with Mrs. Washington.

"Ah, Alexander and Elizabeth!" bellowed Washington as he pivoted to the left. "Such an honor to have you here tonight! Welcome!" He and Hamilton embraced.

Sullivan suddenly found himself in high society's no-man's land, wedged between a Philadelphia power couple and the loquacious Franklin.

"Who's watching all the children?" asked Washington as he politely held Mrs. Hamilton's hand.

"Oh, my mother. She's a saint. You look well, General."

"My manner of living is plain," replied Washington. "A glass of wine and a bit of mutton."

Sullivan anxiously looked to his left at Mrs. Washington, now in a fit of laughter with tears in her eyes, the victim of a Ben Franklin zinger. He sighed and stared overhead as sweat began to roll down his brow. Hamilton inadvertently bumped his right shoulder, causing his body to shift left. He then peered over General Washington's right shoulder to see a line of servants staring back at him, including an elderly woman in a plain grey dress. Next to her stood a stout man with a thin mustache wearing a chef's hat. To his right and one foot forward stood a young woman with an aura of importance. She wore a grey and blue dress and had her gaze locked onto Sullivan's face. He suddenly felt Franklin pull him to the left.

"Martha, I'd like you to meet my guest, Dr. John Sullivan."

"Good evening, Mrs. Washington. An honor to meet you."

Before she could reply Martha Washington sneezed rapidly three times, the force of her airway expulsion enough to jettison a wad of phlegm onto her upper lip. She quickly sniffed but the exudate failed to retreat back up her nostril.

"Oh, my," said the hostess as she turned backward. "Oney, help me."

The servant in grey and blue quickly stepped forward to wipe Mrs. Washington's face. Just then Sullivan noticed another female servant appear from an alcove. It was Sary.

"John, come along," urged Franklin as he pushed farther down the line.

Sullivan stood in shock as Franklin tugged his elbow. Sary looked the same although a bit older, in better clothing and much more mature. At first she didn't recognize Sullivan, but her facial expression soon turned to joyful surprise. Across her face ran a familiar smile as she leaned to her right and elbowed the cook, whispering something into his ear. She then waved energetically with her right hand held low and off to her side.

The remainder of the receiving line was a blur to Sullivan. He soon found himself in a large ballroom being served hors d'oeuvres and cocktails by a host of white gloved waiters.

"Did you see her?" exclaimed Sullivan. "She's here!"

"Of course I saw her," replied Franklin with a mouthful of apple brie. "She looked fantastic. I told you she would be just fine. Now relax and enjoy yourself. Mingle, John. This is a once in a lifetime opportunity."

"Is Oney the one in blue and grey?"

"Yes."

Sullivan just stood alone in euphoria, the wine starting to calm his jitters. "Ben, we found Sary. Now I just have to talk to her."

"Be careful, John. You're in General Washington's home. Remember your promise… do not mention the two words that shall not be mentioned."

Dinner followed with eight guests to a roundtable. Sullivan sat next to Franklin along with a cadre of diplomates from France, their conversation centered upon Franklin's time abroad in the town of Passy. The sage of Philadelphia spoke of his wonderment with hot air balloons while in the south of France, followed by a discussion of their potential role in the future. He then spoke of Marie Antoinette sending her personal carriage to transport him to the seaport of Le Havre for a final sendoff, the Queen hitching her nimble Spanish mules for ultimate riding comfort. Franklin recounted his last journey across the Atlantic during which he invented bifocals and mapped out sea currents based on water temperature readings during the long voyage. Throughout it all Sullivan scanned the room for Sary, but she never reappeared.

Dessert and dancing followed. It was when George and Martha took to the dance floor for the first waltz that Sary returned, standing at attention behind Oney. As the music played and the guests circled around their pirouetting hosts, Sullivan slowly made his way along the perimeter of the crowd. Sary cautiously watched his approach out of the corner of her eye in anticipation. The medical doctor stopped three feet to her left side while keeping his gaze on the dancing Washingtons, the waltz coming to an end.

He leaned in her direction. "Sary, It's so good to see you again."

"Doctor Sullivan," she whispered while continuing to look ahead. "What are you doing here? Where have you been?"

Oney cautiously glanced back over her shoulder.

"Up North for a spell," he answered. "I wanted to come back and make sure you were OK."

"Oh, Dr. Sullivan. That's so sweet of you. I'm just fine. They take real good care of me here."

"You look well." He scanned her body from head to toe, recalling her ragged appearance under the Arnold reign of terror on Elfreth's Alley. "That's a beautiful dress."

Sary smiled.

The crowd began to clap as the waltz ended. Washington spoke a few words of appreciation before signaling the string ensemble to play on. A slow wave of couples took to the dance floor as the music began.

Oney Judge turned back to quickly say, "Here they come!"

"I'm just glad he's gone," continued Sullivan, oblivious to the warning.

"You're glad who's gone?" asked Sary.

The physician began to reply just as the string quartet briefly paused, his voice heard over the crowd. "Benedict Arnold." The music immediately restarted but several heads turned in his direction, including that of George Washington. The commander in chief excused himself from his wife and began a direct path to Sullivan and Sary, the crowd parting as he neared.

"Sary, back to your quarters," ordered Washington.

She spun around and walked away.

Washington then stopped directly in front of Sullivan.

"Doctor, have we really met before?" asked the leader in an inquisitive tone. "Or has Benjamin's memory failed?"

As Sullivan began to respond he spotted a concerned Ben Franklin staring at him from across the room. Several middle aged women in flowing gowns were fawning at his side. Franklin quickly moved his hand back and forth in front of his neck in horizontal fashion, attempting to abort the spontaneous tête-à-tête.

"Yes. We've met before," replied the physician confidently. "About eight years ago inside Pennsylvania Hospital. You were talking to a wounded soldier from the town of Coopersburg."

Sullivan paused to allow Washington time to recollect.

"You asked the soldier about the fishing in Lehigh Creek," continued Sullivan. "He spoke of catching trout with the use of corn as bait."

"Ah yes! I do recall… and then I promoted the young man?"

"Yes! You did, General Washington. Afterwards you pulled me aside to ask my personal opinion of …"

"Don't ever let me hear you utter those two words again," ordered Washington. "Do I make myself clear?"

"Yes, sir."

Washington maintained direct eye contact with the physician. "May I have another private moment alone with you, doctor?"

"Yes, of course."

Washington led Sullivan to another room just off the main hall, closing the door behind.

"I owe you an apology," stated Washington. "Your opinion of that scoundrel was in hindsight, quite accurate." Washington grimaced. "I've never been so humiliated by an individual in my entire life. My only regret is that he lived and Major André hanged."

Sullivan stared back at the leader as a grandfather clock slowly ticked away each passing second, the sound of the quartet muffled in the background.

"So, will you accept my apology?"

"Of course, General Washington. Apology accepted."

"Good. Now, how do you know Sary?"

"Well," answered Sullivan a bit caught off guard by the blunt question. "I used to live with Mr. Franklin on Elfreth's Alley, and of course she lived next door."

"I see."

"She's a wonderful and intelligent woman," continued Sullivan now a bit more at ease before the icon. "I'm sure you're aware of that."

Washington raised an eyebrow.

"I haven't seen her in about eight years," babbled Sullivan. "She certainly looks more mature and if you ask me … "

"Sary is leaving for Virginia tomorrow morning," interrupted Washington.

"Excuse me?"

"Martha is giving her to her granddaughter, Elizabeth… as a birthday gift. Elizabeth turns sixteen on Sunday."

Sullivan stood speechless.

"Don't tell Sary. It's going to be a surprise for everyone."

A spark of anger ignited in Sullivan's heart.

"You may have noticed Oney teaching her the ropes. I'll admit, the girl is a quick learner. She's got the makings of an admirable body servant."

"Wait a minute," stammered Sullivan with an extended hand. He shook his head as if trying to clear his brain. "Did you just tell me that Sary is going to be given away as a birthday present… to your granddaughter?"

"Yes. Isn't that grand? Elizabeth will be absolutely flabbergasted. She hasn't a personal servant yet. All of her friends do, but the poor girl doesn't."

The room began to spin as Sullivan remembered his promise to Franklin just two days earlier, having already spoken one of the two banned words in Washington's presence. He suddenly recalled Franklin's advice from 2020 after speaking to a couple en route to their honeymoon, the newlyweds having just eloped… "Always remember to challenge authority, John… contest the establishment and dare the elite."

"Well, let's say we get back to the party, doctor. Martha is about to sing. She has a lovely voice." Washington went to turn away.

"How can you do such a thing?" growled Sullivan, his temper rapidly rising.

"Excuse me?" countered Washington firmly.

"Give a person away… as a gift? What gives you that right?"

Washington's cordial demeanor vanished. He stepped back in front of Sullivan.

"Never you mind how I handle my servants," growled Washington as he leaned closer to Sullivan.

"They're not your servants. They're your slaves!"

The brazen comment caught the military leader off guard. "Watch your tongue, man," he warned. "Being a friend of Franklin means nothing to me, although I can tell you've been listening to his foolish ideas." Washington curled his upper lip. "Begone from my sight."

Sullivan ignored the directive as his pent-up passion overflowed. He leaned closer to Washington in a semi-controlled rage. "I noticed how you conveniently forgot to mention the word 'slavery' in your new Constitution, General Washington. I consider that a serious omission… because no man should *ever* own another."

"How dare you!" screamed Washington loudly. "How dare you utter such words of insolence in my presence… in my home!" His face rapidly reddened as he continued shouting, some saliva on his lips. "I'll have you imprisoned for defamation of character. Your comments border upon treason! Never in my life have I…"

The door to the room suddenly burst open and in stepped Oney.

"Mr. Washington! Mr. Washington!" she yelled.

"Not now, Oney!" cried out Washington with an extended arm in her direction. He continued to stare down Sullivan.

"But Mr. Washington!"

"I said *not now* Oney! It can wait!"

"But sir, Mr. Franklin has taken ill! He's collapsed onto the floor! Please hurry!" She ran back into the ballroom. "Somebody call Dr. Casey!"

## CHAPTER TWENTY-SEVEN
### BEN'S TWIST
### 1787

Dr. Casey arrived fifteen minutes later to a rather grim situation. In a side parlor lay Franklin, unconscious on an ornate sofa, his legs hoisted high atop a set of pillows. The Philadelphian's eyes were shut and mouth agape, his breathing labored.

"Ben! Open your eyes," requested Casey as he knelt down to take a pulse. "Where's Dr. Sullivan?" he asked.

"Outside," snarled Washington with a scowl. "The scalawag's been banished from my home!"

Franklin let out a tremendous moan.

"It's probably his heart," opined Casey. "He's been battling dropsy for some time now." He placed an ear on Franklin's chest. "It's finally catching up to him."

"Are you sure it's not just overconsumption?" inquired Mrs. Washington. Behind her stood Oney. "I've never seen a man eat so much food!"

Casey gently palpated Franklin's corpulent abdomen. "Perhaps," he said. "The man is prone to overindulge."

"Get him to the hospital and call his family," ordered Washington. "Before it's too late."

Franklin opened his eyes under duress. "I'm fine." He paused to catch his breath. "It must have been the clams. I apologize... please, keep the party going."

"Ben, does it hurt anywhere?" asked Casey.

Franklin clutched his upper chest without saying anything. He rapidly patted his hand on his sternum.

"It's definitely his heart," declared Casey. "Too much salt. I agree, let's get him to the hospital. A bloodletting is in order."

Franklin let out another guttural moan of pain.

"Oney," snapped Mrs. Washington. "Go fetch Austin and Giles to help."

"You better get Hercules and Paris, too," added the General. "We'll need all hands on deck to move Ben."

Oney quickly returned with four male servants and Sary.

"On three," stated Dr. Casey after they positioned a blanket beneath Franklin's frame. "Sary and Oney, you hold the legs and I'll take the head. Ready... one, two, three!"

The makeshift medical team lifted Franklin's body into the air and transferred him onto a sturdy slat of wood from a nearby stable.

"All right everyone," continued Casey. "Each man grab a corner of the plank and watch your backs. We lift on three. One, two, three!"

The wooden stretcher creaked in support of the patient.

"I've a wagon outside," added Casey.

"Use the side entrance," directed General Washington. "We don't want to upset the guests any further."

"I'll need a volunteer to ride with us," requested Casey as Ben began to transport out of the room. "And some blankets, too."

"I'll go!" called out Oney. "Sary. Come along!"

"Yes. You do that, my dear," concurred Martha as she nervously patted Oney on the shoulder. "Take care of Benjamin. Cover him up well."

Ben Franklin was carried down a narrow corridor and unceremoniously medivacked out of the Washington estate into the stillness of the night. Just outside waited the Pagano brothers with their wagon ready to go.

"Easy," said Dr. Casey. "Place him down gently."

They slid his frame into the rear of the buckboard wagon.

"Are those Spanish mules?" muttered Ben.

Into the back of the wagon hopped Dr. Casey, Oney and Sary. Mrs. Washington handed some additional blankets over the siderail.

"Keep him warm," ordered the future first lady.

"Godspeed, Ben Franklin!" bellowed General Washington as he handed a lit lantern to Oney. His servants shut the rear wagon hatch. "Your country wishes you well."

Franklin groaned as the wagon lurched forward, raising his hand in the air as it passed through the main gate.

The transport turned right onto Market Street and headed south, toward Pennsylvania Hospital. About a block away, the approaching footsteps of a man could be heard running on the street. At the side of the wagon appeared Sullivan.

"What happened? Where are you taking him?" gasped Sullivan.

"To the hospital," replied Casey. "It's his heart."

The wagon slowed and Sullivan jumped in.

"John Sullivan, is that you?" mumbled Franklin from beneath several layers of blankets.

"Yes, Ben. It's me. What's wrong?"

"What did you say to General Washington?"

"Nothing." Sullivan looked at Sary as he spoke.

"Don't lie to me. Everyone in the ballroom heard Washington yell."

"That's when Mr. Franklin collapsed," interjected Oney. "They heard the boom in the kitchen. Hercules thought the apple cider exploded!"

"Did you mention any of the words not to be mentioned?" continued Franklin.

Sullivan refused to answer as the wagon continued forward for two more blocks. At the corner of 6$^{th}$ and Spruce Street, Mario turned the wagon east in the direction of the Delaware River.

"Tell me, John. Did you?" pressed Franklin. "Did you use the word slavery in front of Washington?"

Sullivan again glanced at Sary. How dare Washington give her away as a gift, he thought. Anger again started to roil inside him.

"Talk to me, John," ordered Franklin.

"Yes! Yes! I did use the word slavery!" growled Sullivan, his cognitive state in an uproar. "I apologize to you, but not to him. The man needed to be set straight… so I let him have it."

A brief moment of silence passed as the wagon continued onward.

"Very good," muttered Franklin as he gave Sullivan a thumbs up. "I'm proud of you. Somebody had to tell him. Better you than me."

"Hey, where are we going?" asked Sullivan. "This isn't the way to the hospital."

No one answered as the wagon reached Front Street. There it turned back north.

"Mario! You're going back toward Washington's home! Are you crazy? The man threatened to tar and feather me."

Franklin reached his hand onto Sullivan's thigh. "John, relax. Enjoy the ride."

"What?" cried out Sullivan. "What's going on here?" He looked at Oney and Sary. "Where are we going?" In the distance Sullivan spotted the spire of Christ Church through the darkness of the sky. He looked at Dr. Casey. "Edward, talk to me. Where are we taking Ben?"

Casey grinned. "To Pennsylvania Hospital… eventually."

The wagon drove directly into a side shed attached to Christ Church.

"Whoa, Sammy!" bellowed Mario as the wagon stopped before some bales of hay. Antonio jumped off and shut the shed door.

"Alright!" howled Sullivan as he stood. "Can someone please tell me what the hell is going on here? Why are we in a barn?" He looked down at Franklin, his face framed with blankets. "Ben, what are you doing? This isn't funny. I hope you know that!"

Franklin sat up and looked around. "Oney, dim the lantern and get me out of this wagon. For heaven's sake, my lumbago is killing me."

Sullivan's jaw dropped in amazement as the traveling party disembarked without hesitation, the Pagano brothers helping Franklin down.

"Ah, why isn't anyone else surprised to be here except me?" inquired Sullivan. "Am I missing something?"

"John, if there's one thing I hope you've learned from me," replied Franklin as he wiped some straw off his shirt. "Is that you always have to have a backup plan."

"Oh, no," grimaced Sullivan. "Not another backup plan."

"Hence the Casey-Franklin-Judge Philadelphia Freedom Plan," proclaimed Franklin with a raised index finger in the air. "Which up until this point has been played out to absolute perfection." He turned to Dr. Casey. "Except for that 'prone to overindulge' wisecrack, doctor. Perhaps a bit of artistic license on your part?"

Sullivan looked at Casey. "You're in on this too?"

"Guilty as charged," grinned Casey.

"Mario and Antonio, too?"

"Of course," said Ben. "How else would we get you here?"

Sullivan rapidly blinked his eyes. "But what about…" He pointed to Oney and Sary.

"Oh, forgive me," interrupted Ben. "John, I'd like you to meet Oney Judge. Oney, this is Dr. Sullivan."

"Pleased to meet you," said Oney with a firm handshake and a broad smile. She stood beside Sary like a mirror image. "I've heard a lot about you, Doctor Sullivan."

"You have? From who?"

"Sary."

"Ms. Judge is privy to our intentions," stated Ben. "Hence her namesake on the plan's magnificent caption."

Sullivan then looked at Sary in amazement. "Sary? Do you know about this too?"

"No, sir," replied Sary soundly. "I don't know anything. Oney just asked me to come help Mr. Franklin."

"Sary," said Oney. "Listen to me. Mrs. Washington is planning on giving you away to her granddaughter in Virginia… as a birthday present."

"What? What are you talking about, Oney? Don't be silly."

"I overheard her discussing it with Mr. Washington two weeks ago. They're sending you away tomorrow morning. They weren't going to tell you until then. It's supposed to be a surprise for everyone involved, including their granddaughter, Elizabeth."

A puzzled look appeared on Sary's face. "But why? I like it here. My home is here, in Philadelphia, with you and Hercules and everyone else." Tears welled up in her eyes. "I don't want to leave, Oney."

"And you don't want to be Miss Elizabeth's personal servant for the rest of her life," added Oney. "She's a mean spirited woman with a quick hand to the whip."

"So that's why I've gathered you all here," bellowed Franklin with his hands raised high. "In this barn… on this very night. Welcome!"

Everyone stared at the ringleader.

"Alright, Ben," said Sullivan cautiously. "I'm with you so far but do tell me. What comes next in the so-called Casey-Franklin-Judge Philadelphia Freedom Plan?"

"John, I'm sending you home tonight," stated Franklin firmly. "Quite frankly, you've overstayed your welcome in the year 1787."

"I agree one hundred percent. It's time to go. But, what about Sary? She can't be treated like material goods."

"I fully agree. So here comes the twist," continued Franklin. He cleared his throat before continuing. "Sary's leaving, too."

"Excuse me? Can you repeat that?"

"You heard me. Sary's leaving with you tonight. It's our only option."

"But Ben, what about the grandfather paradox?"

"It's time to roll the dice, John. A woman's destiny is at stake here. I'm willing to risk it."

"Oney, what are they talking about?" asked Sary. "Where am I going?"

Oney Judge took hold of Sary's shoulders. "Sary, I love you more than anything. You know that. But if we don't do something right now… tonight, you're headed off to Virginia tomorrow morning and we'll never see each other again." She hugged her tight. "We can't let that happen. This is our only opportunity to save you. So please, listen to Mr. Franklin."

"Oney reached out to me a few days ago through my acquaintance with Hercules," stated Franklin. "She spoke of Sary's fate and asked if I could help arrange her escape. So we formulated a plan with Dr. Sullivan in mind."

Sullivan stared at the cabal before him, trying to calculate the myriad of things that could go wrong. He slowly shook his head in disbelief.

"So, what's happening?" whispered Sary tentatively while wiping a tear from her cheek.

"Sary. You're not going back to Washington's home tonight," answered Franklin. "You're leaving town with Dr. Sullivan."

"But… but, is it safe? Mr. Washington won't take kind to me leaving."

"Yes. Absolutely safe. This will all make perfect sense in the morning light. You're in no danger whatsoever. You have my word on that."

"Sary, you can trust Mr. Franklin," added Oney. "He's on our side."

"Wait a minute," exclaimed Sullivan. "This is all happening too fast. Doesn't she have a significant other, a family? She can't just leave them behind."

"No," replied Oney. "Sary only has me and the others at the Washington estate. There's no one else."

"That's what makes it clean, John," said Franklin. "The cards are all falling into place. Believe me, I've thought this over well. There's no better time for Sary to leave than right now… tonight, at this very moment."

"But… where are we going?" asked Sary.

Sullivan decided to try and answer the difficult question, slowly starting to accept the unfolding scheme. "Sary," he said slowly and carefully. "We're leaving, but in a crazy way still staying in Philadelphia."

"Really? But… Mr. Franklin just said I'm leaving town."

"Yes. He did. So let's just say were leaving for another section of town that no one knows about… in another time. A time where you'll be safe and free."

"That sounds impossible," countered Sary.

"I know it does. But it's true. You have to believe me and Mr. Franklin. It's where I originally came from, before I first met you. Trust me."

"But will I be able to visit Oney?"

Sullivan sighed. "Maybe. Maybe not. I can't guarantee that."

"Sary. You have to be brave," said Oney. "We'll always be together in spirit." She took off a round pendant about the size of a marble from her neck. "Here." She placed it around Sary's neck. "Wear this and think of me. That way we'll always be together."

"Thank you, Oney."

"And best of all, Mr. Franklin said you are going to be a free woman! Free to live and do whatever pleases you. Isn't that worth it?"

Sary's lips began to tremble. "Yes. Yes it is." She grasped the trinket. "I want to be free."

"Well, what do you think, Sary?" asked Sullivan. "Will you go? It would be an honor to escort you to freedom."

"Well," answered Sary thoughtfully. "I surely don't want to live with Miss Elizabeth." She nervously looked at Ben. "And I trust Mr.

Franklin. He's always been very good to me." She next looked at Oney. "And if Oney says we'll always be together in spirit… that's good enough for me. I remember my mother telling me that and it's true." She smiled widely. "And, I want to be free. So… I guess I have no other choice."

"Then, you'll go?"

"Yes. I'll go!"

"Hurrah!" went the combined cry as a group hug engulfed Sary's slight frame.

"Oh, Sary, you won't be sorry!" exclaimed Sullivan. "What until you see where we're going! It's magical."

"Alright. So it's settled," stated Ben excitedly. "Now, let's get our story straight everyone. Gather around."

For the next several minutes everyone agreed upon the same alibi, that while en route to the hospital, Ben demanded a stop at Christ Church for a moment of prayer. Afterwards the wagon turned back toward Pennsylvania Hospital where Franklin was emergently admitted under the care of Dr. Casey, staying there for two days. The escape of Sary occurred just after Ben was carried into the hospital.

"I turned around and Sary said goodbye!" practiced Oney with a shocked face. "She ran off into the night with that no-good Doctor Sullivan. He appeared out of nowhere from the streets." She hyperventilated for effect. "Oh, Mrs. Washington, I tried to talk her out of it but the girl had crazy in her eyes. They must have been planning it for days!"

"Bravo. Bravo," said Ben as he clapped. "A skilled thespian indeed. Make sure to embellish the name 'Doctor Sullivan', that way the onus will be on John."

"What the hell," laughed Sullivan. "At least Washington will remember me."

"Alright everyone," ordered Ben as he placed a hand forward. "Let's everyone put our hands together."

Each conspirator placed a hand atop Ben's.

"Philadelphia freedom on three," said Ben. "One, two… three!"

"Philadelphia freedom!"

"Let's do it!" hollered Franklin.

"Ah Ben," said Sullivan as the huddle broke up. "What about you?"

"Don't spoil the moment, John. Tonight is about you and Sary." He stepped toward Sullivan.

"But, Ben... April 17th, 1790 isn't that far away."

"John, fear not death for the sooner we die, the longer we shall be immortal."

"Whoa! Good one, Ben," applauded Dr. Casey. "We have to remember to write that one down."

"Yes. It just came to me out of the blue," chuckled Franklin. "I've still got it!"

Sullivan just stood in shock.

"John, unfortunately the final and most painful part of the plan is saying farewell to you," continued Franklin with an extended hand. "But our time together, like all good things, must come to an end. It's been a good run. So long, old friend."

"What? You're never coming back?"

Franklin took a deep breath. "No. I have to stay... there's still too much work to be done."

"What do you mean? You've done it all."

"No I haven't. When it comes to the issue of slavery, I'm still behind the curve. You were right the other day by suggesting I take the point on the issue. I've certainly been remiss. So it's time for old Ben to make up for some lost ground before the spring of 1790 rolls around."

Sullivan couldn't bring himself to say goodbye.

"I'm on a personal journey of reconciliation, John... thanks to you. A big step in that process is letting Sary take my place." Franklin smiled warmly. "I hope you understand."

Sullivan nodded his head in agreement. "I do. It makes sense." He shook Franklin's hand. "So this is it?"

"This is it."

"I'll miss you, Ben. You're one hell of a wingman."

"I'll miss you, too. It's been a privilege traveling in your company." Franklin squeezed Sullivan's hand. "But, promise me two things."

"Sure, Ben. Anything. I'll even promise to keep my promise this time."

"When you get back to 2020, check out the secret bin on Elfreth's Alley. I still have access to the house and plan to put in a few surprises."

"Alright," beamed Sullivan. "I look forward to keeping that promise. What's the second?"

"Don't come back."

The finality of the request struck Sullivan hard. He stood silent.

"Let me die in peace with William and Benny at my side, just like the history books will say. By then I'll be tired and ready for the boneyard. Promise me that, John."

Sullivan released his grip and hugged Franklin. "I promise, Ben. I won't come back."

"Thank you."

Sullivan stepped back with a deep sense of accomplishment, looking around at the cast of smiling faces. "Thank you everyone. Thank you for everything you've done. I'll never forget you." He turned toward Sary. "Are you ready, young lady?"

"Yes, I am Dr. Sullivan!"

He reached out and took hold of her hand. "Then let's go."

"Goodbye, Oney!" shouted Sary.

"Bye-bye, Sary! I love you."

"Godspeed!" hollered out Franklin. "We shall rise refreshed in the morning!"

The duo waved goodbye as Antonio pushed open the barn door. They ran to their right toward the graveyard and for the first time in her life, Sary felt free.

## CHAPTER TWENTY-EIGHT
### PIÈCE DE RÉSISTANCE
### 2020

"Who's the club president again?" asked Bliss Bradshaw as a makeup artist applied some rouge to his cheeks. "Wally?"

"No, Bliss. It's me," snapped Attorney Mills as he readjusted his tie. "We've gone over this before!"

"Oh, right," said Bradshaw as he put down a handheld mirror. He looked at a cameraman. "Remember, I want all my face shots from the left of the midline. Never the right."

Before the local media celebrity sat the inner circle of the West Philadelphia Historical Society: Attorney Mills, Wally, Burt and Dr. Sullivan.

"And t-minus two minutes," shouted the producer. "Everyone in their places."

The show that evening was set to broadcast to a national television audience, the topic being the club's recent discovery of a treasure trove of artifacts in the basement of the Zuckerman home. Despite requests from an A-list of evening news anchors, the society chose Bradshaw in appreciation of his previous investigative journalism centered upon the Franklin Wing.

"Where's my teaspoon of honey?" whined Bliss.

"T-minus one minute!"

Sullivan took a deep breath and fixed his collar. Over three months had passed since his return and if his calculations proved accurate, Ben was nearing his death back in 1790. Prior to tonight's show the majority of relics found in the secret bin were already disclosed to the public. However the most important discovery was not, per the request of the National Archives Department in Washington, D.C. Their gag order was lifted earlier in the day, providing the impetus for the hastily arranged broadcast about to air.

"T-minus thirty seconds."

Deep in his heart Sullivan knew that the last item in the cache was Ben's proverbial "second bite at the apple", his personal endowment to the well-being of all Americans and their future generations. How he pulled it off without changing the past was beyond Sullivan's comprehension, but he did it. The physician knew that tonight's revelation would trigger an immediate firestorm across the nation… just like Franklin would have wanted it.

"And five… four… three…"

An aide spritzed some mist above Bliss.

"And go!"

"Good evening everyone, this is Bliss Bradshaw coming to you live from the City of Brotherly Love, and welcome to a special edition of *Bliss on Bliss*." The moderator pivoted his chair toward the historians. "Seated before me are several executive members of the well-respected West Philadelphia Historical Society. They've joined me tonight to discuss their exciting discovery of historical artifacts found inside a home on Elfreth's Alley. Artifacts placed inside a secret, subterranean chamber by one of our nation's founding fathers and Philadelphia's own, Benjamin Franklin." Bradshaw went on to introduce the group of historiographers. "Attorney Mills, as president of the society, can you start off by telling us what got you interested in this specific home?"

"Of course," replied Mills as he stared into the wrong camera. "Some time ago, our society took it upon ourselves to tackle a rather thorny historical conundrum, that being which home Mister Benjamin Franklin lived in on Elfreth's Alley."

"I see," said Bliss. "Please continue."

Over the next several minutes the club president discussed the research carried out by his field team, including their initial contact with Barry Zuckerman, a serpent logo in his basement dubbed Snaky, the legal definition of caveat venditor, a pipe smoking neighbor and a note hidden inside a broken clock with only one hand. It was during his description of the Battle of Bunker Hill reenactment when Bradshaw cut him off.

"Wow, that's quite a collection of anecdotes," commented Bradshaw. "I must admit, your methods seem a bit unorthodox."

"But our madness had its method," grinned Mills. "And in doing so, we unearthed the modern day equivalent of the Rosetta Stone." He followed up the declaration with a deep breath of accomplishment.

"Yes, now getting back to this snake in the basement," redirected Bradshaw. "To my understanding, it's a granite inlay depicting the first political cartoon in our nation's history, that being… Join, or Die. Here's a look for our viewer's at home."

A picture of the segmented serpent appeared on the television screen.

"And this is where the treasure was located?" asked Bliss.

"That's right," answered Wally. "The secret bin was underneath Snaky."

"I see. What prompted you to look beneath the reptile?"

Wally hunched his shoulders while looking at Sullivan. "To tell you the truth, I can't remember why we dug it up. John recommended it." He pointed at his colleague.

The eyes of the nation suddenly focused on Dr. John Sullivan.

"Well," began Sullivan as his brain scrambled for a plausible explanation to uproot the stone. "As you know, the block depicting the state of Pennsylvania is strategically located…"

"I'm the one who dug it up," interrupted Burt. "They let me do it out of respect. I landed on Normandy beach back in June of 1944, under a hailstorm of gunfire."

"I see," replied the moderator suddenly realizing the show was about to veer off script. "Thank you for your service."

"I stuck a crowbar under the block and wedged it open."

"I helped, too," added Wally.

"Me too," clarified Mills.

"It was a group effort," said Sullivan.

"And that's where you found the treasures?" asked Bradshaw. "I can't imagine your surprise. Describe to me what you felt at that very moment."

"I felt tremendous pain!" exclaimed Burt.

"Excuse me?"

"They rolled the granite block right onto my left foot. It broke my big toe in three places."

"We had to rush him to an urgent care center," added Wally. "There was blood all over his sock."

"My toenail still isn't right!"

"Yes. An absolutely amazing story unfolding right before our eyes," stuttered Bradshaw as he turned to the main camera. "When we come back, I'll discuss with these gentlemen the exact contents of Benjamin Franklin's secret vault. Don't go away."

"And… gone to commercial," snapped the producer.

"You guys are killing me!" screamed Bradshaw with his hands thrown into the air.

"I've got to use the bathroom," said Burt as he stood up and walked out.

The remainder of the historical society sat in silence.

"I'm trying to set up a big finish and you guys are sandbagging me with a bunch of crap about a bloody toe, some guy puffing a pipe and caveat whatever!"

"Caveat venditor," mumbled Mills.

"Stick with the storyline!" howled Bradshaw as a hairdresser teased his wave. "For Christ's sake, we're about to shock America! This interview is going to be played ad infinitum! Your great grandchildren will be watching it someday!" The agitated moderator looked up to the ceiling in an attempt to calm down. After several seconds he began to speak in a slow and deliberate fashion. "Now everybody listen. I want Dr. Sullivan to do all the talking from this point forward. Understood? Unless I specifically ask you a question."

Everyone nodded in agreement.

"And five... four... three... back on the air!"

"Welcome back," grinned Bliss. "If you're just joining us, we're about to discuss an assortment of keepsakes excavated by the history mavens seated in front of me." He pivoted back to the group. "Now, Dr. Sullivan, can you describe to our audience precisely what you found?"

"Surely," stated Sullivan confidently. He went on to discuss in detail the exact contents of the bin, including Ben's fur hat, some gold coins, jewelry from the King of France and previously unseen letters from a host of authors such as Washington, Adams, Jefferson and Hamilton. "These letters offer insight into the mindset of our founding fathers, as they struggled to strike a balance between liberty and authority."

"Very well put," commented Bradshaw as he watched Burt stroll back into the group just off camera. "And I see one of the society members is now donning the famous fur hat worn by Franklin himself."

The camera turned toward Burt, the octogenarian proudly wearing Ben's cover.

"Did you talk about the hat yet?" asked Burt.

"Yes, we have Mr. Bilkins," replied Bliss. "Is that the exact hat found in the basement crevice?"

"It is," beamed Burt. "Ben and I had the exact same head size. Great minds think alike."

"All of this stuff is going to be housed in Mr. Zuckerman's home," interjected Attorney Mills. "The letters, the hat, the cannon along with some cannonballs. Barry agreed to donate his home to the city after the house sale fell through. They're going to turn it into a museum. My legal team is orchestrating the transition... the Law Firm of Frederick Mills."

Bradshaw shot a laser stare through the skull of Attorney Mills. While continuing to stare him down he said, "Doctor Sullivan, it's my understanding that you also found a rather special magazine in the hidden cavity. True?"

"Yes," responded Sullivan as he held up a copy of the magazine. "This is a special edition of *Poor Richard's Almanac* placed in the bin by Mr. Franklin himself." The camera zoomed in on the front cover.

"Interesting, and how do you know for certain Benjamin placed it there?"

Sullivan opened the front cover. "He autographed it. Here's Ben's characteristic signature just above the date, that being January 1$^{st}$, 1788, which would be several months after the Constitutional Convention ended in Philadelphia."

"I see. There's also something penned above his signature. Can you read that please?"

Sullivan read the inscription. *"To the future… I hope the republic is well. Please enjoy this collection of personal anecdotes. Remember, the Constitution only gives people the right to pursue happiness. You have to catch it yourself."*

"Ah, classic Ben," declared Bliss. "The man had a way with words."

"The book is replete with Franklin's observations of daily life," continued Sullivan. "In it he touches upon his many sayings, including his all-time favorite."

"Which is?"

"The used key is always bright."

"You can't argue that," chuckled Bliss. "What else is inside the booklet?"

"Ben's thoughts on liberty, democracy and the need to challenge the status quo. He also offers a few predictions for the future and a rather heartwarming story about a servant girl named Sary, and her quest for freedom."

"You can find the story of Sary and other select articles from Ben's special edition *Poor Richard's Almanac* at our website," commented Bradshaw. "Just go to *BlissonBliss.com* and click on the link, *'Ben's Treasure Trove'*. Now, to the final and most striking discovery made within the secret bin, which up until this point has not been disclosed to the public." Bliss flashed his smile across America. "But first, a word from our sponsor. We'll be right back."

"And… gone to commercial," announced the producer.

"Alright! We're back on track, baby," proclaimed Bliss as he gave the group a fist pump. "Let's drop this bomb and get out of here." He took a sip of lemon water.

"Who's going to make the big announcement?" asked Wally.

"I'll do it," huffed Mills. "I'm the president."

"But I'm the incoming president next month," argued Wally.

"I'm a World War II veteran," barked Burt.

"Gentlemen, gentlemen… please," stated Bradshaw. "Everybody calm down. This is a job for a professional. The Blissmaster will do it."

"But you didn't even read the big finish," pointed out Wally. "I'm not sure you understand what it says."

"That's how the Bliss-ter rolls," spouted Bradshaw. "It keeps my reactions visceral and…"

"No," cut in Sullivan. "I'm doing it."

"But, John…"

"No. Listen to me," ordered Sullivan. "I'm the one who got us all involved in this project. I'm the one who told you to dig up Snaky." He looked at each member of the society. "So I'm the one making the announcement." He gazed back at Bliss. "I'd like some time to give a little preface, too."

"And five, four…"

"Take it Sullivan," conceded Bradshaw. "Don't screw up."

"… back on the air."

"Welcome back to our exclusive presentation of the Ben Franklin files. Now, for the moment you've all been waiting for, let's hear about the most important find in Ben's underground hollow, which up until several hours ago has been under quarantine by order of our federal government." Bliss pivoted to Sullivan.

"Dr. Sullivan, please offer your thoughts as to what we're about to witness."

"Thank you," said Sullivan as he looked directly into the camera. "I'd like to remind everyone that Ben Franklin was a civic minded individual. One of his personal mottos was 'doing well by doing good', so what you are about to hear should come as no surprise. Mr. Franklin was also a forward thinker, a man always looking ahead of the curve, hence his nickname during the Constitutional Convention… the Sage of Philadelphia."

"The definition of a clairvoyant," interjected Bliss.

"I've studied Franklin well and the only way to explain his final act is to think of him as a time traveler. Someone among us witnessing the good and bad of modern day society yet capable of transporting back in time to make a difference. So I ask all of you, if possible, what would you do in his situation? What would you change in the past to make society better off today, keeping in mind that you cannot alter what has already occurred between the late 1700s and 2020?"

"A rather interesting premise," commented Bliss. "Perhaps…"

"Bring back dueling," howled Burt. "That way we don't have to listen to these political '*bleep…*' arguing every day. Just let them square off in a field and be done with it."

"Whoa! Mr. Bilkins," chuckled Bradshaw with a wave of his hands. "Thank goodness for the five second tape delay."

"Get tougher with environmental regulations," recommended Wally. "No more plastic water bottles."

"Universal health care," chimed in Mills. "America is lagging behind in that regard."

"All very interesting ideas, gentlemen" said Bliss. "I for one would suggest banning violent video games. I'm no psychiatrist but watching human carnage for days on end can't be good for our children… or adults." He turned his attention back to Sullivan. "Dr. Sullivan, what would you change?"

The question caught Sullivan off guard. He immediately thought of Sary and the plight of her family. "Human rights," came his reply. "Tighten up the laws protecting the basic dignities of every American, no matter what their skin color, religion or sexual orientation."

"Very well," said Bradshaw. "So here we go, America! Let's hear what the so-called Sage of Philadelphia has to say. Dr. John Sullivan, please tell us what Mister Franklin thinks should be changed in today's world? In other words, what is Benjamin Franklin's pièce de résistance?"

"Here it is!" replied Sullivan as a single page, hand-written document appeared on the screen. "The first five amendments to the United States Constitution, signed by all the delegates at the Philadelphia Convention including Mr. Franklin, dated September 17, 1787."

"Unbelievable!" howled Bradshaw. "Only on *Bliss on Bliss* can you see such history in the making!"

"Now, take your time and carefully read through these five amendments," instructed Sullivan. "I'm sure they all sound quite familiar to you. There's the oft quoted first amendment guaranteeing freedom of religion, speech and the press along with the rights of assembly and petition. Number two is the much debated right to bear arms."

"I've never heard of the third," commented Mills as he read it aloud. "*No soldier shall, in time of peace be quartered in any house, without the consent of the owner, nor in time of war, but in a manner to be prescribed by law.* That's what we call in the legal profession, mumbo jumbo."

As the viewing audience scanned the list, Sullivan continued.

"Then there's the fourth which addresses search and arrest warrants followed by the fifth, which are your rights in criminal cases."

"I plead the fifth!" joked Burt.

"Now, to all the history buffs out there watching, this doesn't make sense," followed up Sullivan. "Because the 1787 Philadelphia Convention only generated one document, that being the Constitution of the United States. The first ten amendments to the constitution, better known as the Bill of Rights, were written two years later by James Madison and ultimately ratified sometime in 1791."

"But this record is signed and dated September 17, 1787," noted Bliss. "How is that possible?"

"First off, let me say that the document you're looking at has been carefully examined by the Department of National Archives in Washington, D.C.," said Sullivan. "Earlier today they notified us that beyond a doubt, the document is authentic, along with all the signatures. It's currently being kept at their facility for security purposes."

"Uh-oh," interrupted Bliss with a finger to an ear microphone. "Our producer tells me our phone lines are blowing up." He looked at Sullivan. "Looks like you sparked a fire!"

"Well, kudos to your viewing audience for their prowess," stated Sullivan. "They probably picked up the slight change."

"Which is?" asked the moderator.

"The second amendment. Why don't you read it aloud to the nation, Bliss."

The moderator complied.

*"A well regulated Militia, being necessary to the security of a free State, the right of the people to keep and bear Arms except for weapons of mass assault, shall not be infringed."*

The airwaves went silent for several seconds.

"Do you see it, Bliss?" asked Sullivan in anticipation. "Do you see the change?"

"Hell, yea," replied Bliss with eyes wide open. "Benjamin Franklin just changed the second amendment!"

"Precisely!" agreed Sullivan. "Tell us what you see."

"He added six words—*'except for weapons of mass assault'*. They're not in the existing Bill of Rights," explained Bliss. "I'm sure of it because I own a gun."

"That's right. The second amendment as we currently know it reads, *'A well regulated Militia, being necessary to the security of a free State, the right of the people to keep and bear Arms, shall not be infringed'."*

"Do you understand what this means?" exclaimed Bradshaw as he slowly repeated the words while staring at a monitor to his right, as if in disbelief. "... the right of the people to keep and bear Arms *except for weapons of mass assault*."

"Don't you see what he's done?" asked Sullivan.

"Yes. Yes, I do," came the moderator's concerned reply. "The man has single handedly taken assault rifles off the street!"

"He's made all of America safer," added Mills.

"It's about time!" opined Burt. "Nobody needs a goddamn AK-47 unless you're going to storm a beachhead!"

"But... but, how did he change it?" asked Bliss with a quizzical look.

"Mr. Franklin didn't really change it," countered Sullivan. "But he did somehow find an original copy of the first five amendments, signed by the nation's founding fathers in 1787, including George Washington, Alexander Hamilton and James Madison."

"So this document precedes the Bill of Rights?"

"Without a doubt."

"So... if it came first," muttered Bliss. "Is it now the law of the land?"

"Perhaps," smiled Sullivan. "Time will tell. I'm going to have to leave that decision up to the politicians."

"And the federal courts," interjected Attorney Mills while rubbing his hands together. "Let me be the first to say that we've got a legal brouhaha on our hands!"

"A donnybrook," chimed in Wally.

"A battle royal!" roared Burt. "General quarters! All hands man your battle stations!"

"Yes indeed! For once I agree fully with the esteemed members of the West Philadelphia Historical Society," quipped Bliss. "Ladies and gentlemen, what you have just witnessed is history in the making. It appears that we have a *new* second amendment!

The great Benjamin Franklin has reached out from his crypt and proven once again that he is the ultimate political insurgent. Incredible! Who knows, we may even have another revolution on our hands, but hey… maybe that's the way Benjamin Franklin likes it. Good night, America."

"And… off the air."

# CHAPTER TWENTY-NINE
## EPILOGUE

The controversy over Benjamin Franklin's second amendment pushed America to the brink of civil war. Activists howled and legislators ranted as both sides of the debate flooded the airwaves with propaganda in support of their cause. Gridlock ultimately paralyzed the political process, so in the end, it was the American public that decided the outcome. For the first time in American history, a proposed amendment was put to a national vote, the referendum passing in an overwhelming majority favoring Franklin's revision. The new second amendment was ratified into law on Benjamin Franklin's birthday, January 17th, 2022. On that date, all assault rifles were banned from the public domain.

Around that time in colonial America, Dr. Edward Casey finished his illustrious career as Chairman of the Department of Medicine at Pennsylvania Hospital. During his tenure he championed the cause of military veterans and led a campaign to discourage the medical practice of bloodletting. Up until his final days, he meticulously maintained the hospital's medicinal gardens which to this date continue to flourish inside the walls of the infirmary, drawing visitors from around the world.

Antonio and Mario Pagano carried on as jack of all trades for Mr. Franklin and the Christ Church. Their expertise in explosives led to a massive explosion on July 4th, 1788, the mishap ironically leading to the tradition of fireworks on that date. Their genetic predisposition for gunpowder and combustion was passed down to future generations in so much that their great, great grandchildren founded the Pagano Destruction Company.

Benedict Arnold barely escaped capture after his plot to surrender West Point was foiled. The British granted him a Brigadier General commission and he successfully led enemy forces against the Continental Army in both Virginia and Connecticut. After the war his reputation was thrashed in the British press and he failed to obtain good fortune. He died in London on June 14th, 1801, a spiritually and financially impoverished man. His last words were, "Let me die in the old uniform in which I fought my battles for freedom. May God forgive me for putting on another." He was buried without military honors.

Peggy Shippen was ultimately deemed complicit in her husband's act of treason, her role that of an intermediary between Benedict and the head of Britain's secret service, Major John André. The City of Philadelphia banished her and she fled to London where King George III awarded her an annuity "for her services, which were meritorious". The death of her husband left Mrs. Arnold with a sullied name and heavy debt, forcing her to auction off the majority of her possessions. She died three years after her husband and was buried at his side.

Oney Judge discovered in 1796 that Mrs. Washington was planning to give her away as a wedding gift to her granddaughter, Elizabeth. In an 1845 interview she said, "Whilst they were packing up to go to Virginia, I was packing to go. I didn't know where; for I knew that if I went back to Virginia, I should never get my liberty." On the evening of May 21st, 1796, after setting dinner before Martha and George Washington, she disappeared out the back door and made her way to New Hampshire, where she married a free black sailor and raised three children. She died in February of 1848.

George Mason spent the remainder of his life demanding that the new Constitution protect the rights of the people. He was displeased with the final wording of the Bill of Rights, arguing that it failed to fully safeguard the rights of the individual. Devoted to his convictions, he refused to serve as Virginia's first senator. He stated, "In all our associations; in all our agreements let us never lose sight of this fundamental maxim – that all power was originally lodge in, and consequently is derived from, the people. We should wear it as a breast plate and buckle it on as our armor."

James Madison dealt with his signer's remorse over the Constitution by becoming the driving force behind the drafting and ratification of the Bill of Rights. He served as Secretary of State under President Thomas Jefferson during which he supervised the Louisiana Purchase, doubling the size of the United States. In 1809 he became the fourth President of the United States.

Alexander Hamilton served as the nation's first Secretary of the Treasury and is considered the founding father of the nation's financial system. During his lifetime he was involved in seven successful 'affairs of honor'. However, his eighth affair led him to a dueling field on the West bank of the Hudson River, on July 11th, 1804. There, in Weehawken, New Jersey, he squared off against Aaron Burr, the sitting Vice President of the United States. On the eve of the duel Hamilton penned an intent to 'waste his shot' on Burr. The following morning he was mortally wounded by a bullet from Burr that entered his abdomen just above his hip. Prior to his death, Hamilton and his wife Elizabeth had eight children. Their oldest son Philip died three years before his father, on the same dueling field.

George Washington was inaugurated as the first president of the United States and is commonly referred to as 'The Father of His Country'. His prominent role as a statesman, politician and military leader places him on a short list of greatest presidents of all time. Yet during the remainder of his life he relentlessly pursued escaped slaves, including Sary and Oney Judge. He died on December 14, 1799, after a brief battle with a throat abscess known as quinsy. During the final twenty-four hours of his life his medical team subjected him to a total of four bloodlettings.

His final words were, "Tis well". Upon his death he owned 123 enslaved people. One was set free and the others were stipulated to remain with Martha Washington for the rest of her life.

Walt Stanton survived his gunshot wound from Benedict Arnold and is housed in the year 2065 on the psychiatric ward at the Philadelphia General Hospital. There he enjoys playing checkers with a man claiming to be the Messiah. Mr. Stanton carries the diagnosis of paranoid schizophrenia and despite appropriate care, continues to profess that he's a time traveler. His magical ring sat in a personal belonging's box until it was stolen and pawned by a nightshift employee. It currently resides on the hand of a retired lawman in Whittier, California.

Mingo currently resides over a heat vent in center city Philadelphia, just outside a strip joint called *The Liberty Belle*. He frequently speaks of an earlier time with reference to men such as Washington, Franklin and Hamilton, but no one bothers to listen. Occasionally in the month of May, when the moon is bright on a Friday night, he scales the wall of Pennsylvania Hospital to harvest the root of a mandrake, always careful to keep the wind at his back and an ear full of wax. He enjoys visiting his old nemesis, Walt Stanton, once a week.

Dr. Vincent Pagano married Jordan Ally McCarthy. Together they raised six children on the Main Line of Philadelphia in a town previously known as 'Crankyville'. The memorial plaque in his honor remained in the lobby of the Pagano Orthopedic Institute until the building was razed in 2070 by the Pagano Destruction Company. No fatalities occurred during the event.

Professor Alabaster Bookman stepped down from his chairmanship after the fallout over the Elfreth's Alley debacle. A disciplinary board ultimately found him guilty of actions unbecoming a University professor and he was encouraged to resign. After a futile search for a job as a history teacher in the Philadelphia public school system, he accepted a position as a Ben Franklin impersonator at the Independence Visitor Center. His current online rating is a two out of five stars. He lives with his older brother in Camden, New Jersey.

Barry Zuckerman currently resides in Naples, Florida, thanks to a financial windfall from the sale of his home and a fortune in gold coins found in its basement. He keeps in close contact with the elder members of the West Philadelphia Historical Society, occasionally taking in a Revolutionary War battle reenactment when time permits.

Membership in the West Philadelphia Historical Society exploded after the club's momentous discovery. The name of Attorney Frederick Mills was etched in perpetuity just outside the Franklin House Museum on Elfreth's Alley. The legal eagle is currently retired and spends his free time with Wally Roberts, trying to perfect and resurrect Franklin's three-wheel clock. Burt Bilkins died unexpectedly while visiting the Normandy American Cemetery and Memorial in France. He's buried there among the 9,385 military dead and the inscribed names of 1,557 missing comrades.

Sary adopted the legal surname of Judge in honor of Oney. As a single mother she attended night school and eventually accepted a Franklin Scholarship to the University of Pennsylvania after submitting an award winning essay titled: *"Benedict Arnold – Man, Myth and Monster"*. She recently was granted a Fulbright Scholarship to study abroad in Barbados where she plans to explore her ancestry roots. Seven months after arriving in the year 2020, she gave birth to a set of twins. She named them Freedom and Liberty, yet never disclosed the identity of their founding father.

John Sullivan is the current medical director of the Sullivan Institute, the premier treatment center for Alzheimer's Disease in the United States. His illustrious career was marked by several major breakthroughs in the care of memory loss, garnering him worldwide respect and acclaim. Along with his wife, Theresa, he lives in West Philadelphia with three boys, Quentin, Alexander and Benjamin. He keeps the keys to the time tunnel hanging from a hook in an upstairs closet, behind some dress shirts. After his return to Philadelphia in 2020, he never time traveled again. In 2030 he became President of the West Philadelphia Historical Society.

Benjamin Franklin died on April 17, 1790 at the age of 84. Throughout his final years of life he considered slavery a wretched institution and in 1787 resided as president of the Pennsylvania Abolitionist Society. In February of 1790, just two months prior to his death, he presented a petition to Congress urging them to bestow "liberty to those unhappy men who alone in this land of freedom are degraded into perpetual bondage, and who, amidst the general joy of surrounding freemen are groaning in servile subjection." He's buried in a simple tomb on the corner of 5th and Arch Street, Philadelphia. His last will and testament compelled his daughter to free her slave in order to receive her inheritance.

THE END

# ABOUT THE AUTHOR

**Dr. Michael Banas** completed his undergraduate studies at the University of Scranton. He then attended the University of Pennsylvania School of Medicine followed by an Orthopedic residency at the University of Rochester. His final year of surgical training took him to Los Angeles where he completed a Sports Medicine Fellowship at the Southern California Orthopedic Institute. Dr. Banas currently resides in Dallas, PA with his wife, Theresa. They keep company with Milo, the incorrigible cat, and their two Labrador retrievers, Samantha and Maggie. Dr. Banas specializes in Orthopedic Surgery and Sports Medicine.

Made in the USA
Columbia, SC
03 July 2025